THE
RED BIKE

Tara Delaney

TREATY OAK PUBLISHERS

Publisher's Note

This is a work of fiction. All characters, events, and locations are based on the author's imagination. Any resemblance to actual persons, living or dead, is purely coincidence and unintentional

Printed and published in the United States of America

Treaty Oak Publishers

ISBN-978-1-943658-61-9

DEDICATION

To 'My Bear'
You make dreams come true.

PROLOGUE

I wish I could convey this story without prejudice from an altered state of my mind. It is often very difficult to tell a story with any degree of accuracy after a metamorphosis has occurred. Surely the larvae wrapped in darkness does not perceive the world the same way as the butterfly spreading its wings in spring. However, I will attempt to record the events of the past year in such a way as to remind myself of who I was, and why I changed.

Abbey Gallagher

CHAPTER 1

"Africa?" I repeated, almost shouting into the phone, as the editor of *National Geographic* explained the assignment to me. Their original photographer had to back out of the project and my name came up during an emergency meeting today.

"Yes, I am very interested. Rwanda, too? You're getting us into Rwanda? Wow!" Few photographers had been to Rwanda since the civil war a few years ago.

Opening the door, I waved Ryan in as I listened. "I understand this is soon, but how soon?"

Ryan shot me a quick look, gesturing 'hurry up' with his hand. I raised my palm. He seemed impatient, his eyes narrowing in frustration - so unlike Ryan.

I turned away from him. "Tomorrow? I'd have to leave tomorrow? Um, yes, I can, yes, I can. How long is the assignment?"

Shaking my head at the lead editor's answer—"ten to twelve months, a year?"—I glanced over my shoulder at Ryan, his shoulders up, a confused look taking over his features.

Swiveling back, I said, "No, it won't be a problem. I can make this work. Thank you for the opportunity." I wanted to scream and jump up and down. This was an opportunity of a lifetime, a career changer. I'm going to travel throughout Africa photographing the primate mother-infant bond.

At the same time, my gut rolled, anticipating Ryan's reaction and my parents'. But I couldn't pass this up, not this kind of opportunity. *National Geographic* would be dedicating several months' worth of issues to the subject, all the articles flanked with my photographs.

With no small amount of reluctance, I hung up the phone, knowing Ryan's eyes were on me. I pulled my excitement inward, turned to face him, unable to tell if his root-beer-colored eyes looked more hurt or confused. "Ryan?"

"What the hell! Are you leaving again? What was that about a year?"

I let out a long breath, wondering how to make him understand. "Ryan, let's sit down," I whispered with a hint of caution, nodding toward the couch.

"No, no, we have to go." He glanced at his watch. "Seriously we have to go now. We told your parents—"

"My parents will understand if we're late. I mean, I'll have to tell them about this assignment… tonight."

"That's going to go over well." Sarcasm dominated his tone. Then he shook his head as if he remembered something or had just been brought back to this time period. "Abbey, we can talk about it on the drive over. Sounds like your mind is made up," he said in a flat voice, "but we have to go." His eyes traveled up and down my body. "Are you going to change?"

"It's my parents, not some fancy restaurant." I peered at him. "Why are you so cleaned up? Seriously?"

"It's your birthday dinner." He nodded as if that

explained the change in his usual attire.

Strained silence hung between us as we drove to my parents' house. Ryan's agitation was palpable as he kept looking at his watch, then huffing. He was holding himself back so we didn't have a fight before we arrived for my birthday dinner. I hate birthday celebrations, but my mom insisted, since I had been in Costa Rica on my last birthday. Shit, this time I would announce I was leaving tomorrow for a year.

Looking at him, with his eyebrows pulled in, his mouth straight and hard, I missed the usual affable expression that blanketed his face. "Ryan, I know this is sudden," I said, my words breaking through the thick tension, "but it's an opportunity I can't pass up."

His eyes darted to me, then back to the road, "Ab, it's just that you've been home for less than three months." He paused. "I get it, it's your job and all, but a fucking year, a year," he blurted out.

"I know, it's a long time." Angst poured out with my words. Leaving Ryan for a year meant I could lose him forever. At the same time, if I said 'no' to this assignment, doors in my career would close, doors that might never open again.

His expression lightened. "Ab, let's just have fun tonight, I mean it's your birthday and you are leaving tomorrow."

"Yeah, it's going to a super-relaxed dinner." I rolled my eyes, anticipating my mom's reaction. A smirky smile crossed my lips as I glanced at him. He was giving me an out and I needed to take it. "What kinda fun?" I tried to make my voice sound overly sultry.

Smiling, he said, "The non-verbal kind."
I laughed.

TELLING MY MOTHER AND FATHER during my birthday dinner would be tough. He would get the importance of this opportunity, but she would be more than disappointed. She'd pepper me with questions without any focus on the career-advancing opportunity I was about to embark on. No, she'd push that idea aside as if it were a simple annoyance on the road to a woman's true importance: getting married and having kids.

My leaving wasn't a big deal, although I'd be gone longer than ever before. My family knew Austin was only my base between photography assignments for wildlife magazines. After finishing graduate school at NYU, I'd hung around New York, scrambling for work. Once frequent travel became my life, I moved back to Austin, partly to be closer to my father and brother, but also because I could live more cheaply.

I had spent the last four years saying good-bye on a regular basis. I liked being the one to go, for the most part, leaving my mother behind. Short intermittent spurts had been the only way I could tolerate our living in the same city. Maybe I could use this year to psych myself up to repair our relationship, if I could come home with a ready heart to accept her, along with all our differences.

"Why are you knocking? It's my parents' house." I elbowed past Ryan to push open the double doors of their southwest-style home. The graceful, thick wooden door swung back on its massive hinges.

As I stepped into the Saltillo-tiled foyer and stopped, my back stiffened. Something was very wrong. A strange quiet greeted me, like the stillness before a bad Texas storm, the weather patterns meeting, deciding just how they'll come together to create a fierce wind and sheets of rain, rattling the homes of all the people huddled inside.

Ryan stood behind me in the foyer, his breathing so loud, unsettling.

"Dad… Mom?" I said into the fuzzy darkness.

A commingling of food aromas rushed down the hall, accompanied by the low rustling of human bodies, moving from one foot to the other and shushing each other. I craned my head toward Ryan, understanding why he insisted on ringing the doorbell and knocking like a desperate vacuum cleaner salesman (are there any other kind?). That's how he had warned the crowd of our arrival, and had my mind not been spinning, I might have seen it coming.

The lights came alive as a small mob of familiar faces marched toward me screaming, "Surprise, surprise!"

I stepped back, bouncing into Ryan's chest, turning my head to glare at him, shaking my head. "Christ!" I whispered.

He returned my irritated look with a shrug.

People moved aside, clearing a path for the true star of this party. My mother sashayed through the small crowd like a salsa dancer, rotating her narrow torso from side to side, her voluptuous breasts brushing against the arms of the men who blocked her way. Her feet sprang from the ground as if hot coals were below her. I wanted to throw a bucket of water on her.

"Excuse me, must give my girl a thirtieth birthday kiss," she sang out, as she tapped one of my father's colleagues on the arm.

With every step she took toward me, my blood pressure crept up. I caught myself shaking my head in disgust, watching a fool on parade. She knew how much I hated surprises. She *knew*.

"Happy birthday, Abigail," she chirped, hugging me, leaning her shoulders into me, while her body stood away, keeping the appropriate distance.

"Mom." I started to say, 'what the hell do you think you're doing?' but my father's kiss on my forehead stopped me. "Happy birthday, sweetheart."

"Thanks, Dad," I said, emerging from my trance and turning toward him. A large man, he once upon a time had been an athlete but with the passing decades, his massive chest muscles had softened. Years of sitting at a desk and eating my mother's baking had packed his torso with excess fat.

"Abbey, the big three-O, congrats!" my brother Ethan yelled from down the hall, raising a bottle of beer in the air.

"Come with me, Abigail." My mother pulled my arm. She led me past people ebbing around us down the hall. Frustration accumulated into wet heat in my palms. How little things change.

But I stayed trapped inside my emotions, once again masking my anger with a chiseled stiff smile. If I destroyed this for her, I would destroy it for my father, for everyone. They would all look at my mother and say, 'too bad she has such an ungrateful daughter.'

I just kept telling myself, I'm leaving in less than twenty-four hours and I won't have to see her lipstick smile for a year, or hear her instructions, or listen to all the stories about her charity functions and how much money she raised for this or that cause. I won't have to pay attention as strangers praised her, and then eyed me, as if somehow, I did not add up to all the niceness Rachel Gallagher possessed or the sensuality that rode on her chest.

"What do you think, darling?" She fluttered her red fingertips in front of me to highlight the transformation their living room had undergone under my mother's decorative eye.

"It looks good," I said, my mind spinning as I scanned the room. *Hell, when was I going to tell my family I was leaving?*

Silver and blue balloons floated at the ceiling, trailing long silver ribbons just above the heads of the guests. A large printed thirtieth-birthday banner covered the back wall, and three long tables swathed with dozens of hors d'oeuvres displayed on silver trays stood against the other wall. Lighted candles flickered from every flat surface of the living room, and specks of light jumped off people's faces, creating an almost dream-like effect.

"All for you, dear," my mother called, loud enough that a few of her friends turned their heads.

"Abigail's *thirty*. I can't believe that, Rachel," said Jacklyn, my mother's country club 'we do tennis and lunch' friend. Her emphasis indicated that when the number was attached to my name, it became void of the necessary accomplishments. "My Susan is thirty also, and she's pregnant with her third child," she said, raising her glass in tribute to her daughter as a woman, a mother, a breeder.

'Great, congrats! Your daughter has proved she is capable of doing what stray dogs in back alleys do,' I wanted to snap at her, but of course, I held it in. "Well, congratulations," I said instead.

My mother clasped my wrist and lifted my arm. Her eyes made their way down the length of my body, traveling passed my long straight hair, stopping for a moment at the disintegrating Coca-Cola emblem on my shirt, before moving to my frayed cut-off shorts and at last halting just short of my black canvas high-top shoes. Standing there, I let her eyes attack me and felt like a wax figure in a museum, but they backed off, unable to take anymore visual calamity.

"I can tell you had no idea about this party." My mother arched her eyebrows, smiling at Jacklyn. She had to say it, to acknowledge out loud to her friends that my attire was not appropriate. Suggesting somehow that, had I known, I would have dolled myself up and assumed the same painted appearance of all my mother's friends.

She knew better, and so did I. I didn't even own a fucking dress.

"I had no clue. Had I known I would have worn my good Coca-Cola shirt," I said, twisting my lips into a stiff smile before pulling my arm back as I walked away.

"Abbey," my dad yelled over the soft jazz music. "I want you to meet someone." My father glanced at me and then to a tall man with jet-black hair, dressed like he belonged on the cover of a *GQ* magazine, dark rust-colored, button-down shirt tucked into silky taupe pants with matching belt and shoes. When I looked closer, he appeared to be in his early thirties.

"Martin, this is Abbey."

He extended his hand and I gave it a brusque shake.

"Happy birthday, Abbey," he said in a deep amplifying voice.

"Thanks." Someone came up behind me and then my mother's voice said, "Yes, she had no idea we were throwing her a party."

Once again, her explanation for my appearance.

"Well, surprises can be fun," Martin said, the corner of his mouth turning up.

"Yeah, sure," I rolled my eyes, thinking I'm about to drop a big surprise on my parents.

My mother slid into our semi-circle. "And, Frank, is this the fast-rising young man at the firm you've been telling me about?" My mother inspected Martin and then turned to me with that 'why don't you consider this one' look.

"Yes," my father said. "Martin, this is my wife, Rachel."

"Glad to finally meet you. Frank has told me so much about you."

She lifted her delicate hand in the air to meet his.

"Thank you for the invitation," he said, the next moment taking his eyes off my mother as he shifted back to me. "Abigail, your father tells me you travel the globe photographing wildlife."

"Continue, I'll be right back." My father touched my mother's arm as he excused himself.

"Travel the globe is a little comprehensive, but I do travel a lot."

"But we're encouraging her to use her skills in Austin." My mom stared at me, a pointed smile, almost like it was made of plastic, consuming her face.

I almost said it right then—*I'm flying to Africa tomorrow for a year*—but instead I took a deep breath to assuage my rising anger.

Martin just kept peering at me. Not for a moment did he give my mother that look she so craved. The 'God, you're so beautiful, Frank's a lucky man' look. Not an ounce of him resembled anything close to 'my type' of man, but his utter disregard for my mother and her cleavage endeared him to me a bit.

"Why would you do that when you're doing well with your work abroad?" he said to me.

"Yes, but we feel…" My mother used her soft southern drawl to explain why a woman shouldn't travel alone and certainly not to third world countries. I'd heard her say it a million times.

"My mother feels…" I slanted my eyes towards her.

"Well, you've been blessed," he said staring at me, his low voice dragging across the carpet.

"Yes, she has." My mother slipped her hand around my waist.

"Mom."

"Well, you have been, dear." Her lips pecked my cheek, and I tried not to flinch. "Well, Martin, it has certainly been nice talking with you." She stepped toward him, then touched his arm.

He glanced down at her. "Thanks again for the invite. I'm glad I finally got to meet Frank's family." His eyes moved back to me.

"Oh, the pleasure was all mine." She drew back, her sappy drawl coating everything around us. My mother looked deflated. He hadn't draped her with compliments.

"I'd like to see some of your photographs sometime, maybe over coffee, wine?" he said, erasing her drawl with his deep voice, his eyes fixed on me.

I laughed. "I'll be back in a year."

He wrinkled his forehead with raised eyebrows. "A year! Your father didn't say that."

"My father doesn't know yet, so please…"

"Of course, I won't say anything, Wow, that's a long time to be gone from life."

"Depends, what you consider life."

"Meaning…?" He took a sip of his wine, his pale eyes floating above the rim of the crystal glass.

"That is life and this…" I skewed my eyes around the room. "This is a performance."

He laughed. "Oh, so the beautiful photographer is more comfortable among wild animals than us humans?" He leaned forward. "Is that it?"

It's not that. I've had supporting roles in my mother's theatrical performances all my life, but when I'm photographing animals whose lives are real, based on need for survival, rather than some pretense of a role played in a social circle, my life becomes real, too. I wanted to say, for example, this is my mother's stage, and my thirtieth birthday is only a reason for her to direct a play for some invisible audience where she, of course, is the beautiful, seductive, dramatic Scarlett O'Hara.

"You could say that." I observed my mother across the room. "This is all a game. When I leave here, I don't have to play. Makes life a little easier. I guess I don't have the energy to keep up with the artifice surrounding my mother's country club set."

His mouth turned up in a smug grin. "Very well. Since you do have to play the game this evening, would you like me to retrieve you a drink?"

"No, thanks, I need to rejoin my friends." My eyes darted over my shoulder toward Ryan.

"Well, I'm glad I got to meet you before you run away."

"I'm not running, just doing my job," I said in a blunt tone.

"I wasn't criticizing. I can definitely understand," he said as he cupped his hand on my elbow. "I'm working for your father at the firm, so you know where to find me when you come out of hiding. I'd seriously like to hear from you in a year."

"In a year, you won't know my name," I said, my voice gone flat.

"Doubtful…" He ran his hand gently down my arm to my wrist. "Your father has your picture plastered all over his office."

I could feel Ryan's eyes on me, so I slipped my hand from Martin's. "Well, nice to meet you." I stepped back.

"Good luck."

"Thanks." I walked up behind Ryan. His posture, the way he had his hands stuffed in his pockets and kept pulling his shoulders straight, reminded me of a fifteen- year-old girl thrown into a slinky dress and high heels and then forced to walk down a runway. The uniform—pressed khaki pants and a button-down shirt—didn't match the person.

"Well, thanks for gracing us, Ab," Ryan said, sarcasm tipping the syllables of each word. The Africa bomb weighed on him.

"Come on now." I nudged in next to him, slipping my arm through his, wanting to soften the tension surrounding us.

"You were pretty surprised." Ryan squeezed my shoulder.

"Yes, and you know how much I love surprises." I rolled my eyes at him. If I weren't leaving, he'd find out how pissed off I was to find him in cahoots with my mom.

He looked down at me. "Yep, I love them, too." His tone was pointed.

Ethan laughed. "It's good for you, Abbey. John, this is my infamous sister."

"Pleasure," John said, extending a stiff hand.

Ethan had chosen engineering as a profession, but his personality and manner were more suited to an elementary school teacher. Six years my junior, he still had the face of a young boy, open and without pain. A naïveté lingered in his eyes and his voice had a natural animation that made you want to listen to him.

"Happy birthday, old lady." Sheila's arm crept around my waist and shook my hip like she was trying to make sure no rusty parts fell off. "Jennifer's sorry she couldn't be here, but she's hanging over the toilet praying for morning sickness to end."

I laughed. "Old lady? That's good, coming from you!"

"Forever young." She slanted her eyes toward the

appendage attached to her shoulder and licked her lips like a house cat eyeing a shiny silver unprotected sardine.

Sheila sported a new hairstyle every month; this month it was dyed platinum blonde, cut in a blunt bob with her bangs angled sharply across her forehead. She wore a tight leopard-print skirt, trimmed with a pink ruffle, and a strapless pink top.

But her most prominent accessory hung on her arm, a nineties version of Ted Nugent, a long-haired, earring-infested, rocker-t-shirt-wearing, young twenties guy. He looked up every now and then, between biting and kissing Sheila's shoulder, to nod and grunt in agreement with something she said, as if any words uttered in our conversation could enter his brain.

My mother wove figure eights through the crowd, her hands dusting guest's arms, her Hollywood smile spreading across her face. "You're not eating much, Jim." "Let's not have your hands empty, Bob." And she motioned for a one of the college students she had hired to bring a tray of white wine. "Dolores, you look wonderful," she said to my father's overweight sister, who was standing over the hors d'oeuvres table, cramming fried jalapeños in her mouth.

"Almost time to open gifts," she purred from behind Ryan. She stopped, "Ryan, you look nice." A definite tone of surprise seeped through her voice as she studied Ryan's upgraded attire. He always wore faded jeans, Birkenstocks, and a logo t-shirt.

"I changed, like you asked. I mean, I even tried to get Abbey to change," he continued, his chest rising up, a schoolboy awaiting approval from his favorite teacher.

"No such luck with that!" Ethan chimed in, grinning at me.

I looked at him, scratching my eyelid with my middle finger, making a point of extending it.

"Got it, sweet sister."

"You're a dear," my mother said as she leaned into Ryan. "Now if we could just get you to shave off this stuff." Her red fingernails scratched the edge of Ryan's goatee.

"Well, maybe soon." He tilted his chin toward her touch.

"I like it," I said.

"Fine, dear." Her cherry red lips parted. "But things change."

Before I could answer, she turned toward the table, and Ryan followed her.

"I have some presents under here." She scrunched her flower-patterned silk skirt in her delicate fingers, raised it above her knees, and lowered herself to the floor. She stretched her arm under the white tablecloth, like she was casting a flexible fishing pole. Her full breasts fell against the thin vanilla blouse, desperately wanting to escape between the buttons, the flickering specs of light from the candles acted as a mini-flashlight, illuminating the creamy mounds as they pushed themselves between the edges of her collar.

She slid a wrapped box out from under the table. "Your birthday present," she said, looking up and smiling with pride.

I caught Ryan's eyes staring at the cavern created by the mounds of white flesh coming together above the last secured button of my mother's blouse. Then he shook his head and whirled around, like he had seen something or, worse yet, *thought* something unspeakable. His eyes darted to me and he expelled a loud breath. "Well, are there any other boxes to get?" His voice sounded anxious.

"Ask her." I nodded toward my mother, who stood beside him.

As he repeated his question, he sounded like a nervous schoolboy, instead of the nonchalant Ryan I knew. My mother nodded and clutched his hand to lead him toward the kitchen.

I'd seen signs of a transition in Ryan, as if he'd just taken a sociology class and become aware of social mores. I was trying to understand this, realizing most people did change, at least outwardly, as they made their way in life. But I didn't want it to be Ryan and I. We'd been together almost two years and in that time we'd carved out a sort of natural Oz-land, one where social performances, clothes, money, and saying the right thing at the right time didn't matter.

He understood I couldn't fully commit to him. The relaxed nature of the relationship, along with the assurance I'd always have a sex partner when I returned home from assignments—and, of course, the absolute torture that the idea of my ending up with a record store worker caused my mother—assured its continuation. He never questioned what I did on assignments, or with whom. Our relationship allowed me to breathe easy, avoiding emotional painfulness and insecurity that love brought.

But lately I had sensed an edge of tension from Ryan to go the next step. As if the last few weeks, the words 'I love you' lurked behind every gesture, every sentence, every question. My gut twisted, knowing my departure now would avoid the inevitable. Yet it was risky. Would he be here when I got back? I wanted to freeze him in time, so that in a year maybe I could answer the questions behind his anxious wide eyes.

My mother walked back toward our group with Ryan, her new puppy, trailing behind her, both of them carrying presents. She and Ryan placed all of them on an over-stuffed chair in the corner. I felt like a prisoner watching my captors prepare a torture chamber. I did not look forward to opening gifts while everyone studied my expression to see if I liked theirs.

"All right, everyone, gather around," my mother shouted. her drawl echoing as she twirled in a circle.

Guests moved toward her like moths to a bright light, and she smiled as she coaxed them all into her. Her smile, her perfect mask, her inviting body, and her overwhelming energy mesmerized all of them. I couldn't help but think of the only definition I remembered from physics. Vortex: A mass with a whirling motion that forms a cavity in the center of a circle which tends to draw toward this cavity bodies subject to its action.

That's what we all were, bodies drawn into an empty cavity and subject to her action. Christ, were we ever subject to her actions, like paupers who waited with gaping mouths and empty stomachs to see if the queen would throw us a crumb. And we'd all bow to her and kiss the ground before her, because she was beautiful. What bullshit, I thought, screaming inside.

"Darling, come help with the cake." Her head tilted

toward my father.

He followed her into the kitchen. Someone turned the music low and the movement stilled to give a stage to my mother's laughter echoing from the kitchen. "All right, Frank, not now, later," she giggled.

A low rumbling laughter rippled through the living room.

She made her entrance, carrying a large square cake, the burning candles spotlighting her Hollywood smile as she marched into the room, my father behind her. "Let's sing."

And they did.

"Let's open presents, sit there, Abigail and I'll hand them to you, Frank, take pictures." She said it all with a grin, and each of us obeyed, as we smiled back at her.

I opened several gifts, many things I would store away or donate to a shelter. But I imitated my mother's spurious smile through the whole process, as if someone had pressed it on with a hot iron.

"Are you sure ya like it, Abigail, 'cause if ya don't, I'll march right back into that store and get ya something different, a different color maybe?" my Aunt Dolores said as she bent over a fuzzy lavender robe with yellow and orange flowers embroidered along its sleeves and collar.

"No, really, I like it," I said, forcing the corners of my mouth up.

"I'da got ya something a little, you know, well… sexier." She looked over her shoulder at my father, whose face was expressionless. "But you just don't seem the type." She laughed a wide-opened horsy laugh, revealing every cigarette she'd ever smoked. "Now me, I'd want something a little sexier at your age, but your mom says she can't picture you wearing something like that."

"Right." I grabbed another gift. I glanced at my mother and wondered why every blouse she wore seemed to stretch across her tits. Couldn't she buy a fucking blouse that fit, that didn't advertise her breasts? God, they annoyed me, like intrusive guests that would never go away.

My mother handed me a large flat box wrapped in gold and silver striped paper, from my parents. "Be careful when you pull it out, " she whispered as she hovered.

Instead of ripping it open, I unwrapped the silver paper from the ends of the white box, detaching the tape with care, and lifted the top. Lying royally in a bed of silver tissue paper, my framed work stared up at me.

"Well, Abigail?"

I looked up at her. "I like it." Usually her presents were trinkets or jewelry that held little-to-no value to me.

I studied the photograph and surrounding frame. The golden eyes of the aye-aye lemur nestled in a tree stared back at me. I'd taken the picture ten months ago in Madagascar, waiting motionless at the base of a tree until nightfall for the nocturnal aye-aye. Leaves rustled, and then inch by inch, I turned, aimed, and took one of the best pictures of my career. The background was midnight blue and the edges of the tree branch blurred behind the brown fur of its plump body, its yellow eyes consuming the photograph.

I loved this picture, but the magazine I'd been on assignment with hadn't chosen it for publication. So I'd given it to my parents, along with other pictures from that trip. My mother had had the photograph custom-framed and chosen the matting and antique wooden frame to highlight the brilliance of the photograph.

How had she known this was one of my best photos? I hadn't told either of them. My mother probably pulled it at random from the stack of photos I'd given my father.

Ryan moved to my side. "That's one of Ab's favorites," he said, looking at my mother.

My father kissed her cheek as if to congratulate her, but I still wasn't going to assume she understood me. After all the years otherwise, it wasn't plausible to think she now valued my work.

"Ready?" Ryan pulled his eyebrows up to create a theatrical surprised expression.

"I suppose," I said, without enthusiasm. My heart racing against my will, with all the transitions in my breathing space, I was almost afraid of Ryan's gift.

"Wow, that's a big gift," my father said, as Ryan hoisted a large box wrapped in leftover Christmas paper at my feet.

"Love the paper." One side of my mouth crept up into a wry grin.

"Sorry, well, you know I keep everything, so I thought, paper is paper." He shrugged.

"And you're right." One thing I loved about Ryan was it never dawned on him that Christmas paper for a birthday present wouldn't do. He didn't feel embarrassed until the moment he laid it at my feet. The transition into society wasn't complete.

I tore the red Santa paper to reveal a large box, with a picture of a pop up tent, Coleman, printed at the edges of the white box. I raised my eyes to him. "Is it?"

"Yeah, it's a tent. Your color, too… green. And you can roll it up and tie it on your backpack. Pretty cool, huh?"

My mother leaned forward to inspect it.

"It's a tent," Ryan said, with pride in his voice, as if he had found the perfect gift for any woman and should be awarded a Romeo badge.

"Yes," my mother said, her mouth stiff, disgust shifting the other features of her face before she caught herself and forced her mouth back to its smiling form.

"I love it, Ryan. You're the best." I stood, Christmas paper crinkling at my feet, and wrapped my arms around his neck.

"I guess you can take it to Africa." His voiced sounded strained, like he was trying not to convey anger.

"Africa?" My mom looked over at us.

I glared at Ryan, then glanced at my mother, then to the crowd whispering to themselves and dispersing as if to avoid witnessing the train wreck about to happen. My eyes moved to my father, who stared at me, perplexed. I mouthed, 'talk later,' and he got it.

I didn't have a speech prepared for this. "Mom, I have to talk to you and Dad later. I have an opportunity…"

"Fine," she snapped, then snatched up the pieces of torn paper and stuffed them into a large bag. "All right, everyone, we have plenty of food and drinks left, no one's leaving until it's all gone." She crumpled another piece of wrapping paper between her small hands.

"Here, let me." I bent to pick up a piece of paper.

Her breathing seemed labored as she mumbled something. She shoved the crumpled paper into the sack with an exaggerated angry motion.

"What, Mom?"

"Nothing, darling. It's your birthday and I promised myself I wouldn't say anything about it. Anyway, what's the story about Africa?" She released the paper and stooped toward the floor.

"I have an opportunity with *National Geographic*. It's a year-long assignment in Africa." My words came out flat.

She lifted her head, inches from my face, and peered at me. "When?" she said again, in a hushed angry tone.

I lowered my eyes. "Tomorrow," I said in soft voice. My mom would never create a scene by blowing up in front of an audience. That wasn't in her script when she imagined my party, her party.

"Tomorrow? A year? Africa?" Her tone sounded far off, like her brain had to reach to process the information. Then a wide smile took over her face, her plastic 'I gotta get through this' smile, bereft of any emotion.

"A tent, darling. After almost two years of dating, I guess that's what you two call it. The man bought you a tent for your thirtieth birthday and gave it to you in front of everybody!" Her exhale reeked of disapproval, which said more than any lecture could have. With its soft whistle through heated breath, her sigh asked the all-important question: *Where did I go wrong?*

Why can't she ask me with her words instead of her eyes or a release of breath? Then I could tell her. I could point to the exact time, location, and event.

"Abigail," she whispered as she craned her neck forward. "You should start thinking about marriage, but I don't think

Ryan's the right person and the longer you stay with him…"
Her eyes darted to where Ryan stood.

"Mom, I'm not marrying anybody. Haven't I made that clear, plus I'm leaving for a year!"

She completely missed my point. A year from now, I would still be me and she would still be her. Too often she brought up marriage and children, slipping it into normal conversation, like subliminal messages that would penetrate me without notice

"When were you planning on telling your father and me?" It was an accusation wrapped in a question.

My semi-smile fell as I clenched my jaw. "Tonight. During the small family dinner we were supposed to have, until you decided to make my birthday about you so you could throw a damn party. You know I hate parties." I bit my lip, regretting my lack of control before the words even hit her.

"Abigail," she snapped in a strained voice, grabbing my wrist, "this was for *you*." She blinked as if stifling tears, but right away she shifted from hurt to indignation. "Well, I guess that's your thanks for all my troubles, trying to do something nice for my daughter." Her eyes flitted around the room, making sure we weren't creating a scene, something that didn't match the image she had crafted with such care.

"Really, Mom? Then make it about what your daughter wants, not what you want." I said, my voice flat as I grabbed the bag of garbage. "I'm taking this to the kitchen."

"All right, dear." She patted my back, looking around again to make sure no one heard us.

I moved away from her touch and carried the bag into the kitchen. At the buffet, I picked at the food sprawled across the white tablecloth, sliced some ham, and laid a couple of pieces between a small party bun. My mother, with her perfect-hostess act, charmed all the guests. With his eyes fixed on her, my father extended his hand, she took it and moved into him, nudging against his large frame. He smiled at her and his small brown eyes disappeared into folds of flesh.

Their gestures indicated he was introducing her to someone he worked with or knew from the country club. She offered her hand to the man, shook it, glanced up to my father, patted his chest, then lifted herself on her toes and kissed his cheek, nodded at the man, and excused herself to talk to a friend. My father stared after her, the man said something, and they both looked her way and my father shook his head with pride as if to say, 'Yes, that beautiful one, she's mine. And did you see the way she kissed me? She loves me.'

As though he thought if everyone else believed it, it would be true, she would love him the way he loved her. It wasn't true, no matter how many times she cooed at him in public, nestled her full tits into him at dinner parties, or giggled at his stories. *I knew*. But somewhere inside, the truth and the past nagged at him. Sometimes his eyes narrowed as he watched her crane her head back with laughter at some other man's joke.

People left, coming first to tell me to have a good trip, be careful, write often.

Ryan leaned into me. "We better get you home, you

gotta long day tomorrow and a long night tonight. I won't see you for year, so I want to make sure you remember me," he said pressing his forehead against mine.

I touched his cheek. *I am going to miss you.* His personality reminded me of a platypus, so many different components that didn't go together but were contained in one person. He had a degree in engineering, yet worked in a music store making minimum wage. He played music with his brother at local bars and now was diving into the dot-com world to combine his music with his knowledge of technology.

People described Ryan as laid back, carefree, oblivious to the intricacies of social nuances that haunt most people. He never registered the snide remarks or odd looks of other people. When I pointed them out to him, he'd say, "Oh, I bet they didn't mean it that way" … or "Maybe they had something in their eye."

He tolerated, even enjoyed, our push-and-pull relationship. On those occasions when he drifted away because I was too indifferent about us, I brought him back with a few words and more attention.

But lately his actions were those of a guy intensely in love. *A year?* A low panic came over me at the thought of my mother's words, "things change."

Asking him to wait a year meant I needed to be available emotionally for a commitment when I returned. Would he still be here in a year? I didn't like either option.

"Abbey, what's this about Africa?" My father frowned.

"Dad, it's an opportunity of a lifetime. If I nail this, I can call my own shots, take only the assignments I want."

The pleading tone in my voice hit me. "Dad, I…"

"I'm proud of you," he whispered, his large arms circling me. "It's just that when we get used to having your beautiful smile around, you're off again. I get it, but a year?"

"I know." I grimaced as I peered up at him, "I… I, well, I really have to take this."

He kissed the top of my head. "Just be safe and try writing every once in a while." He pulled back, his eyes darting to my mom, then narrowing on me. "Okay?"

"I'll try, I promise." A small smile crossed my face. He understood how important this was to me.

"Everyone had a fantastic time. Do you agree, Frank?" Her charm rose to the spotlight, mannerisms reminiscent of a starlet in one of those old black-and-white movies. Her head tilted as if her chin were drawing a crescent moon in the air, her lips pursed together, pulling a bit to one side, as her eyebrows formed a theatrical arch when she spoke and looked at all of us for praise.

I wanted to yell, 'Curtain call! Lady, you were done years ago. Get off the stage.'

"Once again, Rachel, you outdid yourself." My father was aware of the words she needed to hear.

As my mother beamed at all of us, I waited for her to lift her skirt and curtsey, the next logical step. Then her eyes flitted toward me. "Well, I'm not sure Abigail enjoyed it."

I didn't look at her. "I did, just not big on surprises." My tone went flat. Then I turned toward my father, giving him a soft smile. "I really love the picture."

"Well, thank your mother. It was her idea."

So, it *was* my mother.

"The photo really stood out among the others. You have a good eye," she said in a soft voice.

"Thanks." How did she know what a good eye was? She had an instant camera. She probably figured it was the thing to say.

"But I still can't understand your affinity for ugly creatures. I guess you see some kind of beauty in them." Her tone shifted to amusement, lightening the air around us.

I rolled my eyes at her attempt at shallow humor. "Mom, I think you're missing the point—"

"I, for one," said Ryan, "am glad this attractive woman finds beauty in ugly creatures."

From down the hall, Ethan guffawed. "Yeah, I bet you count your blessings every day, Ryan."

"Bite me!" I yelled at Ethan.

"Please, Abigail," my mother said.

Then we all laughed at the silliness of the conversation.

I headed toward the door. "We're gone. I really have to get home to pack."

Ethan laid his head on my shoulder and I told him I'd write. My mother patted my back and I was glad my hands were full of packages, so I wouldn't have to feel the emptiness in one of her stiff, rehearsed hugs, where her shoulders touch mine and her torso arches back, clear of any real contact.

"All right then, call me in the morning, dear." She pulled herself up like a marionette puppet, working the strings and lifting her shoulders to match her turned-up mouth.

"I will," I said over my shoulder, as Ryan and I escaped out the door.

On the drive home, Ryan and I exchanged few words. In the midst of a thick silence, we unloaded the car and piled the packages on my bedroom floor.

"Ab," he said as he set the last package against the wall. His solemn eyes halted our methodical preparation.

I pulled two large backpacks from my closet and set them on the bed. "Are you going to help me pack, so we can spend the rest of the night remembering each other?" I made my voice playful on purpose. I grabbed some clothes from a drawer, tossed them toward the bed, then turned back to the dresser.

Ryan grabbed my arm from behind. "Ab, you said you hoped I'd be here in a year. What does that mean?"

"Ryan."

"Come on, what does it mean? Are we finally putting a monogamous stamp on this relationship?" He made quote marks in the air with his fingers when he said 'monogamous.'

"What would be different? When I'm in Austin, we're always together."

He narrowed his eyes into brown slits. "Yeah, and when you're gone to Sudan or Rwanda or wherever the hell, how am I to know you're not going to fall madly in love with some environmentalist or writer or someone you find in the jungle?"

"It hasn't happened yet," I said through a dull laugh.

That was true. Even with the relative freedom my relationship with Ryan granted, I had never met anybody worth trading him in for. I still fucked whomever I wanted when I was gone, but Ryan offered an emotional friendship I hadn't ever enjoyed with any other man.

"You haven't been gone a year before. A year is a long time."

"I know, and I can't ask you to wait. I just said, *I hoped*, but I'm not asking. It wouldn't be fair."

His eyebrows knitted together. "To whom?"

"I'm going to use this year and make some decisions about what I want and that includes you and me. But I just don't think it's fair for me to lock you in."

"I'll decide what's fair for me. But what's fair for you?"

"I don't know."

He stood inches from me. The tension, spray-painted with all the caged words that were never exchanged between us, spread across me.

"You don't *know*, or you don't *want* it. Come on, Ab, you've been my best friend and lover for nearly two years. That constitutes a serious relationship." He took his time as he waved his hands up and down the outline of my body. "Don't get me wrong. I like this."

"But—"

"But a year of not knowing, of just waiting to see how things will be when you get back. I don't know about that."

I dropped my gaze to the floor. Our conversation resembled something written in those cheesy romance novels. "I just can't say for sure what will happen this year."

He threw his hands in the air, as if surrendering, then stepped back. "So, same status then?"

"I guess."

His jaw tightened. "All right, I'm not guaranteeing anything either. A year, shit, a *year*." Defeat twisted through his voice.

"Ryan." I stepped toward him.

His eyes turned glassy. "Just for the record, this is your decision, keeping everything ambiguous for another year. Because if I knew, I'd…"

His toned dropped. "Abbey, I do…" His tongue pushed against his front teeth to form the 'L' sound.

"Shhh." I laid my index finger across his lips.

"We can't say that, can we?" He moved my finger from his mouth. "That would make it too real."

"Ryan, what we have has worked for nearly two years."

But he was right and nothing in the universe can remain in a state of inertia forever. I just couldn't move forward without being filled with dread. I wasn't willing to give up anything in order to promise my life to any man, even this one.

"I guess the deal is, I have been faithful while I waited for you during each assignment, and I don't know if you've been faithful while you're away. Or what you're doing, for that matter."

"Are you asking me if I have been—"

"Nope, we agreed not to tell, so I'll just live with the risk, and *so will you.*"

"I'm trying to be fair to you."

"Let's be real. You aren't being fair to me. You're making sure you aren't tied down, in case you want the freedom."

He turned and walked toward my closet. His ribs rose and fell a couple of times while he tried to maintain his composure. "Forget this, Ab. I'll see you tomorrow for the airport run, because I said I would, but now I'm outta here!"

My stomach churned. "Please, Ryan, stay. This is my last night to *remember* you for a whole year." I laced my tone with a modicum of sultry urgency, wanting him to stay.

When he continued toward the door, my façade dropped, revealing my internal desperation. "Don't go, please!"

I cringed at how needy I sounded, but I couldn't let him leave, not like this.

Ryan whirled toward me. "Shit, Abs, really sick of having this conversation. We'll do it your way but no guarantees from me," he gritted out, throwing his arms up in the air. "Let's get you packed, so we can get to the non-verbal part of the night."

His hands caressed my rib cage up and down, coming to rest just under my breasts. "That part seems easy for you." A tense smirk crossed his face.

With all the doubt visible in his expression, my spine stiffened against the unknown.

CHAPTER 2

One year later ...

Johann moved against my arm, and I jerked. We had sat still as statues for so long, taking controlled shallow breaths in silence. Hiding in the jungle's weave of dense, wet forest for hours, we leaned against one another, not as humans, but as structures for support during the nightfall of the African forest, waiting for dawn.

We were awakened to the nonstop sound of nature's nocturnal children who arise with the sun's closing to become predators of their smaller cousins. A pair of eyes glowing from a bamboo tree stared back at me.

At the sight of a snake sliding on the branch of a nearby tree, I flinched, not from fear, only my body's reaction to the odd sound the snake made. After years of work for *National Geographic* and other wildlife magazines, my camera lens had taken me everywhere and not much startled me, even in the deepest most secluded crevices of the world. I felt proud to have seen closed parts of the earth that others would know only through my photographs.

"Abbey, there, to your left, no fast movements," Johann

murmured, his thick German accent slicing through the humid air.

I rotated my head as if I were a mime performing a street show. My chest pulled inward, the small explosion of my heart caused a slight gasp to expel. A great silverback peered out from behind a large bamboo leaf, his black beady eyes like shiny onyx.

This was the third time we saw him in almost a month, but never this close. The workers had spotted this gorilla family six weeks ago and steered us toward them.

He tilted his head, examining the two humans and the equipment that hung from our necks. I waited, sucking in air, struggling to control my breathing. I longed for the king's approval. He didn't offer any gesture to indicate he would allow us to intrude in his domain, much less to photograph him, thereby making his face as common as a Calvin Klein model.

Before every photo, I allowed my eyes a moment to take a snapshot of the image in front of me, which remained imprinted in my brain's photo album. Those living images had a more powerful effect on me than the printed ones I would later examine on paper. When my eyes first took in what my camera would later seize, adrenaline rushed through my body, triggering my heart to race, only to slow when concentration was necessary to capture the unimaginable in print.

"Christ, Johann. How long do you think he's been checking us out? He's putting his finger to his mouth, as if we were rats in some science lab experiment. I think he's frowning at you."

"Funny. Quiet. I don't want to lose this shot." His blue eyes peered at me from behind sweaty strands of blonde hair matted against his forehead.

"I get first shot," I whispered.

"Abbey," he hissed.

My eyes stayed fixed on my large hairy friend, and with a half-cocked grin I said, "Three nights ago in the tent. Need I say more?"

"All right, I promised," he whispered, his guttural voice dull with defeat.

Movement from the silverback. He approached, studying his human intruders with intense caution. His hairy hand pushed the foliage aside as he edged toward us. I breathed in deep, then inch by inch brought the camera up and adjusted the lens, waiting for the dark beady eyes and protruding mouth to give me a sign. He stopped about fifty feet from us and held up his hand as if waving, exposing his thick leathery palm.

"Now, Abbey."

"Hush," I said without moving the camera.

The silverback stilled his body, his eyes wondered at me. I kept the camera steady while I moved my head to the side, capturing the beautiful animal with my eyes, giving my brain the seconds it needed to record the image, to remember the rush that was mine.

He pulled back his black wide lips to expose his teeth; it wasn't a warning grimace, often displayed when a primate is threatened, but a relaxed grin as though he had me figured out.

I smiled back. We might have been two strangers sitting

across the table from one another and we had just agreed over a cup of coffee to be friends, not to hurt each other. I nodded to him.

Then I shifted my head in front of the camera and adjusted the lens for perfection. Wanting, pleading inside, for the beast of nature to come just a little closer, to feel his husky, hot breath. I snapped pictures as quickly as the camera was able.

Movement.

Through my lens I spotted another gorilla, a female. She kept her body turned to the side, one shoulder rotated inward. The power of the lens revealed an infant buried deep in her chest, though I didn't need to see it clutching her chest to know she was a mom.

Deep in her inky eyes existed the vulnerability of motherhood I had learned to recognize after a year of photographing mothers and their offspring. The baby gorilla clinging to her made us a bigger threat. Her life was no longer her own. It now belonged to the extension nestled against her massive chest.

The silverback turned his head as if to say, 'go back, they're intruders. They seem friendly, but you never know with these human types, they change their minds, jumping between friendship and enemy without notice.' Be alert, was the message in his eyes. He snorted, his massive nostrils flaring, while his eyes darted from us to the infant.

I held my breath and let my finger ride the trigger of the camera, stealing a moment from the gorilla's life. The desire of humans to know all, to see all, to leave no part of the earth uncovered, gave me this job. The infant scrambled higher on its mother's chest, its tiny hands clasping her thick coat.

When the shutter on Johann's camera clicked, I lowered mine. I was afraid the combination of both our cameras, the intrusive projecting lenses, and the greedy sound of shutters might cause the family to grow restless and retreat into their green shelter.

The mother clutched her infant and stared at me for a long moment, as if to see whether I understood her, grasped her fear, her need to protect the young one in her arms. My heart climbed to the bottom of my throat.

"Mom," I croaked in a small whisper, caught in between two worlds. The world before me: a mother protecting her young, and the mother I had at home, who hadn't protected me.

Her stare was exacting, so much so, I had to fight back the wetness settling in my eyes. 'I understand you,' I wanted to say.

But did I? Did I comprehend the sacrifice she was willing to make for the infant she held so closely? I wondered about my own mother. How had she ignored the biological drive to protect, to make her child's life safe, distant from pain?

I studied the mother before me. 'I don't understand, but I respect you. I respect your love, your intense need to protect, and I will not violate it.'

After I spent several months viewing live home movies of primate mothers and their young, the feeling intensified of what has been missed between my mother and me. I'd shot a variety of emotion-provoking photos, which served as a constant reminder of the work ahead of me when I return home. I wanted to find somewhere amongst the ruins of betrayal, misunderstandings, and all the ill words, a meeting point for my mother and me.

I brought my hand up to Johann's camera, cueing him to lower his exposing lens, give the mother what she asked for, a moment of respect. With her torso still turned, keeping her infant shielded from our view (they always shield their infants with their bodies), she nodded at me and then let her gaze drop to my camera.

I drew the camera to my eye, focused, and stared though the lens in disbelief. In a gesture that seemed almost planned, as if she were a model and I had told her how to pose for the cover of some parent magazine, she turned toward me, opening her chest to the camera and exposing her infant. Then she looked down at her infant, tenderness transforming her expression.

I held my breath and clicked twice before she rotated her shoulders to cloak the infant from the camera's lens. God, two pictures of the most spectacular pose, demonstrating the strongest bond in the living world. Only two, so I had to hope one of the photos conveyed what the mother entrusted to me, her most sacred emotion.

She glanced over her shoulder, confirming our friendship, our understanding. Her expression reminded me of a professor who hoped her student understood the lesson that day. I nodded.

At a slow pace, upright, almost strolling, she rambled into the safety of the bush. The great silverback's shoulders lurched forward, and in a flash we stepped back. He swung his head from side to side like a giant pendulum, and then, on all fours, bounded after his family.

We stood, without movement, alone again, longing to see more of our powerful cousins. Neither Johann nor I spoke for minutes. The female mountain gorilla had shown me a truth so vivid and real, yet still difficult to get my head around. She made every decision based on the deep fear that loving another can cause, leading her to an extreme desire to protect.

Johann's article focused on the primate mother/infant bond in the wild. *National Geographic* and *GEO* (the German equivalent) had planned to dedicate several issues to that topic. When I read his words, 'there is nothing more powerful than the bond between a primate mother and her offspring,' I sighed and tried to swallow, but something— anger, disappointment, even longing—caught in my throat. *I wonder if that gorilla mom could give lessons.*

I'd spent the better part of the past year photographing that very bond, taking hundreds of photos of mothers and infants playing, grooming, sleeping, and a few that displayed the fierceness of the mother when her young were threatened.

The photographs could not capture the intense screeches and howls from a mother when separated from her infant or the fearful desperate calls from an offspring to its mother when it strayed too far. I'd heard stories of animal traders who capture infant monkeys to sell as pets on the open market, and I learned the only safe way to take an infant from its mother is first to kill the mother. Often the infant doesn't survive the trip to market, not from a lack of food, or water, but because its heart has shriveled up from despair.

I flinched when Johann touched my arm.

"Damn it, what?" I snapped.

"You were gone. We've been standing here for almost twenty minutes. Let's get back to camp and eat. I'm starving."

"Yeah, me, too."

"Abbey, what's wrong? We got some great shots."

"Nothing," I blurted as my mind caught up with his words. My sun-chapped lips managed a half smile. "This will be an incredible layout."

He curled his arm around my shoulders. "The last months with you have been good, great, I mean."

He always spoke as if searching the air for the right English words to express what came so naturally to him in German. His facial expression was one of grave concentration, even if his words were light.

"Yes," I said, showing him the standard 'I hate for this to end because you're such a great guy' smile I kept stored for the end of a rendezvous. The guy always seemed to be trying to convey that our encounter was of some profound significance.

Isn't it the arrogance of a human to believe I was thinking about him, an experience I can have over and over again, rather than being fifty feet from one of the smartest, most powerful animals that walk the earth? Wouldn't it make more sense that my mind and body were occupied by the moment in time only minutes before, rather than my brief familiar affair with Johann?

In silence we walked to the camp, his arm weightless across my shoulder. When we arrived, several of the workers who had been our guides, operation organizers, and cooks, ran towards us. The darkness of their skin exaggerated their white smiles. Dozens of excited questions wrapped in French were thrown at us.

At best, my French was weak, so rarely did I converse with the workers, but Johann, raised in Germany, found the bordering country's language easy. He told them the tale of the great silverback, nonstop touching his camera, the keeper of all his tales.

I backed away from the commotion into the tent, easing myself out of my sweat-soaked clothes, and wrapped a stiff towel around my body. I left the tent to wash off the grime in the outdoor shower rigged by the workers. They had draped an old shower spigot over a tree, using an ordinary garden hose to connect it to the water supply, a silver tank that they kept full of water. The water was naturally warm, sometimes even hot from the African sun.

I let my towel fall to the ground as I moved under the shower spigot. The stares of the workers, joined by Johann shaking his head, made me laugh. I matched their stares with a wide smile, tempted to grab my breasts and be obnoxious, but I held back. They had seen my naked body several times over the past months, yet the stares never waned.

My skin reddened with the water's touch as it ran down my back and traveled the length of my legs before spilling into the soil. I used a homemade soap to wash everything, my face, my body, and last of all my hair.

As I twisted my hair, squeezing water from the wet strands, it hit me. I'll be 31 in a few days.

We were done, and I didn't have another job waiting, so I would return home to Austin. I'd face my mother again.

The last time I saw my mother she had thrown me a surprise thirtieth birthday party… she knows I hate surprises, yet she still used my birthday as the stage for her social agenda.

Stop, Abbey.

I shut my eyes for a moment and remembered the mother gorilla and her infant. I tried to swallow, my throat thick with anxiety and frustration, not at my mother, but at myself. The primates who surrounded me for the past year had taught me lessons. I understood, now more than ever, that the mother-child bond was indestructible. Things would be different when I saw my mother this time.

I wanted to leave the anger buried somewhere on the African continent, not bring it with me, carried inside, as I had for so long.

"Abbey, my African Queen," Johann said, holding the towel out for me.

I turned the knob and stepped into the towel. He wrapped it around my body, whispering in my ear, "Must you torment me and all these men?"

"One is only tormented if they are weak enough to allow their wishes to override logic." I tossed my head back and walked towards the tent.

"All right, Abbey. Enough of your American version of existentialism."

I took time brushing out my hair while he showered. After he returned to the tent and dressed, he held up a bottle of South African wine. "I've been saving this bottle of cabernet for this… this time, minute, moment… yes, this moment. We should make this a… different night for many reasons."

I laughed. He had retrieved the wrong word. "You mean, 'special,' Johann?"

"Yes. Yes, special." He watched me, his eyes following my naked body through the tent while I searched for clean clothing.

I slid my arms into two holes, letting a gauzy white smock float across my skin, knowing the thin material wouldn't conceal my light strawberry areolas and the dark mound between my legs. I placed my hands on my hips, aware of my disclosure, reveling in its power.

"Johann, how should we celebrate?" My voice low, suggesting the answer.

"Well, let's start with wine, some bush meat, Wein, Buschfleisch." When at the mercy of his nerves, his German took over.

I raised my eyebrows. "Wild bushmeat?"

"Wild." He reached for a bottle opener.

The cook brought in a dinner of wild boar that had been roasting all day. We sat across from each other, pulled apart dense bread, and buried our teeth into the tender meat. Its warm juice captured my tongue, followed by a sip of dry cab, its tartness stripping my taste buds of boar, preparing them for each new bite.

I wanted to toss my wet head back and scream. Hours of deprivation made the usual—a warm shower, tart wine, the coarseness of dense bread in my mouth, the feel of my teeth burying into tender meat, and wet hair lying over clean skin—feel overwhelming, as if the very sensations were only just discovered.

Johann's eyes were fixed on me as we talked about the

silverback's glory and how lucky we were to have snapped photos only a few years after the 1994 Rwandan Civil War. Many great apes lost their lives, the unintended consequence of human destruction.

"We should be able to get high dollar for this piece, Abbey. Don't you agree? We should discuss a price, so we match," Johann said.

"I'm of the same mind, so I'm open to price. You know what I want out of this."

He grinned. "I do?"

"Um, well, and how about a lot of attention that will lead to other jobs. What we have is rare, the photos and your story angle." I sounded business-like, but I wanted him to focus on the goal.

He nodded, realizing this was his shot, too. *Get this right and our careers were set.*

The red liquid halfway up my glass held my gaze, my distracted mind playing my mother's voice, my father's laugh, Ethan's smile, and at the end, Ryan's words, 'Ab,' I hoped he'd say, 'I'm glad you're home,' open and unassuming as he had always been.

Could this be the last time I fell into bed with a man without emotional attachment, just to fulfill a physical need? No more random affairs. Just Ryan. Could I do that? I want to do that.

Until meeting Johann, a German photojournalist with *GEO*, three months ago, I'd been faithful to Ryan during this international assignment. But after eight months of no sex, Johann's rigid lean body and his dry charm got the best of me.

I hadn't wanted any kind of emotional involvement, just sex, and maybe some good conversation. I sensed he thought we had more, and, so the sex would continue, I let him believe that. A few times when my body was entangled in Johann's, scrambling for pleasurable release, I thought about Ryan and if he were doing the same, if he'd caved under months of no sex and still no commitment from the woman he wrote to in Africa every week. His letters had been consistent for the first several months and then nothing for a few months until the letter I'd received just weeks ago, stating he missed me terribly.

"Abbey, where are you?" Johann poured more of the intoxicating liquid into my glass. It took hold, danced in my head, and tickled my crotch, all connected for one mission.

"I'm here, right here," I whispered as I reached across the small table. Leaning forward, I ran my index finger down the length of his arm before grasping his hand and wrapping my lips around his middle finger, sucking.

He moved back in his chair and pulled his hand away.

"All right, Abbey, I understand." His eyes pinched, he almost scowled at me, as if my actions had somehow undermined his thoughts, and I should have known that. "We'll head out tomorrow. You said you're going back to the States. Austin, right?"

He drew in a breath to indicate the importance of his next words. "I'm planning to take some holiday. I'd like to travel with you… to your home… to Texas." He flashed a twitchy nervous smile. "I hear there are some pretty wild animals raised on Texas land."

The way he drew out Texas sounded like Tax…ass.

"Johann," I said in my smoothest voice. I stood, walked to him, giving myself time to prepare my speech so I could get what I wanted.

Light flooded through the thin, net-like sides of the tent, weaving translucence into my threadbare cotton smock, revealing my erect nipples, exposing me. His eyes fogged and his tense lips became pliable as he stared at me.

I wrapped my callused hands around his, holding them in a manner that seemed odd, almost nurturing. With a few words, I could assuage his disappointment, at least for tonight, and we would continue, ending on a peak instead of a lull.

"Johann, it's not you, and of course the past months have meant a lot to me, but I have some things to work out. I haven't seen my family in a year and I need to go home alone."

My words sounded so sincere I almost believed them myself. But soon he would forget me, and his contact with me would dissipate into sporadic e-mails.

He drew me close, pulling the white gauze from my shoulders. Lazily, it slid down my body, revealing my light skin. I stood motionless, letting him remove his clothing. When he touched me, his movements were slow, full of meaning. He was making love to me.

No, why that, I wondered? Why take something primal like fornication and transform it into some psychological purging of our inner selves?

When men made a point of 'making love,' it was like they wanted me to know they were expressing something deeper than two bodies needing to come together, to tighten, then relax for the sake of it, no other reason. But they were inconsistent. How did they decide whom they make love to and whom they fuck?

I resolved long ago to keep it simple. Just fuck and read nothing into it.

Ryan and I had achieved that understanding—sex was for fun. Making the perfect cup of coffee, knowing I liked a squirt of cream and half a package of Equal, washing my Jeep in the Texas heat, and staring at millions of wildlife pictures until two in the morning, those gestures expressed more than jumping into bed.

Now, I wanted Johann and me to come together with the same instincts and force that the animals in the jungle did. I wanted to feel close to them. I changed the course of our interactions, a bite of the lip, a push of the hips, and a tug at the hair that hung at the base of his neck.

"Christus, Abbey!" Words thrown out through heavy breaths. "Christus!"

I answered by letting my mouth run down the middle of his chest, before surrounding his penis with my lips. He reared back, and the animal took control. It no longer mattered what it meant. Tomorrow I would leave.

THE STAGNANT AIR THAT DRIFTED from the smoking section to the non-smoking section tickled the cilia protecting my lungs, resulting in a cough that persisted until I inhaled the open Texas air. No one had come to pick me up, no 'we're so glad you're home, how long will you stay?'

I hadn't told my family or Ryan an exact time, using the

excuse that all the connections came with no guarantees. After flying over three continents, I needed to rest before facing family. I hailed a taxi to take me home.

CHAPTER 3

You can still feel the heavy warmth of the afternoon sun in September. Austin hangs on to summer, like a desperate child to its mother's leg when the babysitter arrives, not wanting autumn and then winter to bury all the sundresses, margaritas, and Jimmy Buffet imitation bands that play at the waterfront bars. I'd grown accustomed to the harsh African sun, so the heat felt natural to me.

What seemed foreign was my own home. Like looking at a picture of yourself in grade school, recognizing all the characteristics—your nose, the color of your hair, your eyes—yet wondering who that person was.

Encumbered by the heavy bags, I pushed myself through the door to a home I seldom occupied. I lowered them to the floor in the foyer and turned to drop my keys in the bowl on the white washed table that leaned against the wall, but the table was gone and a large plant sat on the tile floor instead.

Where is that damn table? Then I remembered I needed a bedside table, so I had moved it a week before I left.

I walked through the small foyer to the kitchen, running my hands over the counter, my palm leaving a path in the thin layer of dust. I opened the refrigerator to find a six-pack of Celis, an Austin hometown favorite, a half-empty bottle of barbecue sauce, and an egg ready to hatch.

Trance-like, I meandered through my condo, dragging my fingers across the sofa, the chair, as if I'd just come home from college and was petting the family dog I'd forgotten. The worn corduroy couch still held the imprints of bodies sunken into the cushions, a sign that life existed.

I looked closer. Ryan's dog, Spartan, had left part of his coat on the sofa. Golden hairs, evidence that Ryan and his furry friend had been here not long ago. The visual of Spartan nestled against a half-asleep Ryan, both snoring as they pretended to watch TV, made my home seem more real, less vacant and sterile.

I stopped at the entrance to my bedroom. Strung across my white down comforter were red rose petals and lying on top of my pillow, a card. I jumped on the bed and rolled across the sea of red, letting the scent of crucified petals torn from fresh flowers fill my nostrils.

"Ryan," I gurgled, between excited laughter, stretching out my arms and legs back and forth like a child making a snow angel. I got up and looked at the vague form outlined in red, a symbol of what little girls were supposed to be: kind, empathetic, and pure. Catholic school had taught me that, but I'd always wondered what was in it for the angel.

The white envelope had fallen to the floor. I grabbed and ripped it open. Even as I tore the flap, I didn't know what I wanted it to say. Splayed on the front of a simple sheet of white paper, folded into a card, was a computer graphic bursting with retro color and shaped into something resembling a heart. Ryan's card read:

> Abbey,
> I missed you tremendously. I have things
> to tell you, but mostly I can't wait to hold
> you.
> Love,
> Ryan

"Ryan."

His printed words made things seem more familiar, and my body relaxed. During the not-quite-forty-two-hour plane ride, my desire to see Ryan had increased, almost rising to an ache.

Indeed I had missed him as a concrete part of my life, not in desperation, but in a complete way. As if during the past year I had stared at the Mona Lisa without a mouth. It was simply strange. While I craved the adventure of traveling and leaving everything behind, I also liked knowing things remained the same during my absence.

I left the flora that decorated my comforter and wandered into the living room. The relentless red glow of the answering machine blinked like mad in the dim light and, after a pause lasting several moments, I did it. I pushed the button to my answering machine.

"Abigail, it's Mom. Are you home yet? Your brother said sometime today or tomorrow, is that right? Call us the minute you walk in."

"Abbey, are you there? Pick-up. Call Mom and Dad when you get in. Mom really wants to see you. You have to meet José, he's great." - from my brother, Ethan.

"I miss you and Africa already. New York called. The

pictures arrived and they're impressed. Call me. I want to talk to you." - Johann.

"I hope you're finally home. I'll be by later." - Ryan.

In the bathroom next to my bedroom, I splashed water on my face and brushed my teeth. After peeling off my khakis and black t-shirt, I slipped under the comforter to try to squelch the travel insomnia. My mind surrendered itself to sleep.

FAINT RINGS CHIMED DURING my last moments of REM. Those seconds before the brain clicks on, yet the body has already responded, jerking the mind awake, sleep abandons the fight to active brain synapses while remnants of a dream run for cover in a dark closet.

I reached out in the dusky room for my small clock, 7:30 p.m. Hours had passed. The phone rang again, then the doorbell, both pulling me into a full state of wakefulness.

I flung my legs off the side of the bed and stood, shaking the last residue of drift from my head. Without a shred of energy, I stumbled to the phone, hoping the caller would just leave a message. But the person kept calling and hanging up whenever the answering machine came on.

"Hello," I said, a notch above audible.

"Abbey, I knew you were there."

"Ethan." I drew out my brother's name through a long yawn.

"How long have you been home?"

"Why? Are you conducting an investigation?" I teased.

The knocking at the door continued, growing in both

volume and pace.

"Just a minute, Ethan, someone's at the door."

I held the cordless phone as I walked to the door. Ryan's transformed face filled the view through the peephole, I looked closer. His chin was clean-shaven, the goatee banished, his hair cut shorter, emphasizing his sharp jaw and square chin. His brown eyes peered back at me.

Ryan's here," I said into the receiver.

"Abbey, call Mom. She's really anxious to see you."

I opened the door, crooking my finger for Ryan to come in. I stood in front of him, with only a pair of white cotton panties preventing my total nudity.

He hesitated as he stared at me.

"Come in. Should have just used your key." I jerked my head to the side and rolled my eyes in exasperation. "Get in here."

When he looked at me, grinning, my heart jumped, surprised at how excited I was to see him.

"What?" My brother yelled from the other end.

"I was just telling Ryan to come in."

Ryan put a large white bag into the refrigerator and took out a Celis. He opened the cold beer and leaned his tall lean body against the kitchen counter. His eyes parked on me, probing my body.

I shook my hand at him to say, 'don't look at me.'

He returned my gesture with a hungry smile and raised his eyebrows, his eyes growing into brown saucers. He let out a cocky chuckle before walking through the living room and then slid open the glass door to the patio.

"I'll be out here, Ab." His grin, made him look younger

than his thirty-three years.

His back hunched forward, his arms bracing against the wrought-iron banister. He could stay out there for hours watching the blue sky darken as the sun edged itself down behind the old red-roofed, Spanish-style houses on the other side of the lake. The glare of the sun ignited the red in the clay-tiled roofs, a fire dance displayed on the rooftops.

He cocked his head to the side like an owl sensing dinner and listened to the trees shifting against each other. We had stood out there a hundred times to watch the sunset, and after it disappeared, I always said, 'Let's go in, I'm hot,' or 'I'm cold.'

'Come on, ten more minutes, come on,' he'd say.

To bring myself back to the present, I shook my head with vigor. "Sorry, Ethan, Ryan just got here."

"Tell him I said hi. I'll see him tomorrow at Mom and Dad's. She's cooking dinner for everyone. By the way, Ryan's on her good side now."

"He was never on her bad side. She just didn't want me walking down the aisle with him."

"Well, that's all changed. Mom's quite taken with him lately. He and his brother are really successful with that new business and he's been at the house a lot to get legal advice from Dad. Somehow he's won Mom's heart."

"Great!" Sarcasm felt like an appropriate response.

"I thought you'd be glad."

"I don't want anyone making decisions for me, least of all Mom."

All right, Abbey, I mouthed before I took a deep reassuring breath, the kind I imagine actors take just before the curtain opens. I'd promised myself not to walk in my old shoes, to behave differently toward my mother.

"Did you say something?"

"No, the TV."

"Damn, I was hoping the jungle would take some of that meanness out of you." He laughed.

"It did, but then I had to come home and face family." I tried to sound more playful than agitated, but no one ever suggested I pursue acting. "I'm glad they're getting along. I guess it means Mom's lightening up a little."

"I think she sees it as Ryan has finally stepped up to the plate."

"What?"

"You can't blame her for being concerned. Last year he was a thirty-two-year-old guy working at a music store, but now he's doing well with his business."

"I'd like to think Ryan hasn't done a three-sixty, but rather that Mom wants to give him a chance because he's a good friend of mine, hell, and yours, too, for that matter."

He laughed. "Okay, Ab, however they got there, I'm just telling you the situation's going to be easier for you. She acts like he's her new son."

"Good, I'm glad, but I need to let you go. Ryan's waiting."

"See you tomorrow."

"All right."

After we hung up, I grabbed a pair of faded Levi's and a white t-shirt from the dresser and threw them on. When I walked out of the bedroom, Ryan was sitting on the couch, thumbing through an old *Texas Highways* magazine, one leg draped over the other, his socks exposed. They were crumpled at his ankles and didn't match, one had a thin red stripe and the other, naked white.

So his new cleaned-up look had not soaked through all the way. Maybe there was still time for me to mess him up again, I thought, laughing to myself.

"Why did you come in so quick? I was going to join you out there."

He looked up and tossed the magazine on the table. "Felt some drops on my arms. But the more crucial question is, why did you get dressed?" His mouth cranked into a slanted smile, and he squinted his eyes as if he could see through my t-shirt and his hands were already cupping my breasts.

"Because I didn't want to tempt you before you feed me."

He stood up and moved toward me to close the gap of old air between us. My heart pulsated in my throat. God, I had missed him. He wrapped his arms around me and I nuzzled into his pressed shirt. A pressed shirt, on a guy who thought an iron was the perfect surface for frying an egg?

He ran his fingers through my hair. "I really missed you. Damn, in a bad way." He pulled my body closer, rearranging his limbs to fit them around me.

"Does this feel weird?"

His light blue shirt smelled like chemicals. Shit, he's dry cleaning his clothes now.

He took a deep breath. "You know what feels weird? While you were gone for a year, my coming to this place and not seeing you." His chest rose and fell in rapid succession. "I don't know how much to say."

"Don't say anything tonight. I missed you, too. Let's just relax. Some music, beer, barbecue. God, I haven't eaten barbecue in so long!" I screamed, throwing my head back with enough drama for a small audience. "Barbecue and a little you, that's what I need."

"You're gonna get a lot of me." He puffed his chest up and pointed his chin in the air.

"Double entendre?"

He squeezed me so tight I thought my ribs would collapse into my organs.

"Ryan you're cutting off my circulation," I gasped.

"Sorry… shit." He shook his head. "I just missed you," he said, as though he hadn't wanted to miss me, but something had yanked him back to me and he couldn't help but concede. He opened his hands, releasing their grip on me.

"Music?" I moved across the room and turned on the stereo. I placed my hands on my hips and watched him, a smug grin on his face, swagger past me toward the kitchen. "What are you doing?"

He grabbed the large white bag with clear grease spots covering the bottom from the refrigerator and held it in the air. "Barbecue."

"How did you—"

"I just knew." He arranged ribs and sliced brisket on a plate, then put it into the microwave.

"Now eat this, listen to some music, drink a beer, and then you're mine." He looked down at his watch. "Hurry, you've got five minutes before I rip your clothes off. A year's way too long for this boy."

"Yikes, you're scaring me," I said in a high squeaky voice.

We sat on the floor and ate. When we finished, Ryan turned the radio off, put on a slow blues CD, *Steak*, by Guy Forsyth, a local young white guy with the voice of an old black man. The music slid across the room, wrapping around my shoulders, escorting me back to Austin. My mind caught up to my body.

We moved to the couch and sat in disquieted silence as if new to this. Not like young lovers, more like middle-aged people, survivors of divorce, and after many desolate years had discovered each other and were coming together, desperate and unsure.

His breathing became deep and deliberate, while mine felt fast and uneasy. He moved his hand from my shoulder to my thigh, to my waist, letting it rest on the opening to my jeans. His fingers were jumpy, the tips circling the metal buttons of my 501s, studying the exact dimensions of the opening, calculating the precise fine motor coordination it would take to get inside.

"Abbey, I just…" His voice shook. "I should tell you…"

He pulled his hand away from my zipper, let it drop to his leg, eyeing it as if it were a misbehaved puppy, telling it to mind, to stay down. "While you were gone—"

"Ryan, we don't have to go there."

I didn't want him to explore all his feelings during my absence, mostly because I didn't know how to verbalize my own feelings. I felt suspended between knowing what I *should* want and being too afraid to want it, but not brave enough to let it go either. It was like spinning and spinning, being in constant motion and going nowhere.

He stared down at his hands. "You don't want to know?"

Relief escaped from his steady tone.

"Let's just worry about now." I took his hand and placed it on my zipper. "I ate fast for a reason."

He leaned toward me, his face intent, and kissed me, as if we were sealing some kind of pact. My whole body responded to his lips on mine, lurching forward in slow motion, begging for him to touch me, but at the same time, my insides churned at the tenderness in his eyes, the gentle firmness of his lips. I hadn't been prepared for his intensity.

"God, I want this," he said, unbuttoning my jeans in frantic movements. He knelt on the floor, slid my jeans off my legs, and then moved my hips to the edge of the couch, positioning himself between my legs. His fingers moved up and down my legs, like a sculptor shaping raw clay into art, then his hands slipped beneath my panties and worked me.

My spine arched. I lay back, pushing my head into the couch, and watched him. The features of his face were tight, as if he held the reins to a runaway horse, trying to control every movement.

With an agitated jerk, he pulled my panties off. He spread his fingers on my knees, moving them up my legs, kneading the inside of my thighs. Then he ran his hands under my barbecue-stained t-shirt until he clasped them around my breasts. I stretched my t-shirt over my head and tossed it to one side. He wrapped his arms around me, resting his head on my stomach.

"God, Abbey I almost forgot you." His voice sounded panicky. "At some point I tried to. I didn't want to, I just needed to so I could go on." He buried his face against my belly.

The ends of his newly cut hair curled up around his ears. I twirled my fingers around the gold loops of hair. "It doesn't matter, Ryan, you're here. We are at the no talkie-talkie point," kissing his forehead, "as in, actions speak louder than words."

He looked up at me, his eyes telling me something I didn't understand.

"Come here." I pulled him up by the collar of his shirt and unbuttoned the first few buttons. He jerked it over his head, then shed his pants and shoes.

He lifted my hips up, as he pressed his face between my legs, exploring me with his tongue, his movements rapid and hungry. I grabbed his hair, holding his head into me. This I could give him, but then I had always been able to give him this.

He pushed my knees up on to the couch, opening me wider. I liked being exposed this way, unfurled. But he wanted me to open my heart wider, revealing something far more dangerous. Alone in the jungle I'd thought I could, but his sharp need commingling with intense desire cut into me. I winced.

"Ryan, come up here now."

He lifted his eyes and panted, "Not yet."

He made long steady strokes with his tongue. The ache between my legs grew stronger. He could feel it, too, making him hungrier. Sharp scattered spasms diffused as they spread down my thighs. "Ryan, oh, God," I yelled.

He stood from his knees, then shifted my legs length-wise on the couch and lay on top of me. His hard penis pressed against my leg as he kissed my chest and touched me between my legs. Spasms trickled from my crotch, teasing me, making me want more. I spread my legs wide, begging him to move into me. I was there, where I had to move forward, have him inside me, so I could get past the ache.

"Ryan, come on, damn it." I dug my fingers into his butt.

On top of me, he slid back and forth, his penis moving against my folds but not into me. He slid his hands under my head, his fingers intertwined with my tangled hair. His breath warmed my cheek. "What do you want, Abbey?" he whispered.

"You know." I wrapped my legs around him. "God." A sticky film of sweat sucked us together like adhesive between our chests.

"More than that," he whispered, as he stared into my eyes.

"Jesus, Ryan," I yelled. "If you don't keep going, my crotch is gonna get pissed off and beg for the nearest vibrator."

His head arched back, as he laughed. "Are you using me, Ms. Gallagher?" His body went still as he steadied his eyes on me. "I want to mean more than that." His mouth turned up into a forced smile, overshadowed by his sober eyes.

I ran my fingers through his hair. "You do, and I'll mention all that in the obituary I'm going to have to write about you if you don't fuck me now," I said, squeezing my legs around his thighs and tugging at his hair.

"Like your choice of words." His tone was edged with acerbity.

He pushed himself up on his arms so that he hovered above me. Then he moved into me, entering me part way at first. I lifted my hips to meet him until he pushed all of himself into me. Then he plunged in and out of me hard and fast.

He didn't look at me, instead he watched himself as he kept thrusting inside me. Then he raised one of my legs and turned me on my side, ramming himself into me even harder, like he had something to prove. One hand used my leg as an anchor, the other reached between my legs and stroked me.

"Come on, Abbey," he growled. "Is this it, is this what you want?"

"Yes," I yelled.

Suddenly, the ache overtook me, the tiny, scattered spasms converged, ripping through my pelvis, sending my whole body into convulsions. But he pounded harder, as his fingers stroked me faster. My breathing came quick and erratic. I rose high, higher, until I exploded, screaming like an animal in the wild.

"Ryan, fuck!" I shouted.

He pulled out of me. Crossed my leg over the other and pulled my hips up so he was behind me, driving into me. His fingers webbed over my back and slipped under me, cupping my breasts, pinching my nipples. I pushed back into him.

When my body wanted to collapse, he slid into me again, thrusting madly as he kneaded my breasts. He spread his hands over my butt, anchoring himself to my hips and pumped me.

"Jesus." He screamed between ragged breaths. "Abbey!"

He thrust upward, fiercely, one last time and yelled out, once, twice and then stopped, his grip loosening on my hips. The weight of his body pushed me down as he softened inside me.

Slowly, he pulled himself out and lay beside me, rubbing my back and murmuring something about, 'making love, instead of fucking, just once.' I tried not to listen.

"Ryan," I whispered, "don't talk."

"I know." He put his hand on the small of my back, his head resting on the edge of my shoulder.

My body went limp, as I drifted away. The phone rang. We didn't attempt to move. My voice came on the answering machine, inviting people to leave a message, then my mother's voice. "Abigail, are you there?"

Silence.

Ryan shifted his body away from mine, slipping one leg to the floor.

"I'm not getting it, not now," I whispered.

He settled back against me.

"Abigail, it's your mother!" her voice blasted from the little black box.

As she talked, I wished I had bought one of those answering machines with a thirty-second time limit.

"We're so glad you're home. I'm sure you're resting. Tomorrow night I thought I'd have everyone over for dinner, we can sing Happy Birthday. Ethan and his man." She cleared her throat. "And you and your man. That would be Ryan, of course. Oh, and Abigail..."

My spine stiffened as she gathered her next words. "We

really like him and well, we can talk more about this, but…"

I held my breath, *Don't, Mom.*

"I changed my mind, I think he'd make a great husband. Enough of that, I'm just being silly, making plans in my head. See you tomorrow."

I was still, my mind paralyzed. I had come home, and once again, just my mother's voice made me want to run.

Ryan said nothing, but his breathing had changed into long, slow steady breaths, patient breaths, waiting for words from his lover. After a moment, I let out the inhale I had been holding. Its release sounded like an exasperated sigh.

His fingers crawled along my spine, sending a chill creeping across my body. "The idea… that dreadful?" he said, a small crack of hurt resonating in the last syllable.

"No, it's just hearing her voice," I said into the cushion.

CHAPTER 4

Ryan didn't go with me to my parents' house. He and his brother Jake had work to do, so he said he'd be a little late. I was glad for the chance to see my mother for the first time without an audience. I jumped from the Jeep and took a few deep breaths before pushing open my parents' door.

After they bought their house in a new neighborhood west of downtown, Austin kept building beyond them and their area soon became one of the sought-after locations: Tarrytown. Two-thousand-five-hundred square feet of living space decorated to perfection, a Texas-New Mexico twist accenting every room, with light blue and turquoise rugs and splashes of color thrown about. A rustic tan leather couch and matching recliner faced a large stone fireplace flanked by chairs upholstered in Native American weavings. A large pine coffee table sat in the middle of the Saltillo-tiled room.

Muted voices from the television hummed as I walked toward the living room. My father sat in the leather recliner with his feet crossed on an ottoman. His hands rested on the rounded slope of his pouching stomach, his head lay cocked back against the chair, and his eyelids fluttered, unable to decide to open or close.

I scooted behind the chair and gave the top of his almost bare head a light kiss.

He shook his head and raised his hand back. "Rachel, yes, I'll get the grill!" His voice was hoarse and full. He grabbed the air behind his head, searching for a piece of my mother.

"Dad," I whispered, nesting my head in the gully between his neck and shoulder.

He bolted up and cleared his throat. "Abbey!" He almost chuckled with a delight so tender, a part of me melted. He stood, taking both my hands in his. "Still the most beautiful girl in the world." He held my shoulders as he looked at me.

"Oh, Dad, you're a little biased." I smiled, moving into him for a hug.

Behind me a female cleared her throat on purpose, and I let my hands slide down my father's arms and turned around. My mother waited, a formed position, watching me, us. She stared at me with that look, the one I needed a tweezers to pull out the judgment and maybe, when all that had been cleared, strands of pride would be left behind. I'd never been able to figure out exactly what that look meant.

"Mom." I walked toward this woman, my mother, determined to remember the love of the mother gorilla and her infant. An innate love, I told myself, as I extended my arms to her outreached hands.

Our fingertips touched. I stepped closer so our hands could grasp, but she would not. For us to embrace was rare, but this time I tried to close in on her, told my arms to wrap around her.

Before I could, she leaned into me and then jerked

back right away. More like a patting gesture you offer a sick person than an embrace of love. Perhaps in some humans, the mother-child bond is not innate.

"Mom, you've lost weight." I glanced at her lean body gone scrawny.

"Yes." She made a half-turn, showing off her new thinner figure.

"But you didn't need to."

She rerouted the features of her face from delight to controlled irritation. "Abigail…" She stepped toward me and cupped my chin in her long bony fingers. "I'll worry about my body and you…"

She looked down, her marmoset green eyes, even bigger than I remembered, because the flesh on her cheeks had melted away. "Worry about yours. I prefer being thinner." She smiled.

I could feel myself trickling away into a dark pool of anger, dragged back into my sixteen-year-old mind. 'I am thin,' I almost yelled.

"Okay, then. When is everyone getting here?" I clapped my hands together like a nervous comic who had just run out of jokes.

Dad looked down at his watch. "Ethan and José should be here in twenty minutes or so. Where's Ryan? I thought he'd come with you?"

My mother raised a few fingers in the air. "He called to say he'd be a little late. He had some business."

"That's right." I tried to wipe any confusion from my face, wondering why Ryan had called to check in with her.

"Frank, get washed up." She patted my father's back.

With both hands, he touched her small waist and if he spread his hands out, his fingertips would meet in a circle around her. He gazed at her for a significant moment.

"Go on, Frank," she said, removing his hands and stepping back. "Quit staring at me," she whispered as he walked by.

"Can't help it," he called over his shoulder. But he hadn't stared at her with desire, something else, not irritation either, more confusion or maybe concern.

"Abigail, follow me. We can talk while you help me with dinner." She walked toward the kitchen. Her powder-blue shift dress snuggled her large chest and fell away at the waist, free flowing to her knees. "We can start making the salad," she said as she pulled produce from the refrigerator.

In the stark light of the kitchen, I noticed something had invaded my mother while I was gone. Age had torn away the last fortress of youth and now inhabited her face. The faint lines connecting her nose to her mouth dug deeper, as age showed its dominion over even the best care and most advanced facial creams.

I almost chuckled out loud. All that shit in a jar, billions of dollars to fight a battle that can't be won. I suppose there is some small triumph from evading its attack longer than most of your neighbors, but in the end, everyone hauls out the white flag. Aging and death remain undefeated.

"Tell me all about the trip." She stretched up on her tiptoes in excitement like a little girl reaching for a balloon.

"Career-wise, it was a great. I think it's going to help me. The magazines will send me copies of all the pictures, so I'll show them to you when they get here. The original pictures went to Frankfurt and New York." I tried to sound warm.

"So, going was... the right decision?"

"Like I said, career-wise, yes." I allowed a few minutes of silence to pass before I said what she needed to hear. "But, of course, I missed everybody. That part was hard, you know, being away."

"Well, you were missed here, too." She smiled and glanced up from the cutting board. "Your hair looks lighter. Were you exposed to the sun a lot? I do hope you wore sunscreen."

"Yes, and a hat, too," I smiled. These are normal questions, Abbey. All mothers ask annoying questions, I told myself.

"Good," she said.

And then, as if waiting for the perfect moment to slip in what she'd wanted to say all along. "I know one young man who missed you terribly."

"You do?" I decided to play her game.

"Ryan." She sliced through a deformed bell pepper.

"Ryan?"

"Have you talked?"

I jammed my thumbs into a crisp head of iceberg lettuce. "Yes."

"Where are things going?"

The sound of the knife hitting the plastic cutting board provided my answer.

"Well, I know where they're going, I'm just wondering when?" She might as well have rammed the question at me.

I ripped the head in half and tore pieces off, tossing them into a strainer. My chest rising, my throat growing thicker, I had to concentrate to get air. I didn't know exactly where and when, but I knew I wasn't walking down some aisle in few days, or months, for that matter.

First step: monogamy.

Maybe I should tell her that, just to see the jolt of shock transform her face. 'Well, mother, I have to stop fucking other men before I can think about marriage. You should've tried that yourself.'

I shut my eyes, opened them, and made myself reply in a calm tone. "You can't know, Mom, because I don't." I let out a breath. "So, of course, I don't know when."

She continued as if she didn't hear me. "You just need a little push, and Ryan isn't that type, but he's going to have to take the lead," she grumbled, almost under her breath, making plans for my future.

"What are you talking about?" I pulled at the lettuce. I just returned yesterday and she's planning my wedding to a man she couldn't stand a year ago. Next, she'll ask me to pick out china patterns.

She left the counter and touched my arm. Her hand felt like ice from digging around in the refrigerator. I kept staring at the fragmented head of lettuce.

"I'm just interested in your life. We barely heard from you for a year. It's hard to write, I know…" She seemed like she was trying to convince herself. "But now that you're home I wanted to…" Her grip grew tight on my wrist.

"Mom?" I looked down at my arm.

Her hand dropped away. "Ryan's been coming around the house a lot, getting advice from Dad about his business, and I'm really impressed with him. He's a good man."

Her last statement sounded almost exasperated, as if her

next words should have been, 'What more do you want? Count yourself lucky you found a good man.'

"I know."

"You've been together a long time."

"So."

"Remember, no one's going to wait forever." Her voice took on a lecturing tone.

"I'm not asking anyone to—"

"You're not?" She raised her eyebrows.

I turned on the water full blast, letting it rush over the torn pieces of lettuce, then swirl around the edges of the sink before disappearing into the drain. Just like my resolve to have a different relationship with my mother. She needs to stay out of my life, I said to myself, watching the gushing water cleanse the lettuce. I shook the silver strainer and set it on the counter.

"What's next?" I felt like a soldier getting my orders for the next hill to take, or, in my case, be overtaken. Yes, swallowed whole by her and her transparent ideas of the way a woman should live her life.

"Cut this into thin slices, only use half." She placed a white plastic cutting board and a purple onion on the counter in front of me.

"Got it."

"That's the concern."

I stared at the purple onion and the wide steel blade of the knife lying beside it.

"You don't know what's next." She spoke with the tone of a high school counselor advising a confused student on their future. "Ryan seems very committed and he's definitely setting himself up to be financially secure."

She lectured while she moved around the kitchen preparing a meal, as if it were the most natural thing in the world. Butter and sprinkle garlic on bread, inform Abbey on the finer points of successful relationships. Baste the steak, list Ryan's marriage material qualities. Put mushrooms in a saucepan, tell Abbey not every woman feels the need to cheat on her husband, just her mother.

Was I kidding myself, believing for an instant there was any hope for a mother/daughter relationship with this woman? My heart had been steeped in anger, simmering for years, and each time she made my life her stage, it soaked in a little more anger. Any hope for us had evaporated in her choices, distilling a mother-daughter relationship into two people who simply tolerated each other. Perhaps that's how it should remain, I thought, tuning out her lecture that was anything but impromptu.

"Do you understand, Abigail?"

"Mmm." I picked up the knife. No one else calls me Abigail.

"Here's the salad bowl. When you're done, just put everything in here and mix it well. I just mean, dear, he's a great catch and if you don't make a move, someone else will." She touched my arm and walked away.

I placed the sharp edge of the knife against the round purple surface, put my other hand over the flat steel edge, and pressed down hard, splitting the onion in half. The purple bulb retaliated and sprayed me with a mist of onion juice.

"You realize that, don't you, dear? Ryan's like your

father, and people like that come along once in a lifetime." She took a bottle of white wine from the refrigerator.

I laughed out loud, and then, like a maniac, I sliced half the onion into bits.

"Abigail?" My mother stared at the knife in constant motion, knocking against the cutting board.

I didn't look up at her. The front door opened and she turned toward the arched doorway leading to the hall.

After I laid the knife on the board, I tossed all the ingredients into the large ceramic salad bowl. Cooking lesson finished.

Ethan wrapped his arms around me from the back. "Big sis." His tone was playful.

I let my shoulders relax, turning to hug him.

"José." Ethan pulled me toward a tall, dark-skinned, dark-haired, very attractive man standing in the entryway.

"This is my sister, Abbey, the one all my depraved thoughts generate from."

"Ah, for that I have to thank you," he said, his gorgeous black eyes smiling as he looked to me and then Ethan.

My mother lowered her eyes and backed away. "I have to see to the mushrooms." She touched Ethan's arm as she walked past.

"I used to think Abbey was the perfect girl, like a princess or something, when I was a kid," Ethan mused.

I rolled my eyes and pretended to shrink, pulling in my shoulders.

José's inky eyes scanned my face, then my body, in a theatrical fashion. "Understandable." He crossed his arms over his chest and smiled, revealing a small gap between his two front teeth, which only added to his already stunning good looks. He was the kind of chiseled perfection you just wanted to touch, run your hands over, while you tried to understand how it was so perfect, yet so natural, making it seem like that kind of beauty was normal rather than a mutation.

"Explains why he's gay, huh," I added, trying to gain composure. We all laughed.

My father emerged, showered and changed. He greeted Ethan and José, and then went into the kitchen to check on my mom.

All three of us strolled out to the back porch.

"Ethan," I said, "I think something's wrong with Mom. Is something going on I don't know about?"

"She seems fine to me," he said.

"I've noticed she lost some weight," said José, "and she was fairly thin to begin with."

"That's exactly what I said to her, and she got defensive." I nodded.

"Maybe she's extra nervous because she's excited to see you. She's probably just eating less," Ethan said. "The fact she's acting defensive isn't news. You guys are always tense around each other. Holy cow, if Mom so much as suggests you do something, you go bonkers."

José smiled. "That's just families." He laid his hand on Ethan's shoulder. He was taller and broader than Ethan. A heather-gray silk t-shirt pulled snug across his back and chest, before folding into his trim waist. His body was built to perfection for swimming. Hell, his body was perfect for anything.

Ethan shook his head. "No, believe me, this is not

normal family stuff. They've gone for months while living in the same town, not speaking."

"So," I said.

"Come on, Ab, you'll sit across the dinner table from her and every time she asks you a question, you look at Dad when you answer, *if* you answer." He turned his brown nondescript eyes on José. "Sometimes the tension gets so thick around them, you feel like you're going to choke on it."

"Oh, please! My brother tends to exaggerate."

"Well, I don't know, I've heard a few stories." José's mouth molded into a knowing smile.

"You better be careful, little brother, revealing family secrets." I pulled my eyebrows together.

Ethan's otherwise-lit face grew serious. "There aren't any secrets, not any more than any other family. You just put some imaginary wall up between you and Mom and now it's going to take an act of God to bring it down. And I'm not so sure you want it to."

All the family frustration swelled around me. "Ethan—"

"Hey, I found the party." Ryan walked through the French doors. He wore pressed khaki shorts with cuffs and a pale blue oxford shirt. Where did all his funky t-shirts go?

"Where'd you get that?" Ethan pointed to the beer Ryan clutched.

"Your dad has a whole cooler full in the garage. Your mom got me one."

"Shit, look at this guy. Mom almost treats him like royalty when he comes to the house. Let's get a few." His eyes darted to José. "You want one, Abbey? It might help you."

"What's that mean?"

"I'm kidding, dammit. You want one or not?"

"Yeah."

"Ryan, looks like you've been working out a little harder." José squeezed Ryan's arm.

Ryan looked at his arm and then back to José. "Who you trying to flatter?" He winked.

"We'll be back with beer," Ethan said as they walked into the house.

Ryan and I sat on the porch railing and dangled our legs. We were both silent, with only the shrill of the katydids in the background and the sound of Ryan gulping beer.

"So, how is it seeing everybody again?" He stared at his beer bottle.

"The same, nothing changes."

He tilted his head, looked at me, and lowered one eyebrow, questioning my lack of introspection. "Ab, everything changes."

"You're right. You're wearing khakis instead of board shorts or worn-out cutoffs, my brother has a new boyfriend, my mother lost weight, my father gained weight, but my mother and I still can't be in the same room for more than five minutes without me wanting to kill her. God, her and that condescending tone she uses when she asks me questions. Questions that are none of her fucking business."

He jerked the side of his mouth up and made a clucking sound. When he ran things through his head, he either made that noise or wiggled his lips from side to side, as if the wheels in his brain did not work unless his face also moved. I used to think it was cute or endearing, something that made me smile, but now it seemed irritating because of the judgment in that sound.

"What?" I shifted to face him.

"She just cares, Abbey. I mean, all parents ask questions, and you don't give a lot up. So if someone wants to know what's going through your head, they gotta ask, then hold their breath."

"Hold their breath?"

"Hoping you're not going to bite their head off."

"Funny."

"Well…" He jumped off the railing to stand between my bent legs.

"Well, I'm not like that… just with her." I smiled and rolled my eyes.

"And…" He pushed, leaning on my legs, tilting his head up to mine.

"And with anyone who happens to be stupid enough to ask me stupid questions when they know I don't have the stupid answer."

Laughing, he let his head drop. "That clears one thing up."

I threaded my fingers through his blonde curls and tugged his head up. "What?" I sucked my lips into my mouth, trying not to smile.

"You're the only one who hasn't changed."

"But I have." I slid off the railing, and Ryan stepped back, raising his eyebrows.

"I've been trying harder with my mother. I just need to get my bearings. The fact that I'm having this conversation is progress." A little encouragement would be welcome after the strained conversation I just had with my mother.

"You're right, Ab, it is." He stepped forward against me, pushing my back against the fence.

"Both of you pounced on me within thirty minutes with the same crap. It's like you and my mom had a plan and I'm—"

"That's not true, but I get it. Sorry, babe, just had a lot of time to think about you." He smiled, bending to kiss me. He jerked his head back and scrunched his nose up, making an exaggerated sniffing sound.

"What?"

"Jeez, Ab, I'm all for trying different perfumes, but I hope you didn't pay a lot for this one because—"

"Shut up! It's onion juice. Christ! I haven't been gone from civilization that long."

He laughed and bent to kiss me again.

"Your beers."

My mother's voice sliced between us, and Ryan pulled away from me.

"José is busy teaching your father the finer points of original art," she continued. "Of course, Frank is mostly interested in the investment value."

They exchanged bottles, his empty one for her full one. "Thanks, Mrs. G," he said, pecking my mother on the cheek. "José found two original prints for me that I'm going to use in the new house." He sounded too proud of himself, too needy of her approval.

"Oh, good," she cooed.

"House?" I couldn't stop confusion from sweeping over my face.

My mother's eyes shifted from Ryan to me. "Ryan, you haven't showed her the plans yet?"

"No, we've been busy." He grinned.

"Oh, Abigail, you're going to love it," she said, extending a bottle of beer toward me. "Here."

I took it, but my hand shook. My mother had recruited Ryan to aid her in planning out my life. Shit, he was even kissing her on the cheek. A year ago, that never would've happened.

She reached down and grabbed my empty hand. "Darling, are you getting sick? Your hands are trembling."

I jerked my hand back. "Don't worry about it."

Ryan stared at me.

"Abigail, I'm only concerned. You might have caught some rare flu or something in Africa."

"I take shots for that."

But the shots didn't protect me from all the various strands of viruses my body had been exposed to, and it was often a matter of luck to come out of the bush without something.

"All right, then." She gave Ryan a sweet smile, patting his arm. "You two have fun and we'll eat in a short while."

Her Texas accent was so thick, I thought I would have to peel it off Ryan. Every time I was gone for a while and returned, it seemed like my mother's accent grew heavier, more exaggerated, like biting into a cinnamon roll and forgetting how much sugar was in it, the sweetness turning my stomach.

"Thanks again," Ryan said.

She floated through the doorway.

I stared into the backyard at the azalea shrubs, their lavender flowers laid to rest and closed off, the two cypress trees, and the large water oak that had been our sturdy playground as kids, ignoring on purpose Ryan's creamy brown circles on me.

"Jesus, Ab, nothing like starting dinner out with a little tension." He lowered his voice and raised his hand as if putting his order in. "Waiter, I'd like a little tension for dinner, medium rare and thick, so thick you need a chainsaw to cut through it."

"Stop it," I said through gritted teeth. "She and I don't get along, all right. Just because you've managed to kiss up to her, and now you're the Wonder Boy, doesn't mean my relationship with her is going to change."

Even as I spoke the words, I was admitting failure to myself.

"I haven't done anything like that. I've just spent a lot of time with your family this past year. Your dad has helped me with the legal stuff and Ethan's done some programming for our website. So, needless to say, I've seen a lot of both your parents and in all truthfulness, your mom has been great to me."

"Super, I'm happy for you."

He moved behind me. "You know what she asked me almost every week?"

Silence.

"If I had heard from you. And if I happened to be lucky enough to get a letter, she wanted to hear every freakin' detail. Each time she watched something on the news about Africa, she'd worry about you being over there and asked your father, me, Ethan, and even José, if we thought everything was okay. Her exact words, 'I hope my girl is all right.' Talking to her about you made me realize what a great lady she is and what great mom—"

"Okay, I got your point, enough." I took a long hard gulp of beer, drowning the lump in my throat.

"Abbey, seriously, when are you going to let go of all this tension with your mom and move on? I mean, how many years can this continue?"

"How many years?" My words came out like a tired echo. "I don't know."

I wanted to bury the past between my mother and me, but I suppose some experiences become so ingrained in us that we can't separate ourselves from them.

My mother's voice called from inside the house, telling us dinner was ready.

CHAPTER 5

The sun slid through my sheer white curtains, threatening to wake me before my sixteen year-old body was ready. I jerked the comforter over my head, enclosing myself in darkness. But even that thick cover couldn't stop the muffled voices rising in anger from downstairs. I sat up and listened.

My parents were arguing, again. Their heated words escalating in emotion, then plummeting into hushed concern, struck me as odd. For most of my life, I had seldom heard my father raise his voice and never towards my mother. Now it had become their mode of communication, making our home feel like a field packed with hidden grenades.

I crept down the hall, crouched against the wall just on top of the stairs, pulled my knees into my chest, and jerked my t-shirt to my toes. I stayed still and listened.

"Goddamnit, Rachel, all these years, all these years have been a farce! I've been some kind of clown in your eyes. Is that it?"

I peered around the wall. My father wore a suit. Dressed for work on a Saturday? He stepped close to my mother, raising his arms, demanding an answer.

"Stop this, Frank. The kids are asleep. You'll wake them and they'll hear."

"Hear what? You obviously don't care what they know and don't know." He turned his back to her.

"Frank," she whispered.

"My children, Rachel! My damn children and I've been..." His voice choked. I was sure my father was crying. "Haven't I been a good father?"

"Yes, Frank." My mother's voice cracked.

"Then why are you willing to destroy that?"

Their words came at me from every angle. *What is my mother doing?* He'd been a great father. As the room fell silent, I inched up the wall, turning to go back to my room. Then came the answer.

"Those were love letters, Rachel, not informational. Love, love, love!" My father's hoarse whisper seemed to grow louder each time he said the word 'love.'

"Frank, be calm."

"Calm! My wife has been, is, remains, however you want to term it. You're in love with someone else. I can't be a fool forever."

She didn't stop him, she didn't say, 'No, I love you.'

"Mom, what are you doing?" I whispered.

After a dead calm, my father sucked in all the air around him, before clearing his throat. "Rachel, did you..."

His voice started off controlled, then it changed, like someone hit him, and he yelled the end of his question. "... fuck him, fuck him?"

"The language," she said, with her melting Texas drawl, as if the word 'fuck' was too offensive for her precious ears.

"The language!" My father roared, his tone full of sarcasm.

I stood frozen in the hallway, as the words of rage spilled from my father's mouth.

"Here's some language you're very familiar with. Infidelity, cheating, making me look like an ass, because for years my life, every decision, every action was about you and making sure you loved me." His voice broke apart as if each word choked him.

A silence below me took over, like a nothingness between them. Then sobbing, powerful aching sobs, came from my father. I wanted to run down the stairs and wrap myself around him, so he would know how much I loved him. *Please, Mom, tell him, tell him how much we love him, tell him you'll do anything to stop his tears. Damn it, Mom, tell him.*

The sobs softened into light hiccups, "I suppose it wasn't enough." His tone was deflated.

"It was." She dragged the words out, but she had hesitated too long.

"Was it? Then why, why go there to see him?" He hesitated. "I've got to get out of here."

"Where are you going?"

"After all this time, and everything we've said..."

"Frank?"

"Work," he said, his voice flat, without explanation. His heavy shoes clomped on the tiled entrance, so I started back down the hallway, closer to my room. I could only see the tops of their heads in front of the door.

"Will you be back?" She sounded like his answer didn't really matter.

"You lied to me. You said you were going to visit your

cousin. I never would've called you there, just waited dutifully for your call. I'm predictable, and you were counting on that. But you didn't count on me finding one of your goddamn love letters, did you?"

"Frank, we've been through this."

He moved closer to her. "Have we? Sorry, it's still fresh on my mind. All of it… the airlines, saying, 'Oh, no sir, her booking says New York,' and the pity in your cousin's voice, it's all there."

His voice took on a sinister tone. " 'You stupid jackass. Your wife's not here. Oh, you didn't know she's off seeing her mad lover? Wake-up, Frank!' That's what she was thinking. You should have heard her tone. She was embarrassed for me. Because I'm a damn fool."

My breathing came hard, my chest rising and falling as I put the story together. My mother had gone to visit her cousin a week ago, and when she returned, all hell broke loose. My dad walked around for days awaiting her arrival, slamming things and talking to himself. He insisted on picking Mom up from the airport himself, and her eyes had turned puffy by the time she walked in the door hours later.

"Are you coming home?" she said in a stern voice.

"Yes, because that's what I do. The same thing I've done for years, open the door every night to a lie."

"It hasn't been a lie." Her tone softened.

"Your smile lies," he said, and slammed the door behind him.

Her tears were my cue to creep back into my room. I rushed under the comforter and lay motionless, with the cotton flowers pulled just under my chin. My mind pasted together their words to form a picture: my mother was having an affair.

I squeezed my eyes shut, wishing that not to be true. It was like some kind of soap opera. The beautiful housewife, two children, married to a successful lawyer, but restless. I saw the way she had invited men's eyes with her big breasts and her straight skirts, just tight enough to show the roundness of her small butt, the way her hips moved when she walked and her breasts bounced freely, waving at all the male passersby.

WHEN I WAS A LITTLE GIRL, I'd sit, my limbs curled over each other in the corner of the bathroom, and watch with admiration and wonder as she made herself perfect for dinner parties with my father. She'd crouch down, resting her butt on her ankles, and I'd stretch on my tiptoes to zip up her cocktail dress and pray I'd be that pretty some day. She'd lift her shoulders and stare into the mirror.

"Well, Abigail, does Mommy look okay?" A wide smile would spread across her lips.

"Mommy's the most beautiful," I'd say, my six-year old hands clapping madly.

"Remember, dear. Show them just enough to envy your husband, but not enough to question your intentions," she'd say, winking.

I'd laugh, not knowing the meaning of her words, the same words she repeated over and over.

All I knew was that I had a pretty mommy, really pretty. My dad said it many times. "How could a man get so lucky to have two beautiful girls surrounding him every day?'

She'd coo and kiss him.

I SUPPOSE THEY'D QUESTION your intentions now, Mother, I thought, as she knocked on my bedroom door.

"Abigail, your brother is already eating breakfast and then we're getting ready to go downtown and do some shopping. You need to get up." Her voice was unchanged, as if nothing in her life was different, as if she hadn't been climbing between the sheets with another man while my father's back was turned.

"I'm not going," I said from under my comforter.

"Darling, you've been wanting to go clothes shopping for weeks."

"I'm sick," I said and then cringed, realizing that was the wrong thing to say. My bedroom door opened. I pulled the comforter over my head.

She sat on the edge of the bed. Her weight made the comforter tighten around me, smothering me under my childhood blanket.

"What's wrong?"

"I just don't feel good," I mumbled from under the comforter. I couldn't look at her.

"Abigail." She tugged at the comforter, I tugged back. "Let me see you. What's wrong?"

"I'm sick, that's all." I hoped she would leave soon because my air supply was running short, and sweat was beading up on my chest and under my arms.

"All right, but then you don't get any new clothes," she

said, moving off my bed.

"Don't need any."

"If you start feeling better, maybe you could find the energy to pick up this room." She shut the door, and I pulled the damp comforter off my head, gasping for air.

I DIDN'T UNDERSTAND, UNTIL LATER, how much that day, the day my father left—or the day my mother let my father leave—would change my life. A week after I overheard my parents' argument, my father's accusatory words, my mother's lack of protest, her confession, they sat down with Ethan and me.

"Your mother and I…" My dad took a deep breath. "…love you both very much and we want you to know that our decision to…"

He looked right at me and I stared back, willing him not to say anything else. Yet the words 'divorce, divorced' kept blaring in my brain.

"Well, we're going to live apart for a while."

"A while? What does that mean?" My eyes fired hate at my mother.

"Abigail," she said, in the same tone she used when I didn't clean my room, or brush my hair, or load the dishwasher the right way.

I put my hand in the air and turned my face from her. "I'm going with you, Dad. I'm living with you."

He stared at me, his eyebrows raised, and then at her.

She has nothing to do with this, I thought. *She's a whore. That's why you're leaving, because my mother's a whore, and I won't live with a whore, better yet, a whore who makes me go to church every Sunday.*

"Abbey, you can't." He stood up from the couch.

"Why not? Why not?" I watched as Ethan moved from the chair and squeezed in next to my mother on the couch.

"You're my father," I said, insistent.

"And…" He stopped and glanced at my mother. The full cushions of the couch swallowed her slim frame. She was stuck, as if the pillowy material had pinned her arms to the back of the couch. "…and your mother needs you right now."

"Well, I don't need her." My long arms flew in the air, flailing out of control.

"Don't talk that way." He walked toward me.

I moved away, stormed over to the couch, hesitated, and directed my eyes at my mother. "I only need you, Dad, only you," I said, my mouth tight and straight.

Tears pooled in my mother's lids and her lip quivered. I lifted my eyes to my father, my voice cool. "Is she for real?"

"Stop this!" he barked.

"I'm packing my stuff." I stomped up the stairs.

"No, Abbey, you just can't."

Ethan whimpered, like he was afraid to be heard. My mother put her arm around him and pulled his skinny shoulders close, resting her chin on the top of his head.

I ran up the stairs to my room and grabbed an overnight bag from my closet, stuffing clothes into it like a mad person. Footsteps rumbled outside in the hall and then Ethan's door opened and closed.

When I walked back toward the staircase, bag in tow, my parents had resumed tossing accusations at each other.

"What have you told her?" my mother said.

"Christ, nothing. Do you really think I sat down and laid it out to her? Jesus, Rachel, give me a little more credit. I do run a successful law firm with this jock head of mine. Somehow I've managed to keep this family well cared for and you in—"

"Don't, Frank, you're acting crazy. If you're leaving, just get out."

"Haven't I, Rachel?" he said, his tone low, hissing like an animal about to pounce on its prey.

I turned the corner. My father's thick fingers gripped the thin material on the sleeve of my mother's crimson blouse. His fist was so tight, his knuckles looked like large pearls.

Crimson, perfect color, I thought. We had just finished reading Nathanial Hawthorne's *The Scarlet Letter* in junior English, and my mother's flimsy red blouse seemed suited to her that day, while her adultery bled my family.

They both looked up at me, and he released his grasp, crimson silk blossoming from his open hand. His face scrunched up as he stared at me while I descended the steps, bags hanging from the ends of my hands.

"I need to go," he said, his jaw tight.

"Dad, I'm coming."

"No." He turned and walked down the hall.

"Please, Dad." I ran behind him and grabbed his arm as he moved through the front door.

"Abbey, stop this. Go back inside."

"Let me come with you. Please, Dad!" I followed him to his car, begging, tears pouring from my eyes. "Dad!" I screamed.

He stopped and whirled around in front of his car, already loaded. "Abbey." He held his arm out and crushed my thin body into his broad chest.

"Please take me with you. I can't live here. Not without you." My words drowned in sobs.

"Baby," he said, while his large hands rubbed my hair.

"Dad, don't make me stay." As I looked up at him, his face twisted in pain as if someone had just cut a limb from him.

"You have to. Someday you'll understand."

"No, I won't!"

I hated the way parents always said that, as if after growing up and making a complete mess of your life, you'd understand their utter stupidity. I wanted to say, 'Yes I do understand, you married a whore, but I'm not one. I'm a good girl and I'll make you happy, Dad. I'll never do anything wrong.'

He got in the car, shut the door, and turned the key, keeping his eyes focused ahead. The roar of the engine covered my sobs. He tilted his head toward me and mouthed, 'Be good.'

My whole body shook with tears. I put my hand to the window and he matched his to mine, the tinted glass keeping us apart. He shut his eyes for an instant, opened them, and directed his stoic mechanical gaze at the steering wheel. The car inched backward and my hand fell from the window.

I took a couple of steps toward the blue sedan and then stopped, my shoulders slack. I dropped my bag and lowered myself to the cement, watching the sedan move into the low shadows that crisscrossed the tree-lined street. It turned right toward the fading sun. I sat on the cool cement with my bag tucked close to my chest until the sun disappeared behind the homes peppering the hills to the west.

After a while, I dragged myself into the house and upstairs. I walked toward my parents' room, gathered my last bit of emotional energy, and slammed my fist against their bedroom door. I waited, thinking she would come, but she didn't.

She never tried to explain anything to me. Instead she went on as if all were normal, talking to me and asking me questions like she had before, except I kept my answers succinct and dry, hoping to end her questions.

At some point, her attempts at meaningless communication ended. A dull silence replaced them.

WE ARE GOING TO BE ONE OF those families now, I told myself. One of the 50% of American marriages that end in divorce and the children live with their moms and see their fathers every other weekend. We were practicing for the part, because there hadn't been a divorce and, as far as I knew, no one had talked to a lawyer.

But every day that I lived in a fatherless house, I grew more certain we would end up grouped into that 50% statistic they quoted in Marriage and Family class, required as a junior in high school. The teacher made us carry around an egg for a week, like it was our baby, so we could capture some understanding of caring for an infant.

No wonder half the families break up. This is the class

that teaches people how to be parents and stay married. Shit, I was sure my mother would do better with a raw egg than with me.

My dad came every other weekend and took us to his apartment, where we swam, ate pizza, and told him stories. Ethan's stories included things about Mom. Mine never did.

"Abbey, are you and your mom talking yet?" my father said between bites of pizza.

"Nope." I stared at the round pepperoni curled at the edges to form pools for the orange grease. I set my slice on the napkin. "Dad, I can't eat anymore pizza."

He smiled. "My cooking skills aren't up to standards. Nothing like your mother."

He kept saying, 'your mother,' as if he were the father of a friend of mine from school and only knew my mom through me. Divorce was inevitable.

"She doesn't cook either."

She had started working at a new clothing boutique owned by a friend, so we were doing the TV dinner thing. It was weird to pull into the driveway after school and stare at a still house. No dark hair passing by the kitchen window to get to the front door, no red lips spreading into a smile to greet us.

"Why?" he said.

"She's working."

He raised his eyebrows and tilted his head. "Working? Doing what?"

"I don't know. I think being a sales clerk at Donna's new boutique. She just started two weeks ago."

Nearly two months since my father left. I'd been so

pissed when she told me I would be responsible for Ethan after school and some Saturdays. I nodded when she told me how I was old enough to take on the responsibility of caring for my younger brother so she could work. But I learned to relish the idea that I would be the one Ethan would turn to, instead of her. I would seize this opportunity to pull him from her protective arms.

Dad had rented a two-bedroom apartment, so Ethan and I could spend the night. It was close to his work, but it wasn't in a great neighborhood, he explained, when we wanted to go explore the area.

He set down his slice of pizza. "Well, good, she's working." He sounded puzzled.

"Dad, I really wish you'd come back. I mean it, it's crazy without you."

"Abbey," he said tugging at the end of my hair. "We, your mother and I…" He set his jaw and took a slow breath. "We need to straighten some things out. Marriages are hard, and it's not simple stuff. Sometimes this happens, people have misunderstandings."

"Dad, I'm taking Marriage and Family class." I rolled my eyes.

"Oh, so you have the textbook on this kind of stuff." He tousled my hair with his thick fingers. "Well, just like wars are easier to write about and read about, the same goes for relationships."

"I'm never getting married."

"Come on, don't say that."

"This sucks, I mean it, Dad, it really sucks."

"Hey, I don't want you saying things like that. You never

used to talk that way."

"Well, sometimes I don't care. If you're not there, nothing else matters to me."

My jaw tightened. "Why couldn't she move out. I'm serious, sometimes kids live with their dads, not their moms."

He shook his head. "You and your mom are a team. You're just having some problems right now."

I stood up. "We are not a team and this problem happens to be permanent. I can't believe she would ever let you leave."

He stood and put his arm around me. "Abbey, I'm so thankful for you," he said, his voice shaking.

I tilted my head up. His eyes were glassy and pitiful. "Dad."

He hugged me, and when the wetness of his pain dripped on my cheek, I determined never to stop hating her. Her.

CHAPTER 6

"When do I get to take this freaking blindfold off?"

"Ab, you're so impatient, I swear. We've only been driving a few minutes. Just put your head back and relax."

"Relax? I've been back two weeks and find out you're into weird sex games, bondage, and shit."

"You wish!" Ryan laughed.

I let my head fall back and tried to feel calm, but when I remembered something, I raised my head. "Ryan, this isn't some… didn't I say I needed a while to get my bearings?"

"Come on, I am kinda clueless, but give me a little more credit than that. I'm not proposing or anything crazy."

Again I tried to settle into a comfortable position and took a deep breath.

"Yet," he whispered.

"What?"

"Jeez, Ab," he chortled, "you're paranoid."

Ryan was right. After two weeks of dodging my mother's questions, realizing she all but had her grandchildren named, I had grown paranoid.

Spartan's hot breath felt too close. His loud wet panting tickled my ear, just before he licked the side of my face.

"Spartan, get back."

"Hey, boy, lie down back there."

The SUV climbed up a hill, turned a corner, and then came to a stop at an angle. "Don't get out yet." Ryan said, slamming his car door shut. "Come on." He opened my door and guided my body out of the elevated vehicle.

With Spartan by his side, Ryan cradled my elbow in one arm and used the other to steer my hips in the right direction. Sticks crunched under my feet and the malleable prickly edges of weeds scratched my calves. Without my vision, the heat seemed even more acute, and a sticky wetness moved from the crown of my head to the nape of my neck before it sucked my t-shirt to the skin on my back.

"Ryan, I really hate this."

"I know you do, Ab," he said. "Ready?" He slid the blindfold from my head.

We stood in the middle of a piece of semi-cleared land that butted up to dense woods. Both his hands on my hips, Ryan turned me in a slow circle. "This is it. You're standing in the living room and this is the view."

His words were so confident that I, too, would see the same panorama. See the same future.

"It's incredible. It really is." I wanted to leave at once, to go away again.

He sidled up next to me. "I'm glad you like it. I've been looking for the perfect piece of property," he whispered into my ear, as if we were in a crowded room.

Then he pulled his head back and his eyes reached into mine, but the confidence had faded. "Ab, I made reservations for next weekend at a bed-and-breakfast in

Fredericksburg. I just thought we could get out of town and have the weekend to… to make plans?"

I rotated my head to take in the preserve. Ryan intended to build a home in a beautiful place and he wanted me to be a part of it.

"Ab, next weekend?"

"Plans?" I said, whittling a few more minutes before I answered.

"Yes," he said.

I took his hand, summoning resolve like someone about to parachute from a plane, who had something to prove to themselves and the other passengers.

"Let's do it." My arms moved around his neck. As I pressed against him, my lips captured his without hesitation, letting him know I meant it, I could do this.

RYAN AND I'D JUST WALKED IN the door when my father's voice came over the answering machine. "Abbey, when you get in, give me a call on the cell, or at my office… not at home."

Something odd in my father's voice, the way he didn't finish sentences. "… don't call home, until I talk…"

I picked up the phone and pushed the off button on the message machine. "Dad?"

"She has to have surgery."

"What?"

"Your mother has… breast cancer." His voice wavered, as if he felt sorry for me, for all women, because we have breasts and some day they may have to be removed.

"You guys didn't say anything the other night."

Over six years ago, my father had called me in New York, while I studied for finals in graduate school, to tell me doctors had removed a lump from my mother's left breast, benign. The almost superior feeling came over me, picturing one of my mom's precious breasts wearing an incision scar, but I had been glad it turned out benign.

"We didn't know anything yet. They found a couple of unusual masses during her last mammogram, a few weeks before you returned and then the ultrasound was cause for more concern. She wanted to wait until after you got back for the biopsies. We weren't really worried because last time it was just a cyst."

He sighed and waited a moment before he spoke. "Abbey, she's going to need you, all of us. They want to perform a double mastectomy."

"Why both breasts? It seems so…radical."

"The results of a biopsy weren't good. The tumors are large. From what they tell me, a protein test indicates an aggressive cancer, so there's increased chance of spreading. They said, possibly stage three A. They'll remove both breasts and some of her…"

He took a deep breath. I could almost feel the weight of it on my end of the line. "… some of the lymph nodes in her armpits to see if it's spread."

"Is that it, no other choices?"

"Abbey."

The low hum of the telephone line.

"She may have known about the lumps for a while but was too afraid to go to the doctor. The doctor said it's a hard thing for a woman to face. I mean, the dreadful possibility of losing her…"

"You think she knew?"

"Maybe, but don't say anything. She's scared, but you know she won't act like it in front of you."

"When?"

"By the end of next week, because they need to be fairly aggressive. After the surgery, she'll start chemotherapy if they find it elsewhere. If they get it all, then she'll just receive low doses of radiation, but they suspect it's already spread."

My father finished explaining as many details as he knew and then said he had to call Ethan. I sat down on the edge of the couch. Ryan sat next to me, stroking my back in slow rhythm, not saying a word.

My mother has cancer. My mother without breasts.

I couldn't imagine her without them, her breasts were her signature. In some ways I had seen them as their own institution. And they should've taken some of the blame for her affair, since their overwrought sexuality served as an advertisement. Many times I'd wished she didn't have her breasts, as they were a source of pride for her.

One afternoon while I packed for college, she'd come in my room to help me. I wanted to ask her to leave, but I didn't. She commented on a piece of clothing, or a book, and nodded and said, "Mmm." She pulled my underwear drawer open and with great care arranged my bras in the corner of the suitcase. All I was able to think was, *leave, please leave.*

"Well, it looks like you inherited a lot, but not everything," she said with a hint of humor, glancing from the shelf of massive flesh resting below her collarbone to the small mounds I called boobs. "Be glad. They can really get in the way... sometimes."

Under my breath, I said, "I am." Then looked at her and smiled. *Where did they get you?* I had thought. *I'm going to college and you clean house and cook.*

In late grade school, I would look at my mother's round, large breasts and know that someday they'd be mine. I was a physical replica of her, just needed the breasts.

Then in junior high school, my friends and I relied on Judy Blume's book, *Are You There, God? It's Me, Margaret* for warning signs that prepared us for our impending surge of estrogen, at which time we would lose all interest in math, animals, the world around us, and would become single minded. One mad strobe light blinking in our once-brilliant minds: BOYS, BOYS, BOYS.

At the same time, boys noticed us, not as competitors or fellow students, but as legs, hips, and boobs. As if with the formation of hips...brains were no longer important. After watching several of my friends lose their minds to puberty, I prayed, "Please God, I don't want to trade brains for boobs."

I guess he had listened.

AFTER A FEW MINUTES, Ryan said, "When is the surgery, Abbey?"

I stared ahead. "Next week. Next week my mother won't have breasts."

"Ab." He pulled my upper body against him and laid my head on his shoulder. "I'm sorry."

I knew then, that I would hear and use that word a lot,

'sorry.' And I would grow to hate it, for all its meanings.

BREASTS AND BREAST CANCER NOW consumed all our lives. Every day leading to my mother's surgery seemed like a march toward an ancient throne in which the once-beautiful princess hands her most prized possession to the gods.

Ethan spent the entire week on the Internet researching breast cancer, informing me that it must be bad if they want to remove both breasts. My father did investigations of his own, and my mother got a second opinion, with the same answer. She had invasive ductal carcinoma, with masses in both breasts. Removing lymph nodes was necessary to determine if it had spread even further.

Ryan backed away from his push for our important talk. I welcomed yet another respite from a decision. The news of my mother's breast cancer was like someone had said, 'it's too windy, you can't jump today, all parachuting called off.' Ryan's focus changed. His energies were spent making himself available to my parents at any time they needed him.

I filled my days by talking on the phone to *National Geographic*, discussing which Africa photographs would be best for the various articles, and negotiating another assignment in the Galapagos Islands. And staring at my own breasts often. They were small, not the eye-catchers my mother's had always been. Yet, I couldn't imagine life without them.

CHAPTER 7

My father, Ethan, José, Ryan, and I filled the waiting room in the hospital yesterday afternoon as the doctors cut away my mother's femininity. Once the doctors told us she was fine and the surgery was successful, the four of us left. My father refused to leave, even though she stayed asleep long after the surgery. He remained with her through the night. He didn't want her to wake up alone.

I didn't want to wake up alone either, so I spent the night with Ryan. We lay in bed, him snoring, and me with my eyes wide open as if I'd drunk a pot of coffee before retiring. Every time I tried to shut my eyes, all the statistics concerning breast cancer Ethan shared with me over the past week marched through my mind. I saw breasts differently now, not as sexy mounds of flesh, but more like big, small, medium—whatever size—time bombs suspended from ribs. I had wondered how my mother reacted when she woke up and laid her hand on her flat chest, discovering they were gone.

BEFORE ENTERING THE HOSPITAL the next day, I grabbed my camera off the front seat of the Jeep. I wanted to see the surroundings protected by the artistic eye of the camera lens, rather than unfiltered through my own eyes, which did not brush the edges soft, intensify color, or subdue imperfections.

As I stepped close to the concrete building, the automatic glass hospital doors slid to the side. The smell of sterility failed to mask the stench of open wounds, cancerous children, and the subtle whiff of fear. Right away, I registered a few mental shots of hollow faces, eyes of regret, prayers of second chances. If each were given a chance to reverse the clock, have their leg back, hold their child, kiss their husband, would they run, hang on, embrace with passion? Or once again would excuses, bills, the lawn, and TV swirl into the mediocrity that consumes so many?

My father paced outside her room. The extra pounds of flesh, accumulated through the years, packed his once-square jaw, and broken spider capillaries framed the edges of his wide nose. His light hazel eyes were hidden under puffy fluid-filled folds of skin, red overtaking his white irises. A white shirt with thin blue stripes was tucked into the belt securing his pants, inches above his butt that had somehow disappeared, like so many men's with age.

It was rare to see moisture in his eyes. Dad did not ever overreact. I had inherited my problem-solving edge from him, a father who approached life's occurrences, both positive and negative, with a deductive strategy, the same way he pieced together a case. His reactions were held until all the facts were organized, presenting a puzzle in which enough pieces allowed for an accurate, if not a vivid, picture.

"Dad." I tapped him on his shoulder.

He opened his hands, engulfing me with his thick arms. I could have lingered in the cocoon of warmth and strength, wrapped in my father's warm bear hug, but he released me, his serious eyes staring into my confused face.

"I want to tell you something before you see your mother." He hesitated, swallowing back tears. "Things look worse than they first believed. The doctor thinks it's in stage four."

"Stage four? What does that mean." I couldn't remember from all the statistics Ethan had shared what stage four meant, but when my father said those words, as if he were choking, I assumed it was bad.

"They found cancer in some of the lymph nodes, so there's a possibility it's spread through the lymph system to somewhere else. They have to do some more tests to find out where it's spread. The prognosis is…" He stopped himself, as if suffocating on the next words. "If it has spread, they'll have to be aggressive with the chemo."

The word 'spread' always meant something bad: cancer, disease, bugs. Spread also meant to destroy, to overtake. Cancer's ugly silent head had chewed away at my mother's insides while she slept, played tennis, baked, and attended charity dances. Because cancer doesn't wave a flag, she continued her life, not knowing the sexy mounds of flesh she had been so proud of served as a petri dish for a thriving cancer.

Two nurses walked out of her room and hurried past us.

"We can go in and see her now," my father said.

I took my father's arm as he went through the hospital room door that would become my mother's temporary home, from two-thousand-five-hundred square feet to a two-hundred-square-foot sterile room.

She seemed so small, doll-like. Her narrow, beautiful features were drawn, tired-looking. She opened her eyelids, exposing rheumy green eyes, the green dull, like grass fighting to sprout after a drought. A faint smile crept to her face. She had aged years with the passing of only a few days.

I fixed my eyes on her face, not letting them wander below her chin. They were desperate, too curious to see my mother's fleshless chest, her large mounds reduced to a flat plain by a doctor's knife.

My father sat in the chair beside the bed, holding her small hand. With the aid of his strong arm, she pushed herself up in the bed. Fighting the pain that showed on her face, she raised her hand toward me, her long fingers signaling me to come, enter her circle, the sphere we would all create around cancer, like planets orbiting the sun at a range too close, parts of life burning.

"Mom." I leaned close, reaching toward her like an awkward infant trying to control its limbs. "Mom." My head next to hers, the odd cadence of my voice as I spoke. With a brief hug, the loss of her body hit me. They were gone, the large pillows that had always stood between us when she drew close to me.

I forced my eyes up to hers. "How are you?"

I pulled back, sounding more like someone she played bridge with rather than her daughter, or like her at those charity functions as she circled the room in an effort to make personal contact with the money.

I arched my back, standing up straight, trying to break

the forced embrace.

"Did you bring the photos?" She strained to sound animated through her weak voice.

"No, but I brought my camera. I wanted to take a picture of you and Dad."

"Abbey, that's not appropriate, your mother is…" He moved back in his chair, turning his head to look at her.

"Your mother is what, Frank?" Her eyes flicked down toward her sunken chest. Her expression looked like she was mourning the loss of a friend. "What, Frank, your mother is incomplete? Is that what you were going to say?"

I glanced at my father's face. His eyes skittered around the room, nervous and edgy. Her comment may have been close to the thoughts running through his head, but why did she have to say it to him, here, in front of me?

"God, no, Rachael," He paused, as if searching his mind for the right thing to say.

"Abbey, I would love it if you took a picture of your father and me."

My eyebrows shot up. "I don't have to." I looked at him.

Why had I even asked to photograph her, to twist into her brain that she wasn't the beauty the camera loved anymore?

"No, do," she said, motioning for my father to sit on the bed next to her. His large frame seemed like an imposing giant beside her small body.

This would be her first picture void of cleavage. From behind the protection of the camera lens, I glanced at the hospital gown lying flat against my mother's rib cage and a bolt shot through me. She had lost the very thing she had packed with so much pride. But the next instant, that bolt of odd victory was replaced with sorrow, not for her, but because her daughter would feel anything but sadness for such a loss.

Peering through the lens, I was struck by my mother's appearance. Although not as wide, the camera still loved her smile, and her green eyes consumed the lens even if some of their brightness had faded. I laid my finger on the shutter and then moved to the side, capturing another angle.

"Enough, Abbey," my father said, as he ran his large knuckled hand over my mother's hair. "You want coffee? I'm going to get your mother some."

"I'll go with you." I stood up.

"You stay with your mother. I'll be right back." He shifted his eyes in my direction. It wasn't a suggestion.

For a long moment, my mother and I just looked at each other. I broke the stare, walked to the window, and dragged the curtain aside. Outside, people helped loved ones through the hospital doors. Feeling my mother's eyes on me, I watched a nurse push a woman in a wheelchair to her car, while the new father held the baby, every now and then leaning down to grin at his wife. They arranged all their baby gear and her stuff in the car. He settled the baby in, then helped his wife into the seat. In unison they waved at the nurse, thanking her.

Women seem so excited after offering the world a new life, but soon they realize that no matter what else they do, the thing that characterizes them is motherhood. I wondered why men are defined by what they create, or manage, and women are defined by whom they take care of? I suppose the answer rested in millions of years of biology. Yet in our human primate society, the notion seemed so unfair because we hail the creators, not the caregivers. If I really thought about it, caregivers are the true creators.

"Abbey, are you lost?" Her voice cracked.

"Just watching," I whispered, before turning to face her.

"Watching what?"

"Nothing," I said.

I stood close to the end of her bed, wishing I could run. Shuffle backwards out of the room, run like I had done so many times before. Turn my back from her eyes. Let her words fall with a thump to the floor, never to be picked up by her daughter who refused to catch the words of a betrayer.

"Come sit." She patted the edge of the bed.

My motions were laggard, as if someone had slowed the shutter on the film. When the picture snapped, I would appear as an apparition, a cloudy outline next to a fading woman. I didn't want to get close to her, not in any way. Catatonic, I sat, pulling my body into its core, then crossed my arms, holding the opposite elbow in each hand, so nothing branched out touching my mother's flesh.

"Mom." The word hung in my throat like peanut butter. I scratched my throat to clear the mucous strain that made my tongue slow. "I'm sorry about this."

"Why are you sorry? For my cancer? You didn't have anything to do with this."

Why was she making this so difficult? Did everything have to be literal?

"I just mean, I'm sorry you have to go through this."

She lowered her head, and I wondered if the tears were

about to pour, but when she lifted it, her eyes were dry. "I'm sorry we haven't spent more time together. You've been gone so much the last twelve years… It's funny, we think we'll do more together, then something like this…"

Her fingers traced down my forearm, sending chills creeping up my spine. I tried not to balk at her touch, but my skin flinched. She felt it and pulled her hand away like a child who had been scolded for reaching toward the cookie jar.

"I wish I'd remembered to bring the photos. I really did love Africa," I spouted, then turned off the words.

Abruptly, I began again. "First, I went to North Africa, where we took the photographs of the macaque, then to Sierra Leone, and then to Ethiopia where I got some amazing shots of baboons in their habitat. But the most incredible photos I took were of the silverback and the mother gorilla in Rwanda. I traveled through Africa capturing nature's wonders on paper."

I shifted my eyes, trying to avoid my mother's acute gaze. "It was tiresome work, sometimes we had to wait days just for one shot, but it was always worth it when we were able to catch a glimpse of the wild on paper."

My speech sounded formal, as if I were at a university symposium addressing a room full of graduate students. I'd never shared much about my travels with my mother, but this day I would rather talk about the lives of those primates who first inhabited Africa than dive into a pool of emotional sludge.

"Abbey, I want you to know something."

Lord, she was pulling me into the game. 'Ring around

the rosy, a pocket full of posies,' taking my hand, asking me to play, 'ashes, ashes, we all fall down.' I hated that game, dragged to the ground because some game demanded you fall, the weight of another pulling you to the dirt. As a child, when playmates opened up the circle, extending their hands for me to play, I shook my head, backing away. And now my mother extended herself, asking me to join in.

I glanced at her body and then shifted my gaze away. I hadn't realized how much dimension her breasts gave her, how the landscape of her body seemed desolate without them. I thought of some of the mountains in Africa that once were covered with lush tropical forest and now, after years of deforestation, stood as naked stark, powerless hills, the soil no longer conducive for vegetation, a wasteland. I looked at her again. I really didn't know what to say.

"Mom, the silverback gorilla is massive." I stood, spreading my arms wide. "And I captured him on film in all his glory. I also got a picture of a mother gorilla and her infant. The first few shots you can hardly see the infant because it's buried in its mother's chest."

"The mom holds the infant close to keep it from harm's way?" she said.

"Yes. She stared at me to make sure I wouldn't harm her baby, then she exposed the infant. But she was never far from escaping back into the bush."

My mother sat up straighter, her mouth pulled downward with pain. The doctor had said her whole torso would feel tender because they removed part of the chest muscles when they took her breasts. "When we removed her breasts," the doctor had said as such a matter of fact. He didn't know what they had meant to her.

"Never leaving the closeness of shelter, in case something might harm her infant?" she whispered.

"The infant also knows who its protector is, his little feet, all four, grip the mother's chest and at the first smell of danger they dig into the mother's flesh," I said, my eyes on the sterile floor.

"Who shields the infant, the mother or the father?"

"What do you mean?" I said, as a slight frown took over my brow. "They both do."

"Would the mother protect the infant from the father?"

I looked up, her eyes, wide circles with moisture floating at the edge.

"I guess. But with the great apes, because the mother cares for the infant more than the father, there is no monogamy." I glanced at my mother's eyes, I wanted to say, 'just like there is no monogamy in human primates,' but she already knew that. "Only in the monogamous species of primates does the father care for the infant, more, or equally, and many biologists believe it's because the father can be sure it's his."

The door opened and my father, slightly slumped, entered, carrying a tray with three cups of coffee and three donuts: fat coated with sugar that had probably sat for a few days. He placed the tray on my mother's bedside table, then stopped.

A lone tear traveled down her cheek. His large thumb wiped it away, and he jerked his head toward me. "What went on?" he said, standing up square, his loyalty to her solid.

She clawed at his forearm, her weak hand reaching halfway around it. "Nothing, Abbey was just teaching me about the social habits of the gorillas in Rwanda."

I stared down at my hands, bigger than my mother's. I'd inherited my father's hands and broad shoulders, and my mother's narrow hips and propensity toward thinness.

My dad's posture eased, falling back on itself. His torso rested on the center of his belly. Her cancer had aged him, too, as the lines around his eyes spread out toward his temples and dug deeper into his sun-kissed skin. The corners of his mouth were reluctant, tense, drawn into downward lines, cutting along the sides of his round cheeks.

"Well, Mom, it's late. I should go and let you get some rest. I'll bring the photos tomorrow." I hugged her, as if she were a hot coal and my flesh would burn if I touched her too long. "Dad." I reached around him, staying in his chest long enough to smell stale sweat woven through the threads of his pinstripe shirt. "Do you need me to stop by the house, get anything on my way here tomorrow?"

"Your father's going home tonight," My mother's tone was firm.

"No, I'm not," Dad said.

"You need a good night sleep and…" she smiled, "and a shower."

"Thanks, honey." He laughed. "I'll head home now, get a shower and a bite, and come back. I'll walk out with you, Abbey." He bent and gave my mother a soft kiss on the lips.

"Bye, Mom," I said as he followed me out the door.

I suggested we grab a bite at the burger joint near their house. Walls covered in Texas memorabilia, picnic tables scattered around the two large rooms, and cement floors covered in peanut shells were all part of the appeal of Wild Al's Burgers.

Dad and I sat across from each other. He ordered a Mexi-burger, oozing guacamole, cheese, and picante sauce, atop a half pound of beef: a taco within a bun. As I bit into my Southwest chicken sandwich, my father stared at me, his eyes drawn in tight as if sizing me up while studying my features.

"Abbey, have I been a good father?" His eyes glazed over, tears pushing against his lids. He, my strong father, awaited approval from me.

"Why are you …Yes, Dad."

"The doctors say it's going to be a hard road if your mother is able to fight this. One of them stopped me in the hall, told me the scans show it's in the liver." The tears escaped his lids and marched down his face. He brushed them away. He turned his head toward the wall, focusing on an old John Wayne painting. "You have always been my girl, but this constant strain between you and your mother has gone on too long, and now would be a good time to make some changes."

The mother gorilla and her infant moved into my mind and I remembered with intense clarity my pact to bridge the gap between my mother and me.

"I know, it's just that we're different."

"Not very," he said, still staring to the side, his voice flat.

As I took a bite of my sandwich, I could almost taste my father's pain, so thick that night, hanging in the air, coating everything. "I know we look alike, but inside we're opposite.

I could never be like her."

"That's not a bad thing to be."

"Okay, Dad."

"Sometimes people make choices, selfless choices," he said, between bites.

"Or perhaps they haven't any," was all I could think of her choice to be a housewife. As soon as the words tripped from my tongue, I wished I could stuff them back, leave them to burn inside of me instead.

His head flew up, his eyes boring into me. "Is that what you think, that she had no choices?" His voice rose into a high painful pitch, and his face turned crimson red. "You have a lot to learn about choices."

"Please, Dad, I know Mom was always there for us. I'm just different," I scooted off the wooden bench, walked over to the counter to get beer, since my Diet Coke wasn't enough to fortify me during this particular conversation. After a few minutes I slid back into the bench, across from my father, and pushed a bottle toward him. "Here, you need this."

"I need your mother to pull through this." He took the beer and swallowed, as if he were swigging something lumpy and thick. "She's been the center for this whole family."

"That was you."

"You're wrong. She gave up everything to make this marriage and family complete. Abbey, your mother and I worked things out a long time ago. You need to let it go. I was as wrong as she was. Please understand that."

"I suppose." I wrapped my lips around the mouth of my long neck beer bottle, swallowing the lies I had absorbed for years. Her lies had become our family's lies.

"You have to know that." He touched my forearm, the ends of his fingers lingering, while he stared at me. A long touch, a steady gaze.

I crossed my feet, uncrossed them, crossed them back, and looked at his hand, then at his eyes.

"I've learned something in my fifty-seven years. I've learned someone's past mistakes are not the measure of their worth as a person today." He lifted his hand. "Let your mother's mistakes go. Forget them and concentrate on what you and she can have right now. She loves you and I know..."

"Dad, you're right. But I really need to go." I twisted my hips around to stand up. His words prickled the back of my neck, since it seemed impossible that my mother and I would be able to repair the past.

"All right, I'll see you tomorrow." He stood up and pecked the side of my face. "I love you," he said, his voice strained, trying not to let the tears come again.

"I love you, too." I stretched up on my tiptoes and kissed my father's cheek.

I left the top of the Jeep down, exposing the wide expanse of the Texas sky. I remembered a chorus to an old cowboy song, 'The stars at night are big and bright deep in the heart of Texas.' It was so true, the Texas sky was wide open and the stars close, making me think, if I reached up and stood on my tiptoes, I could touch a Texas star.

I wanted to wish upon a star, wish I were back in Africa, hiding in the dark Rwandan forest, waking to the sound of nature's nocturnal animals as they preyed on their less advanced neighbors. I had felt safe there. Home, where family members are free to roam while inflicting irreconcilable damage on each other, where transferring destructive behaviors was as likely as passing on eye color, where family secrets fester and destroy, seemed much more frightening than the so-called untamed lands of the world.

CHAPTER 8

As I sat waiting for Jennifer and Sheila among all the other trendy patrons at Dr. Grind's Coffee Shop, my mind bounced between the image of my mother's breastless form lying in a hospital bed (she had been there eight days now) and my father's sorrow. The silent pressure I had interpreted from Ryan crowded in as well.

I pushed all the scenarios for the future from my head and let myself think about something meaningless. Like what constitutes trendy, paying three dollars for a cup of coffee? Knowing the difference between a latte and a cappuccino, or pretending you like the taste of espresso?

I set my camera on the table and stirred my cappuccino, a gorgeous drink, with its billowy froth towering above the rim of the glass coffee mug. Like anything else in life, the first connection was always the best. That moment when the foam tickles the top of your lip, and the creamy milked-down taste of coffee slides over your tongue. I got everything aligned before I took that one first and last best sip.

Jennifer and Sheila had been my closest friends since my second summer in college. I came home to Austin for the summer from college in Madison, Wisconsin, and worked at Baby A's, a Mexican restaurant downtown. I met both of them there, and we were inseparable. I basically lived at

Sheila's apartment.

We repeated this ritual for the next three idyllic summers, where the most important decisions consisted of what flavor margarita we should drink on any given night: mango, papaya, or cactus. So many memories submerged in those luscious drinks.

Through the large glass window, I spotted Jennifer pushing a stroller. Her long hair feathered around her face and a western-style poncho draped over her shoulders. Her smile widened when she caught my eye as she came through the door.

I stood up and hugged her. She laughed and looked at me again, doing the whole inspection thing, throwing her head back, telling me how good I looked. Then we both directed our attention to her new extension, Angelica, who would turn six months tomorrow. Jennifer had dressed her infant in a pink smocked dress, a little hat, and a pair of white booties. Her eyes were closed.

"We need to hope that's how they stay," Jennifer said, "now that she's taking her morning nap."

She rolled her eyes and beamed at the same time when she talked about Angelica. "You have no idea how exhausted I am, how much my life has changed." And then she discussed in detail the deterioration of her body and mind.

Amid my laughter, I thought it was because she'd had a parasite living off of her for nine months and it would probably continue to suck what it needed for years. She ended her horrific description of childbirth and motherhood with statements like 'how beautiful it was' and 'I would never trade being a mother for anything.'

Forever a woman's dilemma, they say motherhood is the most wonderful thing in the world, but what every mother wouldn't do to grab her own life back, to rip it out of the hands of her greedy children.

Her figure faired well through childbirth, adding to it an increase in the size of her breasts.

"They hurt so much and I feel like a cow. My husband Larry is jealous because my breasts are now occupied for the purpose of nutrition."

Though Austin's laid-back style had influenced her, Jennifer exemplified the definition of a Dallas girl. Decorated in a perfect, matched ensemble, she wore a black crinkled velvet skirt with a denim shirt trimmed in black velvet and a silver belt that accentuated her waist. Her skirt draped a few inches below her knees and my eyes were drawn to her black and white boots. I wondered how wearing anything that resembled a cow could be flattering.

"It's good to see you, girl." She grabbed my left hand, stared at my ring finger. "Just checking."

Jennifer was fully aware she embodied the quintessential Texas girl look, talk, walk, and money. That eighties television show, *Dallas*, was not far from the reflection of her life. Her dad was an extremely successful businessman there and she had married the son of one of his best friends.

We teased her when she got engaged, saying she needed to work out just to be able to hold her hand up, due to the weight of her ring. She had laughed, loving the attention that a southern drawl, blonde hair, and a lot of money gets a girl in Texas.

Jennifer and I both knew we were at opposite ends of the

spectrum. But our honesty and sense of humor about our radical dissimilarities drew us closer. The fact that Jennifer never wanted or expected me to change made her a permanent part of my friendship circle. I went to the counter to get Jennifer a cup of decaffeinated coffee and a bagel.

Behind me, inches from my ear, the voice that could coax any president into giving up the secret to the arms code, whispered, "Guess who?"

I turned around. "Sheila. My favorite celebrity." I grabbed her elbow and smiled. "What do you want?"

"Double latte. Well, what do you think?" she said, pointing to her new red hair, cut Pixie-style. Sheila was a host on one of the offbeat radio programs in which the profanity was in line with Howard Stern and her mouth spouted a majority of it, making her somewhat of an icon among the radical college students.

The suffused light streaking through the windows highlighted Sheila's face. Her fair skin looked blotchier, and faint lines formed crescent shadows under her eyes, but her water-blue eyes still set her apart.

Her outfit assured me Sheila hadn't changed. Her cropped pink angora sweater left her body exposed until her tight, black leather pants came to the rescue just below the belly button. I handed her the latte and we sat down with Jennifer.

Jennifer and Sheila exchanged a quick hug, both giving the other the once-over. We took turns looking at Angelica, admiring the way her small lips curled up while she slept, before we settled into the old friends mold.

"All right, Sheila. First, what's that sweater and earring

all about?" Jennifer said, then sipped her coffee.

"The sweater is all about eighty dollars and are you referring to the rings in my ears, my nose, or my belly button?"

I leaned down to inspect the loop in her bellybutton. Sheila's stomach had indentations along the sides and middle formed by muscle development. If my stomach looked like that, I'd dress it up, too.

"I think it looks great," I said. "It shows off her physique."

As I leaned back, my eyes scanned her breasts. They were the same size as Madonna's, full C-cups, and the media had already informed the nation that Madonna had the perfect size breasts. I wondered how Sheila would feel without them.

'Hey, how would you feel if tomorrow they had to hack off your breasts because of cancer?' But that wasn't something you asked your friends.

Yesterday Ethan told me that an average of one out of every eight women would be diagnosed with breast cancer in their lives, so maybe it is something we should discuss.

"Let's not talk about stomach muscles," Jennifer said, rubbing her belly, then skewed her eyes toward the baby.

We all nodded, laughing.

They both wanted to see the pictures from Africa, so I pulled them from my bag. First I showed them the vervet monkey, which I explained had been blamed by some scientists for the AIDS virus. Then the macaques, and finally the great silverback gorilla.

They gasped at my close-up photo of the silverback, and then the photo of the mother and her infant. It looked like I had been near enough to kiss my primate cousin on the lips.

Given the power of the lens, I explained, I had been able to get within fifty feet of the great ape.

"Wow, Abbey, the one of the mother and the baby is amazing. I can especially relate to the way she's looking at her little one, after having Angelica."

"Good," I said nodding.

"He's a hell of a lot cuter than some of the men I've dated lately." Sheila stopped, then looked at me with a question in her water-blue eyes. Her red lipstick mouth wore a smug grin. "Speaking of men, how is Ryan?"

"Good question," Jennifer added.

"Ryan's fine. He seems to be doing well."

"Seems to be doing well!" Jennifer squawked. "He and his brother have turned that small internet music business into a million dollar winner. Is there more to this story, Abbey?"

Jennifer played with the gold loop dangling from her left earlobe. "Seriously, what's happening with you and Ryan?"

"I don't know," I said wincing at my own staid words.

"Come on, Abbey. You've been saying that for what, almost three years." Sheila stared at me. "In all fairness to Ryan, make some decisions. Either let him go, so he can have a life, or confirm his feelings and delve into it with him."

Her words were condemning. The reality was that Ryan had made a decision to move forward in our relationship. His actions were telling, even if he kept his words masked.

My fear kept me on some edge. I couldn't move forward, so I ran, making excuses to Ryan the last few nights why I couldn't go there, how I needed to be alone. Really, I didn't want to be alone, but the thought of answering the questions disguised in his tender kisses, his prolonged hugs, and his intense looks over coffee made me feel like a brick weighed heavy on my chest.

"Ryan's probably my best friend. In some ways I can't imagine being in Austin without him. He's been such a part of my life here, and there's a lot of security knowing he'll always be here. But I don't know if I can say, this is the one, this will work forever, he'll never leave me, I'll never leave him."

I had found it so easy to let Johann go, making it clear I didn't have the energy or time to make a long distance relationship work. Poof... he was gone and I didn't feel any loss. But the thought of Ryan not being in my life left me feeling bereft.

"Ryan's a great guy, Abbey," Sheila said, the current in her eyes still.

"Yeah, he is." The fear I had stuffed into the mattresses of strange men seemed to emerge whenever the idea came up of Ryan and forever. "Maybe you're right, I need to let him go. God, that seems almost as scary as saying 'I do.' "

"Why don't you just give it a real shot?" Sheila said. "Jump in, Ryan's ready to catch you. I saw him a few times during the last year and all he could talk about was you."

I sat up straight and looked her in the face.

"One day I ran into him here after you'd been gone probably eight months and he told me he was going to move on, that he needed to forget about you. He was hoping you'd give a little more in your letters. He said you still seemed non-committal and he had to try and date other people." She flipped her eyes down and then back at me. "Sorry, Ab, but I agreed with him."

"That doesn't seem to be what he thinks now." I tried not to let surprise enter my tone.

She smiled as if a fond childhood memory had just played in her head. "No, it's not. I saw him again, not even three months later and I asked him how his new Abbey-less life was going. He said, it's not, after a couple of months of trying to forget you, he decided he was sick."

"What?"

"Sick in love, and all the extra time with your family made him more sure you're what's right."

I let my chin sink into my palms and briefly I shut my eyes. That explained the months of no letters and the subsequent letters where he made it clear how much he had missed me, a desperate edge to his penned words.

Sheila continued. " 'Forever,' that was his exact word. I think he's hoping that when you saw his dedication, you'd give a little."

"You think?" Jennifer said.

"I'm not ready for the whole family thing, and how can anyone be sure this person is the one?"

"Can anyone ever be? It's sort of like a lottery. Sometimes you marry, 'the one' and sometimes you just marry. A lottery for love." Sheila grimaced, like the whole thing was futile, something you could never win.

"How depressing, Sheila," Jennifer said. "Abbey, I understand not wanting to hook up with Ryan a couple of years ago when he was a struggling musician, working in a music store, but he's probably worth close to a million by now."

"So, now he's rich enough to fall in love with, Jennifer?" Sheila leaned across the table. "That's depressing."

Jennifer's eyes flashed to the ring on her finger. "Money doesn't hurt. I can guarantee that."

"Well, neither does a good lay," Sheila said.

Jennifer rolled her eyes. "Anyway, none of us is getting younger."

"Thirty-one is young," I said. The whole conversation sounded inane.

"Once you get married, you find out there are more important things than sex." Again, Jennifer's eyes shifted to the infant sleeping in the stroller.

"Wait a minute. This coming from the girl who swore she would never marry a guy who doesn't go downtown," Sheila blurted.

"Well, I didn't." Jennifer grinned. "Larry and I have a good sex life."

I never understood why married people refer to sex as a separate life. 'We have a good sex life,' not speaking about any other biological process as a disjointed entity 'we have a great eating, shitting, or sleeping life.' So once you get married, sex must take on a life of its own, a life you have to feed and nurture, or it will die, and one day you will say, 'our sex life is dead.'

That concept seemed altogether pathetic to me. Had that happened between my parents? Had their sex life died and my mother sought relief somewhere else? I felt so sad for my father. He had always adored her and then was willing to forgive her. 'Forget it, put it aside,' he'd said. I almost told him I couldn't.

"I certainly won't be going out with that friend of Larry's anymore." Sheila stared at Jennifer.

"Forgive me for trying to do you a favor. His daddy has a huge business and he's not doing too bad himself. He's a great guy." Jennifer's twangy Texas accent looped around her words and buzzed in my ears like a bad heartbreak song.

"Great, his daddy has money. What has he done? He played football in college because he talked about that for an hour, right before he crawled on top of me and said…" Sheila leaned in close, spread her fingers on the table and opened her mouth wide. Using her low husky radio voice, she said, "I need you to want me, baby, I'm going to give you the winning touchdown."

"Oh, tell me he didn't say that!" Jennifer snorted.

"He did, just before I crawled out from under him and left."

"God, how old is this guy?" I said.

"Thirty-five." Jennifer said, still laughing. "Isn't Ryan sounding better and better all the time, Abbey?"

"Enough about Ryan. I need to head out."

Sheila leaned toward me. "Really, Abbey, you should decide something, so you can at least keep Ryan's friendship. Everybody's got a breaking point, even Ryan."

"I'm listening, Sheila," I said, without looking up from my coffee.

I took a deep breath and absorbed Sheila's heavy perfume. The air around her smelled like a fortune teller's parlor lit up with incense.

"I need to get to the hospital." I swallowed. I should have told them earlier but I didn't want the emotional dramatics that would escort the news. I chose my exit as the stage to announce my mother's condition.

"What... the hospital?" Sheila sounded confused.

"Yeah, my mother was just diagnosed with cancer and she's getting chemo-therapy, so I need to go visit her."

"You didn't say anything." Jennifer reached across the table to touch my hand.

I concentrated on keeping my hand still, taking in her sympathies.

"What kind of cancer?" Sheila said.

"Breast."

Both of their eyes grew large and round, fear dilating the pupils, and they tried to keep their mouths straight. As women, we knew ovarian cancer as the silent killer and breast cancer as the maimer of our bodies. What a choice: die or have your body disfigured.

"She had a double mastectomy last week, and they found cancer in her liver, so the next step is chemotherapy."

Without any conscious intention, both their chests sunk in, pulling their breasts closer.

"I'm going to start doing those self-exam things," Jennifer said. "How is she taking it and all?"

"I don't know, she's pretty sore and tired from what I can discern."

But I couldn't tell them how she felt inside, because I didn't know. I wondered if my dad did, if she'd told him.

"How would anyone react to having their breasts removed?" Sheila said with a tone of sarcasm.

"You're right, dumb question," Jennifer said. "You should have told us sooner, Abbey. You can't keep these things to yourself. That's what we're here for."

"I just wanted to hang out with you guys and not have this whole meeting turn into something emotional."

"That's what friends do, talk about our lives," Jennifer said.

"I know."

I tried several times to pull myself from their probing questions, more so when they entered the territory of my emotions. I half-expected one of them to ask me if I were concerned for myself because of the genetic factor. Christ, if another nurse told me that I now had an increased chance of having breast cancer, I'd scream.

They both were aware my mother and I never communicated on any level. They attributed it to different generations, the same reason they didn't communicate with their parents. They did not know the depth of the chasm between us. It would have revealed something about her, along with my father, I didn't want to make public.

At last, they let me go. I hugged them both and then, as I made my way to the door, my friends exchanged lingering whispers of concern.

After I climbed into my Jeep, I clenched my jaw, fighting the swell of emotion that pushed behind my eyes. If I got cancer, I knew they'd be here for me, and Ryan would, too. They weren't placeholders in my Austin life. I was connected to them and my life mattered to them.

When death becomes a real thing, it makes you wonder who will miss you when you're gone. Would I miss my mother if she died? God, I wanted to miss her.

CHAPTER 9

Nothing at the hospital had changed: the walls still a pale aqua blue, the smell of rubbing alcohol still permeated the halls, and the faces of those hoping for another chance occupied the waiting room.

I rode the elevator up, listening to the conversation of two sons, early thirties, discussing their father's funeral, and then the alternative, if he did live; the cost to care for the man. They hoped it would not come to that. He would die in peace and fast. In peace, I thought, without dipping into their bank accounts to sustain his life.

When I was ten, my grandmother, my father's mother, lived with us her last few months of life, and we all had taken care of her. Somehow, though, she'd nurtured us, providing a mission for us as a family, chores that focused around a woman who had given so much in her life.

But my generation had seen the folly and emptiness of giving and we were most concerned, it seemed, with how tragic events would affect our pocketbooks or our intense, busy social and business schedules. I was one of them.

In slow motion, I edged through the door to her room. My mother sat on the bed, doubled over, gagging. I plunked down beside her. She used one hand to prop herself up and the other hand to shoo me away. "Go on, Abigail," she said in a strained voice.

"No, Mom." I grabbed the pink kidney-shaped bucket and held it close to her chin.

Her torso jerked forward and vomit spewed from her mouth. I put one arm around her to steady her.

SHE HAD DONE THE SAME WHEN I was twenty, home from college. I stayed out drinking with Sheila and Jennifer. The last thing I remembered was Jennifer's brother making us Texas Tea, a drink we would never forget, consisting of several hard liquors, iced tea, and 7-Up. The next time my brain registered my whereabouts, I was leaning over the toilet. I felt a hand on my shoulder, the other one whisking my hair aside to keep it from falling into the toilet, while I wrenched my guts out.

My mother helped me walk to my bed, made me lie down, and then undressed me. She tugged for a few minutes at my tight jeans, then lifted my shirt off, talking to me the whole time like I was three, 'Can Abigail lift her arms and help her mom?'

I did as she instructed. She pulled the covers up and stroked my back, telling me I would feel better tomorrow. Her petite warm fingers ran up and down my back. I said in a little girl's voice, 'I like that, Mom.' I remember thinking how wonderful her touch felt on my back and how I never wanted her to stop.

The ends of her fingers touching my skin was the last thing I remembered before I woke to a throb in my head and the sound of my parents' voices rising and lowering in an argument down the hall. My mother lied to my father, telling him she heard me come in soon after they went to bed.

I had pulled the pillow over my head, not wanting to hear her. I hated that she made me a partner in deception, using my indiscretions to justify her ease with dishonesty.

"SHOULD I CALL A NURSE?"

"No, I'll be fine," she said, just before she retched again, her body letting go, splats of bile dropping into the pan. "Please get me a warm cloth."

I reached over the bed to try to wipe her mouth but she grabbed the cloth from me, wiping it herself. Our eyes met for a long moment and her jaw quivered with a blend of anger and sadness.

"Mom."

She lay back on the bed, breathing deeply, trying to regain her composure. I brought a glass of water to her mouth and she lifted her eyes, studying my gesture, my motive. She moved her hand on mine to steady the glass and then drank from it like a scared thirsty child that a stranger had found.

I set the glass on the bedside table. The water splashed on the sides of the glass. I felt shaky.

My perception was skewed, corrupted by my own anger and self-importance. It was hard to see who she was, even as she struggled to hang on to her life.

I was a member of the club of those who grew up not wanting for anything, never having experienced a war, or a depression. What we needed, we always got, and what we wanted was on the way, because our parents, the ones who did suffer, whose parents were immigrants or impoverished, swore their children would never feel a loss for anything.

Instead we delve in self-pity, conjuring reasons why we're not more successful, or happy. Why our marriages don't last, or we haven't found our way. Our fingers cannot help but point toward our parents as we lie on the psychologist's couch and claim, 'it's because they forced me to go to school' or 'they didn't hug me enough.'

I knew this, but somehow couldn't stop myself from feeling like her choices cheated me.

My eyes were drawn to a colorful bouquet of fresh flowers stuffed into a glass jar. "Mom, did Dad bring you fresh flowers?"

"No, Dad claims not to have sent them. I think he's lying though, because there's a new bouquet twice a week."

"They're nice."

"I should rest. You don't need to stay here," she said, her voice reaching just above a whisper.

"Mom." I pulled the Africa pictures from my bag. "I finally remembered the photos."

I had always shown the photos of all my adventures to my father, but I'd make my mother beg to be a part of my life, only showing her my work after my father viewed them.

"Yes." She moved her slight frame into a sitting position.

I flipped through the pictures, trying to imagine myself, the little girl, plopping down next to her mother on the beach, her hands full of seashells, crossing her legs in excitement as she showed them to her mother. Each one wrapped in a brilliant story of adventure about the sea. Her face would grow more and more animated with each wild story that accompanied my colorful shells.

My mother's tired eyes grew bigger and a smile eased across her face as I told her the different stories, hiding in a tree, awaiting a picture, endless hours spent in a Jeep getting to the next country, trying to remain still as insects feasted on my arms in the bush. She pointed to the mother and infant in the background.

"I have a close up of them," I said, pulling two eight by ten photos from the manilla envelope.

"Abigail," she whispered. My name spoken in a way I hadn't heard from her since I was a little girl, pride emphasizing every syllable.

"Oh, Abigail," she said again, pushing her torso into an upright position.

We both stared at the picture.

"Mom." I wanted to soak up her pride and be a part of the mother-daughter moment that seemed to be happening as we stared at the dyad.

"There's been some talk that this photo may win the Alfred Eisenstaedt Award."

A slow deliberate smile crossed her face. "And it should. Only a gifted photographer could have evoked the trust of her subject in such a way, as to capture this level of emotion on paper. You have the gift."

How did she know? Only people in the business know what it takes.

"Have you ever taken… I mean, has photography ever interested you?"

What if this talent had been begot from my mother?

"No… no, I was just… struck." She spoke as if she had to think about her response.

She pointed to the picture. "How long does the mother keep the infant with her?"

"You mean attached?"

"Yes, like that." She tapped the image of the infant.

"At least six months, and then the infant hangs on the mother's back for another year, venturing only a short distance for several years. They stay very close to their mothers for eleven to twelve years, at least within hearing distance."

"How can their mothers keep them so close, for so long?"

"It's physiological. Mom. That's where they want to be. They feel safe there."

"What about the monkeys from South America, the ones you took pictures of two years ago. How long do their infants stay with them?"

"Not as long. The further you go up the evolutionary chain, the longer the gestation period, and the longer the mother cares for her young directly."

"Until humans." She shut her eyes.

"Humans?"

"Yes, we don't keep our young protected and safe for very long, not long enough," she said, regret woven through her words.

"That's right. The very thing separating us from the Great Apes, supposedly our ability to reason, allows us to go against our own biology."

"So, the power of our brains interferes with the natural order of life." She opened her eyes and turned her head to look at me.

"But our brains have allowed us all this technology," I said, moving my gaze around the room, focusing on the machine that pumped a gray substance into my mother's arm so she would not become dehydrated and another machine that allowed little drips of hope to seep into her bloodstream: chemotherapy. The only promise of life, destroy the bad cancer cells. Along with them at least a third of the good cells, and when it is all said and done, the bad guys die and enough of the good guys live to sustain a human organism.

"Yes, and isn't it glorious? They're going to keep me alive as long as they can, so my family can wait on me and suffer, disrupting their lives."

I hated to hear her talk like that; she sounded like a martyr and if there was one thing she wasn't, it was a martyr.

"Our lives are not disrupted. And they believe they can kill the cancer," I said, with emphasis. "You have to think positive."

She stared blankly at my shoulders, not responding.

"Mom."

She lifted her arm and laid her hand on my shoulder. "You really should wear sunscreen."

She moved the tips of her fingers in tiny circles as if assessing the damage. Her skin felt dry and rigid, as though her fingerprints were being engraved on my freckled shoulders.

"Abigail, how many times have I told you to wear

sunscreen?" Her voice was stern. "Oh, darling, why would anyone want to scar beautiful porcelain skin?"

"Mom, really?"

The expression in her eyes and the tone of her voice took me back to when I was a little girl, wearing my new Barbie doll hot pink swimsuit. She'd slathered sunscreen on my shoulders before I ran through the sprinkler, lecturing me on the value of protecting my skin. I had yanked my arm taut against her grip, wanting only to run through the water shooting into the air.

"Abigail, take care of your skin. You'll be happy you did." Her voice dropped off.

My mother's eyes closed and in a short time, she was asleep. I leaned over the bed. Her skin looked like the inside of an old clamshell; ashen peeling layers. It wasn't my mother's glowing skin that she had babied all her life, proud that people could not believe she was my mother. Now she looked old enough to be my grandmother.

Both the beginning and the end of life rob us of all dignity. In the beginning, someone slaps you on the ass just to hear you cry, and in the end, no one hears your cries.

The outside of my fingers trailed the edge of her prominent jaw. I pulled away, not kissing her cheek. She was lost in sleep and it wouldn't matter. The gesture, a difficult one for me, couldn't be wasted. When I thought of the possibility of losing her, longing tried to settle into my heart, but the old fury pumped it out.

It was too late for us. No amount of resolve could break through all the blocks of anger I had built into a thick wall over the last fifteen years.

CHAPTER 10

Six months had passed since my father left, and every day, every minute he stayed away, my hatred for my mother grew at an exponential rate, like a sprinkle of yeast mixed with water. The water was seeing her, the whore, walk through the door after work, dressed perfectly, every hair in place, lipstick unsmudged, eyeliner highlighting her green eyes, tits bouncing as she wiggled up the steps. She seemed unmoved, untouched by the hell she had caused.

Meanwhile, my father was falling apart. He had gained weight, as if he found some solace in fast food. And his eyes always seemed puffy. Extra tears rested just below the skin in case he needed them, and surely he would. It was a bad dream.

I hadn't ever seen my father cry. Now every time he dropped us off, his eyes never stopped blinking as we walked backwards down the stone pathway to our front door, his lids trying to keep the tears trapped under his skin.

I couldn't stand the sight of our kitchen any longer. The garbage overflowed with TV dinner boxes, frozen juice containers, and empty wine bottles, leftover from the alcohol my mother nursed every evening after work as she sat on the couch and ate a frozen diet dinner, watching some sappy movie and talking to Ethan during commercials. She kept up a solid image to her friends when they called to invite her and Dad to dinner or a party.

She would say, 'Oh, Diane, I'm so sorry we'd love to, but we're so swamped. This is such a busy time in school for the kids and they're so involved. You understand.'

This was her standard answer to ward off any suspicion that Mrs. Rachel Gallagher was not leading a perfect life.

I tied up the trash and took it out, tossed a load in the wash from the stack of dirty clothes, loaded the dishwasher, scrubbed the counter, the entire time cussing under my breath at my mother.

"Abigail, you're having a little fit. Is something wrong?" Her haughty voice pricked the back of my neck.

I turned from the dishwasher to face her. Her hip was pressed against the wall of the arched entryway and she held a glass of white wine in her hand. My eyes bounced from her long polished fingers to her shoulders. I couldn't look her straight in the face.

"Think you could do your job," I said in a flat tone.

"I just got home from my job!" she said, a sharpness to the edge of her voice.

"Oh, good, Mom, from your salesclerk job. Great!" I turned to finish loading the dishwasher.

"I'm sick of your attitude, Abigail. Don't you talk to me like that." The wine on her tongue exaggerated her drawl.

I slammed the dishwasher shut. "Like what?"

She stepped toward me. "In that disrespectful manner. I'm your mother and I won't stand for you treating me like this," she said, as the wine sloshed against the sides of the crystal glass.

"The first part's my bad luck, and the second part's

yours. You have to put up with me. I'm your daughter, remember." I smiled.

"Go upstairs. I don't want to see you the rest of the night."

"You won't, don't worry," I said, as I walked to the stairs.

After a quick shower, I called Amy. She was a couple of years older, already in college, and much more fun than the girls my age. Since Amy's parents used to hang out with my parents, we grew up together, until her parents' sordid divorce years ago.

Then my parents discouraged me from playing with her. They said her mother had lost control of Amy and she was a bad influence. But after my father left, Amy's parentless house had been a refuge for me, especially on the days I didn't make it to school. Amy was a pro at writing excuse letters.

"Amy, I'm in for that party tonight."

"Great, I'll come and pick you up."

"Listen, just honk," I said. "My mother's being weird."

"Gotcha. Remember try not to look too high school. This is a college party."

"I'm gonna wear that skirt I got with you the other day."

"Cool, and a tit shirt."

"Okay," I laughed. Amy's tit shirts made her quite popular with the collegiate males.

When Amy honked, I stuffed some money in my pocket and ran downstairs

My mother stood at the bottom of the stairs, her pale pink blouse hanging out of her matching skirt and mascara smeared under her blurred green eyes. "Where do you think you're going, young lady?" she said, placing her hands on her hips. "And dressed like that."

She reached over and touched the hem of my faded denim skirt. "No, no, no, I don't think so, Ms. Abigail, you're not going anywhere like that."

"Mom, get out of my way." I moved to the side.

She took one sliding step on the tile and stationed herself in front of me. "I mean it."

Her eyes widened with concentration as she tried not to sound drunk. "That skirt barely covers your bottom and that top is way too tight. No, no."

"Move." I glared at her.

"No, I won't let you leave dressed like that."

I edged past her, closer to the front door.

She turned and grabbed my arm. "Listen to me. No daughter of mine is walking out of this house looking like a slut. What would your father say?"

"What would he say, Mother?"

"Abigail, go upstairs and change."

Amy beeped the horn again, louder and longer. I twisted my arm from her grip, and walked toward the door. Her presence behind me was palpable. I grabbed the doorknob.

"You want to dress like that? So you're trying to look like a slut on purpose?" she yelled.

I spun around and laughed. "I learned everything from my mother."

"You...!" she screamed and raised her hand, open and violent, then she swung and struck my face.

I didn't react, because I couldn't believe she would. I touched the side of my face and looked at her.

She cradled the weapon hand in her other hand and stared at it as if it were badly injured. She looked up at me as tears rolled down her face.

I backed against the door, still clutching the side of my face. The stinging spread across my jaw and down my constricted throat, and enveloped my heart. My mother had never struck me before.

"Oh, Abigail what have I done? I'm soo..." She reached toward my face.

The honking started again, knocking me back into reality. I opened the front door.

"Lord, I'm..." She tried to speak between gulping tears.

"The word is 'sorry,' bitch." I slammed the door and ran down the driveway toward the glaring headlights.

"Girl, what the hell are you doing in there?" Amy said, twisting her neck toward me. "Shit, girl, little heavy on the blush. I said look older, not like a clown."

I touched my stinging cheek. "I ran into something unexpected."

"I guess so. Here put some powder over it, and drink some of this." She handed me her purse and a large plastic glass.

I sniffed it. "What's in it?"

"Just drink it. It's vodka with a little lemonade."

As I drank a few gulps, my tongue shriveled from the taste, my lips curling into my mouth cavity. The bitter taste of vodka, a taste I wasn't familiar with, had conquered the small dose of lemonade.

Amy had sprayed her mousy brown hair into an erect waterfall of bangs, which jutted from her forehead and fanned her face. Her blue eyes were disguised behind a ring of black eyeliner and tons of mascara, upstaged only by the purplish red lipstick caked on her lips. Her boobs tried to escape, squeezing themselves out from both sides of a leather halter top, and her matching black leather skirt rode up her legs while she drove, revealing red lace panties.

I handed her the plastic cup.

"Drink some more," she said, pushing the glass toward me.

The red stop sign came fast, too fast, along with a car creeping into the intersection from the other street. Amy didn't stop, she just bounced her body up and down to the loud music.

"Stop!" I screamed.

"Shit!!" She slammed on the breaks and we spun into the intersection. Vodka and lemonade splashed everywhere.

"Oh my God, oh my God!!" I kept saying, my subliminal Catholicness emerging as I fought back the urge to cross myself.

"Shut up, we're fine. Shit, you're making me nervous."

A man jumped out of the car we almost hit, screaming and yelling. "What the hell is your problem, didn't you see the stop sign?" He hollered and pointed, but Amy just kept driving through the intersection.

"Yeah, all right, I made a mistake."

"Mistake? You coulda killed someone."

Amy reached back and grabbed a t-shirt from the back seat of her Camaro. "Here, wipe that shit off your legs. If you're lucky, some guy will lick it off your crotch," she said, smiling as she twisted her butt against the furry seat covers.

"Excuse me?" I crinkled my forehead and made a disgusted face.

"Shit, girl, you've never been eaten out?"

"No," I said, not wishing to explain, and thinking that the whole concept of a guy putting his mouth down there made me sick. Just a few nights before I had watched *Coming Home* with Jane Fonda, and I couldn't get the scene out of my mind where the paraplegic guy lowers himself on top of her naked body, then slides his head between her legs. It just kept replaying in my head. All they showed was her throwing herself back on the sheets, gasping and crying out.

Then it struck me, that's what married people do with their secret lovers behind their husband's back, the disgusting stuff. Shit, my mom.

"No? Well, you're missing out." She laughed hard and long. "I think John's screwing some girl from his little junior college, so I'm a free woman tonight."

John had been her high school boyfriend and they continued dating after graduation. He attended a local junior college, said it was like thirteenth grade without the hassle of high school rules. Amy was in her freshman year at the University of Texas in the heart of Austin.

"Why?"

"I don't know. He's acting weird and I can't decide if it's all the coke he's putting up his nose or if he's fucking someone else, 'cause he's sure not interested in fucking me. But this guy I met last week is supposed to be here tonight, so John just might be history. Hell, maybe I'll keep them both." She chuckled at her clever solution.

"Both," I said, shrugging my shoulders.

"Hell, yes, this is a woman's world, baby. Shit, Abbey, you gotta lot of growing up to do. Let's start tonight." She parked on the side of a residential street lined with cars, then leaned over and touched my bare leg. "If anyone asks, you're eighteen going on nineteen and you're a history major at Southwest Texas State. All these people are from UT so they won't know. Just a minute," she said reaching into her purse. "Here, put some of this on." She handed me tubes of mascara and lipstick.

"I'm already wearing mascara."

"Not enough. Remember, eighteen going on nineteen, not sixteen going on seventeen. Oh, and I'm twenty-one." She pushed open the car door and swung her legs out one at a time.

I finished applying more mascara and a touch of the scariest color lipstick I had ever seen. No, maybe, I had seen it, in the movie *Bride of Frankenstein.*

The house was crowded with smoke and body odor. It wasn't just cigarette smoke, but a commingling of tobacco and pot. Amy led me by the arm out the back door, where people circled around two silver kegs. We grabbed a couple of plastic cups and handed them to the guy manning the keg dispenser.

"Step right up!" He motioned to Amy and me.

Amy stepped forward, nudging herself into his side.

"Hey, Amy, is that it? Yeah, Amy."

She made a fake pout, pushing out her bottom lip. "You didn't forget me, David, did you?"

He looked down at her overly tanned flesh oozing out of the leather top. "Damn, no, I never forget…" He stared at her tits and then fixed his gaze on her eyes. "… a great set of eyes,"

They both laughed.

"This is my friend, Abbey. She's a freshman at Southwest Texas."

"Good-looking friend," he said, perusing up and down my body.

Amy grabbed David's chin. "Got any good lookin' friends for her, 'cause you're gonna be occupied."

"That's okay," I said, taking the foaming cup of beer from him.

They laughed again. "That's okay?" he said, taking another gulp of beer.

"I mean, you don't have to set me up." I felt silly and all at once so young and stupid. I wanted to go home.

"Fuck, set you up? Have you looked in the mirror? You'll be fighting off these fucking primates in a few minutes."

I followed Amy and David back into the house. Anyone could tell that a bunch of guys lived there. A few weeks' worth of cooking splatters covered the stove, while a stack of empty pizza boxes leaned against an overstuffed trashcan.

Most of the corners of the house were occupied with couples making out, as if they were alone, ignoring the house packed with people. Guys rubbing their stiff jeans against the legs of girls, girls grinding their tits into the chests of guys. Male hands disappearing up t-shirts and under skirts, acting surprised when the girl opened her eyes from passionate kissing and removed his hands. 'What? What? Oh God, I had no idea my hand was squeezing your tit, ass.'

The girl would laugh, give him a scolding look. and then nudge closer and start kissing the crazed primate. When he thought it was safe, or the beer made him brave and her numb, his naughty hand would find its way to her tit or ass once again.

Sure, this is a woman's world, I thought, remembering Amy's comment in the car. We provide the roads, but they're driving the cars.

"Rod, I want you to meet someone," David said, turning toward me.

"God damn! Hellooo!" Rod stood from the couch. He took my hand and kissed it. He was massive with a huge chest that seemed to expand when he smiled.

"He plays football," Amy whispered in my ear.

He looked just how I pictured a Viking: tall, over six feet, broad, muscular, blue eyes, pale blonde hair, and tanned. He had the straightest, whitest teeth.

"Hey, we're playing a little game of quarters. You in?" he said, still holding my fingertips in his huge callused hands.

"I guess."

"Come here." He motioned for me to sit next to him on a worn couch, positioned in front of a coffee table covered with puddles of yellow liquid and glasses.

I sank into the couch next to the Viking. Amy and David squeezed in next to me.

"You know this game?"

I shook my head.

"All right, I'll tell you the rules." He scooted his large torso back and talked into my ear. "First, how old are you?"

I swallowed. "Almost nineteen," I said, staring at my

creeping hemline.

"Good, good. Okay, you have to try and bounce the quarter into the glass and if you're successful, you make someone drink. Got it, Princess?"

I loved the way he growled 'Princess' in my ear. "Got it, and you're in trouble," I said, plucking the quarter from his fingers, the liquor making me feel cocky.

"I hope so!" He laughed, a deep Viking laugh.

I aimed like I had seen some of the others doing, then bounced the quarter. It jumped off the table onto the carpet.

The whole table whooped and clapped. "Let her try it again." A skinny guy at the other end of the table yelled.

Amy bent over to pick up the quarter, seizing the opportunity to expose heavy mounds of cleavage and the edges of her tanned butt. As she bent over, David grabbed her by the hips and pulled her down on his lap. "Meet your new seat."

She laughed and handed me the quarter.

The alcohol made me feel braver, haughtier, and I liked it. The guys at the table watched all my movements, hoping for a glimpse of illegal flesh. All their eyes were fixed on me as I leaned forward to study the edge of the glass, the angle I should bounce the quarter at, as if there was truly a science to a beer game.

I smiled, feeling the power of being pretty. A woman's world, yes, that's right. If you're smart and pretty, it's your world, and they have to make room for you. All those silly boys and their raging hormones have to make room for you. As I bent forward to bounce the quarter, I rubbed my bottom against Rod's leg.

"In! You drink," I said, placing the glass in front of Rod

for show.

"Okay, Princess, but you're gonna pay." He grabbed the glass with one hand and placed the other hand on my knee. The heat of his hand soaked into my skin while his rough calluses scratched my knee. He finished the glass and slid his hand between my knees.

I flinched.

"Take it easy," he whispered. "The calluses are from football. You'll have to come see me play. You got a boyfriend?" His lips grazed my ear.

"No," I said from behind my hair.

"Good." He slid his hand up my thigh and rested it inches below my skirt.

I missed on the next attempt. Rod grabbed the quarter and bounced it right into the cup, and I drank. Then again, and again, until I could barely hold my head up.

"Hey, she's had too much," the skinny guy said, and I looked up.

"Where's Amy?" I said.

"They went to have a little fun." Rod slipped his hand under my skirt.

I shifted my hips back.

"Come on, Princess. You wanna have fun, too, I can tell."

I scanned the house. The crowd was thinning.

"Come on, Rod, she's real drunk. I think—"

"Dan, stay out of it." Rod tapped the thin guy on the chest. "Back off, pal."

The skinny guy stepped back. "You okay?" he said, looking at me.

I hated the pity in his tone. "Of course." I smiled up at Rod.

He shrugged his shoulders and walked away.

"He's my roommate, kind of a stuffed shirt, but an okay guy."

"Skinny." I laughed and then rubbed my hand over Rod's thick chest.

He kissed me, jabbing his tongue in and out of my mouth, then he slid his finger underneath my panties and inside me. My pelvis moved back, his hand moved with it. My stomach felt achy and the feeling crept down between my legs, gripping his finger. I wanted him to touch me. Touch me and call me 'Princess.' I felt wanted and I needed it to continue.

"You want to see my new truck?" he said, sliding his finger out of me.

"Yes." I let him lead me out the door and down the sidewalk. I was like a robot and he had the controls. He opened the truck door, and I stood on the sidewalk looking in.

"Nice truck."

"Come on now, let's not play games. Get in."

I didn't know what he meant by playing games, but I crawled into the truck.

He climbed in and said, "I know where we can go." He put his arm around my waist and slid me close to him.

He drove, country music blaring from the radio. He steered the truck with one hand and fondled my breast with the other, stopping only to take a drink of beer from the bottle I had squeezed between my thighs.

I liked how his large hand kneaded my breast, like he

couldn't get enough, like I was valuable. I forgot, for a few hours, how fucked up my life seemed and I wished he would keep driving. I could listen to sad country songs about how people screwed their lives up, drink beer, and feel his big hands on my breasts. We could drive out of Austin, past San Antonio, all the way to Mexico, and I could disappear there, make my mother regret her stupidity.

"You know where I want to be, Princess?"

"Huh." I said, lost in Mexico on some beach.

"You know where I want to be right now?"

"Where?" I smiled and flipped my hair toward the Viking.

"Right where that beer bottle is." He spread his hand across my thighs, dragging it down to the beer bottle.

I opened my knees, releasing the bottle to his hand. The touch of his rough hand tingled my thighs and wove into my panties. I imagined being his girlfriend, running to him waving my arms after he won a football game. 'That's my boyfriend,' I'd say to all my friends. I'd strut his powerful frame in front of my mother and say, 'look what I got.' I remembered my father played football in college and I smiled.

When his finger went into me again, I sighed. Oh God, it felt good.

"You like it. Damn, you do." He parked the truck.

I sat up straight and moved his hand away. "Where are we?" I couldn't see any houses, only the edges of trees slanting back and forth outlined by the weak light of a silvery moon. "Where are we?"

"Chill, Princess. I just thought we could be alone away

from the party. I've got some more beer back here." He turned on the overhead light and grabbed a six pack from behind the seat. "Have another cold one," he said, handing me a beer.

I had already drunk too much.

He put his arm around my shoulder. "You wanna date a football star?"

"Maybe," I said, smiling coyly. It's a woman's world, I told myself. "Maybe."

"Maybe." He snorted and chugged his beer. "Drink up, we got some business to tend to."

"I need to go home," I said, taking a drink from the bottle.

"Not yet." He took the bottle from my hand, finished the beer, and threw the empty bottle behind his seat. "All right, Princess, how bad you wanna be my girlfriend?"

The inside light illuminated his face and I didn't like the lusty way his eyes smiled at me, like I owed him something.

Acid churned my stomach, and all at once I wanted to be home under my flowered comforter. I scooted away from him. "I need to go home. It's—"

"Cut the shit." He slid toward me on the vinyl seat. I backed up against the door. He reached behind me and locked the door. My heart jumped in my throat and I tried to speak.

"Please…" I squeaked.

"Don't fuck with me. You know how many girls would kill to be out here. I didn't spend all night with you for nothing. You're not gonna get away with prick teasin' ole Rod. Nope, sorry, Princess, that ain't gonna fly."

He crouched on the seat in front of me and jerked my hips forward. The back of my head hit the door. My whole head pounded. He pushed my shirt and bra up, leaned in close to my face. "I'm gonna make this nice for you."

"No, no!"

He acted like he didn't hear me.

Again, I said, "No," and still, he didn't listen to me.

He lay on top of me, his large frame pushing my body into the stiff vinyl. I tried to get my hands up to push him off, but I couldn't move. He sucked one of my nipples while he unbuttoned his pants. I squirmed back and forth. Scared, I tilted my head up and bit him on the shoulder.

"You fucking bitch, goddamn it," he said, rubbing his shoulder.

"Take me home."

"Ha." He smashed his body into mine. He was so heavy I thought I would suffocate. He pushed my skirt up to my waist. I tried to get my hands to my waist and pull it down, cover my body.

And then the terrible sensation of cotton panties sliding down the length of my cold legs, wrapping around my ankles like chains, paralyzed me, as I realized the inevitable. I tried to twist my hips, but they didn't move. He had his thick thighs between mine, forcing my legs open.

"Please," I whispered.

He pushed his hips into me and then he entered me, hard and fast, thrusting past any barriers. "You're gonna like this, Princess," he said, his voice proud and generous as if he were granting me a wish.

Pain shot up my body. His force pushed into me again

and again, his weight crushing my pelvis into the seat. Then he yelled out as if he had just scored a touchdown. I closed my eyes, begging the tears not to come. Within moments, he pulled up his pants, saying we better get back.

I lay there motionless, praying it had not happened, not like this, feeling more exposed than if I had been standing on a street corner with no clothes. The pain was intense, almost unbearable, yet fleeting in the spot from which it came. It dulled and trickled through my body, to remain as an unsettling ache that localized nowhere but seem to come from every part.

"Come on, Princess. We gotta..." He glanced down, the blood evidence of what had just happened, his words stopped. He tilted his head and stared between my legs. "Shit, shit, are you a fucking... oh, God, you're a virgin. Shit!" he screamed.

I reached down and jerked my panties up, and then pulled my bra and shirt down. My slut outfit.

He pounded the steering wheel. "Are you? Shit, shit, shit. Why didn't you fucking tell me. Shit!" He pounded again, stopped, looked at me again, studying me in the diffuse overhead light.

I pulled my arms and legs tight into me, wishing I could disappear. I felt it all seeping from me, his rage and my innocence, caught in my white panties.

He fired up the engine and tore out of the dirt road as if in a race. He drove like mad until he reached the highway. I clutched myself and wiped away the lone tears that had squeezed from my pinched eyes.

We drove in silence, no music, just the lingering echo of

his howl when he thrust inside me.

"Shit," he whispered. He took a deep breath like a little boy about to bat. "How old are you?" he said, concern ringing in his voice.

I buried my head in my hands.

"How old?" his voice rose.

"Sixteen," I said between my webbed fingers.

"Shit, shit! What the fuck? Why did you lie? Goddamn, you know how old I am. Fucking twenty-two. Shit, shit," he shouted and hit the steering wheel.

I looked at my watch and knew my mother had to be going crazy worrying about me. "Could you drop me off at my house?"

No answer.

"Please," I said.

"Whatever. Shit, shit, I gotta fuckin' sixteen-year-old sister at home. Shit."

I stared straight ahead.

"Sixteen. Shit!"

He pulled the truck into a small late night convenience store and kept the engine running. "Tell me where you live."

I told him with careful precision so I wouldn't have to repeat myself. So I wouldn't need to talk again.

"Okay, I'll take you home." He slid toward me. I scooted closer to the door. "Now I gotta tell you something."

I looked up at him and cringed. He didn't look like a Viking anymore.

"Look, you can't tell anyone about this. I mean it. I would be screwed. I'm up for a big contract with a pro team and shit..." his eyes darted from side to side. "This could ruin everything." His eyes fixed back on me as if I were to blame.

I just sat, motionless, moved my gaze off him, and stared straight ahead.

"Come on, we got a deal. I'll take you home and you keep your mouth shut." He slid back and put the truck into gear. "Deal?" His tone demanded a response.

"No problem." I bit my lip, trying to stop my bottom lip from trembling. It's a woman's world? Really?

He stopped in front of my house. "Stay there," he said, jumping out of the truck.

I started to open the door, but he jerked the handle from the outside, flung the truck door open, and extended his hand to me. "Always a gentleman," he said, smiling.

Unconvinced, I didn't want to take it, but he blocked my way. He helped me from the truck and then kissed my hand. "Our secret, Princess," he said, winking.

It occurred to me that he didn't know my name. I was just another naïve princess.

I jerked my hand away and walked across the lawn to the door.

"Not a word," he yelled, before driving off.

A sad quiescence settled in me as I crept into the house, but I didn't know if I had let it in, or if it had always been there. My mother had left the light on in the entryway. I took off my shoes and tiptoed down the tile hall, every muscle tight and shaking, waiting for my mother to scream my name from her room, demanding an answer to my whereabouts at two a.m.

I took one step on the stairs and stopped. There she

was, her stocking legs pulled into her chest, her pale pink skirt lying across her thigh, exposing her white lace slip, her hands clasped together, the ends of her pink polished fingers intertwining and resting under her chin. Her black hair fanned across a red couch pillow.

From a distance, she looked like a painting, the fair maiden. I set my shoes down and walked toward her. An empty bottle of wine sat on the floor and next to it a crystal glass lay on its side.

I stared at her. I wanted to crawl next to her, have her wrap her arms around me like she did when I was a little girl, and tell me a story about a princess who falls madly in love with a real prince, then drift off to sleep as she said the words, 'the end.'

Her warm breath a rhythmic brush against the back of my neck until I fell asleep. I always knew this version of her would disappear by morning, but I had loved feeling her soft body against my back and pressing my toes into her thighs. The back of my head resting on her chest, so that the rise and fall of it was like being rocked gently to sleep.

I backed away. That mom was gone and so was that Abbey, that princess. She knew what princes were like, she read the end of the story. The end my mother changed for both of us.

I grabbed my shoes and ran upstairs. I soaked a washcloth in warm water and scrubbed the triangle between my legs until it was raw and hurt more. The harder I scrubbed, the faster the tears fell, filling the cavities behind my eyes. My face was puffy with pain, as if all the fluids in my body had rushed into my skull.

From the mirror, a slut stared back at me, my puffy face, the canvas to black mascara circling my eyes and purple red lipstick smeared across my chin. I scrubbed my face until it was sore.

"That was it," I whispered to my reflection. "That was it."

A tender touch, sweet kisses, and professions of forever love did not accompany my prolapsed innocence. Just some jock getting off.

CHAPTER 11

A breeze tickled the back of my neck, carrying with it the coldness that the death of summer brings. I had promised to meet Ryan at the lake and talk. 'Talk,' that request seemed so overwhelming.

Standing at the bank, a boy used a stick to poke a turtle that found refuge on a dead tree trunk that had fallen into the lake. The turtle pulled his head into the shell that protected his soft body. The boy's mother jerked him away from the lake, scolding, steering him away from danger.

I stared at the lake, the daunting water.

I WAS TEN AND WATER HAD filled my lungs, I spat, losing control, my arms flailing. My mother's voice echoed off the water. I opened my mouth to cry out for her but nothing came. I was filled with ocean water.

Her hand wrapped around my arm, I knew it was my mother because her long nails cut into the soft flesh on my arm. I wanted to tell her she was hurting me, but the words drowned in all the water my small body swallowed.

When I woke, I had some vague memory of an ambulance siren. Her face hung above me, her hot tears dripping on my cheeks. Tubes emerged from my small arm, traveling to bags hanging from metal coat racks. I shook my head, as a guy in a white shirt leaned over me. Turning my head to the side, I coughed, and salty liquid spewed from my nose. I gagged as if I'd been choked. "Mom."

I found out later that my mother held my hand on the ride to the hospital and was there every time my eyes opened for the next four days, until she and everyone else were convinced I suffered no brain damage. She did not leave my side and, with love and concern rippling in her voice, called my name over and over, "Abigail, Abigail,"

I'd swum out too far. My mother said, 'stay close,' but I didn't listen. At ten, I thought myself a great swimmer, a survivor of four years of swimming lessons, so my mother's warning seemed unwarranted. Later I told her I was sorry and she'd nodded and looked at me like I was a precious artifact.

A TALL, LEAN JOGGER WEARING parachute running pants, a windbreaker, and headphones passed me. His hair, long, like Ryan's used to be, before… before what, I thought. What made him so different now?

A golden retriever brushed my leg. I thought at first it was Spartan until the furry creature kept going down the path ahead of its owner. I whirled around. The runner was a woman, probably about forty, not Ryan.

He and Spartan had been inseparable since he graduated from college, and I often thought Ryan smelled more like Spartan than a man. All of the images of Ryan and Spartan raced through my mind. Our camping trip at Lake

Buchanan, northwest of Austin, two years ago, Spartan, Ryan, and me, along with gallons of rain. We were determined to sleep under the stars, but the stars soon gave way to thunderous clouds and we slept in Ryan's truck, the three of us, one wet bundle.

Spartan would rest his snout on the table while Ryan and I read the paper. When Ryan wasn't looking, Spartan would snatch a donut. I'd laugh and Ryan would chase Spartan around his apartment with a newspaper. Spartan always managed to escape under Ryan's bed.

Then Ryan would throw me to the floor, tickling me, claiming I had prior knowledge of Spartan's clandestine activities. I would raise my arms, surrendering, promising to do anything as his prisoner. More than one Sunday morning had led into an afternoon of sex and stale donuts.

Earlier in the week, as we sat drinking a cup of day-old hospital coffee, Ryan said there are certain relationships one could never escape, due to the depth of emotion, the shared experiences, or the blood connection.

Perhaps Ryan was right. Even if I tried to break free, I was chained to my mother because the brain was so clever and capable of storing memories that aren't voluntarily recalled. Rather, sensory experiences trigger them so they become indelibly printed on the mind's canvas. Memory chains: a smell, a vision, or a touch brings back one that triggers another, leading to a whole sequence of memories and before you know it, you are transported to your brain's storage vault of old movies.

The smell of lilacs always made my mouth feel full, as I played in the backyard while my mother baked. I could almost taste the thick country gravy and buttery biscuits, leading to the vision of my mother pulling biscuits from the oven and swatting my father on the butt, telling him to wait for dinner. The clumsiness of a man's hands struggling with my zipper causes the stale smell of beer to swell in my nostrils, then a sharp pain shoots through my groin and my body flinches.

None of it conscious, but a shared connection of the mental and the physical, as if my body was the remote control and my mind the TV.

"AB, OVER HERE." RYAN WAVED his arm in the air, like a member of a construction crew standing on the side of the road, signaling cars to slowdown. I walked toward him.

"I just got back from the hospital. Your mom seems… well, she looks drained. It's weird to see her like this."

"I know, she was really tired yesterday. The combination of the surgery and the chemo has wiped her. But the nurses told me she's getting up and walking around."

We took a few more steps ahead in silence until the movement of our legs became synchronized. I slid my arm around his waist as we walked.

"Your mom is strong enough to pull through this."

"She may have the strength, but it's going to take a lot more to beat this. It's an aggressive cancer."

"Your mom's aggressive."

"That's true."

"But you're holding up okay, Ab? I mean, being there for her."

"I don't know if I'm doing it for her, my dad, or me. You were right about letting go of the past between my mother and me. But it's weird, not like it's one event. Our past shapes us, so it is part of us, and letting it go is impossible. Well, at least too painful, like cutting a part of your flesh away. I thought I would be able to open up my arms, reach out to her, and together we'd say 'sorry' and the past would be mended. It doesn't work that way, as little as I'm able to do it, she seems less able. Oh, sure, now that she's sick, she's more needy, but that's not about her and me."

"The reason she's reaching out doesn't matter as much as the fact that she is."

"And what am I supposed to do? Open myself up, justify her actions, overlook the implications her foolishness has had on my life? What if she doesn't beat this and I have to tell myself all over again that I don't need her, just like I did in high school? No thanks, I don't have the energy for that."

"Jeez, Abbey."

"It sounds cold, but that's reality. Believe me, I want her to beat this so everybody can go back to normal."

"To the way things were?" Ryan raised his eyebrows.

"Just normal," I said.

"Normal?"

"Okay, functionally dysfunctional."

Ryan laughed. "Oh, Abbey." My name had a hopeless trail to it.

"So let's get to the big talk," I said, plucking the words out of thin air and tossing them out there. Sort of like throwing someone a fastball when they were prepared for co-ed softball.

He stopped, wrapped his long fingers around the sleeve of my jacket, and pulled me into him. He twitched, because he had probably been talking himself into this all morning. "I just want us to move forward. A lot of things are falling into place for me, except you. You just keep standing on the sidelines, not wanting to enter the game. It's making me crazy."

I nudged my arm away from him and strolled to a picnic table next to a tree. Ryan followed me in silence.

He slid into the bench across from me. "I didn't bring any of this up the first couple of weeks because I just wanted us to hang out and know each other again. Plus, I'm a chicken. In some way, not having anything definitive gave me hope. When I finally got myself ready to lay it on the line, we found out the news about your mom."

I turned my head and stared at the still water. He wasn't asking me anything yet, but the question was coming and the answer was already swelling in my throat. The truth in Sheila's words, 'move Abbey, one way or another, move,' but I couldn't. I felt like my mother had tied me to the train tracks fifteen years ago, the ropes had rotted away, but I was still stuck.

Ryan spoke again. "I did a lot of thinking and arguing with myself while you were in Africa and I thought you were doing the same. Even though we've talked, I haven't heard anything definite. I think you can tell by my actions, I'm still here after a year. But *your* actions... one day it seems like you're in, the next day I'm just some guy you're sleeping with. And now all this talk about the Galápagos Islands assignment... so once again, you'll leave everything up in the air with us." His breathing, shallow, and his words came faster.

"It's just all this stuff with Mom," I said.

"I know, Ab, but your mom wants us to be together, to move ahead with this relationship."

"My mom has nothing to do with it. Why are you talking to her about it anyway?"

He took a deep breath, released it with a long sigh. "She's talking to me. The point is, not your mom, not anybody, it's us."

"I postponed the trip to the Galápagos Islands for a month. Hopefully, then Mom will be through with this, so we can all go on with our own lives."

"What's the point?"

"I'm not going anywhere for a while," I said. "I'm staying until—"

"I'm not saying don't go, or go, I just want to get some things straight with us."

"Why are we talking about this now? I don't even know what the next months will bring. Please."

"But you never know, do you, Ab? None of us does, but you're waiting to have your whole future laid out for you before you'll make a decision today. That doesn't make sense."

Before answering, I played my words in my head. 'Ryan, I care about you, I need some more time. No, Ryan, you're not who you were when I met you. Ryan, I haven't ever been able to commit to anyone, I guess you're as close as I have ever come to loving someone, but is that enough? Just coming close?'

Could I really ask him for more time? I had a year to get it together. Then I come home to find out that my mother and Ryan have decided I need to commit… and… shit, my mother's breasts are gone.

"Ryan, I don't know what to say right now. So much is up in the air. If I were going to commit to someone, it would be you. But…"

He raked his fingers though his hair. "I don't like where this is going," he said, staring to the side as if he were speaking to someone else.

I stood and scooted in next to him. "I know I… I can't imagine not having you as a friend."

"You won't have to." He squeezed his lips together.

"So the right thing would be to just let you go. But that seems impossible."

Ryan squeezed his eyes shut. "So you're saying…"

"I can't commit, but I also can't imagine someone else having you."

A muscle in his jaw flinched. "Abbey, I told myself after you'd been gone almost six months that I needed to move on. And I tried…" His voice shook. "Well, I was here when you got back, wasn't I?"

I nodded.

His arm slid around my back and he pulled me close. "You have it all. You're beautiful, smart, outstanding in your career. Yet this thing with your mom is crippling you. If I could erase your sixteenth year, I would."

But there was so much more to my sixteenth year than my mother's indiscretions. It had just been easier to lay all the pain at her feet and then cover it with anger. Why are painful past experiences so much more raw and nearer to the surface than the joyful ones?

"My fear is, I let you go, you get it all worked out, and then some other guy with a foreign accent gets an amazing woman."

"Foreign accent?"

"Well…"

The acuity of his words sliced through me.

"So what are you going to do?" I said.

He squeezed my shoulders. "I don't know, Ab. The conclusion is you still don't know, so I need to think about my next step. But for now, I'm going to that party tonight. If you're still up to it, Jake and I can pick you up."

I let out a breath. He wasn't walking away, not yet. "I'm up for it. Matter of fact, I need it."

He pecked me on the lips. "Then we'll be by around nine… F.r.i.e.n.d." he said, drawing out the last word.

"Thanks," I said.

He sauntered toward the parking lot, my eyes followed his blue windbreaker until it slipped into his new SUV.

RYAN HAD ACTED STRANGE EVER since they picked me up for the party, and he was drinking beer like it was water. He handed me a beer. "Here, Madame," he said, bending and waving one hand in the air.

"Don't you think you should slow down? You never drink like this," I said, concern ringing in my voice.

"Hey, Ab, I got a few things to drown, and I'm not driving." He tipped the bottle and let a third of its contents flow into his mouth. His eyes squinted at me as he swallowed.

Later, after a few drinks, while an old friend of mine and I were engrossed in conversation, a petite woman with long bleached-blond hair and coconut sized breasts, wearing a tight crop top and a short skirt, came over and put her arm around Ryan. In her drunkenness she asked him why he dumped her after two months—'no explanation, you just stopped calling'—she insisted she had the right to know.

His face floated between soft pink and crimson. His eyes darted and shifted between her and me. Jake, Ryan's brother, put his arm around her, explaining this wasn't the best time to get honest answers from Ryan, since he'd had too much to drink. Jake managed to pry loose the suction she held on Ryan, and they edged away.

"Why did you break up with her out of the blue?" I said.

"I don't want to go there." His speech unsure, every other word slurred.

"Was she your attempt to go on?" My voice drizzled sarcasm.

"Let it go, Ab."

"Why?" The beer made me bolder and less controlled.

"You don't wanna hear the answer." His voice grew louder and the cadence more erratic.

My brain was slow, not conscious of the people staring. Something angry and jealous rumbled inside of me. I had never seen any of the girls he had gone out with, and, though I told myself that was what I wanted, having a woman who belonged on the front of *Playboy* materialize before me, certain Ryan had fucked her, made me turn ugly. And the beer wasn't aiding the control of my tongue.

"Yes, I do. You obviously enjoyed her." I reached up and pushed his chest.

"What the hell are you doing?" He glanced down at his chest where my hands had been.

"Asking you a question you can't answer." My chin jutted out like a boxer, readying for a fight. I puffed my chest up to him, demanding a reply, becoming aware of the horrified stares.

He backed up. "You want an answer? You'll get one." His eyes grew wide, his hands writhed together as he shifted his weight from one foot to the other. I knew then, I'd shoved him past the point of control. "You want to know why, Abbey?"

I spun my head to locate the blonde bombshell, but instead Ryan's brother strode toward me, a puzzled look masking his ruggedly handsome face.

"No, Ryan. Stop," I said, with an angry urgency. A scene assembled and I was one of the players, instead of an onlooker.

He dropped to his knees.

"Ryan, get up. You're drunk. I'm sorry, I don't care why."

A group of half-drunk partygoers circled around us. I imagined, as I did so many times growing up, when my parents wanted to take pictures in public, that I was Sabrina the TV witch, and I could blink myself out of the situation.

"I'm drunk, but how I feel stays the same." He cupped one hand on his heart. "I broke up with her and everyone else because I want to be with you."

"I won't hear this." I turned around.

He grabbed my hand and held it against his cheek. "You know what?" Tears hung at the bottom of his lids. "There will never be anyone like you."

I tried to pull my hand back, darting my gaze around the room, seeing all the eyes on me, watching my reaction while he made a fool of himself and me.

He kissed my hand, then he lifted his head toward the sky. "I love you, Abigail Gallagher, with everything I have in here." He let go of my hand and hit his chest.

I didn't know how to react.

Jake came up behind me. "Abbey, let's get him out of here. He's really drunk." He touched my arm. "You're shivering."

"Just a little cold." It was the chill left over from Ryan's words, 'I love you' that made me shudder, like a cool unexpected wind whispering over a half-naked body basking in the sun.

Jake pulled Ryan up from his knees. "Come on, bro, let's go. You've had way too much tonight."

"I do love her," he wailed all the way to the car, tears flowing down his face. His head bent with his arms flopping in front of him as he staggered, like a little boy walking home after losing his first baseball game. I followed a couple of feet behind the brothers, wishing I had brought my own car.

"I know you do," Jake said, tousling his younger brother's hair and then stuffing his loose limbs into the back seat.

I got into the front seat. No one talked during the twenty-minute drive to Jake and Ryan's apartment. The image of my mother and another man manifested in the foggy darkness. I rolled down the window, enough to let my head clear and the image to flow into the moving air.

Ryan's sniffles scratched at my heart, but I didn't look at him, acknowledge the tears, the words. I told myself he was drunk, he meant nothing with his words. I almost believed it. Within a few minutes, Ryan passed out.

Jake and I dragged his limp body up a flight of stairs and dropped him onto his bed. "Give me a minute," I said.

"You want a ride home or you just gonna stay?"

"I hate to ask, but I don't think he's going to want to see me tomorrow."

"He's not gonna want to see anybody tomorrow," Jake said with a forced laugh, as he ambled back down the hallway to the living room.

"One minute," I called after him.

I refused to be my mother, lying on my husband's bed, writing love letters to another, with no thought of the family I was destroying. I knew no better way to prevent this than not to feel love. Or at least this was what I had told myself for years.

I pulled Ryan's sandals off, laughing to myself at his odd-looking feet. The second toe longer on one foot than the big toe. Rolling him on his side, I unbuttoned his shirt, releasing his arms from the sleeves.

I sat on the edge of the bed and dabbed his face with a warm wet cloth. His individual features were odd, but together created an endearing face, the kind babies smile at, and dogs lick. His creamy brown eyes were set close together. When they were open, flecks of gold, close to the pupils, created an amber hue. Long honey-colored eyelashes surrounded them, lending a feminine quality to his eyes. His amazing mouth was generous. Full ruddy lips with a prominent scar branching off the right side of his top lip, one branch reached the bottom of his nose, plastering him with a permanent smirk even as he slept.

I ran my hand down the lump of his Adam's apple to his chest, both nipples were surrounded by swirls of light brown hair, the rest of his chest, smooth. My fingers rode the ridges that comprised the two-pack he had gotten at the gym, then to his navel, where hair that originated at his groin became a presence.

Above the edge of his shorts, I laid my hand flat on his lower stomach, the palm of my hand absorbing the heat. I imagined sliding my hand under the waistband into the dark cave created by his sunken stomach and stiff shorts. I left my hand there, resting patiently, at the mouth of his shorts.

Twisting my ankle, I pushed my shoes off my feet, letting them drop to the floor. I slipped into the bed and nudged myself next to him, my cheek on his chest, my mouth centimeters from his nipple.

I wanted to feel close to him, wedge the picture of the blonde and her coconuts out of my mind. My lips moved nearer to his nipple, the full of my tongue licking it, then I kissed his nipple, sucking it like a baby to its mother.

His hips rotated and his back rose from the bed, arching. His hand moved around my back, urging me close. My eyes traveled down the pathway that led to the cave, his pink arousal growing, pushing his shorts up to expose its swollen head.

I untangled myself from my clothing, unzipped his shorts, and moved myself on top of him. I wanted to give him what I could. I braced my hands on his chest, straddled him, and eased him into me. Slow rhythm at first, and then frantic, thrusting my hips back and forth on him.

His eyes opened, my hips slowed. He put his hands on my hips. "Abbey." He pulled me in close, so my head touched his. "I'm a fool for loving you."

"I'm a fool for not letting you," I whispered into his curly blonde hair where his ear was hidden.

He rolled on top of me and moved into me with such force that my body twisted and I cried out. He squeezed his eyes shut, until his body quivered and he had given everything. He opened his eyes and when the contorted expression of orgasm eased, he mouthed, 'I love you,' and collapsed beside me. He whispered my name until sleep overruled. "…Abbey."

Ryan's soft snore filled the dark room like elevator music, as if coming from everywhere. I felt for my clothing, dressed, and slipped from the room, clutching my shoes to my chest.

Jake startled when I tapped him on the shoulder. He had dozed off in front of the static television. I took him up on the ride home, enduring his odd stares. I didn't want to be there when Ryan awoke.

The next day, on the phone, Ryan tried to apologize, but I pushed past the whole night, telling him I had little memory of the evening, thanks to the beer. I had no desire to broach why Ryan had professed his love or why I had felt compelled to make love to him.

After that evening, the word 'love' found no place in our vocabularies. When I considered mouthing the word, I reminded myself of all the people who had bought into the whole love thing, only to find themselves walking down an aisle leading to a road full of potholes. I knew where it forked, a choice between walking ghost-like through a love-less marriage, or destroying a family by leaving. Neither seemed like a fairy-tale to me.

I learned a long time ago that love equaled vulnerability. But there was power in sex.

In one encounter, Ryan and I had blanketed all the emotions that swooned to the surface, burying them under sweat and orgasms. In an instant, sex could bury old anxieties or create new ones. I was sixteen when I realized I didn't have to connect sex with anything but physical pleasure, and that the power came when you could separate sex from love. A useful lesson.

CHAPTER 12

It had been six months since my father left. We continued our catatonic walk through our daily lives. School mornings I got up, got ready, and drove Ethan to his school, and then made a decision on whether to attend school or go to Amy's house and drink. Amy had finished college finals, so I skipped a lot of school or left early so we could lie out by her pool and drink, smoke pot, and talk about boys.

I told her about Rod, the football player, but I twisted my version to fit more into the perimeter of a woman's world. A world where women only did what they wanted, one where they had choices. I told her it wasn't fun, not something I was dying to do again anytime soon.

She told me the first time never is, you just have to get it over with so you can move on to the fun.

I wouldn't link emotion and sex anymore. All those movies where the guy walks toward the woman as if he is being drawn to a powerful goddess, slowly undresses her, kisses every inch of her tender delicate skin, and can't say "I love you" often enough were fairytales designed to suck women into some ideal fantasy, so men could get off. What a sham! I was done with fantasies!

Amy and I sat on her bedroom floor, leaning against her bed, smoking a joint and drinking mostly vodka mixed with just enough lemonade to help us swallow the liquor. I pulled the harsh smoke deep into my lungs and held it for a few seconds, puffing my cheeks up like a bullfrog. "Good," I said expelling the air and handing Amy the fat joint.

Amy took a long drag and exhaled.

I'd felt sick all morning at school, and trying to concentrate on calculus in the afternoon made me queasier. So I skipped my last two classes and drove to Amy's. Her mother didn't come home before seven, and that was just to change clothes before she ran out the door to her boyfriend's house.

"Does John, David, or whoever..." I laughed at the litany of men in Amy's life. "...tell you they love you during sex."

"Sometimes," she said, taking another drag, sucking the last potency from the joint, "but they don't mean that shit."

"Nobody means it. Look at my parents. They always use to say 'I love you' to each other, to Ethan and me. My mom couldn't hang up the phone without telling my dad she loved him. What a fucking joke."

"Yeah, I know. Within ten years, my parents' 'I love you' turned into 'fuck you.' "

"Why say it then?"

"Guys say it so you'll think this fuck with them means something."

"What?"

She giggled. "Some profession of love, that they might want to marry you or something."

"Oh, that's what we're all looking for." I adopted a thick Southern drawl to imitate my mother. "Oh, you love me, do you? Thank Gawd, now I'll devote my whole life to you, yes, and when I get sick of it, I'll find someone else to sleep with and destroy this life we've built together because I love you and you love me… one happy, fucking family."

Amy roared. "Yes, darling I love you, the roses are proof." She changed her voice to a deep male voice. "While you're smelling the roses, I'm gonna fuck my secretary in your bed."

"Your dad?"

"Yep. He sent roses to my mother's work that day, the card said, 'Thinking About You.' And the funny thing is, I was here. He thought I was at school and I was sitting right here, thirteen years old, home sick."

"Shit, what happened?"

"The front door opened, I thought it was my mom, so I peeked out my bedroom door. A blonde woman was mashed between the wall and my dad. I stepped back in my room, but left my door cracked. He never heard me. I don't know how he could through all her moans and 'Yes! Yes! Yes!' "

I laughed. "Moans?"

"That's what you're supposed to do. They gravitated toward my parents' bedroom. Right there," she said, pointing at the wall.

"God."

"They went after it. She screamed like someone was murdering her."

"God."

"She kept yelling my father's name. I wanted to kill him."

"Do you hate him?" I said. "'Cause I hate my mom."

"No, I'm used to it. That's how it is, someone's gonna

get screwed, literally."

"Fun!" I rolled my eyes.

She stood up and jumped on her bed, then flopped back on the bed. "It can be."

"I don't think so." I turned to look at her. She lay on her back in a pair of white lace underwear, the kind you get at Victoria's Secret, not Sears, and a short t-shirt. She had thick athletic thighs, a round hard-looking butt, a short waist, and big boobs that sloped from shear weight.

"Come up here," she said, rubbing the bed next to her.

I slid on my stomach, propping my head on my hands so I could look at her. Her face looked so clean and young without all the make-up.

"Ab, I'll be gone this summer, visiting my dad in California. We'll see who he's sleeping with this month," she said with a laugh. "But you need to know a few things before I head out. I don't want you out there and clueless," she said, turning on her side, her boobs falling beneath her shirt.

"All right, shoot. I'm a fast learner."

"First, they can't fuck you around if you fuck them first. Anyone."

"Meaning..." I raised my eyebrows.

She sat up. "You have to have the same attitude as guys. Don't go into it looking for love, or forever, or any of that shit. Just the orgasm, folks, that's all," she said in a cartoon voice.

I knew what orgasms were. Between school textbooks, Nathaniel Hawthorne, and Edgar Allen Poe, I'd managed to squeeze a few *Cosmopolitan* magazines into my reading repertoire. "Okay," I said, sounding sheepish. I didn't want to say I'd never had one and probably wouldn't.

"Okay? I just gave you some of the best advice of your fucking life and you say 'okay.' "

"Okay, great," I said, flashing her my best wide-toothed grin.

"Second, when they start talking about love, they're just looking for someone to do their laundry, cook their meals, and have their babies. I guarantee, if you ever get married, you'll be screwed. Bored and lonely. Look at your mom. That's why she's seeing someone else, she's lonely."

"Bullshit," I said, flipping onto my back. "She's a whore. Anyone who'd throw away a family and my father… he's the best. She can't be lonely."

"Everyone gets lonely."

"Whatever. She's had this lover guy for a long time, from what I can gather. What a fucking cheat! Meanwhile my father stayed faithful. Really, he's crazy about her, so this is killing him."

"My point! Whoever loves the most, loses. Just don't do it. You don't have to love someone to get off."

"All right, I got it. Men are for our sexual pleasure, nothing else."

She twisted her body and propped her hands on either side of me, caging me. She arched her back like a cat, swooping her face close to mine. "That's right, smart girl."

"But where's the pleasure?" I looked up at her. There was nothing remotely pleasurable that night with Rod, unless humiliation and pain equated pleasure, and I knew better. But I liked Amy's concept of using boys.

"I was hoping we'd get to that." Her face hung inches from mine, the odor of smoky vodka blew from her mouth as she spoke, and her thin hair brushed against my cheeks. In the background President Reagan on TV talked about the Cold War and what a powerful country we lived in, the most powerful.

"This is lesson number one. We'll cover everything over the next few weeks before I leave, and then you'll be ready for a fucking fun summer." She giggled in my ear. "Topic number one is oral sex, you choose: blow jobs or the pleasures of getting your box licked."

I covered my mouth with both my hands. "Ugh, they both sound gross."

She rolled her eyes and pushed herself back up. "You have the deepest belly button." She circled my belly button with her index finger before letting her finger slip in. "Choose one. Neither is gross. Blow jobs give you power and the other gives you a lot of pleasure." She laughed long and wickedly, tossing her head back, her fingers resting on my bare belly.

My breathing seemed to speed up, out of my control. "I should go."

She moved on her side and nudged close to me. "It's okay for me to teach you what I know." Her fingers moved around my belly and stopped at the ridge of my swimsuit. "Just say which one. I think pleasure, and tomorrow I'll teach you blow jobs." Her fingers dipped below my suit, running through my hair before sliding into the wetness between my legs.

Christ, last month a slut, now a lesbian, what next?

"But…" I closed my eyes.

"Abbey, I'm going to walk you through everything so you'll know if you ever need to tell a boy how," she whispered in my ear. "Believe me, you'll have to teach them and they're slow learners." She giggled.

"But I… I'm not."

"No, and neither am I. We're friends, and I care for you. That's why I'm showing you."

I opened my eyes. Her body was propped up with one hand, while the other hand, slow and gentle, touched me down there. She looked at me like she really did care, like she loved me, and it felt good to think maybe she did care.

"You do this to yourself?" she said.

I shook my head.

"Oh, Abbey."

She eased my bathing suit bottoms down my legs and tossed them to the floor. The flying blue bird sailed to the soft carpet. I felt so vulnerable, uneasy, yet I knew I was safe.

"Take off your top." She slid her hand from my crotch and ran it up my stomach. "You choose. You want me to stop, leave your top on, but if you want to learn how to feel close to someone, take it off." She bent her head and kissed my stomach.

"I just…"

"You just don't think you deserve to feel good? Well, you do. All women do." She spoke with confidence, as if giving a speech at a women's rights rally.

My heart throbbed in my throat. I didn't want to do this, but I also didn't want her to stop touching me.

I unbuckled the small gold design that held my bikini

top together in the front. The blue cups slid down my side, unveiling my compact mounds. My pink nipples were erect and hard, like tiny red flags waving on top of hills of snow.

"They're beautiful. Now touch them."

"Amy!" I sat up and propped myself on my elbows. I stared down the length of my long body, thinking it was beautiful and how stupid I was for letting that guy misuse it. From now on, I call the shots, I told myself.

"This is kinda unfair," she said. "I'll take off all my clothes, too."

"That's not what I'm saying."

She stood up on her knees and pulled the cropped t-shirt over her head. Her boobs were even bigger than I thought. She smiled and stuck her thumbs inside the rim of her panties, shimming her thick thighs as she slid them down to her ankles. Then she dropped back on the bed, lifted her legs in the air, and pulled her lace panties off her feet.

I couldn't help but stare at the pink flesh, wearing a light brown mink coat that appeared between her legs. I had never seen it from that direction.

She moved in next to me and held my hand. We took turns smoking another joint and laughing at the fact we were both naked in the middle of the afternoon. Then she explained the details of oral sex to me. "Someone kisses your body and their tongue roams between your legs and your hips lunge forward, wanting more."

As she spoke in a secretive tone, a ticklish feeling from my stomach trickled to my crotch and over my pelvis. She held my hand tighter, describing how a boy's tongue would move in and out of me, licking my most sensitive part, while a warm wetness settled in our connecting palms.

"Do boys like doing that?" I said.

"Good question. I've gone out with some guys in college who won't go down there. I won't date them."

"They won't?"

She turned on her side again, her bare breasts rested on my arm. I tried to ignore them, but I couldn't help but register their silky weight.

"Some are just selfish, but some are afraid 'cause they don't know how, but you can teach them." She crinkled her nose. "But only if you know what to teach."

"All right. What do I do?" I whispered. My whole body felt heavy and slow from all the pot and vodka.

She laid her hand over mine and then moved my own between my legs. It was so wet and warm down there. "Move this finger back and forth until you feel a sharp chill." She tapped my middle finger, and I wiggled it around.

My back arched.

"That's where I'm going to put my tongue." She gave my chest a light kiss. "Move your hand out of the way."

I slid it to the side. She kissed a trail down my stomach to the inside of my thigh. Her hair tickled my stomach and I giggled, but then my body shrunk back from her touch. "Nooo..." jumped out of my mouth as my legs slammed shut.

She jolted up. "Abbey, I'm not going to hurt you."

A lone tear ran down my cheek. "It's just... well, Rod, I didn't want to, he forced."

Amy, crawled up near me, "Oh, Abbey I'm sorry it

happened that way. Trust me, I won't hurt you. I want you to take control. Don't let men ever have the upper hand." Her eyes bored into me as she spoke with authority. "Got that, Abbey?"

Another tear slid down my face. "Got it," I whispered.

Her thumb wiped away the wetness on my cheek. "Lie back and let me show you how good it can be." Then she crawled between my legs, opening them with gentle prodding.

She looked up, giggled, and whispered, "Play with your nipples."

I did everything she said because it felt nice. So much nicer than Rod ramming his penis inside me without asking.

She told me everything she was doing and then she said, "I really care about you, Abbey. I want this to feel good."

I believed her, so I opened my knees and let her mouth kiss the wetness between my legs and then she licked me, and my hips jumped. I stopped touching my breasts and gripped the sheets, balling them into my hand so I could hang on to something while my body lost control.

She slid a gentle finger into me, spread me open, and explored me with her soft tongue. My hips rose to meet her mouth, just like she said. Then tiny flesh spasms, like someone was squeezing my upper thighs, a sensation my body begged for and tried to pull away from at the same time, fused together and exploded, shooting through my whole body.

I screamed and laughed, hysterical laughter.

She laid her head on my stomach and hugged my shaking body until I was still. No wonder people are so fixated on this stuff, I thought.

"That's lesson number one: pleasure."

"Lesson learned," I said, running my fingers through her hair.

She raised her head, looked at me and grinned. "Tomorrow, lesson number two, blow jobs. Power!" she cried in triumph, flinging herself back on the bed, her fists beating the air.

"Power," I echoed.

CHAPTER 13

The wind was chilly, but a warm mist floated up from the ground, softening the sharp air. Almost three weeks had passed since my mother's breasts were removed, and already their disappearance seemed like part of forgotten history, logged away in a dusty book. Now she had to focus on keeping her life, leaving her no time to mourn their loss.

I thought about the wife/parent mask my mother had worn her whole life, a fixed smile adorning it, appearing centered and satisfied with her supporting role to my father. For the public to see, she'd cherished all the memories of family, decorating Christmas cookies, my first communion, shopping for school clothes.

Yet the uncertain edge to her voice, when as a young girl, I had asked questions exploring her marriage to Dad, made me think she had taken the role, unsure if the movie would be a success. When my father walked out, the real woman emerged from under the perfection of a painted parent mask. It seems more painful for children to watch that mask peeled away than it is for parents to lose it.

I entered their house without announcing my presence, expecting to find it empty, but my father sat in the center of the living room floor, surrounded by clothes, water-stained boxes, and old photographs, staring blankly at picture albums filled with our family's history.

He jerked his head around. "Abbey, what are you doing?" His face was puffy and red, his features twisted with agony.

"I came by to see how you are." It sounded like a reasonable answer. "I just left Mom, sleeping." I knelt down next to my father in the sea of memories.

The redness lingered in his face even as he neutralized his expression. "I'm going through some things here, trying to straighten the house up a bit. In a few days, your mother comes home." He stopped, glanced down at an old dress.

"Dad?"

"The doctor said she can go home once she gets through the next few days of chemo. They'll move a hospital bed in here. She'll go to the hospital for her chemo treatments. Maybe she'll do better at home. In a couple of months they'll see if all the chemotherapy has halted the cancer in her liver." He dropped his head, burying his face into the old dress.

"Dad." I moved close to him and laid my head on his hunched back, my arm resting on his shoulder.

"We can't lose her," his words gurgled.

"You'll never lose her."

He turned, staring into my eyes, inspecting the way my hair fell to my shoulders and the small cleft in my chin, examining every feature on my face. "Abigail… what a beautiful name. When your mother told it to me, I thought, what a beautiful name…"

His eyes darted away. He flipped a few more pages in the album, and in an abrupt move, stood up. "Can you help me get some of this stuff organized, moved out of the way? They'll put the hospital bed in the living room because it's downstairs. I need to get back over to the hospital."

His tone was controlled, as if my reassurance had wiped away any signs of emotion. My father and I read the same book on emotions, so it was odd to see him burying his face in my mother's old dress, crying like a schoolboy who had lost his way. I hadn't seen him like this since the last time he almost lost her, but that was to another man.

He straightened his shirt, smoothed his thinning hair back, and bent down to put on his shoes. "Is Ethan having flowers delivered to your mother?"

"I don't know. He never mentioned it to me."

"Strange. See if you can get Ethan over here to help. Him and his…" he inhaled. "Do you like José?"

"Ethan's happy. What more can you ask for?"

"That's overly generalized for a woman who puts men through a series of grueling tests, knowing they're going to fail anyway."

"Dad, that's not true."

"Case in point, Ryan."

"Ryan's a different story."

"I know what your problem is, Abbey."

"What?"

"You haven't found anyone who compares to your wonderful dad." He touched the side of my cheek.

"That's it, Dad."

He walked to the door. "I'll see you tomorrow."

"Dad, don't stay too late. You need sleep, too."

"I won't," he said, as he slid through the door.

I called Ethan. He would be here in an hour. My dad could've arranged the house himself and I could also do it myself, but no one wants to put their hand into a dark bag of memories by themself.

I grabbed the watch and cufflinks my father left on the coffee table and went upstairs. The smell of stale sleep filled my parents' room. Rumpled clothes lay next to the four-poster bed. One side of the bed was perfectly made, while the other side bore the signs of my father. The unevenness of their bed probably made sleep an implausible feat for him.

I set his cufflinks and watch on the dresser next to my mother's opened jewelry box. I glanced at the row of rings nestled into red velvet slits. Next to her wedding ring was her friendship ring. I always liked that ring, liked what it stood for.

JUST PRIOR TO MY SIXTEENTH birthday, before my mother's betrayal of my father, she and I were in the kitchen making cookies for the debate club bake sale. My eyes were fixed on her right hand, elegant and graceful, with a gold ring shaped as two hands, embracing a heart wearing an elaborate crown. I'd watched that hand put on lipstick, sign checks, pluck the lint from my black Sunday coat, carefully brush her thick hair.

At last I had to know. "Mom what's that ring?"

She set the milk on the kitchen counter. "What does it mean?" she said, smiling.

"Yes, I always remember you wearing that ring."

We sat at the table and she spread out the fingers of

her right hand. "This is an Irish friendship ring. The hands symbolize friendship, the heart love, and the crown loyalty. You wear the heart facing in if you're taken. And obviously my heart is taken."

"I like that." I examined the ring closer. "Who gave it to you? Dad?"

"No, a very dear friend." She wore a Mona Lisa smile, a hundred emotions and meanings entangled in a quick upturn of the lips. She was gone for a moment, distance settling into her eyes.

"Mom…" I whispered.

Then, without a word, she stared into my eyes as if they were tiny crystal balls, and she was watching a fantastic scene. She stood and wrapped her arms around me.

Not a sad moment, but a lump formed in my throat. I hugged her back and knew I should ask her something more. I'd felt happy, yet, somehow empty, like something was missing, something she couldn't say.

I WONDERED IF ALL MY MEMORIES of us were tainted, dulled from my knowledge of her lover, like a splattering of black paint on a beautiful portrait. Its beauty is still unmistakable, but you would never buy it, claim it for your own. I can't remember events without somehow seeing her longing for another man, darkening them. Our recollections of moments are somehow changed because of life lived since.

I slid the ring onto my finger and stared at it. Who gave her this ring? The bottom of the heart faced in toward my hand.

The front door opened and I put the ring back into the velvet lined box. "It's about time," I yelled down to Ethan.

"I was hoping you'd have most of this done by the time I got here," my brother hollered back up to me. "What is all this? It looks like Dad brought stuff up from the basement. What was he doing?"

I stood behind Ethan, this time taking in the extent of chaos my father had created. "He was really upset when I got here, thumbing through old albums and clutching some of Mom's clothes, crying. He's really scared."

After Ethan lowered himself to the floor, he picked up clothes and put them back into boxes. "Abbey, what do you think?"

"About Mom?"

Nodding, he folded each dress with care, as if to display it in a store window.

"She doesn't look good and—"

"What?" His eyes darted toward me.

"It'll be hard to beat this."

"I don't want to believe that." His eyes dropped to the dresses he was refolding.

"Then let's not, for Dad, for them both. Let's assume she'll make it." I hoped my face didn't reveal my lack of confidence, so I smiled, my mother's smile.

Ethan gave me a puzzled look. "Was Dad searching for something? Some of this stuff is older than you."

"Why don't we get to work?" I gave the soft flesh on Ethan's arm a light pinch through his chambray long-sleeved shirt.

His clothes were always fresh and pressed, and he took

care in his presentation. Although he possessed an under-stated attractiveness, his face would not draw strangers' eyes. Ethan was the kind of guy, once you started talking to, you never wanted to quit. He listened with intent and asked sincere, non-intrusive questions, and he always touched you during a conversation, signaling his understanding.

"Hey, careful." A genuine smile crossed his face.

"This project requires a drink." I walked toward the kitchen.

I poured us both a glass of boxed white wine, the only thing stashed in the back of the refrigerator. I didn't want to guess how long it had been there, since my mother would not allow box wine to pass over her lips. "For you, darling, a superb month for boxed wine." I bowed a little as I handed Ethan his glass.

"Dad must have bought this. I can't imagine Mom drinking wine from a box."

"Yeah, Mom probably said, 'Dear, can you pick up some wine while you're out?' " I imitated her high pitched drawl and delicate hand movements, the way she twirled her fingers in the air, closing them together to form a budding flower. "And Dad comes back an hour later with a five gallon box of the cheapest stuff he could find."

"Yeah and don't you know," Ethan added, "they prob-ably had company and Mom made him turn right back around, telling the guests that he forgot some crucial ingre-dient for her leg of lamb. Meanwhile she wrote down the name of a French white, saying, 'Please, Frank, come back with something that requires a corkscrew.' "

I laughed and took a sip that turned it into a swig. It

wasn't the kind of wine you sip and savor, it was the kind you squeeze your nose and gulp. "Poor Dad, he thought he was doing great by saving so much money."

Ethan took a large box to the basement while I taped up some of the other boxes. When he stayed gone longer than necessary, I wondered what he was doing in the place of our childhood secret meetings, where parents were excluded. He came down the hall carrying a medium-sized box covered in water stains.

"The idea is to put things away, not take more stuff out."

"I saw the writing on the edge of this box. It must have been under some of the other boxes that Dad was going through."

"What writing?"

He set the box on the floor, bending his knees and sitting beside me. "Look, it says, 'modeling photos.'" Ethan opened the box and pulled out a plastic bag full of photos.

I acted somewhat interested, leaning over Ethan, drinking the tart wine. My mother had done some catalogue modeling in Dallas and those weren't my type of photos, for the most part lacking any artistic flair.

"Jesus, look at her." Ethan held up several black and white photos of our mother in sultry poses. They looked like professional modeling photos.

I reached over Ethan's shoulder and grabbed more photos from the bag. There were so many, some of her in swimsuits, ball gowns, tight jeans, and one of her in a fur coat open so the edges of her full breasts were peering out from beneath the animal skin. Another one of her surrounded by sailors, she, smoking a long cigarette, blowing the billowy smoke in the lusty boys' faces, again a healthy amount of cleavage pushing out through the cups of the dress.

Ethan and I gorged on the images of my mother that portrayed her as sensual creature.

"Christ," Ethan said, handing me a large photo.

I leaned against the back of the couch, my eyes reaching into the photo. My mother, Rachel, bent over, her arms draped on the back of an executive's leather chair, her legs spread, forming the most perfect upside down V. Black hair fanned over her bare back, its thick ends spreading over her ribs, concealing most of her exposed breasts. The jeans covering her butt were so tight that the seam buried into the crack of her ass, her eyes searing the camera with a look that said, 'I dare you.'

"Let me see that one again," Ethan's face was flushed and I wondered if it was the wine or the erotic pose of his mother. "God, these pictures… did you know?"

I shook my head. These photos hadn't been taken for a Sears or J.C. Penney catalogue, where my mother had worked.

The quality of the photos, paired with the overwrought sexuality displayed without crudeness, was the work of an artist. Only a photographer with an exacting eye and a passion for the art could bring to the surface my mother, Rachel, a woman I had not seen.

The photos were the work of one person. I could only assume a man, because the sexual tension between her and the eye of the camera was palpable. He had brought something out in her, and she, the willing subject, opened herself to the artist, pulled something from him, like a symbiotic dance that moved off the paper.

I had experienced the same give-and-take dance with the mother gorilla. My mother's response to that photo was based on experience. She knew the trust it required for subjects to reveal themselves before the artist's lens. She had been able to do just that, reveal herself. Not just her skin, but also the woman beneath the skin.

"I'll get us some more wine." Ethan's words came out breathy and unsure. As he bent over to get my glass, his hand seemed unsteady. Rivulets of sweat dripped down his temples, as if the salacious pictures of his mother undermined his own sexuality.

I imagined the photographer, how he must have felt adjusting the lens as he peered through it at her spread legs, jeans glued to her skin, and those green eyes, their demand not masked by the black-and-white film.

How could he have taken those photos without pulling the jeans, with all his force, from her body and calling her dare?

The other photo showed sailors clambering around her, but she had no time for them, only for the person behind the lens. A thin veil of white silk slid over her erect nipples and eased down her taut legs, creating a scant shroud that failed to conceal the faintest darkening between her thighs. The camera seemed to sense her body was bare beneath the white sheath.

Ethan and I drank more wine, letting the acid taste blur under the inebriation. We organized most of the boxes, stored them away once again, and rearranged furniture so a hospital bed would fit. She had once conveyed such fantastic control in photos, but now cancer dictated her life.

We left the box containing my mother's pictures sitting in the middle of the floor. When the work was finished, we scurried back to the photos like middle school boys who had found their father's stash of *Penthouse* magazines. The poses and costumes were endless and our eyes' appetites were insatiable.

We flipped through photos of her in front of an old English pub, the wind blowing, lifting her skirt to reveal a black garter and the borders of black lace that rescinded into the contour of her hips. Ethan handed me a color photo, crushed red velvet material wrapped around her erect body as if she were a toy soldier. A man standing a foot from her held the end of the fabric and the viewer knew, if the man walked away, the fabric would unroll, leaving her naked under Big Ben.

I peered closer. Only the man's hands and a fraction of his body had been caught on film. He must have set the camera by timer and then allowed himself to become part of his own artistic product, something few professional photographers will attempt.

Then came the photo that made me ask Ethan for another glass of stale wine. A large, eight-by-ten color photo of Rachel in a low-cut, shiny emerald gown, her anxious breasts bursting from the plunging neckline. The material followed the curve of her body with a slit starting at her upper thigh and dropping to the floor. One leg perched on the edge of an antique gold sofa and her fingers spread like a fan below her breasts, but my eyes were drawn to the man on his knees, one hand reaching up the black hole of her dress and the other balancing a camera to his eye. He had captured himself in the middle of creating. His work revealed a genius quality and there was something wild and dangerous about the man with the camera, the man to whom I was sure my mother's iniquity belonged.

Admiration for this man shifted into anger. He had to be the lover my father spoke of. So she had loved him even before my father.

None of it made sense. Why leave him and marry my father, then continue an affair with him?

My eyes stayed on the photos. She had never been this raw with my father. If she was real with the man behind the camera, she had played the part of the happy housewife with my father. She could have won an Academy Award for her role, had she not been caught.

"I'm so glad I never saw these pictures when I was young." Ethan set his glass on the floor and walked towards the bathroom.

"Why?" Without knowing where the answer lay, I could conjure no words.

He looked back at me and rolled his eyes. "When I get back, let's put these photos away." He shook his head. "Far away."

Ethan disappeared down the hall, and I put all the photos back in the box, but stopped when I saw shiny green fabric under other dresses and more photos. At first, I jerked my hand away from her dress, his dress. Then inch by inch, I pulled the edge of the emerald green satin, until the dress slid into my arms. I sat shaking, looking at it, running my hands over it, kneading the slippery material with my fingers.

Then I gulped the last of the wine and ran upstairs with the dress in my hand. My heartbeat rose to my mouth as I entered the bathroom connected to the master bedroom. I stripped all my clothes off and eased myself into it, the thick satin gliding over my bare skin. The rich fabric fell into the cavern created by my hipbones and brushed against the hair between my legs. The edge of the green dress grabbed my small breasts and pushed them toward my collarbones.

I lifted my leg and watched in the mirror as the slit spread open, traveling up my leg like a row of firecrackers. I twisted my auburn hair into a knot, piling it high on my head, and then painted my lips with a tube of my mother's blood red lipstick. The mirror reflected the same sultriness my mother had possessed.

"Abbey, where are you…?" Ethan sounded annoyed and a bit drunk.

"I needed to use the bathroom, too," I said in a monotone voice, my eyes watching the mirror as my mother stood before me, in me.

"Let's finish up." Ethan peered around the corner. "Christ." He shut his eyes and cranked his head away from the mirror.

Behind my mother stood her son, the son she had taken great care in nurturing. She was drawn to his vulnerability and she used it to bring him in close.

"Take off the dress!" he croaked, still shielding his eyes.

"It's just a dress," I whispered. But as I spoke, my body trembled underneath the emerald sheen.

Lowering his head, he walked into the bathroom. He didn't look at me, but rather at the reflection in the mirror.

The wine had slowed his speech and his movements were cat-like. He sat on the counter, his knees curled to his chest, his feet in the sink, staring into the eyes of his mother.

I leaned against the wall and turned my head toward the mirror. I didn't want her to leave. I wished I could have bent forward and touched her, sucking from her the energy and sureness her body radiated in the eye of the camera.

"Abbey," he said, bending his head over his shoulder and redirecting his eyes toward our mother. "When I was young, I convinced myself I would marry Mom someday." His statement attached itself to a brick and fell to the floor.

My chest tightened at his words. I hesitated, because I wanted to hear more about the woman who had snatched the heart of the men around her and then toyed nonstop with their obsessive need for her approval.

"It's normal for young boys to want to marry their mothers." I turned my body toward the mirror and rested my arms on the counter beside Ethan. My arms bent, I leaned into the mirror, revealing small mounds creeping out from the emerald dress.

"No, it was more than that. I saw Mom the way she looked in the photos." His words became breathy as he stared at my reflection, his mother, in the glass.

"What do you mean?" Under the parent and the devoted wife mask was a different woman. The one who had cheated on my father, I told myself in disgust.

"One night I..." His voice cracked. "I had a bad dream and when I cried out, she came to me, pulling me into her arms. Her slippery robe, I suppose it was silk, had fallen open when she reached for me. I rested my head on her bare breasts and my lips were pressed against her flesh." He sighed, as if his words were painful. "She held me in her arms and let my tears trickle onto the crevice between her breasts, I lifted my head and I saw her breasts."

He stopped, considering his mother in the mirror, staring at the dark shadow created by my breasts, as if his mind imagined her. "When she saw me staring, she quickly closed the robe."

Drops fell from his lids as he placed his hand on my mother's reflection in the mirror. "That night I would have given anything to feel her breasts, they seemed so perfect."

He slid his hand down the reflection to the top of the slit. His head bent and tears swam down his face. "I was only nine, but she was so perfect, and I have never had that desire for a woman since. And never for Mom again, just that once. Christ, I have run it through my mind a thousand times."

I threaded my fingers through his hair and brought his head against my chest, holding him tight.

"Abbey," he whispered, arching his back away.

"Don't say anything," I said as I rubbed his back and rocked his head against the green fabric covering my chest.

I forced myself to imagine it, a child needy for the safety only a mother's arms can provide. For that moment, I could pretend to be the mother who bore the child from her womb where she kept him safe, until nature unwittingly forced her to relinquish him to the world before his time, his tears making her body ache to have him back inside the warmth of her body.

CHAPTER 14

The dull light smothered the indistinct horizon, as thick gray clouds concealed the sun's descent in the west. The moisture in the air turned cool with the approaching weak autumn, and my skin felt clammy as if a horrible dream had become a daily routine. My father wrapped his arm around her waist and guided her one slow and careful step at a time to the wheelchair my brother manned.

Ethan's hands rubbed her shoulders before grasping the handles of the chair and wheeling her into the house. She glanced over her shoulder, touching his hand. He smiled and she answered with an upward movement of her lips.

HER PRECIOUS BABY HAD BEEN torn from her belly before he was prepared for the harsh world; she begged the doctors to keep him inside. She gave him up eight weeks prematurely and wasn't able to nurture him the first month of his life. He lay sprawled, like an injured bird, tubes springing from every orifice, in an incubator attached to a breathing machine.

My six-year-old eyes followed the rhythm of his small chest, up and down, as my father held me in his arms so I could see my new baby brother through the strange glass.

For the next month, the hospital became my mother's home. She wasn't present at home for meals, to pull the covers to my chin, or to attend my first school play.

As I stood on stage, I missed her bright hopeful face. My father made up for her absence, clapping so hard that day, I was sure his hands would be bloody. When I went to hug him after the play, he bent down on one leg, his strong grip shaking my shoulders. "Oh, Abigail, you were the best, the most beautiful star I have ever seen."

My father meant his words. He was the first parent to stand during the applause, giving lead to the other first grade parents. No one could wipe away the smile cloaking my face that day.

Dad explained that Mom felt uncomfortable leaving my baby brother or she would have been there, too. I soon learned my mother was more like a critic from the newspaper, rather than a parent who thinks you're a star if you stand on stage and sneeze. Whenever my mother did attend my plays, she assailed my ears with advice after I took my first bow.

'Smile more, Abigail. Never turn your face from the audience. Don't let the others upstage you.' Then she'd demonstrate how I should keep my body open to the rows of excited parents. She told me it was all in an effort to see me be the best. But my father already believed I was the best.

Once my brother was released from the hospital, our family's life revolved around him, making sure he ate, gained weight, and breathed clean air. We had air humidifiers and had to be careful where we carried the struggling infant.

Because Ethan was allergic to pine, Dad bought a fake Christmas tree. My brother was allergic to everything and remained sick the first ten years of his life.

Mom kept him close to her. He needed her extra attention so she pushed my father and me to the side, as cheerleaders to my brother, and she, the coach to the struggling player. But even he suffocated under my mother's thick blanket, reaching for me at age ten, my greedy sixteen-year-old hand jerking him from my mother's claws.

He became my project and I gained pleasure from guiding and shielding him, while my mother's heart ached to have him nestled once again in her bosom of influence. When most sixteen-year-olds would have frowned at their ten-year-old brother's intrusion, I had welcomed him and even enjoyed his questions and the intrigue that being an older sister afforded me.

THE FIRST COUPLE OF WEEKS she was home, we ran circles around my mother, serving her, trying to appease her desire for perfection. I spent most of my daytime hours at their house, not for her, but for my father. I shopped, ran errands, kept the house clean, even cooked by my mother's explicit instructions, allowing my brother and father to keep a vigil by her side during those first days. Her walk was unsteady, so she sought the crutch of my father or brother for mobility.

Our conversations fluctuated between something that resembled a mother and daughter to benign niceties and brief salutations, as if I were a friendly nurse hired to care for a dying woman.

At times, the cloak of discomfort smothered us both and when it did, I lay down with her, shutting my eyes just to escape the angst that defined our relationship. I could sense the dissembling of the family psyche, like hidden grenades waiting to explode as we marched towards my mother's ineluctable gravestone.

How could it be, that with modern medicine, they could not detect the insidious disease earlier and halted its destruction on her body? The word 'malignant' described the kind of cancer whose growth was tenacious, lying silent until it could inhabit yet another community of cells, until there was not enough of the organ left to fortify a human life.

As she slept, I filled a water jug on her bedside table. Tuesdays and Thursdays were my mandatory days to care for her. After a couple of weeks, my father arranged his schedule at the firm so he could work from home a few days a week, and every Wednesday Ethan left work at noon to take my mother to the hospital for treatments.

On Thursdays we were alone together all day. She slept a lot the first week, but by the end of the second one, she seemed to be feeling better, which made me believe the chemo was working. Instead of my mother, the cancer was dying.

It was strange to look at her, knowing she housed the monster, cancer. She had once been driven to precision in her appearance, which the lens of the camera longed to capture, absorbing her very essence and exploiting it so beautifully on paper. Without any hesitation, she'd given herself to the camera.

The photos Ethan and I had discovered teased my mind. When the pictures were taken, she could not have been more than twenty, and I wondered how much time the affair between her and her photographer had extended. Neither my father nor my brother knew who sent the flowers to my mother every week, but I did.

I leaned against the kitchen counter and squeezed my eyes shut.

DRESSED IN HER EMERALD GREEN GOWN, Rachel took his outstretched hand. He whirled her into him, gazing into her green eyes, their color magnified by the sheen of her gown. In defiance, she stared into his eyes, her lips straight and serious.

He twirled her out, never letting the tips of her delicate fingers escape his touch. She circled him, his body turning round and round so his eyes remained fastened to her form. Her sensuality danced on the perimeter of his ownership because she would not, could not, keep herself still.

"ABIGAIL," MY MOTHER'S FAINT VOICE called from the living room.

She had enmeshed herself with my father, keeping her lover on the outside looking in, and now with her inevitable goodbye, he dared to come closer, sending flowers to our home twice a week, my father's home. She had not been the same way with my father; no intrigue surfaced in her eyes whenever she looked at him. Familiarity and comfort spilled from her expression any time they embraced or posed for the camera.

Rubbing the drowsy mucus from her eyes, she said, "Did your father come home for lunch?" She reached for a glass of water.

"No, he had to stay at the office to straighten some things out. He said he'd be home around dinner time."

With a weak gesture, she invited me closer. I sat in a chair near her bed, facing the large window, the frame to our tree-filled backyard. An old rope dropped like a lifeline from the branch of a large water oak in the middle of the yard, and above its frayed and knotted end, a wooden board twisted in the wind.

My bottom had spent many sunny afternoons on that board, swinging high as my mother pushed me, singing an old Patsy Cline tune, while bread baked in the oven. She would look at her watch and say, 'bread is ready' and I would trot in the house behind her floral dress and wait with excitement as she pulled the fresh bread from the oven.

She'd let me sit on the counter and watch her prepare the roast or ham for dinner. I stayed by her side until my brother woke from his afternoon nap, and then she shooed me away while she fed him from her breasts.

I felt my mother's stare and turned to look at her. Since she'd been home, she was gaining a healthier demeanor. Something about being in a hospital makes everyone look like they're at death's doorstep. Maybe it's the color of the walls, the overly washed hospital gowns another sick person wore only hours before, and the stark lights.

My mother pushed the button to raise the head of the

bed. Clearing her throat, she looked at me with grave seriousness. I hoped she wasn't going to launch into an 'I may die speech.' Not with all we had left unsaid between us.

"Abigail, I want to ask you something."

Lord, I can't enter into this conversation. 'More time, Mom, I need more time,' I thought as I scanned her face.

"Yes?" I tried not to sound like a scared child.

"I really want Thanksgiving to be special this year."

"It always is."

"Yes, but you're here this year and I—"

My mind was able to finish her sentence. This was a disguised 'I may not make it' speech.

"I want this year to be perfect and I'd like to invite family and friends. What do you think?"

"Fine with me. I mean, you're the queen of that kinda stuff."

"I need your help." She waited.

"Doing?" The familiar anxiety that came from being a part of her events made its way under my skin.

"Sending invitations, shopping, and cooking. I want this Thanksgiving to be the best."

"It'll be special all right, if I'm cooking. I barely passed Home Economics." I stood up.

Her face formed an exasperated look and then an instant later she replaced it with a smile. "We'll work together. Since I escaped that hospital, I'm feeling better, less tired. I can write everything down, but I just wanted to make sure you will take over from there."

Did most mothers have to ask for their daughters help four weeks before Thanksgiving, especially when they were fighting cancer?

She slid her legs off the bed. "I can't lie here all day."

"I thought they said 'rest.' "

"Until I feel ready to get around. And I'm certain of one thing. I'm tired of this cancer wasting my days."

I held back a laugh because that statement sounded so much like my mother. She had become disgusted with cancer, therefore, she was not going to yield to it. Again, it made me think she may make it after all, she may beat this insidious robber of mothers, wives, sisters, and daughters.

My mother's determination, something I often saw as selfishness, was coming through. When she wanted to do something, the things that got in her way were not huge problems, but minor nuisances. Her plan would be carried out regardless. Seeing the same attitude in the face of cancer made it seem more noble than selfish.

She reached for the stainless steel walker my father had bought for her at a medical supply store two days ago. He explained she would only need it temporarily, until she felt strong again. She acted irritated when she looked at it for the first time and I'd listened to my dad say it's not permanent, over and over.

I jumped up and moved it closer.

"All right then, Thanksgiving," she said.

"Of course, Thanksgiving."

She pulled herself from sitting to standing, using the walker. The way she stood, her legs spread more than normal and her protruding lower stomach—which the doctors explained was due to fluid retention and an enlarged liver—made her look like a pregnant grandma. I had to look away.

She took a few steps and stopped, taking deep laborious breaths. With each of her struggling breaths, my own breathing became more difficult, as if I were trying to suck in oxygen for her.

"Mom, are you—"

She raised her hand, and then in a moment of pure sincerity, she craned her head over her shoulder and smiled. She took another deep breath and then pushed out the word, "Thanks," and turned her head back.

"Yes," I said to the back of her head.

Her smile was the vulnerable real one I had seen in her modeling photographs. Who was she before she learned to paint on a perfect smile for all her friends and my dad's co-workers, hell, even her own husband and children? Who was the young woman in the photos, and how could my mother have kept her buried for so many years, only to emerge sparsely in the midst of her cancer struggle?

Those questions could not be answered without knowing who the man was she had held onto for so long.

Wanting to see more of Rachel, I scanned the photos in the living room. Encased in old ornate gold frames purchased at estate sales, family photos lined the fireplace mantle and shrouded one wall. My mother had an affinity for wealthy dead people's stuff.

In one photo, my mother sat in a chair, coddling my brother. My father stood on one side and I on the other, with my hand on the chair, all eyes cast on my baby brother, my mother, the queen, holding her prize.

When my parents at last brought Ethan home from the hospital, my father had carried my new brother through the house, showing him his new home, introducing him to the world, saying, 'this is a tree and this is your dad's chair.'

My mother watched, pride oozing from her pores. My father observed her bathe my brother, even holding his tiny head up when she requested. Both so impressed with the new life they had created.

Had they been drawn together like this with my birth? Had my dad introduced me to the world like he was a real estate agent and I a prospective buyer, convincing me this was a great place to live?

I examined a picture of myself as an infant, my mother cuddling me in her arms, as she sat on a blanket spread across the grass. My father must have taken the picture, gleaming behind the camera. I scanned every one in a way I had never done, searching for the young Rachel, the seductive, almost magical Rachel, among our family photos. She could not be found.

No doubt the camera belonged to her. In every picture she stood out as if the people surrounding her were background, but her love relationship with the camera was gone. Why had she traded the man behind the camera for my father? I asked myself that question almost every day since Ethan and I had discovered the modeling photos.

"What are you doing?" she said as she emerged from the bathroom wearing pants and a white blouse, her thinning hair combed and pulled into a small bun. Dad had moved some of her clothes into the hall closet, so she didn't have to struggle up the steps to their bedroom.

"Looking at family photos."

Using the walker to steady herself, she plodded to the

large chair and sat. I waited for my father's overstuffed chair to envelop her.

"How did you meet Dad?"

"At a park. I told you that years ago," she said, a modicum of defensiveness creeping into her tone.

Her change in timbre cut through me. Her lies leeched out any empathy I might have felt, and irritation took its place.

I shifted my weight to one side and crossed my arms over my chest. "What were you doing before you met Dad?"

"Abigail, this is silly. I worked at a bookstore and did some catalogue modeling."

'That's a fucking lie!' I wanted to shout.

The caliber of pictures tucked away in the basement wasn't that of catalogue photos. Rather, they were the kind of pictures that comprise the portfolios of top models in cities like Milan, New York, and Paris. The quality of those photos meant my mother had the makings of a first-rate modeling career. With her striking features and long lean body, the camera loved her. She was going to continue the lie that she was some small town girl who made her way posing for catalogue pictures and selling books.

"How come you never pursued modeling further? You're attractive enough, and if you weren't going to college, why not modeling? I mean, more than catalogues?" I stared into her eyes, waiting for her answer.

The features of her face stiffened, her mouth hardened until it looked like she couldn't move it.

"Well, why not? I mean, you seem to like the camera." I was digging, wanting to hurt her. I took a step toward her.

"Abigail." She smiled, but it took muscle work, forcing the edges of her mouth up to create a rigid mechanical smile. "I didn't want that. I…" she shoved the words out, "wanted a family, children…"

"You did?" I raised my voice.

Her eyes widened. "Of course," she whispered, with the conviction of an unsure witness during cross-examination.

Violet, red, and burnt orange wiggled in my peripheral vision. I tried not to look. Instead I took another step toward her, turning my head from the flowers, the outward evidence that my mother's affair had continued during her entire marriage to my father.

My dad, hopeless in love, had chosen to forgive her. His naïveté made me sad and her abuse of his love angered me.

"So, you're glad your life has been about your family?"

"Yes, Abigail," she snapped, as if she had a right to be irritated by my questions.

"And that's what you want for me, marriage and family, happily ever after, me and Ryan? Is that what you think?"

"Where are you going with this? I just think Ryan would love you forever and that's important. After all, he's devoted to you."

"So, that's enough?" My voice escalated to a yell.

"Please. I'm…" She shut her eyes for an instant, but I didn't care if she was tired.

Why was she trying to sell me on something that had made her miserable and caused her to live a double life? Her logic was so fucked up. She had fallen deeply in love with a man and his camera, gave that up, and married my father, all the while continuing an affair with the man behind the camera. The whole time raising a family and trying to sell me on the concept of love and marriage. That's like a lung cancer spokesperson selling cigarettes, stupid.

Again the flowers pulled my eyes. Damn her. "Mom, who are the flowers from?" I glared at her.

I walked toward the flowers. She followed me with her eyes. The clock by her bed read 5:30. That meant my brother would arrive from work in a few minutes.

She gave me a blank stare, but no answer.

"Yes, Mother. These damn flowers, who are they from?" I picked up the vase.

The poison inside me boiled. Never answers, just unresolved questions. I didn't care why she gave up modeling, I just wanted to know why she betrayed my father all those years.

"Abigail, please stop. I don't know. Why are you asking me all these questions, and now… let's just try to—"

"Why not?" I screamed, still holding the vase in my hand. I wanted to throw it, along with the gray water and flowers, against the wall, watch the fading flowers fly everywhere while the vase shattered. But tomorrow would bring another delivery. They'd been coming twice a week since my mother went into the hospital and continued when she came home.

Her eyes moved to my hand, a look of consternation dominating her face. "Put the flowers down." Her speech was slow, but her voice squeaked, giving her fear up.

"I know who sent the flowers. Who can't get enough of the beautiful Rachel?" I slammed the vase on the table. Water splashed up and sloshed across the surface.

"What are you talking about?" The words caught in her throat, making the end of the sentence barely audible. My insult showed on my mother's face and no doubt bitterness and disgust beamed from mine.

I turned, walking toward the kitchen. "Nothing, Mother. Ethan will be here in five minutes. I've got to go," I said, grabbing my coat and running for the door.

"Please come here, let me…" Her sandpaper voice faded as I shut the door behind me.

My heart raced and I stopped outside the door to steady myself before driving.

When I got home, I stripped to my underwear and fixed myself a gin and tonic. I nursed it while I ate a Lean Cuisine frozen dinner. I hadn't listened to messages since yesterday, so I pushed the button and sat back in the chair.

"It's Sheila. Some people from work are going to a happy hour Thursday night at that cowboy club, Dallas. I know, I hate country music, too, but hey, half-priced drinks and some free food. Five o'clock. See you there."

Click, then the next one.

"Ryan, just calling to see how your mother is doing. If your family needs anything, let me know. I'll stop by tomorrow. I'm thinking about you, Ab."

He was pulling away, adopting the role of friend versus boyfriend, and I missed him. When I took time to think about anything besides my mother and her life, I wished I were with Ryan. Thoughts of him playing the guitar, making up silly songs as he went, his hand slipping "quite accidentally" from the small of my back to my butt filtered through my mind. But when I was with him, I wanted to get away.

"Abbey, we are nearing the end of the month extension. If you want the assignment with the Galápagos turtles, you need to act. I can put off the editorial department another couple of weeks. That's all. They love your work, but they need someone to go soon. If you can't do it, give me a call."

I'm taking that assignment, I told myself. I'm leaving. I will leave here, her.

"Abigail, Mom. We need to talk."

With the edge of my fist, I pounded the stop button. I couldn't listen to her. No, we don't, I thought, angry with myself for prying. Now she would feel she needed to talk to me. And the flowers. I didn't want to hear her theory about the flowers, because she knew who the sender was.

I swallowed the rest of the gin and dressed in a hurry to see if I could catch Sheila at the nightclub. I put on a pair of tight Levis and a white blouse, tied its hem in a knot, just above my waistline. With the tube of red lipstick I had stolen from my mother's bathroom, I decorated my lips.

After scanning the nightclub and finding no Sheila, I headed for the door, but instead veered to the bar and ordered a drink. I had never sat in a bar alone, but that night a buzz from the alcohol would help me forget my unanswered questions and my mother's answers in the form of questions. With her impending death, I had a desire to resolve things in my own life. The life my mother hadn't chosen, the one stored in a box, wielded more impact over me than the life she had lived as a wife and mother. But why had she chosen to leave it, yet hang on to it?

The music became the background for the scene that drew my attention. Across the bar a couple in their forties cuddled in a corner of the smoky room. I couldn't quit staring at them.

They seemed to be engrossed in each other, oblivious to their surroundings. He caressed her cheek and then they were lost in a long passionate kiss. She stretched her neck back and laughed at something he said or perhaps the wicked movement of his hand below the surface of the old pine table. They acted as if they had been forced into making some public appearance, but they'd rather be home, naked, wrapped up in each other's bodies.

I wondered if they were married, if they had been united for a long time and had maintained the passion of newness. I searched for gold bands but their hands moved nonstop over each other's skin, and it was dusky and crowded in the bar, so I couldn't find any symbol of marriage on their fingers.

I created my own story for them. They were married, all right, to different people and had to escape into a dark corner of a rustic bar so they could feel the thrill of each other's touch. Marriage, what conspirators the union creates.

I was finishing my third gin and tonic when a hand reached in front of me and placed a fourth drink on the bar. I turned, making eye contact with a tall dark-haired cowboy who wore Wrangler jeans held up by a western-style belt with a gold ornate buckle. He had on a starched white shirt with silver snaps.

"Does the lady care for another?" He lifted his hand from the fresh gin and tonic.

"How did you know what I was drinking?"

"Well, ma'am, I was standing next to you at the bar

when you ordered your last drink, and forgive me for being so straight with you, but a man could hardly not notice you. Name is JimmyJohn," he said, extending his hand.

God, he's one of those Texas boys with two names. I thought they kept all of them trapped in West Texas. An old friend from high school had attended Texas Tech University in West Texas and when she came back, she made me laugh until I cried, telling me the names of some of the guys she'd gone out with JohnDavid, JimEd, BillyJoe. All of them had double first names.

"I'm Abbey." I gulped the last of my drink, not offering my hand.

"Much obliged, Abbey." He tipped his hat. "Mind if I join you?"

"I suppose." The alcohol chipped away at my inhibitions. I grabbed my jacket from the stool next to me and the long legged cowboy moved in.

"What's a beautiful woman like you doing in a bar by herself?" His mustached mouth stretched into a grin.

Why do people question a woman's presence at a bar alone, but never a man's?

"Same thing a good-looking feller like yourself is doing in a bar by himself." I threw out my best Texas drawl; the alcohol made my tongue slow so the drawl came naturally.

"Touché." He smiled and brought his beer up to toast my glass.

"Where you from?"

"Canyon. It's in West Texas just north of Lubbock, south of Amarillo, but I've been living in Austin for a couple of years."

"I thought that was a regional name."

"Whadda ya mean?"

"West Texans seem to have a proclivity for naming their children dual names. As if a two-year-old doesn't have a hard enough time learning one name, they add an extra name for the poor kid," I said with a smile.

A deep guttural laugh exploded from his chest. "You know, ma'am, your cynical attitude makes you even more beautiful." He twisted the sides of his handlebar mustache, then stood up and gestured toward the dance floor, indicating we should dance to a George Strait song. "Care to dance?"

I placed my hand in his and allowed him to lead me to the dance floor as if we were at a high school homecoming dance. He held my hand and my waist away from his body during the song, gliding me across the dance floor like a Raggedy Ann doll.

When the music slowed to the twang of Reba McEntire, the cowboy pulled my slack body into his. His excitement pressed against my navel as he slid his leg between mine to the rhythm of the music. One dance turned into five. When the D.J. pushed the country music to the side and put on some rock-n-roll, it became more fun to be a spectator, watching cowboy butts starched up in Wrangler jeans, wiggling to the beat of rock and roll.

"Do you want another beer?" I grabbed my purse.

"Oh, no, ma'am. I mean, yes, I do, but I ain't lettin' you buy." He marched toward the bar and returned with another round. "Just wouldn't feel right havin' a woman pay for my drink." He set the glasses on the table.

My eyes played tricks on me, people's twins started to appear. I blinked several times and took a deep breath, trying to focus on the dark-haired cowboy gazing at me.

"Damn, you're one beautiful woman."

I stared at the ice cubes floating in my clear drink, watching the twisted lime, fighting to break through the ice.

"Are you all right, ma'am?" He rubbed his rough hand on my back.

I leaned into the West Texas native, opened my eyes wide and batted them like Mae West. "Are you going to call me 'ma'am' when we are..." I hesitated, knowing that referring to sex as fucking would do little to protect my image of a fair lady to the cowboy.

"When we are...?" The side of his lips curled toward his nose.

"Yes, you know." I tried to focus my eyes.

He ran his index finger down my temple, over my chin, then he leaned into me and kissed my lips as if we had spent a lifetime as lovers. I returned his tongue penetration with a sloppy aggressive kiss. I couldn't rein in my tongue and I caught my hand resting on his leg miserably close to his groin.

He glanced at my hand and smiled. "How 'bout we get outta here?"

He took my hand like it was the grip of an old red wagon and led me outside to his truck. I fell into the truck. The gin had infected my whole body, yet I wanted more. I just didn't want to feel. I needed more gin to numb my confusion and the nagging feeling I had endured since high school that my mother was someplace she didn't want to be, that it was all an act.

"I'll give you a ride home and we can get your car in the morning. You're in no condition to drive now," he said, looking over his shoulder as he backed out of the parking lot. "Which way, sweetheart?"

"Get on 183 North, yes North…and then… then I'll direct you, Mr. Cowboy." I slid close to him, walking my fingers up his stiff jeans to the bulge between his legs. "Are you a happy cowboy?" I fondled his ridged jeans.

"Yes, ma'am, but we're both gonna be in trouble if you don't take that there hand off my privates."

I rubbed his crotch until the friction made my hand warm. "Why is that?" I buried my tongue in the cowboy's ear.

"Hey, ma'am, we're gonna have a wreck." His hand brushed passed his ear and then he removed my hand from his crotch. "Be a good girl."

"Oh, I'll be a great girl." My foolish words slurred as they spit from my mouth.

"When we get home," he said, patting my knee as if I was some young schoolgirl and he had a lollipop waiting for me.

Men always think they are doing you a favor when they're fucking you, I thought. When you moan, the guy believes he is the greatest fuck you've ever had. If you don't, they wonder what's wrong with you, instead of what's wrong with them.

After several convoluted directions, I was able to point the cowboy on the right path to my house. I stumbled inside and made a line for the gin in my cupboard. If I was going to have sex with Mr. Cowboy, I wanted my blood stream to have a healthy ratio of liquor to red blood cells.

"How about some gin?" I grabbed a glass.

"No, thank you. I don't think you need any either." The cowboy's tone transformed from playful to lecturing.

"You don't? Well, that's not a very fun attitude." I sauntered my loose ligaments over to JimmyJohn and plopped myself on his lap, bottle of gin in one hand and a glass in the other. I set the glass down and swigged the gin from the bottle.

He extended his arm, trying to reach the bottle. I leaned back and held the bottle of gin from him. He wrinkled his face up and frowned, "Seriously, ma'am, that's enough. You're gonna hurt tomorrow."

My spine become rigid when he said the word hurt. I gulped some more gin and JimmyJohn reached for the bottle. The bottle slipped from my hand and smashed to the hardwood floor. Glass and gin sprayed all over the floor.

"I need to get outta here and let you get to bed."

I tried to unbutton his stiff jeans.

"I don't think so," he said, removing my hand from his zipper. "It wouldn't be very gentleman-like of me to make love to a sloppy drunk. I'd rather see you again under different circumstances."

"Make love?" I repeated, laughing, barely able to hold my eyelids open. "We're going to fuck." I straddled his thighs. "And it will be the best fuck of your life." I pulled my shirt over my head.

He twisted his leg from under my thigh, escaping my wrestler hold and stood. "Might have been, but I doubt that. I don't take too kindly to a woman with a mouth like yours."

I groped for him, sticking my tongue out and running it over my lips like some desperate whore afraid her john might leave and she wouldn't make enough drug money for the night.

He pushed my hands away, shoving me back on the couch. "Listen, you go to sleep. I'm leaving."

"No, you can't. Look at me. Look how beautiful the wonderful Rachel is, and I can fuck like a racehorse. You can't leave," I yelled, throwing my arms in the air.

"What a waste," JimmyJohn, my cowboy, whispered as he walked to the door.

I tried to get up, follow him, beg him to stay, but when I stood, a sharp pain stabbed my foot. I fell back to the couch. A blurry red stream dripped from my foot. In my drunkenness I didn't care. I pulled a sharp piece of glass from the center of my sole and fell back onto the couch.

CHAPTER 15

"Abbey, Abbey." From a distance came Ryan's muted voice. I tried to lift my hammered head, but the couch had sucked my head into the cushion and my lids were glued to my eyeballs.

His voice got closer. "Abbey, oh my God, Abbey!" A hand circled my ankle.

I peeled the lids from my eyes. Ryan's face floated above me as he wedged in beside my listless body. The light pouring in the large window assaulted my pupils and I shut my eyes. Someone was pinching the nerves behind them.

"Abbey, what happened here?" Ryan said, the moist air from his mouth settled on my cheeks.

Fighting the chain that held me down, I lifted my head. The blood vessels in my brain pounded like someone had lit fireworks in my skull. My stomach rolled over, bile splashed up my throat. "Ryan, I'm going to be…" my head fell back to the couch, "…sick."

Ryan got up, went to the kitchen, opening and closing cupboards. He put a bowl up to my chin and propped me upright. Arm around my shoulders, he held my poisoned body as my guts traveled up my esophagus destined for the pan. My body convulsed and when it had rid itself of all the undigested alcohol, it continued to ripple, punishing me through a series of dry heaves. Flashes of foolish words and actions toward a stranger in a bar hung on the periphery of my memory.

Ryan's long-fingered hand touched my bare back. "Abbey," he whispered, stroking my hair. "I'm going to carry you into the bathroom. You can't walk, and there's glass all over this floor." Frustration and concern threaded through his tone.

"Ryan, please leave. I'll be fine." I hated sounding pitiful, the focus of need.

"You're not fine and I'm not going anywhere until I'm sure you are." He hoisted my limp body from the couch and carried me to my bed, then explained how he was going to take off my jeans so I could shower.

We both exchanged odd looks as I reached for the buttons of my jeans. I kept still while he struggled to yank them down my legs, awkward in his handling of such tight jeans. I was more concerned about how my noodle legs would support me in the shower than what Ryan might be thinking.

"If I get you to the bathroom, do you think you can remove these and take a shower by yourself?" He touched the leg edge of my bikini cut cotton underwear. "You need to rinse this cut." He looked down at the dried blood covering my foot.

I smacked my lips together. Cotton was growing in my mouth and the taste of bile coated my tongue. "I don't think I can." I looked at his puppy face. "Why did you come by?"

"To see how you were. I thought it was strange your Jeep wasn't here, but when I called your parents' house earlier, they said you were at home. I came in to see if you were all right."

"Why?"

"Your mom said you were upset yesterday, asked if I'd check on you."

"Damn her."

"She just cares about you and she knows this is hard on you. Hell, it's hard on the whole family."

"Let's not talk about my mother."

"Where's your Jeep?" He offered me a hand to sit up.

"I left it at Dallas Nightclub last night." I propped myself on the edge of the bed.

"How did you get home?" His brown eyes wide, questioning me.

"Ryan."

His eyes investigated my face as if they were the fingers of a blind man exploring a stranger's features. "Never mind," he said in a tone of defeat. "It doesn't matter."

"It does," I said as I brushed his arm with my hand. My lack of explanation would snip the weak strands that kept us together.

"No, Abbey, we're friends, you don't owe me an explanation."

"But I…"

'Nothing happened because the cowboy didn't want me' didn't seem like a good answer. Although Ryan had taken his time backing away while trying to assume the role of friend in my life, it was still painful for him, just as it had been for me when I saw the blonde. Human relationships are crazy fucked-up things.

He tossed me a quizzical look. "Let's get you a shower." He held me up while I brushed the coating off my teeth and splashed some water on my face. I turned and leaned against the counter. He knelt on the floor, pulled my panties down my legs, helping me step out of them. He lifted his head, his eyes creeping up my legs as he stood. He shook his head. "Christ, Abbey, I—"

"It's okay." I touched his face, but he moved and my hand fell to my side.

"No, it's not okay."

"You're helping. I don't expect anything more."

"Nothing can happen." He sounded like a priest convincing an adolescent to stay clear from the throes of sin. "This needs to be a friendship without sex. Maybe you can do both, have sex and be friends, but after three years, I can't."

That's why Ryan had been pulling away, needing a distance that would allow for a friendship without physical intimacy.

"I know." I raised both hands to my temples.

He blinked as he stared at his jeans. "I guess I can take these off." He slid his loose faded jeans from his long legs, revealing boxer shorts covered with bright green frogs. I had to hold down the laughter in my throat.

"What?"

"Nothing," I said through weak giggles.

"I like these." He yanked his t-shirt over his head, then turned on the shower. "Let's just do this." He reached for my arm.

"You're going to take a shower in those?" I looked down

at his frog underwear.

"Well, I'm not going to be naked."

"Come on, Ryan, I don't want anything to happen either. We've known each other forever. It'd be like brother and sister. I won't look, and anyway you'd have wet underwear all day."

"First of all, I don't know any brothers and sisters in their thirties who take showers together. Besides, I know you. You just can't help yourself when you're around Peter." His eyes scrunched into slits and a smile consumed his face.

"Oh, yeah? Well, here, let me try." I said, batting at his boxers, still weak as I leaned against the bathroom counter.

"Patience, madwoman." He crawled out of the loose shorts.

He held me around the waist and guided me to the shower. I leaned into him, enjoying the heat of his naked body against mine. The hot water cascaded down my body, making me feel human for the first time since my eyelids opened. Ryan squirted some liquid soap into his hand and offered it to me.

"You do it," I said, as I braced my arm against the tiled shower wall. I needed to feel his acceptance envelop me.

"Abbey."

"Please."

He ran his slippery hands over my shoulders and down my back, hesitating when he reached the small of my back. Then his hand followed the curve of my bottom, then down my legs. Breathing became an effort, my chest, dipping then expanding to the rhythm of his hands. My lungs relaxed for a moment when he cleaned my cut foot. He refilled his hands with the soap and rubbed both hands up and down my belly, avoiding the land mines above and below.

I wrapped my hands around his wrist and slid them up to my chest. He stood behind me, pressing into my butt, his soapy hands washing my breasts with care, even tenderness.

He whispered in my ear, "Why are you so destructive, Abbey? What are you trying to prove?"

I turned around and hugged him. His trembling arms encircled me, the arms of a man trying to control a jackhammer. The dam broke, the one stopping the tears that had hung in my throat for two months, and the salty river ran down my cheeks, mixing with the shower water. When he tried to release me, I held him tighter.

"You're crying?" He couldn't hide his surprise.

I choked out a "no," sucking in my breath, trying to stop the tears.

Holding my hand, Ryan stepped from the shower. He grabbed a towel and wrapped it around me. I dried my body. He turned away from me, dried himself, and wrapped the towel around his waist.

"You feel better?" He faced me again.

"Much." I lowered my head, feeling awkward, as if we were young teens, seeing each other's bare bodies for the first time.

"Let's get some aspirin down you and then off to bed."

I swallowed a couple of pills and Ryan helped me wiggle under the sheets and blanket.

"I'm going to clean up the glass while you nap. Later I'll take you to get your car." He kissed my forehead.

I grabbed his arm and pulled him closer. "Thanks for

taking care of me."

"We're friends, remember?" He stiffened against my pull. "Friends."

It was a declaration, something he had thought about and now would make come to fruition. He took a stance. I sensed it in his stiff shoulders, the way his body fought back from yearning. The way he stood back firm from my touch, as if he was a recovering alcoholic and I was a bottle of booze.

"Will you hold me?" I hated the way my voice begged.

He backed away, staring at the ceiling. "Seriously, Abbey, there's nothing I'd rather do than slip under those sheets and be with you, hold you, be inside you, but I'm not going to, because I'll be right back where I've been for years, wanting you, and that's not a fun place to be." He walked toward the door. "I'm going to clean up."

"Why?" I already knew the answer. How could he keep extending with nothing but insouciance in return?

He stopped. "Why what?"

"Why isn't it a fun place to be?"

"Shit, this is stupid. You know why."

He was right, but I didn't want him to leave. I rolled to my side and propped my head on my hand. "Well, why?"

He stood in the doorway, motionless.

"Ryan?"

"Let me tell you a story," he said.

"All right."

"Remember the stories I told you about growing up, how my parents were real poor when I was young? The house I showed you in Victoria, Texas, remember?" He kept his eyes on my face, locked, so I could not turn my head.

"Yes."

"When we lived there, a boy my age had a brand new red bike. I thought it was the most beautiful bike I'd ever seen. I asked my parents for one, but they said 'not this year.' So I rode his bike when he let me, but I could never take it home. I always had to leave it at his house because it wasn't mine."

He went silent, as he stared at the wall. "I dreamed about that red bike, thinking next year I would get one. I thought about waking up and seeing my red bike sitting on the front lawn. Riding it to play with friends, then riding it home because it was mine. I spent a whole year with all my eight-year-old thoughts swirling around that red bike. The next year came and my parents hugged me, saying they still could not buy me a bike like Tom's. I made myself quit wanting it, made myself not think about it, or else the aching would start again. I realized how destructive it is to long for things you can't have."

"But you've had me." My own statement reeked of vapidness.

"No, Abbey, I've had your body, sometimes your mind, but never your heart. You keep it locked away, bound up tight so no one can get to it. I'm tired of trying, just like I got tired of wanting the... red bike." He choked on the last two words, then stepped back, out of my room.

He had never stopped wanting the red bike. He'd just made a decision not to think about it.

As Ryan swept my indiscretions into a garbage bag, the scraping of glass on the floor kept me tossing. I tried to stay awake, think about Ryan's words. The wall I'd built to keep my mother out was thick and I had locked out everybody.

MY HEAD DROWNED IN THE pillow and the day was dead before I woke again to Ryan's voice.

"Abbey," he said, "your car's out front. Jake went with me to get it. Everything's cleaned up."

He leaned over the bed and kissed my forehead. "Take care and stay away from the gin."

"Thank you." I grabbed his hand. "Ryan, about my Jeep and the way I've been—"

"Never mind. We've already decided we're better off as friends." His tone was flat.

"Have we?" I felt a desperate need to have him back.

"Jesus, Abbey, why are you dragging me down this path? You haven't wanted to talk about us in any real way since we've been together and now you want to talk!"

I squeezed his hand. "I just didn't think I could do the relationship thing before."

His eyes bore into me. "Spare me the semantics. 'I can't do this' is what I've heard over and over again from you, sometimes loosely disguised, but basically the same thing. It means nothing! 'I found a new man' means something. 'I discovered I'm a lesbian' delivers a message. But 'I can't do this' is void of any meaning."

He pulled away and towered over my bed, crossing his arms over his chest.

"Okay. I just freaked out because it seems like you've changed, the business, the sports utility vehicle, all that boring yuppie stuff."

My voice started out soft, but the volume escalated. "Now you're building a house. All the things we said were trivial and meaningless. We were going to do real stuff with our lives, travel, make music, save the animals, hell, save the world."

I preached, turning my palms upward. "Remember, we weren't going to be part of those ordinary people, living in some numbered house, in some neighborhood some- where?" I let out a soft scream to show him the maddening effect this kind of life could have on someone.

Ryan forced his lips straight, diminishing the usual natural grin. "That's your reasoning, Abbey? So if I'd go back to selling records for minimum wage, you'd want me?"

His tone projected a challenge. "You'd marry me because I didn't have a future? That makes a hell of a lot of sense. I'm calling bullshit on that one. You were putting me off when I was that guy. Now I'm a guy with a future and you're still doing it. This is on you."

The words 'marry me' shut me down. I didn't know what to say.

"Come on, Ab, be honest with yourself. What is it, really?"

His question by itself made me want to cry, even though I didn't know the answer, not enough to say it.

"I just thought we both agreed we didn't want our parents' lives, remember? It's like you're selling out." I patted a spot on the bed next to me.

Ryan shook his head and refused to sit for the chat I wanted.

"I already called bullshit on your lack of commitment before I changed. Also, depends. What's selling out?" He shrugged. "Tommy, the kid down the street, got the red bike, but three years later his parents divorced. I didn't get the bike, but my parents held on. Not sure they always wanted to, but they did. They gave me something, security, and I've been thinking about it a lot lately. About my parents, your parents, those are the real heroes. Not all those people going off on self-fulfilling crusades. It's the people living in all those boring neighborhoods, struggling each day to stay married and raise their children, so those kids feel safe enough to travel and discover themselves, the way you have. I realized just who the real heroes are, and it's the very people I've avoided being like."

He spread his arms wide. "Now I look at my parents, your parents, Joe and Ann, the neighbors down the street, married for thirty-five years, and I wonder how they did it. I see your father, desperate to hang on to your mother, because he had something so many people wish they had, and he wants to grow old with the love of his life. I want that."

I swallowed the tears. "But that's the problem. Not everything is what it seems. I have no desire to have what my parents have. My mother does not warrant the title of hero."

Ryan clenched his jaw and shook his head. "You asked why I changed, and I told you. I know who the heroes are. You're right, we *are* in different places."

He threw his arms up and walked toward the door. "The place you're at is killing you. Maybe you should do like the

rest of the yuppies you despise, pay some fucking psychiatrist ten thousand dollars to tell you that you hate your
mother. For Christ's sakes, get it over with."

"That's not fair. I'm not like them."

He raised his arms in the air again and hurled his words
like stones. "You're not? Why? You don't have a big house?
You don't care about money? You're worse, Abbey, because
you run to remote places and hide behind the lens of some
camera, then criticize people who are just trying to love, the
whole time blaming your anger on your mother. Well, look
in the mirror, I bet you'll see your mother."

"Stop!" I screeched.

"Because we're actually saying something? Make a decision to go see a psychiatrist now. Tell him how confused you
are because you hate her and she's dying. Or go after she
dies and tell him how much you hate yourself because you
didn't love her when she was alive."

"Damn it, Ryan, you're a bastard." I shook my fist at
him, my body shaking. A strange wetness streamed down
my cheeks.

Only a few feet from the door, he stared at me, as if
he knew he should hug me, say he was sorry. He stood
motionless as he watched the salty water drip from my chin.
"Abbey," he said as he handed me a tissue, "I'm leaving."

My words were waterlogged. I let him walk out and
cried even harder when the door slammed shut. Tears
marched down my cheeks, each tear representing a different
sadness. Most of them I couldn't name, couldn't give them
purpose. I thought about the first time I had been drawn to
his smug grin, the one that was forever painted on the face
of the old Ryan.

CHAPTER 16

A little over three years ago, I fell for that grin at the Oasis, an outdoor bar/restaurant with several decks overlooking Lake Travis. The Oasis, a place where Austinites gathered to celebrate the sunset. People watched with anticipation as the orange orb faded behind the hills that courted the lake to the west. When the sun disappeared, leaving behind a faint pink glow reflecting off the blue lake, the crowd stood, clapping and cheering. The round of applause went to the star of the ball, who would make her next appearance after a night of rest.

I turned from the bar, a margarita in each hand, and smashed into a nice-looking guy, drinks covering both of us. The sticky liquid oozed down my arms and dripped from his beard. Through laughter I said, "Sorry about the margarita bath."

"No problem, saves me some bucks. That's what I was drinking."

"Yeah, now you can just lick it off your shirt."

His mouth crawled upwards, his eyes smiling at me, an impish grin consuming his face. He cupped my elbow in his hand and brought my arm to his mouth. Tilting his head slightly, he licked the sweet intoxicant from my skin. I wanted to back away, yell 'weirdo,' but I didn't. I stepped closer.

"At that rate, it'll take you all night," I said, controlled, without removing my eyes from his expressive root-beer-colored circles.

"I hope so."

I jerked back my arm. "I need to order a couple more drinks and get back."

"Someone waiting?" He kept his eyes on me.

His lips, tongue, and rough edges of beard were gone, but my skin held their imprint. "Yes," I said, with a slight thread of guilt.

"In that case, let me buy you two more and send you and your sugary skin on their way." He turned and, despite my protests, bought me two margaritas.

He handed me the drinks. "Nice to meet you. I'm Ryan, and you are… Sugar girl?"

"Hardly. It's Abbey. No one would ever use the word 'sugar' to describe me."

"All depends on the circumstances, doesn't it?" He winked. "Again, nice meeting you, Abbey..."

"Gallagher, Abigail Gallagher. Thanks for the drinks."

His image stayed with me even as I talked with my date, one of my brother's set-ups from school. Later, I excused myself to the restroom, and went on a quick search for Ryan, the Margarita Man. As the night pushed the sun farther behind the hills leaving dusky light, the Oasis was a muted maze of stairs, tables, and bars, and all the bodies seemed like small mice scampering past me in every direction. I looked for him, but to no avail.

How many guys in Hawaiian shirts, shorts that looked like boxers, golden hair and a beard, wearing Birkenstocks could there be? A lot, I decided, remembering I was in Austin. I left without a second encounter.

I AWOKE THE NEXT MORNING TO loud knocking at my front door. Groggy, my head hanging on to a numbing headache, I rolled over. The red block numbers on the clock read eight-thirty. I thought it might be my brother because he was the only person I knew who would just drop by unannounced.

The person leaned on the doorbell as if I was hard of hearing. "All right, Ethan, hold on," I screamed. My face scrunched up with irritation as I grabbed the door handle, pulling it open.

There he stood in the same boxer shorts, Hawaiian shirt, and mussed hair, unevenly cut, the ends looping up, creating a true bed head. He held a bag from McDonald's in one hand, in the other, a silver thermos. "How did you know it was me?" he said, a smile peeking out from behind his mustache and beard.

"I thought you were Ethan, my brother. What the hell are you doing here? How'd you find where I live?"

"I looked it up on the Internet, not hard. But this certainly isn't the kind of greeting I expected."

"Excuse me, I forgot the trumpets. You're here, so what do you want?" I rubbed my eyelids.

He dug in his pocket and handed me an envelope. "This is for last night."

I returned a puzzled look.

"Cleaning bill," he said.

"What?"

"Yeah, it's a very valuable shirt. Are you going to invite me in?"

"No. I, um, mean..." I looked down at my robe.

He held up the McDonald's bag. "Someone's got to help me eat all this."

"Well."

"Really, I'm not a weirdo, I just wanted to share some breakfast."

"That sounds exactly like something a weirdo would say. Just a minute." I slammed the door shut and ran back to my room, threw on a t-shirt and pair of worn gray sweatpants.

I opened the door and moved my body sideways. "Come in."

"You didn't have to get dressed up just for me."

I rolled my eyes, then followed him through the foyer and watched as he made himself at home, setting two places, using McDonald's napkins and plastic forks, at the small granite breakfast table. Then he displayed a breakfast of muffins, eggs, sausage, and hash-browns alongside the napkins. "Do you have any coffee mugs?"

I smiled. "Yes"

"This is gourmet coffee, ground the beans this morning. I just can't break down and drink Mickey D's coffee."

He poured us both a cup. We shared breakfast, and spent the morning laughing at his stories about him and his brother. They were in a band together and had also embarked on several businesses, most of which had failed. He made it clear he was not designed for the nine-to-five business world, and it was just a matter of time before he and his brother got a break with their band or a business took off.

Later we sat on the sofa and I showed him pictures of animals from all over the world. I told him that my chosen profession, as a freelance photographer specializing in wildlife, took me away from home most of the time, but I had bought a condo in Austin so I could see my brother and father between assignments.

He asked about my mother and I said, "And her, too." His eyes squinted with concern but he didn't probe and I didn't offer any explanation. We talked about travel, the places we had both been. After two cups of coffee and four hours of conversation, last night's margaritas and too little sleep settled in my body. I craved rest.

"I really need a nap," I laid my hand to my forehead. "Too many margaritas."

"No problem." He stood. "Well, thanks for sharing breakfast with me." He winked. "My number is on the bill."

I followed him to the door. He stepped outside, turned and smiled.

"Question?" I said, smirking.

"Anything," he said, raising his arms in the air.

Holding on to the door-frame, I swung my body toward him. "How did you know I was alone? I mean, I had a date last night."

His hands grabbed my sides, easing my body into his. His fingers spread across my ribcage. Powerful long fingers. He tilted his head forward, his beard coming towards my face, he opened his mouth, my lips opened in response. He buried his tongue into my mouth, then licked my lips. He lifted his head back. "I saw him." He grinned. "You're too much for him."

"And you're cocky." I pulled away, but he moved forward and we were drawn into each other, locked in a kiss that made my headache dissipate and my stomach twist.

"I have neighbors," I said in a hushed voice.

"Lucky them," he said.

I planted both hands on his chest and pushed him back.

"Sorry, I'm getting ahead of things." He stepped back. "I've got to get out of here. Let me know when you want to pay your bill."

I watched him stuff his long legs into a small red truck that was clinging to its last days. After stepping back into the house, I grabbed the envelope from the kitchen counter. It read, 'You owe me pizza, beer, and a movie.'

I threw the bill down and ran outside. His truck was taking its time backing out of the long driveway that led to my condo. He saw me and stopped. He stuck his head out the window and yelled, "What's up?"

My face turned hot, like I was on stage before a large audience and everyone was waiting for my line, but I'd never read the script. A long minute passed and I wanted to run back inside.

"Abbey?"

"Your bill, uh… I don't know."

"Let it go. I kinda got carried away with myself. Didn't mean to freak you out."

I walked to his truck, balancing on the balls of my feet because the pavement steamed with early afternoon heat. I put both elbows on the ledge of the truck window and rested my chin in my hands. A glint of sadness, of unrealized dreams, inhabited his eyes and I wondered what this fly-by-the-seat-of-your-pants guy was running from.

"I'm ready to pay you back. I knew it was an expensive shirt when I saw it, probably belonged to some ancient Hawaiian god."

The corners of his mouth turned up, his cocky grin returned, and bits of insecurity seemed to evaporate in the sun.

"So how about it, pizza, beer and... maybe, *Titanic*?"

"*Titanic*?" he said. "No way, I don't want you to see me cry on our first date."

"I just thought something really long would be good." At that moment, I wanted to fill my hands with his pinkish cheeks. They looked as if he spent time in the sun often. When he smiled, small indentations formed below his eyes on both sides of the rosy balls.

"Is seven okay? That would give me time to...." he looked down, eyeing his disheveled clothes. "Well, take a shower and put on some clean clothes."

"Seven-thirty and you bring the beer," I pecked him on the cheek and walked away.

Seven-thirty seemed years away. I bought all the ingredients to make homemade pizza, picked up the movie, then called my brother for instructions.

He laughed. "You're cooking?"

In spite of his laughter, I got the recipe and felt confident that I could make the pizza.

After a shower, I twisted my long auburn hair into a knot, and put on my shortest denim shorts that sucked to my round butt, the material stopping an inch below my cheeks at the top of my long legs. I rummaged through my closet until I found the white embroidered shirt with small pearlescent buttons I'd bought in India.

When the knock at the front door came, my hands were twisted in dough, and a snow flurry of flour covered the counters. By this time, I realized that trying to make the pizza myself wasn't a great idea.

I yelled for him to come in. He walked into the kitchen, set the beer down, and stared at me, then broke into laughter so hard, he bent at the waist.

I stared back.

"Abbey, you're making the pizza?" His eyes grew wide as he scanned the mess that seemed to conceal every counter of my kitchen.

As I stood among the shroud of ingredients strewn around the kitchen, taking in his obvious understanding of the big failure underway, my face flushed, a combination of embarrassment, irritation, and anger. How did he know I wasn't a cook?

A little too fast I jumped. "Yes, damn it! I know how to make pizza."

"Sure you do." He cocked his head to the side. "Let me help."

"No. You sit down and drink a beer while I make this fucking pizza." I flipped him a caustic smile.

"Chill," he said, with a shrug of his shoulders.

I never finished the pizza and I think it was he who suggested we order out. Leaning against the counter drinking beer and talking, I learned he had a computer science degree from UT Austin, but music held his passion, so he'd turned down several jobs, upsetting his parents to a terrible degree.

I listened more than I talked. When his questions translated into a personal inquiry of me, I twisted them back toward him. He answered them openly, talking without hesitation about fears of mediocrity, failure, and worse yet, a contrived sort of happiness that most people developed because the world said that money, cars, and a big home should make us happy.

Inside I agreed with him, never wanting the ordinary and not being content, always pushing for more. I looked with pity upon those women who made having two children, living in a house in "the right" neighborhood and the one family vacation a year seem like heaven. I told myself they were missing the world, they would die and not realize all the exciting places and things that existed.

"Why did you and your last girlfriend break-up?" He had told me they'd dated for more than three years, so it seemed like a reasonable question.

"Well." He took another swig of beer, emptying the bottle. "The answer makes me seem like an ass."

"Slept with someone else? If so, that makes you normal." I handed him another beer.

He blinked at me, then raised his eyebrows.

"There are only two species of primates in this world that are monogamous, the Gibbons, a monkey from Southeast Asia, and the Tamarin monkey from Brazil. I guess the interesting part is that in both species the males and females are the same size."

He nodded and took a swig.

"Also, the males care for the young more than the females.

Not like humans, we aren't designed to be monogamous."

He wore a puzzled look as I ended my speech. I didn't often divulge my primate theory to men, saving it instead for my girlfriends on those nights when the wine flowed nonstop. With wine, the topic of men and relationships sooner or later came to the surface. I used the primates as an example of how unhealthy it was to be glued to one guy. My girlfriends would laugh, cheer the notion, and then go home to their steady boyfriends.

"No, wrong answer," he said, "but I enjoyed the monkey lesson. I take it your relationships don't last long."

I let the last bit of hops flow down my throat, "And why is that?" I placed my hands on my hips.

He alternated moving his palms up and down like a scale weighing something. "Let's see, monogamy," he said, raising his eyebrows, "and long-term relationships. Somehow, the two seem to be synonymous."

"Depends on the security level of the individuals in the relationship. Anyway, let's talk about something else."

"No, I'm interested in your perspective."

"Well, I'm interested in why you broke up with that girl after three years."

"Okay. She wanted to get married, have kids. I don't really know how I feel about marriage, but no way on kids. I refuse to bring a child up in this world." His smile flattened. "But I am into monogamy."

"That's good for you," I said, trying to end the conversation.

He slid down the counter, moving his legs sideways until his hip leaned into my side. His large brown eyes searched my face. "And you, how long do your relationships last?"

He stood dangerously close, his warm breath brushing against my cheek. I thought to move away, but I didn't want to. I wanted him to shut up and kiss me.

"Longest?" I flicked my eyes away from his intense stare, realizing the answer would say something about me. At twenty-eight I had never had a relationship last more than a year, aside from my ninth grade boyfriend.

He nodded. "Longest."

"Eight months, average relationships have been two to three months. However, I think that says something about men." I cocked one eyebrow, indicating my point had been made, then bent to grab a couple of beers from the refrigerator.

He moved behind me, his torso bending into me and before my hand reached the beer, his hand traveled up the back of my knee, "Can I?" he whispered.

"Please," a breathy answer escaped my mouth. His touch, the urge in his voice traveling between my legs making me clinch, wanting to feel him.

His fingers slipped under the edge of my shorts, squeezing the bottom of my butt. A gasp escaped my mouth. I shut the refrigerator door.

He pressed himself into me. "Can I touch you here?" he whispered as his long fingers lay on the front of my leg, his fingers inching toward the edge of my shorts.

I nodded. "Mm..mm."

He slid his fingers beneath my shorts, the tips searching the groove between my legs.

"I agree with you, Abbey. It does say something about

those men's level of security," he whispered in my ear as he unzipped the front of my shorts with one hand, while the other hand loosened my hair from the knot on my head, letting it fall to my shoulders. He buried his nose in my damp hair and breathed in deep while his hand explored between my legs.

"Yes." I pushed my crotch toward his touch.

"They must have been incredibly insecure men to let a beautiful woman like you go." He pulled his hand from my shorts. "And yet, you probably still linger with them." He sucked my wetness from the tips of his fingers. "I'm sure forgetting you is no easy task." He gave me a wry smile.

I put my arms around his waist, pulling him in so I could feel him. His tongue teased my mouth, but when I opened mine to kiss him, he pulled away and smiled. I grew impatient and grabbed the back of his loose curled hair, drawing him in and kissing his full lips hard, dragging my teeth along his bottom lip.

"Do you have a condom?" I murmured, my breath ahead of my words.

"Uh, huh." He touched the edge of my chin, "You on anything?"

"I'm on the pill but don't sleep with anyone without a condom, unless it's serious." I spoke fast, wanting to get back to our physical communication. I grabbed the back of his hair, pulling him in again, kissing his neck, then his jaw.

He chuckled under his breath. "Serious…what's that for you, two weeks? Then break up a couple months later."

I jerked my head back, giving him an overexaggerated stern look, knowing he was referring to the average length of my relationships. "What? Think you might want to shut up or your memory of tonight is going to slide from a night of great sex… to you blew the chance to get laid."

He guffawed, wrapping his arms around my lower back. We both bent to the kitchen floor, my butt on the woven rug, while my spine pushed into the tile floor. The evening began there, led to us falling asleep, my butt to his stomach, his arm under my head, and ended three days later when he left my house.

CHAPTER 17

There was a certain urgency among my family to recreate all the unions from the past, so we gathered for a family dinner. My mother hadn't told my father about our fight a week ago, else my father would have said something to me. His solidarity to his cheating bride was stronger than ever.

Whatever it was she said we had to talk about didn't come up. Maybe my mother didn't want me to know or was too scared to tell me. Anyway, she didn't broach it again.

And as for me, I acted cordial, but the words exchanged that day set us back and I wondered if it would be possible for us to come together at all before the end. I still arrived to be with her on my scheduled days, Tuesdays and Thursdays, but a morbid silence occupied the moments between our few words and in some ways, I felt as weak as she looked. I didn't have the energy to pretend, to go on striving to be close to a woman who refused to give up living a lie.

I just wanted to get it over with. Each day her tenacious illness chipped away at my world.

Dad cooked fajita meat on the grill, while Ethan and José were in charge of beans and rice. My job was easy: prepare all the condiments to go with meat rolled into a tortilla, sour cream, guacamole, grated cheese, and diced tomatoes.

Mom lay propped on a lawn chair in the screened-in back porch, watching my father.

Less than three months had passed since my mother first learned cancer was running wild in her body. Her pain seemed to intensify daily until she spent almost all her moments grimacing and rubbing the small of her back, like the pain was born there.

That day, as I watched my father ease her into the lawn chair and lay a knitted blanket over her thin frame, I knew she wasn't going to live. The cancer had not yielded.

She tried to conceal the grimace with bright red lipstick and fashionable clothes, but I saw through her forced smile to a dead woman. Cancer had already crossed the finish line, raised both its fists in victory, but it would allow her to stay a while longer, so she could feel its triumph tromp through her body.

Other than during a few breakdowns, my dad didn't believe she would die. Day to day, he was confident she would live. I wondered what he thought when he helped her shower or change clothes, looking at her plagued body, so far from the woman he had married. How it felt to kiss her? Like kissing the cold ground.

Only sprigs of hair were left on her head. Today she wore a dark wig that curled around her chin, in the style of Jackie Kennedy's hair, in a way her own hair never did. It had been thick and straight and she always let it grow past her shoulders, even after fifty. She thought the longer length made her appear younger.

She was right. On several occasions, men twenty years her junior turned their heads to take in all of her, followed her precise walk with their eyes, wishing they knew a woman like her. She swam in the attention; I saw it in her coy smiles, her half curtseys when men complimented her, the tilt of her head when men looked her way.

"Abbey, can you bring me a large platter?" my father yelled from the back porch.

"Just a minute." I finished chopping the last tomato and grabbed a plate from the cabinet.

"Christ, you two. Enough! You haven't been able to keeps your hands off of each other since you got here."

Ethan stepped back from José in front of the fireplace. "Come on, Abbey, he just got back from Santa Fe this morning. We haven't had any time to be together."

"Boo hoo, I'm broken up," I said, rolling my eyes and walking past them.

José laughed. "I thought gay men were supposed to have the market cornered on the mordant sense of humor."

"Oh, no," Ethan said with a chuckle. "Abbey definitely wins that award, and we have yet to find the seed of its origin."

"Excuse me," I said in fake huffy tone. "I have a very light and jovial sense of humor."

"Light," José said. "Yes, very light."

Ethan snickered and leaned into José, kissing him on the cheek.

"All right, I'm leaving you two for a couple of minutes, so use it wisely." I walked toward the back door.

"Here, Dad." I handed him the platter.

"Thanks." He took the platter from my hand and stared at me for a minute, I felt my mother's eyes join his stare.

"What?"

Dad glanced at her, then at me. "Nothing, I was just thinking, what a wonderful woman you've turned out to be."

"Dad." My face heated from his words and I wished he hadn't said that in front of my mother.

My mom raised her eyes and stared at my father, as if they were having a silent conversation. Then she looked at me and again that dichotomous expression penetrated me.

"Well, I need to finish in there." I turned to walk away, trying to sound casual.

Once inside, I ran to the bathroom, cupped cold water in my hands, and brought it to my mouth. My mom seemed an odd cross between proud and agonizing, an expression I noticed since I was a teenager, one that always made me want to retreat into my little girl body. I sat on the edge of the tub and put my head between my legs, my breathing was labored. I wished I had a paper bag.

"Where's Abbey?" Dad called to Ethan, his voice carrying down the hall. "We're ready to eat."

After I splashed more water on my face, I joined my family for our evening meal. The tension churned, rising in the room. Tension that comes when everyone pretends to be polite, acts as if you only met yesterday.

The table remained quiet through the whole meal, broken-up only by José's interjections on the new gallery he had opened. He had been doing a lot of shopping and design work the last month.

I nibbled a few bites, even less than my mother. I couldn't bring myself to eat. The forced family unions came across as so surreal. No one talked about it in front of her and everyone whispered about it when she slept. I was tired, not of helping, just so fucking tired of myself in the middle of the murky cancer war.

Following dinner, I insisted on cleaning the kitchen, encouraging the others to retreat to the living room. After I cleared the table, I loaded the dishwasher. First, the dishes went straight across, lining the back, then the larger bowls in front, and only cups and glasses on top. I'd learned years ago, from my mother, the specific way to do everything in life. As I finished wiping the kitchen counter, laughter filtered in from the living room, along with the sporadic tapping of piano keys.

My mother sat on the piano bench, my father, in a chair beside her using his broad hands to support her back, and my brother had nudged in next to her on the bench. José stood, one hand on Ethan's shoulder.

"Come on, Mom, one song. I'll play with you," Ethan said.

"No, no, you play, I'll listen."

Ethan played an old Ann Murray song and they all sat still. I leaned against the piano and let the notes float around my ears.

Then my mom and Ethan played a Linda Ronstandt song, "Love Is A Rose," and they hummed the tune.

My father threw his head back and clapped his spare hand to his knee. "Bravo, bravo."

"I'm leaving if you all break into Johnny Cash and Dad starts singing 'Black Sunday.'" I tried to sound light.

José concurred. We were having fun. It was one of those

family pictures you see on sitcoms where the family gathers around the piano and struggles to sing a variety of out-of-date songs from a limited repertoire.

My mom moved her hand from the keys and lovingly stroked my father's arm. "This one is for you, Frank," she said in a hoarse voice.

Ethan laid his hands in his lap and tilted his head to watch my mother sing.

She cleared her throat.

Her fragile hands played the keys, bones clicking on ivory boards, as she sang the words, "I'm on top of the world looking down on creation and the only explanation I can find is the love that I found ever since you been around."

She sang, her neck arching upwards like a sparrow during the first spring days. A strained voice now replaced her dulcet tone. My mother never would've sung without a clear and clean voice in the past, something unthinkable, but not this day. Death was too close for such cares, or perhaps she knew she would never sing without the sound of sickness afflicting her voice.

Tears filled my father's eyes.

"Oh, Frank," she whispered.

"Please, keep singing," he said.

Please don't, I thought. For Christ's sake, the whole marriage has been a farce and now in front of us she professes her love for him, *sings it*, no less.

She warbled again in her raspy voice, her eyes on him. "The only explanation I can find is the love that I found ever since you been around. You put me on top of the world..."

I couldn't stand it. I leaned forward and hit the keys

with the palm of my hand. My fingers hit several keys and the sound, muddled musical notes, bounced off the walls, assaulting my ears. Someone jabbed my side.

"Abbey," my brother said under his breath, a disturbed look on his face.

"Sorry, I tripped."

I stepped back from the piano. If I'd been fifteen years younger, my father would have told me to go to my room and never come out. When he looked from my mother to me, a commingling of anger and sadness distorted his face.

My mother just stared at the ivory and black keys, her face washed blanche.

"I have to go." I said, shaking by head. "I have to go."

I grabbed my jean jacket from the couch and made my way to the door. Why didn't I let her have her moment, if not for her, for my father? God, she's dying, Abbey, I told myself, disgusted with my own actions. But every time pain of her loss swelled in me, I smashed it with old bitterness.

I was just outside when Ethan came up behind me. "Goddamn it, Abbey, what was that all about?" He grabbed my shoulder.

I didn't turn. "Nothing, I told you I tripped."

He circled me until he stood in front of me. "Are you really this fucking selfish and, God…" He tossed his head like he was dog flinging water from his hair. "…screwed up, because I'm telling you, this isn't how normal people with good parents act."

"You're giving me a lesson on normal?"

"That wasn't fair." He yelled.

I had rarely seen Ethan angry enough to raise his voice.

His nature didn't allow it.

José walked up behind Ethan. "Sweetheart, enough," he said.

"Jesus, José, you saw that shit in there," he said, turning to look at his lover.

José slid his arm around Ethan's shoulders. He stood at least four inches taller than Ethan and he was also muscular, more masculine looking, something that had never occurred to me. But what I also saw was how much he loved Ethan and how great his desire was to protect and nurture him, just like my mother had done.

"Did you hear that stuff about me not being normal?" Ethan said.

"She didn't mean that. She's the last person who'd think that." José bore his intense black eyes into me. "Right, Abbey?" His words were stated as a fact, not a question.

Inside, I was crumbling. I didn't even feel comfortable in my own skin. As I stood there looking at my brother and José, and witnessing his unconditional love for our mother and then the love between the two of them, I wanted to scream.

I hung my head and stared down at my own feet. "No, Christ, Ethan. You know I don't see you like that."

"We don't know how much longer we have with her," he said, his tone softening.

"Oh, please, as if she and I ever had anything together."

"She's always been your biggest cheerleader. You should hear her tell her friends about your travels. She even boasts about all the men you have chasing you. I think her exact words were, 'Abigail just has so many options, that's her problem. Someday she'll make a decision. It's hard for her to choose just one, with all those men out there vying for her attention.' "

"She should know."

"You don't let up, do you? What do you mean by that?"

"Nothing, you're right. I am just this fucked up."

"I just think you should take a deep breath and try to see her for who she is."

"I do. I have to go."

"I'm really worried about you. You can't keep turning your back on everybody."

"Aren't you curious about the photos we saw?" I said.

"No. Mom has a right to her secrets and her life, just as you do."

"I'm out of here. I'll see you tomorrow."

"Abbey!" Ethan called after me.

"Let her go," José said.

DOES SHE HAVE A RIGHT TO her secrets? I whispered to myself. Does she?

The nights were growing cooler, fall being sucked away by winter.

I had intended to go home, sleep off the anger. But I couldn't. For someone who seemed to have everything going for her, I was dangerously close to throwing it away. Some of it, I already had, and I wanted to, as if the more I punished myself, the more pain she'd feel.

I went to the convenience store and decided on a six-pack of strawberry wine coolers. They would remind me of a less complicated time. At the checkout stand I was struck by one of those cheesy tabloid magazines that was professing the latest story on Oprah, 'Oprah's Secret Life, Three-Way Love Triangle.'

I laughed as I pictured Oprah standing up on stage in the middle of her show and giving everybody who had ever said anything bad about her 'the finger.' I wished she'd do that just once. Tell all those people who acted like overly critical mothers to 'fuck off.'

But then she wouldn't be Oprah, the mocha angel, delivering everybody pieces of their lost spirit in the palms of her generous hands. I smiled thinking about her handing me a piece of my soul. 'Here, Abbey.'

I hoped I'd be humble enough to accept it. But she couldn't deliver my spirit to me because I didn't even know where to tell her to look.

I swigged down strawberry wine coolers and drove around the Texas Hill Country, stopping at random to stare at the luminous circle in the black sky. It reminded me of the times Sheila, Jennifer, and I grabbed the cheapest crap sold at convenience stores, stuffed the bottles in our backpacks, and climbed the stone steps leading to the top of Mount Bonnell, which overlooks the winding Colorado River and furnishes a view of West Austin's twinkling night lights.

We'd taken turns creating scenes for our future. I said, 'Okay, ten years from now, Saturday at six o'clock.' Then Sheila or Jennifer gave a detailed description of what they would be doing at that precise time between gulps of syrupy wine coolers. We laughed, until we almost cried at some of the possibilities for the future. None of mine had included caring for my dying mother while still disdaining her.

After parking my car on the side of the road, I walked toward Sheila's house, staring down at my feet, encouraging them to keep straight. The street light illuminated the complicated pattern of pearl strings crisscrossing the sidewalk, a sort of natural hopscotch board left behind by slugs crossing from one green swatch to another. Sheila's two-bedroom cottage rested in a strange neighborhood, an amalgamation of trendy yuppie homes and run-down shacks where people displayed their treasures on the front lawn. Her radio show would end in a few minutes and unless she was going out, she would be strolling up the sidewalk soon.

I sat on the cold cement step in front of her house, beside me the two remaining wine coolers. I opened another one and cried. Between sobs I drank sweet strawberry liquor. I bent over and rested my chin on my knees, then stared at the sidewalk and cried some more.

Most of my own miseries were not made by others, but were a product of my own mind. Why hadn't I just asked her about the other man, heard with my own ears her story? But then I would know the whole truth, and it may be more painful than the bits and pieces I had melded together creating my own story.

I would rather punish her by remaining knotted, letting her witness the twisted thoughts of her daughter spurred by her weakness. I had been so engrossed in my misery that I didn't notice Sheila coming until a pair of lime green, square-toed, vinyl boots on the sidewalk appeared at my feet. I lifted my head, mucous running from my nose and tears streaming from my eyes. I wiped my face on the sleeve of my denim jacket.

"Abbey?" Sheila sat beside me, trying not to stare at my swollen face.

"I'm completely fucked up. The most fucked up person I know," I said between sobs.

"Let's go inside." Sheila tucked her arm under my shoulder and pulled me to standing.

I reached for my last wine cooler.

"Nope, you don't want that."

"Yes, I do. I'm sorry I should have gotten you a six pack, but I'm so fucking selfish I didn't even think about it."

"That's okay. I gave those up for Lent at least eight years ago and I've never looked back. Pretty brave of me, huh?"

I smiled beneath my tears.

Inside I dropped to the couch and Sheila fixed me coffee. She returned with two cups and sat beside me.

"Ab, you're just having a hard time because of your mother."

"No, that's what's making the way I am so obvious to everyone, but I've always been like this."

"Like what?"

"Fucked up."

"All right, just drink your coffee."

I sucked in, pulling the tears back. "Ryan and I really broke up. You know we were doing that whole 'friends' thing and then, well shit…"

"The 'friend' thing is hard to just jump into, especially when two people have been together for a long time and when one side has other expectations. That may work in books or movies, but in real life two people need distance before they can go into that whole 'friends' mode. You know, get the longing out of their systems."

"Well, I don't know if we'll ever get back to being friends. I've been so distant to him."

"I think you'll be friends again."

"I don't know." I sniffed some of the mucus back into my nose. "I even managed to piss Ryan off, which is a pretty hard task. The last time I saw him, he was definite about ending any possibility. I mean, we're really done."

"I talked to him the other night."

"What did he say?"

"Just that you guys needed time to figure things out."

"Because I'm thirty-one and I don't even know how to name it."

"Name what?"

"How I feel. So it seems easier to be alone and figure things out for myself."

"It's not, Abbey. It may seem easier now, but it gets harder later because the pain, the anger, it doesn't just leave. It stays, waiting until we're vulnerable, and then it erupts."

"I know. Christ, I feel like I'm in one of those oubliettes and I can't find the one door."

"What the hell is an oubliette?"

"It's a dark room where they used to put people a long time ago to forget about them," I said. "Sort of like a dungeon,"

"Most people would have just said hole, as in, I feel like I'm in a hole. But not Abbey."

I smiled at Sheila's twisted expression. "I'd have to dig

myself out of a hole. I don't want to work that hard. I just want to find the door and poof! I'm out, free from all this bullshit." I opened my hands as if smoke would emerge by magic.

"You'll find the door."

"I hope so, because I can't see anything in here."

"Because you don't want to."

"But I do, it's just so mixed up inside my head. I wish my mom and I could be normal, not have all this stuff between us. I just can't seem to let it go. If I could do that with her, then maybe I would be able to have some kind of relationship, without feeling like I need to keep at least one foot out the door. But instead, I fuck other guys when I'm on assignment, just so I can tell myself over and over again how much I don't need any one person."

"It's life patterns we get into, and sometimes we don't even know why we do those destructive things. You only know certain aspects of your mother, and those are what drive your relationship, but we don't see all of our parents. For years I resented my father because he left my mom. In turn, I have spent how many years making fun of men. Destroying any relationship that even bordered on seriousness. All in an attempt to prove I was right about men. It's like I had ascribed to one train of thought, influenced by what I saw with my father, so I've spent most of my twenties proving myself right. But I was wrong. I was wrong about why my father left my mother, and I was wrong about men. Nothing is ever one dimensional."

"Damn, Sheila, that was intense."

"Yeah, well, I know, but I've been proven wrong. Men

aren't that bad."

I clasped my hands over my ears. "Is this really Sheila I'm talking to?"

"Well..." A wide grin consumed her face.

"What?"

"I met somebody and he's the opposite of who you would have pictured me with. An accountant."

"Big question, has he reached puberty yet?"

"Yes," she said laughing. She was well aware of her reputation for hooking up with much younger men. "He even owns a home in the suburbs." Her tone was taunting.

"I can't hear this now. You're throwing in the towel, too?"

"No, just taking off some of the armor," she said winking. "You should try it."

"All I can think about is sleep. My head is too jumbled to process all this."

"Just crash on the couch."

I slipped off my shoes and laid my head on a musty pillow.

Sheila tucked a blanket under my chin. "Tomorrow we'll get some egg burritos and entertain ourselves by looking for some doors," she said, chuckling.

When she reached the entrance to her room, she turned around. "It really is easier when you let people in, Ab."

CHAPTER 18

Ethan called me last night while I was lying on the couch, babying the residue of my hangover, and asked me to come by his place on my way to see Mom. He'd found a special tea, some 'cure all' he'd gotten from an herbalist friend. The herb guy claimed the tea would boost Mom's immune system and help increase her appetite, which was disappearing along with her hair.

He had hinted that perhaps when I gave her the tea, I could also apologize for ruining the family gathering two nights ago.

I drove the stretch of highway that cut Austin in half east and west. Short ugly mesquite trees, attempting in vain to reach the status of majestic red oaks, their branches like the arthritic fingers of an old woman, and knotted live oaks, equal in width and height, crammed the strips of green along the highways. During early spring, bluebonnets and Indian paintbrush were sprinkled throughout Austin and the Hill Country, adding color to combat the starkness of the encroaching asphalt. But in late fall, nature was muted and seemed to blend with the hard surfaces.

Austin was growing faster than anyone had imagined. After an invasion of the technology world, even the native Austinites traded in their Birkenstocks, braids, and guitars for the promising jobs and stocks of the dot.com world. Some said the coexistence between the musical nature lovers and the technology geeks was impossible, but Austin had somehow managed to put both in the ring without any injuries. Perhaps even a mutual respect had evolved.

After parking in front of my brother's house, I plodded to his front door, as if waiting for some laggard part of my body to catch up. I knocked, hoping he was awake at 8:30 on a Saturday. I had told him I'd stop by sometime today, and the hour was early for me as well, except I hadn't been able to get a good night's sleep in a while. So, at the first hint of sunlight, I welcomed the chance to leave the unsettled night between the sheets.

"Who is it?" Ethan's muted voice came from inside.

José opened the door. "Your sister."

I raised an eyebrow, my eyes skimmed his slightly mussed hair and the blue silk robe covering his body. "Did I interrupt?"

He looked at me with an exaggerated frown, his black eyebrows sliding down over his eyes. "What do you think? If it was a choice between sharing a cup of coffee with you and some bedroom fun, do you think anyone would have jumped up and answered the door?"

"Got it." I walked past him into the kitchen.

Clad in a pair of white designer briefs, my brother stood at the counter, grinding coffee beans, his eyes squinting without contacts.

"Ethan, can you put some clothes on?" I said.

"Cover up this sexy body?" He ran his hands up and down his narrow chest. But in a few seconds he came back from his bedroom wearing a pair of jeans and open button down shirt.

"I already called Mom and told her about the tea." He sounded excited, as if he believed some herbs soaking in hot water would provide the answer.

Ethan's relentless research about breast cancer had already taken him on a couple of wild goose chases and I had the feeling this was another. On Ethan's prompting, my mom got weekly massages, drank freshly squeezed juice, burned incense, and learned to meditate.

"I saw her yesterday and she looked really drained. Seeing you will help, if you can manage an apology for the other night."

Without meaning to, I crinkled my nose.

"What?" Ethan said.

"Why does everyone think, if only I'm nice to Mom, that will save her?"

"No one thinks that, Abbey, it's just…"

He motioned for José and me to sit down as he placed fresh pastries and coffee cups on the table.

After a slight hesitation, I sat, not wanting to engage in a lengthy conversation about my mother. In my eyes, we could never have a conversation where my mother's infidelity did not figure, at least subtly, as the fork in my family's history, while all relationships with their understandings and misunderstandings got scrutinized under the exposing lens of deceit.

Now everyone expected me to file away the past and examine everything under the new cancer-scope. Her disease changed things today, but just because a person gets sick doesn't mean history is rewritten.

"Abbey, Mom's been worried about you. You were gone so long and now you come back to this. I think she even feels, as crazy as this sounds, guilty for this, and you and…" He took a long sip.

"And what?" I set my cup on the table.

Ethan always wanted everyone to get along, making him a sort of glue in our family. He had managed to become the center, bringing our family together six years ago when he 'came out' his freshman year at Southern Christian University. He left after his first semester, finishing his degree at UT Austin. He faced an abundance of ridicule and unwarranted shame.

It floored me that in the nineties, society still cast judgment on a person's sexual orientation. Both my parents and I agreed to serve as a united front. My father didn't want anything to affect Ethan's promising future, least of all the religious beliefs of others. Since his freshman year in high school, I knew he was gay. He and I talked, always skirting around the issue. I remember feeling proud that he knew who he was and what he wanted, no matter how much it deviated from society's ideals.

When he visited me while I attended graduate school at NYU, I took him to The Village and introduced him to a couple of gay friends so he could see just how normal they were. I remember telling him, 'Who gets to decide what's normal? A bunch of puritanical white males with predefined roles as kings of whatever social organizations they belong to? No. No!' I pounded my fist on a small wooden table at my regular coffee shop.

He had rolled his eyes and told me not to confuse him being gay with my undefined feminist take on men, which was my excuse to run from men and had nothing to do with his sexuality.

"Even with the cancer, you can't seem to cut Mom a break. And then the idea you may leave again, take that assignment in the Galápagos Islands, is adding more stress. God, she doesn't need it."

"That's my career, and because of all this family stuff, I'm jeopardizing even that. It's all I have." Emotion crept into my tone.

"It's not like Mom planned this. Let's chill with the hostility." Ethan barked, shaking his head.

"She's trying to wedge herself back into my life. After how many years of not caring, now she wants in, so she can fix it, make sure I end up just like her." My voice wobbled a little.

"Maybe." José sat up straight at the table. "Can I say something? This is a family thing, but…" He slid one hand across the table, resting it on Ethan's hand. "Ethan and I have been together for almost a year and I feel like part of your family."

"Of course, José, you are family." Ethan's tone was dusted with sweetness.

"Maybe your mom just wants you and her to understand each other. That doesn't mean be best friends, simply acknowledge her as the mother who loves you and appreciates you. She just wants to see you happy. Time seems to be running out, so she wants to pull you close and make sure your future is good. Ryan appears like the answer to the second issue, so maybe she's being a little too pushy about the marriage thing."

His eyes focused on his coffee the entire time he talked. He reminded me of one of those social workers or counselors who appear on all those daytime talk shows to mend families.

"Point well taken," I said, with a contrived smile. I tried to comprehend everything. If I had just walked in on one of those group therapy sessions, I'd be the newcomer. Everybody took turns urging me to see my resistant troubled self clearly.

He tipped his head, acknowledging my comment, his dark eyes staring at me as if he saw past the anger and sarcasm to the pain that I stored deep. Ethan squeezed his hand and they shared a moment of appreciation.

After a short silence I cleared my throat. José's soft, defined manner made it seem safe to be honest, however crude my explanation would be. Maybe I could at long last say how I felt.

Holding his coffee mug, Ethan got up from his chair. "Anyone need a refill?"

José and I both declined. Ethan went to the counter and poured himself another cup.

I looked down at my charcoal drink and then up at José. Just talk Abbey, I thought. "You're right, José."

Ethan cleared his throat. "Wow, this is a first."

I kept my eyes on José, who had raised his hand, signaling Ethan to stop.

"Oh?" José's eyebrows twitched until they arched.

"It's just that this tension between my mother and me

wasn't born when I became a wildlife photographer and started traveling, or even because of Ryan, none of that. It's been present for fifteen years."

Almost catlike, Ethan crept toward the table, easing his chair from the table, sitting without distraction or noise.

"Ahh," José said, "Ethan told me your parents were separated for a while when you were in high school, but I suppose his memory isn't as acute as yours. He was only ten, right?" José shifted his eyes toward Ethan.

"Yeah, ten, and I don't really think about it that much." Ethan looked at me. "As a matter of fact, I would've forgotten it, but your intense anger since then keeps it fresh. I've never understood why."

Ethan hadn't known about the affair. I was the one who overheard my father's accusations. My brother only knew they were fighting, never about what, and I hadn't told him because he was ten and I didn't think he'd understand. Since then, I kept it to myself as my silent ammunition against her.

"You blame your mom?" José said to me, free of accusation.

I nodded. "I know why they split."

"Why?" Ethan said in a casual tone, as he sipped from his coffee cup.

I shifted my eyes to Ethan. Was I about to destroy their strong bond with a simple confession? And if I truly hated her, why hadn't I done this years ago when Ethan was more fragile? I wanted to believe it was to protect Ethan, not because I felt any loyalty toward her.

"Mom had an affair."

"Oooh, that explains things," José said.

Ethan wasn't taken back, his expression showed no surprise. He nodded. "I knew it was something like that."

"Did you hear them arguing?" I squinted at him.

"No. I didn't put it together until years later when I thought back on it. Two people don't progress from everything is okay to bitterly fighting, to separation, and then to talk of divorce, if something didn't happen. It wasn't like it was all boiling up for years and then they split. It came all of a sudden, so one of them must have been having an affair. When I really thought about it, I knew it had to be Mom."

"Yeah, Dad would never do that."

"I didn't make that assumption based on Dad having superior morals, but Mom's personality and looks. She gets a lot of attention and, let's face it, she's always been beautiful to a striking degree. Dad, well, we can just say, there's a surplus of men who look like Dad."

José laughed under his breath.

I glared at him and the lines of his mouth went straight.

"That's great logic, Ethan," I said.

"Well, I'd never suspect Ryan of having an affair, but I wouldn't blink with the knowledge you were—"

"Thanks! Don't compare me and Ryan to Mom and Dad."

"Why not? Same situation, Dad's devoted and so is Ryan. The only difference is…"

"What?"

"Well, Mom understands Dad's value and maybe she made a mistake, but it was once, and she's more than made up for it by being devoted, if indeed she did have an affair."

"Oh, she did! Anyway, I understand Ryan's value. We've just had a more open relationship."

"Ryan was okay with that?" José might as well have been trying to push a pillow between two Sumo wrestlers.

"I guess not, but that isn't what I'm talking about here."

"Well, actually," José said, "it kind of is."

Ethan and I both looked at him.

"Go on," Ethan said.

"Shall I explain, Abbey?"

"I guess." I shrugged, not sure where he was going.

"Abbey already knows this. She's too smart not to." He looked at me. "It's just scary to change."

I lowered my gaze and stared into my almost empty coffee cup. My heart beat faster. José understood and now would lay it on the table, right in front of my little brother.

"Let's hear this." Ethan said. "José has a great sense of people. Maybe he can even get to the root of Abbey."

I saw the truth in Ethan's comment, in the way José looked at people without judgment.

"At the same time your mother supposedly cheated on your father—"

"Please, José, forgo the 'presumed innocent until proven guilty' words. I know without a doubt, all suspicions have been confirmed."

"All right. When your mother cheated on your father, you saw it as cheating your whole family. Not only did she hurt the man you cared for and admired, she diminished the hope, the youthful dream of falling in love forever, and attached to that was her life. Like if I tried to sell a particular piece of artwork, expounding on its value; the care that went into creating it, how the piece will bring you joy, and how, of course, I have work by the same artist hanging in my very own home. Then you catch me throwing it in the trash, disregarding the very beauty I had spent hours elaborating on. You'd feel betrayed. With your mother's affair, your dream of love was destroyed, and you found it simpler to walk away, maybe even run from anything beautiful, such as love, in fear of seeing it ruined, reaffirming your beliefs. So you—"

"Please." I rested my forehead in the palm of my hand.

"I think you understand," he said.

Although his words were laced with empathy and spoken without judgment, hearing them was like someone carving them into me with a razor blade.

We sat in stillness, not a word said, and minutes ticked past all three of us. José was half-right. My mother's betrayal ruined any fantasies I had about love and the happily ever after. But as he spoke, the images that fueled my pain and justified my fear and anger came to the surface, until the truth sat beside me like an ugly but necessary piece of furniture.

"It's not just that, José."

My brother and José looked at each other, then at me.

Poor Ethan, I thought as he gripped the armrests and shifted in his chair. I was at last going to say it out loud. Something I hadn't admitted to anyone, not the real truth. I had kept my stone of anger buried, taking it out and polishing it when I wanted to remember why I hated my mother.

"When Dad moved out, my mother lost all authority

over me, in part because she was off in her own world, and also because I wouldn't let her wield it. Anyway, I was on a mission to… well, I partied a lot and one night I drank way too much and…" My eyes got damp. "Well, there's no other way to say it, I was raped." A couple of drops dribbled down my cheek.

"Ab." Ethan whispered, his eyes also glassed over.

I couldn't look at him or I'd lose it.

"And your mother wasn't there for you?" José moved me forward, gentle as he could.

"Not then, nor during the subsequent outcome. I learned the only person I could rely on, or even trust, was me." I touched Ethan's arm. "Ethan was too young and I didn't want to destroy Dad's image of me. My mother was so wrapped up, she couldn't even see it. And even with all the tension, she was the one I wanted to be there. So I felt justified in my anger toward her, still do. Only now, I want it to end so we can have something…" I sniffled. "…but sometimes I think, why bother? If she doesn't make it, I'll have to go through that same feeling of losing her again. When I was younger, I knew the affair was her choice. The cancer isn't."

Ethan got up, tears dripping from his eyes. He squeezed José's shoulder. "I'm going in the other room. Ab, I just don't want to listen to talk of Mom dying." He wedged behind me, wrapped his arms around my shoulders, and whispered in my ear. "I'm sorry you had to go through that." He squeezed me tight, before pulling away and walking toward the bedroom.

Tears slid down my face and drizzled onto the table. José

got up and returned with a paper towel. I blew my nose.

"Sorry," I said.

"Let's not apologize for hurting, because you'll have to get in line." The corners of his mouth turned up. He poured more coffee into our cups before sitting down.

"Boy, did you ever pick a great time to become part of this family." I wiped away the tears and rolled my eyes.

"Actually, I think I did. Any other time, I wouldn't have gotten to know you. You're a lot more complex than just a beautiful, pissed off woman."

I laughed. "I'm glad Ethan has someone like you."

"Ooh, that was full of sincerity."

"You're right, it was. It's in there."

"Someday, I'll tell you my story. I only understand you because of who I've been and who I'm working to be."

"You're the first person, José, I've ever said the word 'rape' to. When I told the story to Ryan, I made it sound consensual, because it was the first time. I just didn't want anyone feeling sorry for me. I mean, I was drunk and willingly got in his truck, drank beer, let him feel me up. I didn't say it was rape because it makes me sound so pitiful, so stupid."

"No, that's how it makes him sound. You were a victim and I'm sure that loss of control and the results... do I presume you got pregnant?"

I nodded, glad Ethan wasn't in the room anymore. It's one thing for me to allude to it, but to have to hear it was another.

"That's a lot for a high school girl to handle, especially alone."

"It was, but I did… I just made the decision, went through with it, and then moved on."

"You didn't really. I mean, you know that."

"Yeah, but I'm done. This has been too much therapy for one day. I'm afraid I can't afford your bill."

"You're clever at escaping."

I reached across the small breakfast table and squeezed José's hand. I blinked as if my eyes were being squeezed at the same time. "I've never verbalized all this. I suppose that's part of being screwed up."

"Or scared," he said.

"I'm more comfortable with 'screwed up' than 'scared.'"

"Well, we've hit a stopping point for today's therapy session," he said, a grin taking over his face. "I'll get the tea. I think Ethan put it in the cupboard." He went to a cupboard and returned with a small pale green box.

"Are there any special instructions with this stuff?"

"Not unless you consider boiling water special instructions," he said with a chuckle.

"I think I can handle that. Tell Ethan I said bye." I picked up my car keys from the table.

José walked me to the door.

"Thanks." I tapped his arm and promised to stop by his new gallery sometime soon.

"We'll do it again!" He smiled.

"Let me recover from this session."

He put his hand on my shoulder and aimed his black eyes at me. He was so terribly handsome. "Abbey, you'll be fine. Just be honest with yourself."

"If you weren't already attached to my brother, I'd be

after you," I said.

"You're forgetting… I prefer men."

"Logistics! Okay, if I was a man and you weren't attached to my brother, I'd be all over you."

"That's a lot of 'ifs.' Meanwhile there's Ryan, who's not gay, isn't dating your brother, and has a great butt."

"Hey!"

He laughed and raised his hands in the air. "Sorry, couldn't help but notice. Seriously, if you were as open with Ryan, you'd both come to a different place. He'd understand your reluctance, and you'd find out you can trust him. Just a prediction."

"All right, Freud." I tilted my head to one side. "Take care of my Ethan. I didn't mean to hurt him."

"He'll be okay."

I turned and walked down the sidewalk to my car. A long sigh escaped my mouth, as if after fifteen years I could breathe again. When I got in my Jeep and turned the key, tears fell, trailing at first, then faster, and what had begun as a small cry released into a giant sob.

I put off delivering the green tea. I'd call my mother and tell her I had a cold. I didn't want to be disheveled when I saw her for the first time since I ran out of the house.

I was messed up, but I didn't know how to get back, to quit being afraid, to stop walking on my own heart. The pain of the past had been embroidered into the threadwork of my life, and it seemed almost impossible to pull those threads out without the whole thing unraveling.

CHAPTER 19

The last week of classes during my junior year of high school, I couldn't concentrate. Between the absence of my father, the queasiness washing through my gut every morning, and the new knowledge Amy had bestowed on me, I was always distracted.

My math teacher asked me to stay after class. She scrunched her forehead and then with considerable effort pulled her eyebrows up above the gold rim of her thick glasses, so her eyes could escape their sight wheelchair. She asked me if everything was all right, if I were having 'problems' at home?

Why do people pay all that money for eyeglasses if they're just going to contort their faces so they can look at you free of the thick lenses?

I reassured her I was fine, but the way she shook her head and asked again told me she didn't believe me. Hell, there were three days left of school and only two weeks before Amy left for California, and I planned to spend every day for the next two weeks at her house.

My mom and dad were communicating with each other by phone. The conversations started out civil, almost nice, but often ended in attacks over silly stuff.

It's funny how grown-ups break up because one person

is cheating, and then they bring up every other little thing and throw it in each other's face. Once someone has slept with another person, the fact that she's been doing his laundry for years and he leaves pens in his pants doesn't really matter.

Shit, why even bring up her flirting? Everyone can see it has already gone past that. She's not flirting anymore, she's fucking. At that point, how relevant is any of it?

I asked my dad if they were going to get divorced and he just grimaced. I think he wanted to, I really do, but I also believe he couldn't bring himself to do it, and I know she wouldn't. The other night, she screamed on the phone, 'You don't understand, I do, I do care and I'll never, ever file for divorce.'

She was so melodramatic, it was like listening to the contemporary version of *Gone With The Wind*.

Day by day my queasiness morphed into an uncontrollable need to throw up. Every morning for the past two weeks, I turned the shower on while I puked in the toilet. Ethan complained to my mom that I was taking too long. I was more worried about what the throwing up and growing boobs meant than upsetting Ethan.

One Sunday morning when Ethan and my mother went to church, I got my answer. When I said I was sick, my mother stopped arguing. It's hard to argue with someone who won't speak to you, so we marched past each other in silence. I liked it because I could do what I wanted, without having to concoct some story to cover myself.

The home pregnancy test reading was positive. I sat down on the toilet seat and cried. That was it and this is what it got me, I thought. Then I panicked, wrapped it up, and buried it deep in the trash.

I knew what I had to do, and on Monday I made the appointment for the following Wednesday, including a pre-appointment and a follow-up. That morning I sat at the breakfast table, my eyes down, lids heavy from lack of sleep, and willed my mother to turn around and hug me, say she was sorry for messing up my life. 'If you put down the paper and say you love me and you're sorry, then I won't go without you.'

I looked at my bowl of soggy flakes, raised my eyes, and stared at her. She wore a turquoise robe with her hair piled high on her head. Without the make-up and tailored clothes, she looked more like a mom than a beauty queen. She shuffled around the kitchen, holding a phone to her ear, talking to someone from the country club.

I could tell by the way she cooed and laughed, her fake canned laugh. She stuffed two pieces of toast in the toaster and stood there staring at the metal box, waiting for it to spit her breakfast out.

I willed her to notice me. 'Come on, Mom. It's up to you, get off that phone, look at me, ask me what's wrong, rub my back. It's your choice, whether I do this alone or with you. Please Mom! With you, so you can hold my hand, cry because I'm in pain, stroke my hair, tell me it's okay. God, Mom, I need you, get off the fucking phone.'

The toast popped in the air, she buttered it and stood at the counter eating small delicate bites while she listened to some bitch from the country club on the other end. I took my bowl to the sink, washed all the flakes down the drain, and let the bowl drop just enough to make a loud noise, not enough to break.

"Abigail!" she yelled, covering the phone.

I turned around. "Sorry, Mom, it slipped."

"Be careful," she muttered, then into the phone she said, "Karen, you must be so excited. When's the wedding?" She waited for the answer. "Of course, we wouldn't miss it for anything."

I stared at her, penetrating her with my eyes. Begging her to hang up the phone.

She looked up at me, lowered her eyes, and then turned back to her toast.

I carried the carton of milk to the refrigerator and thought about letting it slip from my hand, spattering across the floor, splashing up my mother's legs. Maybe then she'd hang up the damn phone.

She twisted her body, the cord wrapping around her torso. "Your daughter's one lucky woman," she laughed. "A life of luxury."

I set the milk on the shelf, slammed the refrigerator door hard. The large metal box shook from the force.

She covered the phone. "Grow-up, Abigail. For God's sake, start acting your age," she hissed.

"Oh, I am, Mother. I am." I hushed, walking past her.

I SIGNED IN AT THE front window using a fake name and waited. While thumbing through *Better Homes & Gardens* and *Woman's Day*, I pretended to read the best cherry pie recipe in all of North America. Everyone else had someone.

A young twenties girl was wrapped in the arms of her boyfriend, I suppose. Another girl sat with her mother, holding hands. Tears streamed down her face and she never looked up from the olive green carpet.

When a woman's voice called my fake name, I stood, smiling. "I'm ready."

The crying girl looked up from the carpet and stared at me in disbelief. I shrugged my shoulders, suddenly feeling odd and out of place. Shit, I didn't know the standard protocol on how to act during these things.

A woman who I imagined my parents describing as handsome sat behind a long metal desk cluttered with papers and files. She had blonde hair with veins of silver creeping in along her temples and clear blue eyes. She introduced herself as Mrs. Davis.

I stared into her concerned face and wondered how she could act like she earnestly cared about every girl who stepped through the door who had made the same stupid mistake as myself.

But she seemed to; her shoulders tilted forward when she spoke, as if she yearned to reach out and hug me. The more she leaned forward, her face growing softer with sympathy, the more I slid back in my chair until I could feel my bottom pushing out the back.

The counselor, Mrs. Davis, pulled her chair out from behind the desk and faced me. "You put Baptist for religion," she said, glancing down at an open manila folder.

I wanted to say, 'great you can read, I'm impressed, and I lied about religion, too, just like I lied about my name. I don't want you to know me.' But I think she did care.

Perhaps she had her own children and she hated to think that one of her church-going, flower-dress-wearing, ballet-practicing little girls could ever be faced with this choice.

"Yes."

She raised her eyebrows and leaned forward again. "There are other options."

I leaned back. "Not for me." I'm not your crusade, lady. Just get me through this and feel good about yourself because you're counseling all us wayward girls.

She smiled and touched my knee. This all seemed rehearsed, like they had a script hidden in the manila folder that told them when to smile, lean forward, touch, and frown. "Who came with you?"

"No one."

She sat up straight, her face shifting between deep pity and surprise. I didn't care for either expression. "But we can't allow you to drive home alone."

"I'll take a taxi." I skewed my eyes to the bouquet of daisies beaming from a vase on the corner of her desk.

The corners of her mouth softened, her handsome face turned grandmotherly. "All right. Follow me," she said, clutching the folder to her chest.

I struggled to lift my legs away from the vinyl chair. The cracked surface pulled me back, sucking them to it. I stood and rubbed the back of my legs, then followed the blonde Statue of Liberty down the hall. Nurses passed by with their heads cocked, half-smiles, no teeth showing, as if all expressions were etched on their faces.

She spread her hand on the door and craned her neck toward me. "In here," she said, nodding for me to enter.

In the middle of the white room was a large silver table with suspended metal stir-ups, and positioned strategically at the base of the table a large clear glass vacuum. It looked like one of those heavy-duty, steam-cleaner kind of vacuums. Something people use to suck years of dirt from the bottom of their carpet.

"Are you all right?"

I kept staring at the vacuum. The word "mommy" slipped from my mouth.

"What?" She placed her hand on my shoulder.

I took a step back, letting her hand drop. "Yes."

"Yes?"

"Yes, I'm all right." And I flashed her one of those false smiles I'd seen my mother paste on a million times.

"You need to put this on and sit." She patted the table. "I'll be back in with the doctor."

I held the hospital gown and nodded.

"See you in a bit." She backed out the door.

I put the gown on and edged up onto the table. The cold metal penetrated the thin white sheet and slapped my skin, and my body arched away from the table. I forced myself to lie still. Silent, pushing all thoughts from my head.

In minutes she returned with the doctor. The procedure was standard, they said, and they both smiled down at me while my childhood was sucked away. She tried to hold my hand, but I wiggled it loose. I didn't need anyone to hold my hand.

In the recovery room, I was just another young face recovering from a mistake. I sat in a reclining chair with a thick blanket on top of me.

"Rest here for thirty minutes, or as long as you need. Then I'll see you before you go." She touched my shoulder. "I have something for you." Her tone was grave. "So this doesn't happen again." Then she walked away.

Next to me, the crying young woman rubbed her puffy eyes as she wept. I looked at her. "It'll be all right." I used Mrs. Davis' words, because I didn't know what else to say.

"N… n… no." Her sobs turned into wails.

I just wanted to leave all these sad faces and forget this, forget everything about this whole event. I felt sick inside, not just from emptiness, but all the things that filled me up, all the lies, the manipulation that needed to occur in order to dispose of a mistake. I had lied about my name, my age, and my circumstances, and now I sat alone with all my memories and lies.

The girl next to me stopped sobbing and turned toward me. "Did you name it?" All the features of her face pinched up in agony of an emotional or physical kind, I didn't know.

"Ah… no, no." Nervous words spit from my mouth. "I didn't think about it. I didn't think."

Her face muscles relaxed and the wrinkles smoothed away. Her short blonde hair was cut in a sporty style, and her grayish eyes seemed older now than when I saw her in the waiting room. She wiped her face on the blanket. "How come your boyfriend didn't come?"

"I didn't tell him." I turned my eyes away from her stare.

"You're better off. Smart girl." She sniffed so hard I had to look and make sure her nose was still on her face. It sounded like a snort an old farmer would make in the morning.

"You know why? I'll tell you why," she said. "I dated this guy for a year. He's a pilot for a commercial airline." She smiled like I should be impressed. "He'd been telling me for the last three months that he had filed for a divorce, but when I told him I was pregnant, he freaked. Said he couldn't leave his wife, then he stopped calling me."

Her tears spilled over again. "He sent me a money order in the mail… for this." Her words cracked and turned into sobs.

A woman's world? Boy, we sure got a good thing going. Amy was right about using men for what we need and moving on. 'Someone's gonna get screwed, literally!' Amy's message rang in my head.

I leaned over to her. "Sorry that happened, but let me give you some good advice." I talked with authority as if I were the older one, instead of the other way around. She pulled her tears in and looked at me. "The key is never to need them, just use them for your needs."

She scrunched her face up in agony and bawled again.

I went to find Mrs. Davis. I had to get out of here before the young woman told me what she named it. I didn't need any more details about the result of her affair with a cheating commercial airline pilot.

Mrs. Davis gave me a three-month supply of birth control pills. She pressed them into the palm of my hand and instructed me on how to take them, emphasizing I could not miss one day. I wanted to say, thanks, this will get me through the summer.

I drove around. I couldn't go home. I thought about going to see my dad, to ask him to hold me, but I didn't think I could look at him right now.

I went through Sonic to get a chocolate malt and ordered two, one for me and one for Amy. That's where I'd go. I hadn't told Amy, but I knew she'd understand, even scold me for not telling her earlier so she could have gone with me. She'll probably think I was pretty mature for handling the whole thing by myself.

I carried the cold malts to the door and knocked. No answer, but Amy's car was parked in the driveway. So I knocked again. No answer.

Tears balled up in my throat and I sucked some of the malt through the plastic straw. I knocked again, and then walked around back to the gate leading to her pool. At the sound of splashing, my heart jumped. Thank God, she's here.

I pushed the gate open with my butt and turned. "Amy, look what I got!" I called, lifting the malts up in the air like a kid at the fair.

"Shit. Abbey." She crested her head to look at me. She was in the far corner of the pool naked, her legs wrapped around someone, his large hands clutching her hips.

I took a few steps closer. I couldn't see his face, but his voice traveled across the water. "Is that your little sister?"

"No, silly." She laughed and hit his chest. "You know her."

He tilted his head to the side and looked at me.

My eyes dropped down to my chocolate malt. I was going to drink them both, they were both mine.

"You look like shit, girl, you all right?" he said.

"You okay, sweetie?" Amy turned around. Her arms

splashed through the water's surface as she walked toward the steps, but he yanked her hips back into him.

"Let's finish what we started. She can wait inside," he growled.

"Is that all right, Abbey? … I got some good shit. It's in my jewelry box. Get a few tokes and then we'll compare notes."

"Yeah." I squirmed, then stared to see if that was really him.

"Put my malt in the fridge. Thanks for thinking of me, Ab." She held her hand above her eyes as a visor against the afternoon sun.

I didn't move.

"Go on!" he yelled. He bent his head and nibbled her shoulders as if hungry, then he lowered his voice, "Her voice sounds familiar, but I don't know her. Maybe one of my sister's friends," he said and laughed.

It was Rod. Amy knew what he'd done. God, how could she do this?

She turned back to him and giggled. "Never mind, it's not important."

Their words were quiet but still ricocheted off the still water and echoed in my head, 'It doesn't matter, it doesn't matter, someone's gonna get screwed, and guess what, Abbey, it's you. Your best friend screwed you.'

I shut my eyes and shook my head to stop the message blinking in my brain.

"You some kind of voyeur?" he yelled above her head.

I kept staring, my eyes glued on the wreckage before me. My stomach churned from the betrayal.

"Bye-bye, Abbey," she said cupping her hand and waving that beauty queen parade wave.

I backed up and ran through the gate. The sun had baked the inside of my dark car, the black upholstery absorbed the heat and burned the bottom of my thighs. I propped myself up so my legs could adjust to the heat and I caught my face in the mirror. I did look like shit, my hair was stringy from sweat, and gray crescent moon shadows arced under my eyes from lack of sleep.

"Well, Abbey, are you tired of getting screwed, literally?" I said aloud. "Yes."

The tears broke from my eyes. I wiped them and told myself to stop, but they kept coming. I rolled down the window and threw the malts on the sidewalk.

I thought about driving away, maybe to another state, except I wasn't interested in going to any of the states around Texas. I drove through the hills, along the lake, past all the upper middle class homes squished together among the trees.

As the sun started its downward decent, I meandered through neighborhoods, staring into the windows, dim lights shining on children running around, the head of some woman as she stood in front of the kitchen sink, her arms swaying back and forth while she washed dishes. Faint sounds of laughter and noisy shouting came from backyards.

What a stage all the homes were, for such a grand play. A one-act starring a mom and a dad, with young children playing the supporting roles. When the curtain opens, you think it's going to be all smiles and laughs, but by the time it closes, you're crying, wishing you had never bought a ticket to this performance.

Aimless without a destination, I drove along the highway leading out of town, staring at the dying sun. Bit by bit, the encroaching blackness buried the yellow ball. I'd only had my driver's license for a few months and wasn't allowed to drive after dark, but I didn't care. For the first time I noticed my t-shirt was wet, soaked with sweat and tears. Tears, with no feeling behind them, yet deliberate and insistent, trickled from my eyes.

I wanted them to stop because I wasn't sad. I didn't care. You have to care to be sad, I told myself. I quit caring some-time between when the life was sucked from me, and when the melted malts splattered on the sidewalk. There had been a point where the sadness sort of fell into a pool of useless feelings that hardened in me.

I decided then, driving down the dark road, I would not allow myself to engage in the act of thinking for think-ing's sake, skipping from one fantasy to the next, like all my girlfriends. I would use thought only for solutions, not possibilities.

An hour out of town, I realized what I needed to do. I turned my car around and wiped my face with the end of my t-shirt. When the edges of the capitol dome pierced through the skyline. I drove towards it, knowing the closer I got to the lighted dome, the closer I was to my father's apartment.

I ran up the stairs, forcing a smile, and knocked. The door flew open, "Jesus, Abbey!" Dad screamed.

I walked in.

"God, where have you been?" He hugged me and

his body trembled. "Your mother is out of her mind. It's almost midnight. She said you left this morning and never returned, no call, no nothing. What's going on?"

He gave his speech with an authoritative tone, but he asked the question with concern and then stared at me as if the answer lay somewhere in my stringy hair, tear-stained face, disheveled clothing, and hollow tired eyes. And he was right.

I stared back at him.

"Abbey," he whispered trying to break my trance. Then he took me by the shoulders and led me to the couch. "Come here, sit down."

I sat and faced him, not taking my eyes off him. He asked if I wanted a glass of water. I nodded. He hurried to the kitchen and returned with the glass, then sat beside me and held the glass to my mouth like I was a toddler just learning to handle a real cup. I tilted my head and drank. He set it on the table.

"Abbey," he said, rubbing my back. "I need to call your mother." He spoke soft and slow, enunciating each word and studying me to make sure it all registered, but I looked straight ahead. "All right?"

I gave a slight nod and tightened my jaw. I wasn't going to cry.

He walked toward the kitchen, glancing over his shoulder, as if nervous to leave my side. He picked up the phone.

"Dad," I said without inflection, a scary steadiness to my voice. To my own ears, I sounded more like a judge than a sixteen-year-old girl.

He stopped dialing and hung up the phone. "Yes?" He took a step toward me.

I kept staring at the wall across the room. "Tell Mom we're both coming home or..." I steadied myself, holding him under sharp scrutiny. "... no one's coming home."

"Abbey—"

"Your decision." I buried my eyes into him. "Either way, I don't care. But I'm only living there if you are. So what will it be?" I clamped my teeth together, struggling to keep my composure. I had never talked to my father this way before.

He gazed at me, taking me in, I wasn't little Abbey anymore and he knew it. It wasn't about height, boobs, hips, or periods. Rather, it was facing the fact that my parents dropped my hand and I had to scramble to find someone else to hold it.

In the end, I just held both hands together, because I figured out I was the only one who will never leave me.

He picked up the phone, dialed a number. He walked as far into the kitchen as the cord would allow and talked in a hushed tone. His voice reassuring, then emotional, then angry, emotional, and then reassuring. He hung up the phone, walked past me to his room and returned with his briefcase and a large gym bag.

I lifted my eyes to him. "What's it going to be, Dad?" I knew the answer, but I kept my mouth straight and serious.

"You're a smart girl, aren't you?" He said it like he used to when I beat him at Monopoly. Triumph would transform the features of my face and I'd say, 'Oh, Dad, it was just luck.'

The corners of my mouth crept up. "That's what I've

been hearing lately, but the jury's still out."

He held his arm out, his brown leather briefcase dangling from his hand. "Let's go home, sweetheart."

I stood and moved next to him, his arms pulling me in close. As my head settled against his chest, I wondered if he knew, if he could tell I had been stripped bare of all my goodness.

CHAPTER 20

After I spent the morning thinking about my next step while walking around Town Lake, I arrived at my parents' house with the herb tea. I'd lumped all the events that occurred during their separation into one pile of blame that rested on my mother.

Now, as I sorted through some of the memories, I realized the blame grew from anger, which sprung from pain. I didn't really hate her. I hated myself, and she hadn't been there to change that.

When I walked in, mother was sitting at the dining room table, surrounded by envelopes and cards.

"Mom."

She looked up from her work. "Abigail, I didn't know if you were coming." Her tone sounded thankful.

"I told Dad last night when I called."

The conversation with him had been cold. When I mentioned to him I would stop by with the tea, he said, 'Only if you think you can treat your mother with respect.'

I agreed, then thought, 'Does she treat you with respect?' This, despite the fact I now realized they both had the relationship they wanted. He chose to stay with her, and she chose to give up another life.

"Sometimes he forgets." Mom smiled and looked down

at her envelope.

"Where's Dad?"

"I made him take a nap. He's exhausted and his obsessive doting is making me a bit crazy." She giggled under her breath.

I giggled, too, only to indicate I understood. Not because I felt like laughing and certainly not like giggling. Had the past couple of weeks happened? Did I cuss my mother out and ruin her song of love to my father? Because she acted like none of it happened.

"Here's the tea Ethan's been talking about." I set it on the table.

She stared at the pale green box containing Ethan's latest hope, and her lips made a small smile. "That's good. Is Ethan doing all right?" Her gaze rose from the tea to me.

That question struck me. She was still a mother to Ethan, more concerned about how her disease was affecting him than how it was destroying her own body. She would never stop worrying about him, but what about me? How was I doing? Had she ever asked Ethan how I was doing?

"He's okay. I mean…"

She waited, her concerned eyes resting on me.

I pulled out a chair and sat facing her. "Mom…" I pushed down any edge to my words. "It's hard for him because he cares, you're his mom."

I said it as if that encompassed everything: you brought him into this world, you fed him, you protected him, and you nurtured him. Hell, you're his mom. It sounded so blank, even though it meant a lot. It meant everything.

"He just wants to help," I added.

"I should tell him I'm feeling better. The chemo treatments are over, so I'll have a little reprieve, and then they'll do some more tests. But I'm tired of this house." She glanced around the dining room and the adjoining living room. I expected her next words to be, 'what a dump!'

Ethan, Dad, and I had been responsible for keeping the house clean and our definition of clean was different than hers. One year, she fired four housekeepers in a row because she felt certain she did a better job, so my father gave up on the maid idea.

"I can do some cleaning now," I said.

"No, the house is fine. I'll have someone come in and clean it before Thanksgiving. Right now, I'm not worried about it, I'm just tired of being in this house. I'm like a prisoner."

"I'm going to José's new gallery tomorrow. Do you want to come?" The invitation came out of my mouth before I had a chance to process it.

She pulled her lips into her mouth, like she couldn't decide whether to smile or cry. She sat back in the chair, composing herself. "Yes, I would like that a lot, Abigail."

"Okay, that's what we'll do." I let a soft sigh escape my chest.

"Yes, that's what we'll do," she echoed, an apprehensive grin spreading across her face. She reached up and adjusted the dusky blue scarf that covered her balding head. "Could we go to lunch, too? If you have time."

"I have time."

She nodded.

"And I want to," I added.

"You pick the place. Nothing too fancy, I'm not at my best." She laughed and I wondered if all the medications made her punchy or if this was her way of facing the decline of her appearance. I'd expected her to be bitter and angry.

"You don't have to worry about that."

She shifted her gaze to my face. "Good." Then she smiled at me, telling me she knew I understood.

I pulled myself back from reaching across the table and hugging her. At that moment it seemed natural, but our history loomed large in my mind and it seemed like a huge feat to overcome. Not the history of offenses, but the sort of non-history, nothing shared.

"I better fix you some of this tea." I stood, reaching for the green box. "Ethan will kill me if I don't get some of this in you right away."

"Abigail, forget the tea... really. Get us both a Diet Coke. I can't consume one more antidote. All these cures are making me sick."

"Right." I laughed. She had a point.

I poured us both Diet Cokes and sat down at the table. "How many have you done?"

"Only a few, since my handwriting isn't that steady. You have nice..." she lifted her pen. "I like doing it. It's something to do." She wouldn't ask me to help with the Thanksgiving invitations again.

"Why don't we do it together? It'll go a lot quicker." I reached for a pen.

I sat at the dining room table for the rest of the afternoon, addressing envelopes and applying stamps. My mother slipped between 'excited child' and 'refined Rachel' during our conversation about our outing. We tossed several restaurant ideas between us, but in the end she wanted me to choose.

And that decision seemed almost overwhelming, because I *did* want my mother to have fun, have fun with her daughter.

THE NEXT MORNING I CHANGED shirts six times, three of them were t-shirts, but not the shabby, hole-blossoming ones I usually wore. I decided on a blue sleeveless one under a white linen shirt, worn open, and a pair of jeans, my least faded.

I slammed on the brakes of my Jeep in my parents' driveway. Shit, I was more than twenty minutes late. I hadn't meant to be late. Shit. I knocked, opened the front door, and raced down the hall toward the living room.

"Abbey," my father whispered from the kitchen. I took a couple of steps back and leaned into the kitchen doorway. He signaled for me to come closer.

"What?" I said.

He put his finger over his mouth. "She's in there waiting."

"I know, I'm late," I whispered, following my father's lead.

"That doesn't matter. I just want everything to be okay today. Can you keep it light, Abbey? She's so happy. I haven't seen her look forward to anything in so long."

"Don't worry, Dad. I didn't invite her to destroy her."

He smiled. "I didn't think so, but tension has a way of

creeping in when you two are together."

"Not today, Dad," I said with grave sincerity. "I promise."

"That's my girl," he said, patting my shoulder.

She sat on the edge of the large chair in the living room, wearing flat black boots and a long black blazer over a taupe cotton dress. A scarf with pastel geometric shapes was wrapped loosely around her neck. She had on the Jackie O. wig again. Her make-up was soft, although it couldn't hide her hollow cheeks and sallow skin. Still, she looked pretty. I needed something besides jeans, I thought, studying her.

Her arms rested on her lap, pulling the fabric of her dress tight over her protruding belly. Her belly kept growing, the effects of cancer in the liver, as her arms and legs got thinner, making her look like a potato with toothpicks. She had to hate it. How did she justify her body to herself?

"Abigail." She turned to look at me. "How long have you been standing there?"

"Only a second. Sorry, I'm late."

"I didn't even notice." She smiled.

Was there any sarcasm in her voice? No, none, maybe a bit of humor, because it was obvious she had been sitting perfectly still, as if posing for another portrait, for a while.

"Shall we?" I said, extending my arm to help her get up.

The metal walker stood behind the chair as if it had been hidden, stored away. She pulled herself up. I leaned against her, balancing to control the slight shake in her body as she tried to conceal her weakness. Two mounds on her chest told me she had gone to the trouble of wearing prosthetics, or at the very least a well-padded bra.

We walked together, arm and arm, down the hall, stopping at the kitchen entrance so she could say goodbye to my father. He leaned down, kissed her forehead, and then he kissed her on the lips.

Dad touched my arm, his eyes focusing on me, a grateful peace smoothed the features of his face and I recognized the words behind his half-smile. 'Thank you, Abbey. For me, for her.'

For some strange reason, his expression didn't make me proud, but rather ashamed that my father would almost drop to his knees in praise because his daughter was taking her dying mother to lunch. Something mothers and daughters just do without the imminence of death.

"Rachel, don't you think you should take the walker?" my father said from behind us as we reached the door.

She looked at me. "There's not enough room in Abigail's Jeep for a clunky metal walker."

"Surely we can get it in the back, since it folds down," my father said, walking up next to us.

I glanced at her, then looked over at my father, raising my eyebrows. "Really, Dad, I've got a bunch of junk in the back and we don't have time to clean it out. Besides, we're fine."

She tightened her grip on my arm. She was still Rachel, albeit with the wig and the padded bra, refusing to be seen in public with a metal walker.

Once behind the wheel, I took more care than usual. The shocks in my Jeep were crap and my mother's body bounced like a small child on a horse. Her knuckles turned white as she hung on to the edge of her seat, but the natural smile never left her face. It was so different from the one she used for her friends.

From the corner of my eyes, I watched her looking out the window and then back at me. I didn't shift in my seat, keeping my eyes on the road, not wanting to enter that queer moment when you meet someone's stare and then you both look away, changing the preoccupation of your eyes.

My mother and I hadn't had a history of fun where such a stare would make us laugh that knowing laugh, or smile in fondness at one another because we were both thinking the same thing. No, I hadn't wanted to share anything with her.

But now as I drove, I wondered if there was time, if I would become attached, and then later have to let go again.

I'd been justifying the past and cleaning out some of the anger. She had her reasons, and one never understands the complexities of human relationships. At least she and Dad were still together. All silly excuses for her behavior, but they allowed me to view her life with a modicum of understanding.

'So, Abbey, you're moving towards the 'F' word, the word that is supposedly a major construct of modern religion, yet somehow, doesn't seem to stop people from killing and ridiculing each other over meaningless religious differences. You're forgiving your mother,' I thought. Then the real possibility of her death made my stomach turn over.

"There it is, Mom." I tilted my head to the side, "The greenish one. I'll have to go around the block, because this is a one way."

José's art gallery, Broken Visions, was an old mossy-green stucco house with burnt orange shutters, just off the main downtown strip, 6th Street. It was nestled between a lawyer's office and a vintage clothing store.

I helped my mom from the Jeep and we walked up the stairs, arm in arm. She tried to balance herself on her spindly legs, but I supported most of her weight.

His gallery screamed 'Art.' Two wicker rockers on the front porch had been painted yellow, and offered cushions covered in material that resembled a Picasso abstract. The sun bounced off the multiple colors in the stained glass door.

My mom stopped in front of the door, slid her arm from mine, and balanced on her thin legs. She straightened her skirt, pulled the jacket over her protruding belly, closed the bottom two buttons, then neatly tucked the edges of her own fuzzy hair back into the front of her Jackie O. wig.

"You look good, Mom." I wanted to offer her that.

"That's relative," she said, reaching for my arm again.

When we opened the front door, a tintinnabulation of bells sounded throughout the large front room, alerting the owner a customer had arrived. José walked from a backroom. He smiled when he saw us.

He was expecting us.

I'D CALLED HIM LAST NIGHT and he sounded excited and slightly proud over the phone. "Well, Abbey..."

"Don't say it. I just want to do this, nothing to do with your clever counseling skills the other day.'

"Good to know! I'd hate to think I chose the wrong profession," he said.

I'd hung up, laughing.

JOSÉ GAVE US A TOUR OF HIS gallery. Each room was arranged like a sitting room, with comfy oversized chairs covered in bright velvet fabrics. Four large rooms each had a different feel: contemporary, traditional, dark, and another that was just plain weird, or as some would say, 'funky.' Once José noticed my mother's difficulty standing, he suggested we sit, and he would bring us some herb tea he had just brewed.

My mother looked at me and made a face. I had to hold back a laugh.

"José," I said, "do you by chance have any Diet Coke?"

"Well, yes, but—"

"Mom and I are taking a day off from green, herb, grass, whatever tea. We're going straight for the saccharine today."

"Can do!" José said, then he disappeared into the back of the gallery where he had a small kitchen next to his office. People didn't just come to his gallery to view things but for 'the experience,' he'd boasted on the tour.

My mother tossed her gaze toward the ceiling. "Don't ever get sick, Abigail. People will force you to consume things you hate and do things you don't want to."

"I wouldn't be good at that," I muttered.

"What?" She leaned forward in the purple velvet chair.

"Today, we'll do what we want to. We'll pretend…" I almost said, 'pretend like you're not sick.'

But I was already pretending, acting like we had a history as a mother and daughter who enjoyed each other, adopting the AA mantra of, 'fake it until you make it.' When I wasn't analyzing every statement, every look, it seemed like we were having fun.

"I think we already are." She smiled.

José returned, carrying an antique-looking gold tray with two crystal glasses filled with chemical-laden caramel liquid and a small platter displaying an assortment of gourmet cookies. He placed the tray on the table that separated the two overstuffed chairs. "Here we go, beautiful ladies."

My mother nibbled on a cookie and drank her Coke while José explained where he gets all his paintings and sculptures, and how he judges art. He told us he'd just discovered a new artist in Lake Tahoe and he was trying to get his hands on more of her work.

"I'll be right back." He returned, holding a painting of a woman being sucked down a well. The paint swirled around the canvas, creating her face and the effect of her being caught up in a downward spiral.

My mother stared at the painting, mesmerized by it. "José, that painting is almost haunting." She leaned closer to study it.

"I get the same feeling when I look at it for a while," he said.

"There's a lot of dimensions within that woman," she said. "What's the artist's story?"

José launched into a biography of the artist's life and her disdain for abstract art, as she sought to create dramatic realism on canvas through oil medium, and incorporate other organic materials into her work. For instance, a piece of twine had been covered with paint, becoming part of the canvas as well as the woman.

My mother went on to say how there was more to the

painting than she could see, rather almost something one could feel.

Their analysis of the painting buzzed around me, not touching me, I was not a part of it. Amazing, my mother could even entrap a gay art curator's sincere attention.

"Abigail." My mother turned toward me.

"Huh?"

"Dear, tell us what you see in the painting," she said, with an air of an art history professor seeking to enrich the clueless student.

She was the only person who thought they could address me in such a way, and I hated it. Always calling me 'Abigail' and putting me on the spot. Shit, what did I see? A woman going down a fucking well, and she doesn't look too happy about it either.

José moved the painting in front of me and they both looked at me, waiting for me to say something profound. I remembered why I didn't hang out with my mother.

"Who do you think she is, Abigail? Make up a story, anything," she pushed.

I stared at the painting, letting my mother's words trip into my brain. Then my gaze bounced between her and the painting, as if studying them together. "Well… maybe she's not the woman we see here. Maybe she's someone else, or hell, even a few people, and this is who's being presented to us." I pointed at the portrait. "This is who we get to see, but the other women are hidden, buried deep inside her and we'll never see them."

"Well, then…" my mother whispered.

José leaned his head to the side of the canvas and gaped

at me in disbelief. Did he realize I was talking about my mother?

"Abbey, that was incredible. That's exactly right. That is… Wow… Few people would see that without knowing."

On the receiving end of José's praise, my back became erect.

"There are six other women painted under this one. Each of her paintings is like that. I have one displayed in the next room that has twenty people painted under the actual portrait you see. It can take her up to a year to create a portrait."

"Wow, I guess that's why I like photography. You take a picture, develop it, and it's done. The crucial time lasts only seconds."

"But it's no less an art," my mother said. "As a matter fact, that crucial time makes it even more difficult because once it's gone, you can never get it back. So, in order to be a photographer of your caliber, you have to possess an innate gift. Then have the patience to hone it, along with a love for the subject before your lens, or at least an understanding of your subject, just as this artist has for the women she creates on canvas. The difference is, you may only get a moment to connect to your subject, where as she can take months."

"Good point," José said with a nod.

"I hadn't considered all that."

My mother had experience working with a gifted photographer and now she was saying that about me, her daughter. I shifted back into the chair, needing support. I felt disconnected with the daughter I had always been.

"Rachel, I want to show you a sculpture I think you'll

appreciate," José said, offering his arm to my mother.

She stood and moved in beside him, grimacing in pain. Then she attempted to master the features of her face, raising her eyebrows from a frown, pulling her mouth taut, and at last bringing the edges of her lips into a soft smile.

"I'm sure I'll appreciate it if you selected it, José." Her Texas drawl gushed.

"Come, Abigail," she said, looking down at me.

"You go on ahead," I said. "I'm not big on sculpture."

When they left, I got up from the chair and moved closer to the portrait José had leaned against the wall. How much time had my mother's photographer taken to understand her? How lucky he had been to know her, to have seen the real woman behind the portrait. That one is the woman I've never known or only saw glimpses of, the small town Texas girl, the model, the wife of Frank, the neighborhood beauty, the cancer fighter, the country club friend, the mother of Abigail and of Ethan, different mothers, separate women. How many women were painted behind my mother's portrait?

My mother's giggles wafted in from the other room and I realized again how much other people enjoyed her. They didn't see her as fake or contrived, or maybe they did, but they didn't care because she engaged them, fed into their need for attention. She understood this because of her own need for attention. It was an exchange of sorts, she fed them, and in turn they fed her.

They returned and my mother's sallow skin looked flushed. "Oh, Abigail, I'm glad you stayed out here. José has some pretty interesting sculptures back there."

He gave her a playful wink. "And we wouldn't want sweet Abigail exposed to anything of a provocative nature."

"Certainly not," my mother said.

"Mom's face looks like you just made her sit through a porno flick."

"Abigail!" she laughed. "Well, he does have some very revealing art, that's all I'll say."

"Thanks, José, I bring my mom here and— "

"I forgot about that new shipment when I took you back there to show you the bronze hummingbird sculpture." He looked at her with an apology grazing his face.

"It was an education. We'll just leave it at that," she said, sounding coy.

Noon approached and people meandered into the gallery.

"Excuse me, I should probably see if anyone has any questions," José said.

My signal, it was time for the changing of the guards. I stood, and José slipped his arm from my mother's as I eased my hand under her elbow so she wouldn't lose her balance.

"Feel free to stay as long as you want. It's been a pleasure," he said, half-bowing in front of my mother, then bending to kiss her hand and staring up at her with his midnight black eyes.

"Oh, José, it was our pleasure," she cooed.

"Oh, yes, it was!" I said, rolling my eyes and lifting my shoulders in a playful, exaggerated motion.

José stood and came toward me, leaning into me like he was going to kiss my cheek. Instead, he whispered in my ear, "Smart ass."

Before he sauntered away, I remembered I wanted to ask him a question. "José, is there a story about the woman in the portrait?"

"Ah, that's another interesting thing about this artist. Each portrait has a rather fascinating story behind it, but you don't get to learn about it until you buy the painting."

Without thinking about it, I glanced at my mother; she was already looking at me. Then we both shifted our eyes back to José.

He took a step back and thanked us again before tapping a potential customer on the shoulder and asking him if he had any questions about the painting he had been admiring.

I DECIDED ON A PLACE THAT served Euro-Asian cuisine, with a low-key atmosphere and, most important, dark. I asked for a table in one of the corners, thinking my mother would feel more comfortable away from the crowd. We talked at first about José's gallery, his eclectic choice of art, and then about José himself, how handsome he was.

"Do you also see it, those eyes?" She leaned across the table and spoke in a low conspiratorial tone.

"Of course, I see it." We both laughed.

She sliced a bite of her seared tuna and scooted it around the plate with her fork before she put it in her mouth. She didn't have an appetite, she explained, but she tried to force herself to eat.

She sipped from her glass of water and then cleared her throat. "Speaking of good looking, how's Ryan?"

"You're not putting Ryan and José into the same category, are you? If so, Ryan has totally fooled you, because José is the kind of man who causes people to drop their jaws and stare, and Ryan, let's just say, you don't notice him until he's at your feet."

"But once he's there, you'd never want to tell him to go away," she said, tossing her gaze around the room, as if innocent of any further goal.

"I don't want to talk about Ryan."

"But, Abigail."

"Mom."

"I'm just going to say one thing," she said.

I know you are, I thought, cupping my chin in the palm of my hand and resting my elbow on the table. I looked up at her. "All right, go on."

She set her fork down and took another sip of water. "It's just that when you think about your life in a long-term way, someone like Ryan…" She stared at me. "You know what, Abigail? If it's not Ryan, whoever you choose, on your timeline, will be who's right for you."

My chin almost slid off my hand. "Mom?"

"Some people are meant to be friends and, hell, there are lots of men out there."

I smiled and sat up straight. I hadn't met 'Rachel, my friend' before, never knew she was one of the women painted behind my mother's portrait.

"Exactly." I said, clinking my water glass to hers, but I knew, even as she spoke, I had had a host of men and few were as genuine as Ryan.

"But keep in mind, Ryan would make a great husband and he desperately loves you. That counts for a lot—"

"Stop." I held a finger in the air. "You said one thing."

"Okay, okay, but can't you just see him as a father—"

"Mom!" I hit my fork against the glass, calling the conversation to a halt.

"All right."

"Anyway, from what I can tell, kids are a pain in the ass." I slipped a stir-fried shrimp into my mouth.

She furrowed her eyebrows and smiled at the same time. "That's cynical, Abigail, because children are wonderful and they're definitely worth any pain."

As she spoke, seriousness changed her expression and she stared at me and past me at the same time. "You won't see it as pain. Whatever decisions you make will come from love, not pain. The pain comes when your children hurt or even worse when you can't be there for them…"

She slid her hand across the table and touched mine, as if unaware or not in control of her own actions. "Or when you know decisions you had to make will hurt them, and you won't be able to stop it."

A long silence plopped down next to us. What has been said revealed so much about what hasn't been said.

"How was it?" The waiter reached for my almost empty plate.

"Great." I slid my hand away from my mother's touch.

She moved her hand from the table and smiled at the waiter, that perfect country club smile. "Yes, very nice, really enjoyed it."

He looked at my mother's nibbled tuna and then at her, his hand hesitating before he picked up the plate. "Finished?"

She nodded.

He gave her an odd look and lifted her plate. "Dessert?"

"No, that's all right," I said.

"Let's have dessert," she said. "We could share something really fattening."

She wasn't hungry, but somehow sharing a decadent dessert would mean something to her. Maybe it would signify that we shared something in this new reality.

With my approval, my mother chose a chocolate pâté. The waiter arrived, carrying a large white plate, displaying two dark squares of what looked like condensed chocolate mousse surrounded by swirls of a raspberry cream sauce.

We shared the dessert, both taking turns making low moaning noises when the chocolate hit our tongues. I tried to answer my mother's rather judgmental, but observant question, concerning the waiter's appearance. Half his hair was dyed an orange-red and the other jet black, he had more earrings on his face than I owned.

She wanted to know why some people go out of their way not to be attractive. I went on about self-expression and individuality and she nodded, saying it wasn't that individual when a third of the people of the same age alter their appearance using abstract art. She had a point.

When we left the restaurant, I turned toward the highway that led to my parents' house. "Let's not go home yet," she said. "I want to buy you something. There's this boutique."

"Mom, I don't wear that stuff." My tone was pleading, not frustrated.

"It has everything, dressy things, jeans, tops you'd like,

more like dressed up versions of t-shirts than old lady tops. You'll see."

She spoke with care, but also with desperation, like this was something we had to do. Fatigue was settling into her body. We had been gone from the house nearly five hours. She was tired, since her usual routine included a couple of hours napping every afternoon, even when she'd spent the day watching TV.

"But, Mom, aren't you tired?"

"I'm never too tired to shop," she laughed.

I laughed also. Again, not because I thought it was funny, but just to indicate I understood her.

"All right, I do actually need some stuff," I said, turning the corner on the next street to avoid the exit to the highway. "Which way. Mom?"

"Back downtown, it's on the corner of Lamar and Sixth."

"I'll have us there in fifteen minutes."

"Good," she said and laid her head back. In a few minutes her eyes were shut. "Just let me rest a bit, so I'll be ready when we get there," she said in a soft voice.

"That's fine," I said, as I steered my Jeep onto First Street toward downtown.

A lot of firsts today. For all the many things my mother had tried to get me to do, go shopping, get our nails done together, go to lunch, share anything, I had disregarded her, in an effort to punish her. But I'd also convinced myself she wasn't the kind of woman I'd spend time with, even if she weren't my mother. That she was shallow, self-absorbed, lacking interest in anything not linked to her precious country club friends or her appearance, yet in only a few hours I had visited an art gallery and done lunch with a complicated woman.

My mother's breathing deepened. When I shifted in my seat to look at her, her head was bobbing on the end of her neck like one of those toy dogs sitting on the dashboard of an El Camino. I made a U-turn at the next intersection and headed back toward the highway.

"We'll go shopping another day," I whispered.

CHAPTER 21

I dreaded the holiday in which more American families get together than any other, Thanksgiving.

Without her saying it, my mother had decided this would be her last Thanksgiving, and knowing it made the impending day seem like passing some point on the way to her death. She wanted it celebrated with extravagance and precision. She prepared a guest list of family and friends, a food list, and a chore list, assigning each of us various tasks around the house. I was left to cook, under my mother's direction.

I slid the turkey from the oven, then basted an artful mixture of butter, Worcestershire sauce, and spices from my dead grandmother's recipe. My mother had already demonstrated the technique a few times and I assured her she didn't need to escort me into the kitchen each time; I was capable.

She said, "Of course you are, Abigail."

I nodded, smiled, and strolled into the kitchen.

Did the Pilgrims feel the strained air between family members on that first feast, or did the anxiety come later when they realized they had gorged on the vast majority of their stored food and faced starvation the winter following their celebration. Everyone in my family seemed to be desperate, starving as they reached out for some morsel of emotional food to help them survive the deterioration of the woman who was at the core of their lives.

For years, I had thought of her at the center of my life in a destructive way, like a worm munching, chewing bit by bit from the middle of the apple until only seeds remained. But bit by bit, I was pulled into her and her toward me. I had pushed her away years ago, although at the same time, she had also allowed me to leave her.

Now we were both inching toward each other.

I sat at the kitchen table, watching the turkey cook through the oven door, as if my intense stare would speed the cooking process, making the day progress and reach its end faster.

"The oven works without you there."

I turned stiff lips into a smile and looked at Ethan, then shifted my eyes and smiled wider at José standing behind him. They both looked sharp, dressed in nice dark pants and pressed pale-colored shirts.

I looked down at my faded jeans, ran my hands over my worn gray turtleneck sweater. My wardrobe was limited to jeans, one pair of black pants, t-shirts, and a few sweaters. I prided myself before on the simplicity of my life, but now I felt awkward, since the house would soon be filled with family and friends.

"Where's Mom?" I walked past my brother and José into the living room. It seemed empty since they'd rolled her hospital bed into the guest bedroom downstairs.

"She's upstairs. Dad's helping her get ready." Ethan said as he turned down the collar on José's shirt.

When I reached the top of the stairs, my parents'

giggles halted me. My mother, teasing my father on his lack of fashion sensibility and he, in turn, commenting on her hundreds of pairs of black shoes. I peered through the door that had not been swung shut all the way. The late morning light slithered into the room through a large bay window and circled her, making her thin body almost translucent as the sunlight penetrated her paper skin. My father stepped in front of the beam, casting a shadow upon my mother.

She lifted her arms like a little girl on her first day of school. He slid the dress down over her arms and helped her pull it until it fit into place, then leaned in to kiss her mouth.

She touched his cheek and they kissed again, their lips united for a long moment.

He pulled away and smiled. "Be careful," he said patting her frail hand. She let out a weak laugh.

I knocked and nudged the door. "Mom, Dad," I said in that odd tone you use when you feel like you're interrupting something intimate.

"Come in," Dad said, pulling his shoulders back in surprise.

"I was going to ask Mom…" Begging my brain for the next words, I looked at my father.

"Yes?" My mother whispered. Her voice had grown weak along with her body.

"I'll leave, so you and your mother can talk."

"No it's…" My words tripped on my tongue.

"I have things to do downstairs." He shut the door as he entered the hall, leaving us behind.

The light rippled over the bed, then dissipated, soaking

the carpet that led into the darkness of my mother's closet. Outlines of boxes and neatly arranged clothes looked like soldiers lined in a row, readying themselves for a fight.

"Abigail?"

"Mom." I flashed my eyes at her, my voice abrupt, jumpy. "Can I borrow something to wear for dinner? I can't wear this. I just can't wear this sweater." I pulled at the soft material. "I've been wearing the same thing forever. God, I don't even own a dress, not one that fits."

"Of course." She steadied her arms on the metal walker and pulled herself up, shuffling her feet toward her closet, her legs moving like a wounded deer.

"I hate this sweater." I yanked it off and tossed it to the floor. "I have no clothes and if I were going to buy some, I wouldn't know what to buy." Panic dominated my voice.

My mother raised her eyebrows for a second, frowned, then gave me half a smile. "It's all right. I have a lot of dresses and you can borrow anything." Her hand skimmed the cloth soldiers that hung in perfect order. She reached up and turned on the closet light. "You choose. What do you like?"

"I don't even know what I like." I swallowed the thick swell of anxiety creeping from my stomach. I pulled my faded jeans from my body and walked to the closet. "Whatever you think, Mom. I don't know. I don't know. Where have I been?"

As I stared at all the dresses, pants, and shirts made to fit my mother, it dawned on me they would also fit me. A tear wound its way down from my eye to the edge of my nose before falling into my mouth.

"It's okay, you'll look beautiful in anything." Her slight arm touched my back and I let my head fall to the side, resting it on her bony shoulder. "You'll figure out what to wear."

"No, Mom, you're the one who knows," Another tear drizzled from my lid.

"I never knew, I just did. I'm like that great ape, holding my infant close, waiting to run scared," she said, her voice raspy, like speaking was difficult.

My eyes drifted to her in confusion. Why was she saying that now and what did she mean by almost apologizing for protecting me, as if that explained the cavern of emptiness that had existed between us?

"I need to show you something." She stumbled as she reached into the closet and I caught her. Her pale skin felt clammy, a cool film coated it. "Bring me to the bed," she said, between forced breaths. "I have to shut my eyes."

I lowered her to the mattress. "I think you would look beautiful in the long blue skirt and a cream sweater," she whispered, holding her hand slack in the air and pointing to the closet, her eyes remaining shut.

"Yeah, that'll be perfect. I'll wear that," I choked out, trying not to burden her with my sudden onset of emotion.

After I dressed in silence, I helped her down the stairs and watched as her theatrics moved to center stage, hugging and kissing everyone, telling me to get drinks, ordering Ethan and my father to get that dish, open the wine, bring another glass.

We did as we were told, all the worker ants preparing and gathering food for the queen. I had learned that the trick to destroying an ant colony was to kill the queen; once she was dead, the others died alongside her. I wondered if we would all die, our family becoming disjointed parts of a unit that had worked in the past, perhaps dispassionately, but it worked.

The clumsy quilted mitts that covered my hands made me feel like a clown at the circus. I reached into the hot oven. Bending, I tried to pull the huge turkey out, but some of the juice splashed on the sides of the pan and splattered on my face.

"Shit, stupid-ass turkey," I cried, backing away from the oven, ripping the mitts from my hands and splashing cold water on my face. "Fucking bird—"

"Hey, you're being awfully hard on that dead bird, don't you think?"

His voice nestled in behind my ears, and my body froze over the sink. For the first time since I'd met Ryan, I was concerned about how I looked. What would he see when he looked at me? My heart felt like a sponge that kept growing under my sternum with each word he spoke.

He ran his long-fingered hand across my back. "You okay?"

"Yes," I whispered, unsure I meant it.

His hand dropped from my back and when I turned, Ryan slid his hands into the mitts, lifted the cooked turkey from the oven, and set the large pan on the counter next to the stove. After he took off the oven mitts, we both stared at each other.

"Ryan, are you staying for dinner? I mean, it would be nice if you stayed... if you want to." My voice sounded awkward, like a nervous teenage girl, as my mind tried to grip my senses and bring me back to the controlled Abbey I needed to be.

"No, I just came by to drop off some wine and say Happy Turkey Day," he said, eyeing a bottle of red wine on the counter. "I think it's one of your mother's favorites."

"And that is?" My question was sincere. I really didn't know.

"Malbec, a grape from Argentina."

"Oh."

A small, tentative smile crossed his face. "She says, next to France and Napa, some of the best reds come from Argentina."

"Makes sense." I shrugged.

He stood on one side of the kitchen as I leaned against the counter on the other. Neither of us attempted to cross through the fog of confusion that hung between us.

"I guess my mother knows about a lot of things I never really thought about." I looked down at the Saltillo tile floor, studying, for a moment, all the shades crammed into one square tile.

"Yeah, well, I'd better get in there and say hi to the rest of the gang before I make the trip to my parents' house."

"Thanks for assisting me with that evil bird."

"No problem. I enjoy helping damsels in distress," he said with a smirk as he turned toward the dining room.

His tweed coat spanned the width of his back and it felt like a string of ache stretched the length of my body, from between my legs to my heart.

"Ryan," I blurted out.

He turned around. "Yeah."

"Your jacket looks nice. I haven't seen you in a blazer before."

He smiled. "Likewise, with the skirt."

"Mom's."

"Fits well." He stepped toward the dining room. "Well, I'm gonna hug the folks before I go."

With one desperate, unplanned move, I lunged forward and grabbed his arm. We both looked down at my hand coiled around the sleeve of his tweed coat.

"I'm sorry, I shouldn't have been so cavalier, not with you." The words spurted out of my mouth.

He looked into my eyes, then down at my hand, and back at me. "Ab, I pushed too hard. I wanted things to work so bad, and I just thought after a year, and the things your mom said... you and I wanted the same thing. I tried to sort of break away, date someone else, but I couldn't... I truly believed we had a chance. You were right, it was between us, and I didn't mean to drag your mom into it. I haven't said anything to your parents about us breaking up. That's our business and yours to tell."

One corner of my mouth turned up. "My mom doesn't need to be dragged. Anyway, she's not the reason I treated you so carelessly."

"You know what," he said, twisting his arm from my grasp and cradling my hand in his. "It really doesn't matter, it's probably for the best. We both want different things and that's okay. We'll always have the friendship, and as for the other part, maybe it's not in the cards and that's something I'm adjusting to." His hand drifted from mine, and he smiled the stiffest smile I had ever seen. "I'm doing good. I am."

We stood in proximal quiet, while in the not-so-distant next room, the echoes of family and friends drifted around us.

"Let me ask you a question," Ryan said. "What happens to a beautiful bouquet of flowers when they're laid on the front step, the giver rings the door bell, but the receiver never opens the door?"

Ryan was famous for convoluted analogies, so I had gotten good at deciphering his riddles.

"What happens to love if it's never received, never caught?" I said.

"Something like that. Anyway, the flowers, do you think they wilt away, eventually die?"

"Maybe the giver rang the doorbell when nobody was home."

His eyes shut, deliberate, measured, as if he hung on to the idea. "Maybe."

"Or…" I whispered.

"Or?"

"Someone was home, but they were too afraid to answer the door."

"Ab," he said, his eyes narrow and serious. "If the giver knew that, he'd have bust open the door and laid the flowers at her feet. Problem is, he doesn't have a clue what's going on inside the house."

"Ryan!" My father's deep voice burst though the kitchen.

Ryan backed farther from me and turned, offering him his hand. My father tugged him into the living room and the salutations flew as my proud father presented Ryan to more family and friends. My mother almost begged Ryan to stay for Thanksgiving dinner, and he, polite as always, backed out of it, claiming he had to get to Victoria to see his 'other mother.'

She crooned, "Oh, Ryan, Abigail really is going to miss you."

My mother was right.

I stood in the kitchen alone. My heart fell so low, as if it no longer rested beneath my ribcage but had sunk to my feet. I splashed more cold water on my face, this time to wash away the hot tears that pooled in my eyes. Why hadn't I just said, 'Ryan, I think about you all the time and there is no denying that I love you and I don't want to become a stranger, not to you, not to myself.'

"Happy Turkey Day, Ab," he said, passing by the kitchen for the front door.

"You too," I croaked, as the front door shut.

"I'm supposed to help you carve up that bird," José said as he walked into the kitchen.

I turned from the sink.

"Hey... what's wrong, you all right?" His voice was soft.

"That damn turkey spattered some hot juice on me."

"All those turkeys are out to get us."

I smiled. He took a knife from the drawer, and we went about cutting the turkey while everyone else shuffled around us, escorting vegetables and side dishes to the dining room table. My mother's failing voice told everyone where to place the dishes.

After a few minutes of silent slicing, José said, "He's a

great guy, isn't he?"

"My brother is a great guy." I knew for whom the adjective was meant.

"The other great guy. Your great guy."

"Well, not mine anymore."

"That's up to you."

"I already screwed it up."

"Is that easier for you?" he said.

I sawed at the top of one of the turkey's legs.

"Come on, does a friendship as true as his scare you, so it's easier not to get that involved?"

I stared at him, his thick black lashes curled up, almost reaching to the curve of his black eyebrows. I understood, as I gazed into his ink-colored eyes, why my brother loved him. What I found difficult to understand was his capacity for love. Where had it come from?

A couple of weeks ago, he told me over soy-enriched lattes that his parents had disowned him, shortly after his high school graduation, ten years ago. He was the youngest boy from a large Hispanic Catholic family and his dad said that his 'deviant behavior' had brought disgrace to the other seven brothers and sisters. 'Oveja negra,' were the last words he heard from his father as the door had slammed shut behind him.

"José, we already went through this. I've been involved with plenty of people." I sliced through the last of the joint and jerked the leg away from the giant bird.

"I'm sure of that, but I mean emotionally, not physically. Long after that intensity from a first kiss is gone, friendship continues to strengthen, making the thousandth kiss better than the first."

I took a deep breath, putting the last of the sliced turkey on the platter. "José, that may work for you, but for me, the idea of being with the same person forever is… b-oo-ring." Maybe he has to love, because love was ripped away from him, I thought.

"I know you a little better than that. You meant to say 'scary,' didn't you?" He winked as he picked up the platter.

"Here we go again," I said. "Boring. Boring." I followed him into the dining room.

"So scared," he whispered in my ear after he set the platter on the table. With the sensation of his words tunneling into my ear, my spine stiffened.

Everyone gathered at the two large tables we had set up for the occasion. My mother assigned seats so her followers scurried about until they found their places, all the time smiling at the queen. My father and I were seated on either side of my mother, with my brother and José next to me. Aunts, uncles, and friends of my parents were arranged in some efficient social order around the table.

With my mother's prompting, my father led the occasion with a prayer, one of thanks for family, friends, and the abundance of food. His words of praise were simple, without emotion, as if he were working hard to keep the emotion from creeping into his voice.

"Abbey, you look quite beautiful. Never have I seen you… well dressed," said Candace, my mother's friend, as she passed the mashed potatoes in my direction. "I mean, *so* well dressed. It's amazing how much you resemble your mother. You should be proud."

I forced my eyes to stay focused on the serving bowl, certain my mother recorded my reaction to her friend's claim.

"Thanks." I offered a gracious smile over the pile of mashed potatoes, coaxing my dry lips to curve, seem appreciative. Turkey, mashed potatoes, beans, rolls, stuffing, and corn overtook the china, and the decorated pattern almost disappeared between the swelling portions I had heaved onto my plate.

Muted voices mingled from both tables, complimenting the food, making Christmas plans, talking about how Austin is growing. "The traffic is terrible," someone said at the next table.

My cousin Derick had come with his pregnant wife, Carolyn, both of whom I hadn't seen in seven years. They made several comments before dinner on how little I had changed. "Same old reserved Abbey."

His wife's voice traveled across the table. "Abbey, how long will you be staying in Austin?"

The chatter chilled to a dull, achy silence as eyes shifted toward me, while forks kept their continuous path from plate to mouth. I looked down, searching for an answer in the maze of vegetables and potatoes. How long would I stay?

"I don't know," I said, my eyes still on my plate, my voice rushed, my answer tenuous.

"A while, won't you, Abbey? You won't be leaving the country for a while, right?"

My Aunt Dolores' head bobbed up from her trough of food. "Abbey." A high-pitched squeak escaped her full mouth, bypassing the food that packed her cheeks.

Flashes of heads discreetly rotated toward her rounded jowls. Anticipated stillness rushed in, as she swallowed the last of the food storage she had packed into her mouth.

"Surely you'll stay until your mother... as long as Rachel needs you to. For goodness sakes, she'd do the same for you." With these last words, Dolores added an emphatic edge to her voice.

The feasters put down their forks.

Aware of the eyes on me, I pushed my chair backwards and stood. "Does anyone need anything else to drink?"

"That's right, isn't it, Abbey?" Her squeaky voice stalked me as I hurried toward the kitchen. I was afraid the pitch would shatter my glass.

I opened my mouth to speak, but my mother's strained voice cut in. "Abigail is an exceptional photographer, and if she chooses to take another assignment soon, that will be the right decision."

I reached the arched doorway to the kitchen and grabbed the side of the wall, my breath caught in my chest.

"Well, she may be great and all," Aunt Dolores blurted, "but you need her and if she needed—"

"Dolores, enough." My mother's sharp voice rose, sounding like a shovel scraping on a cement driveway.

I let out a deep breath and I walked into the kitchen. *Thank you, Mom.*

The shallowness of perfection dominated the day, making it impossible for me to eat. Everyone smiling, chatting, acting as if there wasn't a dying woman in the room, as if they had not all come to say goodbye, as if this would not be the last time most of them would see her body while warm blood still pumped through her veins.

Throughout the day, people told me I looked just like my mother. I half-expected a metamorphosis to occur. My hands, the strong long fingers would shrink into tiny delicate digits brushed with red tips, and my small compact breasts would grow fuller with large erect nipples from feeding children, and my hair would adopt a darker tone.

With her death, somehow, she would still reign and I would be trampled from existence. Then I wondered how much of her was already imbued in me and if being like her was such a bad thing.

I carried my plate to the kitchen, found my camera, checked the battery, the film, and the flash. When I finished, I resisted the desire to sneak a swig of some of my father's liquor, like some naughty high school kid.

Instead, I hid behind my camera, the eye of the lens capturing the idiosyncrasies of family gatherings.

CHAPTER 22

The cancer marched on in my mother's body. Ethan and I found out later that she had chosen to discontinue all chemo a couple of weeks before Thanksgiving and that it hadn't stopped at her liver but also grafted itself to her bones. She was losing more and more fluid and now she was hooked to a morphine pump.

The home-care nurse came once a day to check her vitals and the morphine pump, set up on a drip the nurse controlled. I asked why they didn't let my mother control it, since she was the one with the pain.

"We don't want to overmedicate her," the nurse said.

How can you overmedicate someone who is counting the weeks until the grave? She would be dead before addiction set in.

A numbness crept into my body, spreading like a red wine stain on white linen. At times I wasn't even sure of where or who I was. I plodded through the daily routine of caring for my mother and watching my father become more and more disheveled, needing to be reminded to bathe, like some six-year-old boy.

I liked being numb, so as not to think about all my unanswered questions, the gnawing feeling I had from the unknown. My mother and I stuck to our regimen of exchanging a collage of sentences. If they were all pasted together, perhaps they would create some meaningful picture, but alone they led to more questions and confusion. She wanted to tell me something. Daily, I thought about getting back to the box that held evidence of my mother's past, but Ethan insisted I leave it alone.

Her country club friends drifted in and out of our house, sometimes making an afternoon event out of their charity work. One afternoon two of them whispered in the kitchen as they refilled their tea. "Did she ever smoke?"

"No, and she wasn't a big drinker either."

"Maybe it was stress. They say stress can do that to you."

It was funny how we needed an explanation for another's early death, equating it to some lack of judgment, so we can cross ourselves off the list of potential cancer acquirers. Don't smoke, do eat a lot of fruits and vegetables, don't drink, do yoga. So we can tell ourselves with some frail reassurance that we're immune. Or even better: it strikes one out of eight, she has it, so statistically I won't get it.

'I don't think cancer is that calculating,' I wanted to say as I marched into the kitchen, bringing their whispers to a halt.

SINCE WAY BEFORE THANKSGIVING, fake Santas and trees decorated in silver and gold, along with green and red blinking lights, impregnated every store. The Christmas season bombed my senses. I wandered around the store trying to remember what my mother asked me to get.

I pushed the cart from aisle to aisle, wishing I had made

a list, hoping the visual cues would trigger my memory. I swung the cart into the cereal isle and almost hit a woman in a short dress and heels. "Excuse me," I said.

The guy with her turned around. It was Jake, Ryan's brother.

"Abbey, how's your mom?"

"She's doing all right," I said, my voice monotone.

"Sorry." He turned his head toward the woman. "This is Diane. Diane, this is Abbey." He stalled, then looked at me as I nodded at Diane. "An old friend of Ryan's."

"How is Ryan?"

Jake's smile vanished. "How do you think he is, for God's sake?" His question was swift and clean, like a blade slicing to the bone

The girl folded her hands together and cast her eyes downward. Jake didn't wait for an answer. His mouth widened, like Cheshire cat's, a toothy grin stretching across his face, his expression transforming within seconds. "He's great. As a matter of fact, he's seeing someone." He looked through me as he spoke, discarding my humanness.

His words yanked me from my fog. "What?"

"Seriously." A haughty air edged his voice.

"Really?" I tried not to act surprised as this new revelation stabbed me.

"Did you expect him to wait for you?" He glared at me, as if I had an answer to his question.

Jake was acting as judge and jury in the case of Ryan Weston vs. Abigail Gallagher. The conclusion: Abigail found guilty of butchering a decent heart in millions of unrecognizable pieces. Now, Abigail, did you really expect him to sew the pieces together and place his mended heart on the butcher's block so you could cut it apart again?

Heat stung my cheeks and, suspecting my flushed face would give me away, I expelled my mother's line that had let her back out of all emotional downpours without opening her raincoat and getting wet. "Of course, not." I smiled. "Nice to meet you, Diane." I pushed my cart past them.

Jake whispered, "There goes the black widow."

But I didn't turn around. My stomach twisted into tiny knots. I had forced Ryan out of my life, telling myself what we had was a friendship mixed with some sex, nothing deeper. I let my best friend go, and now he would spend the rest of his late nights laughing and talking with someone else.

She would get his life: wake up to him sitting in a chair, drinking a cup of coffee while he watched her sleep, listen as he sang crazy songs while strumming his guitar, fight with him as he dragged her from the bed at five a.m. to watch the sunrise over the lake, and laugh as he chased Spartan around the house with the newspaper for stealing his chocolate eclair from the coffee table.

A thirty-minute trip to the grocery store lasted two hours. All of the aisles looked the same, pears turned into apples, and a list of food whiffled through my mind. I was forgetting things and would have to return to the same grocery store, the same aisle, and look at the same food. I couldn't remember all the things that should be in my cart.

I trudged up my parents' driveway, hugging two paper sacks in each arm against my body, the last of the afternoon light wasting. Would the roses bloom next year without my mother there to prune them, wearing her straw hat and green garden gloves, my father fixing her a late afternoon cocktail after her long day of work?

My father always said, "Your mother's roses look wonderful, don't they?" – his way of digging up a compliment for my mother. Yellow, red, and white roses with pink tips circled the brick house, my mother's beauty encasing our homestead.

I unloaded the groceries and went to ask my mother what I forgot. Her bed was empty, the sheets pulled back, halfway draping the floor, a white pillowcase covered with a mixture of auburn and gray strands of hair.

"Mom?"

No answer. I had only been gone for a few hours.

"Dad?" I ran upstairs and in my parents' room a string of clothes lay on the floor, and drawers had been pulled open.

I raced back to the kitchen to call Ethan, then I saw the note on the counter.

'Abbey - Went to the hospital. Dad.'

I read the note again. I should rush to the hospital, see to my father, sit by my mother's bed, wait. I did not. I called out, "Mom, Dad, Ethan…" … listening, making sure no one was home.

The phone rang and I jumped, spooked in the dark house. I rummaged through the kitchen junk drawer, searching for a flashlight, found one. I stared at the phone until the ringing ceased.

As I walked from the kitchen, the smell of vomit emanated through the living room. I held my breath, walked past her bed, and breathed again once I reached the end of the hall near the garage. Holding the flashlight in one hand, I opened the door to the basement and used the other one to brace myself on the flat wall as I descended the steep steps.

The only light came from a bulb hanging by its own cord, sufficient for a storage place, but too diffuse for a searching expedition. The same dank basement that had been a fort for a thousand childhood adventures was now a wasteland of family memories, broken forty-fives next to a record player, a deceased Singer sewing machine my mother refused to throw out because she had used it once upon a time to make baby clothes, and three fake Christmas trees, boxed and stacked next to several cartons containing decorations of Christmases gone by.

The dark basement made me lonely, not for people, but for memories. Mental projections of me loving someone left the screen white, blank, until the reel wound to my brother and father, but even those images seemed like slides taken with over-exposed film, mere shadows.

Where had Ethan put the box of my mother's memories? I held the flashlight close to the stacks of large cartons, reading the labels, the lists of contents: Ethan's baby clothes, Christmas decorations, fishing gear, and books.

I moved the boxes to the side, lifting them one by one, so I could make out the descriptions. Where did Ethan put the photographs? Did they disturb him so much that he had tucked the box into a dark corner disguised behind others full of family memories, or was that its hiding place all these years, hidden from my father's eyes.

Driven to submerge myself in parts of the past that were connected with the future, and knowing soon my mother's life would also be the past, I needed answers while her life was still in the present.

After much searching, I located the box. Gray electrical tape covered the top. Ethan had sealed the box in such a way as not to let the old memories escape. I peeled the tape from the top of the box and opened the flaps. I held the flashlight close to the box, and sat on another box, which was hard, probably filled with books.

I pulled more pictures from the box. The edges of some of the photographs had turned a haunting blue from the dampness that seeped through the cardboard box.

Again, I examined the picture of my mother and the photographer. Two old dresses and magazines, along with yellowed photographs, were in the box, a collection of her past life. The dresses were from a different time and the magazines were old. I flipped one of the pictures over. Written in twisted looped penmanship, not my mother's precise script, were the words:

You are something to behold forever, 1966

They were lovers before I was born? She had carried this affair through her life or at least the remnants of it. I studied every picture, every date, trying to decipher a beginning and an end to the love affair, but something about my mother told me there was no ending. Perhaps it was all her. She bore some naïve torch for a man who was long gone.

The back of another picture read 1968. That year, she posed for photographs made with another man while she played the beloved newlywed to my father?

I shoved all the pictures back in the box and pressed the tape on the lid. Setting the flashlight to the side, I moved boxes and hid the box under other family memories.

Damn her. Damn her and her façade. We had all participated in a charade of sorts, with my mother as the director.

I ambled through my parents' house, interrogating myself, asking questions like a lawyer putting together the pieces to a dubious crime. Once more, I examined the photographs lining the mantel and arranged on the creamy wall.

The timeline was skewed, but even my sharp mind couldn't find any explanations to fill the gaps, making it complete. Pieces were missing, yes, but even more strange were the peculiar expressions and subtle body language between my parents, all captured on paper. Even on their wedding day, in one of the pictures, she glanced his way like he was her brother or a man she had been married to for twenty years after the passion of love dwindles, giving rise to a fondness from a life of memories and shared responsibility.

THE NEXT FEW DAYS WERE more than confusing. Scenes from my mother's life projected on my mental screen: Rachel dancing in our backyard, sipping mint juleps, pulling my father's arm, enticing him to leave his lawn chair and dance to a waltz tune on the radio. The day she hesitated when my father asked her, among angry words, if loving her was enough, and how she didn't beg to keep him home. My mother holding her premature infant son in her arms while I looked on. Her breastless form lying in a hospital bed, life slipping away from her.

One night, driving home from the hospital, I tried to imagine my parents' on the day they got married. A ceremony between the husky ex-football player turned lawyer and the delicate, chiseled china doll, an avatar of femininity.

Their wedding seemed disturbing, yet familiar, the picture on the mantel, she in a white dress inflated by her large bosom, the gold locket around her neck hiding between the white pillows, and he in a dark double-breasted suit. They were both smiling, not at each other or even the camera, but someone who stood on the periphery.

At once, it occurred to me I had never seen their marriage certificate. At the end of my street, I twisted the wheel, turning the Jeep around, and sped up the highway toward their house. That night I raided my parents' room, rifling through drawers, emptying and refilling boxes, filing through books, retrieving old photographs of my brother's birth.

I never found the marriage certificate. I left their room exposed, as if a savage had ransacked it. Although the pieces had been put back together, I had ripped it apart, inspecting, searching for details of their private life.

I found his picture, my mother's lover in a small wooden box, stuffed behind the shoe rack in her closet. I remember her reaching behind that shoe rack Thanksgiving morning before she became dizzy. Was she getting ready to reveal her secret to me? She had never let him go. He had lived with us in my father's house. I returned him to the safe box of secrets hidden from my father and tucked it under my arm.

I went to my father's office and combed through

business papers, bank statements, any piece of paper with printing, I touched. I remembered the stories of Ethan's birth, his milestones, his first words. Where were mine?

In the lower drawer of my father's armoire, I found my brother's birth certificate. He was born in Austin, Texas, at St. David's Hospital.

I shuffled more papers and envelopes, and at the bottom of the drawer lay a manilla envelope with my name printed on the front, but it was too thick for a birth certificate. I opened it, ripping the tongue from the envelope and slid the papers from its mouth. Legal papers with small formal printing filled the white sterile paper. My mother's precise signature danced across a line at the bottom of the last page. Planted on the line next to my mother's name was my father's blocked signature. The third line was etched with a dark firm print, that of a judge.

I read a scattering of words, *Father unknown, Abigail Wiley became Abigail Gallagher 1972, adopted by Frank David Gallagher.*

As if someone had halted time, I sat at my father's desk, spreading the papers out like pieces to a complicated puzzle and stared at the words shrouding the forms. My eyes burned, tears splattered onto the paper, disintegrating the two words 'father unknown' into a small pool of black water. I wiped the moistened words with my fingers, smearing a line of black ink across the paper.

Father unknown? Unknown to whom? Me, the hospital, the courts, but not my mother.

Then the pictures of my mother, her lover, and the dates scribbled on the back of the photographs flashed in my head like a bright strobe light, harsh and disturbing.

I pummeled the wall, pounded my feet, and hurled things around my father's office. I screamed a wail, fueled from some dark place inside me. I paced about the room, yelling, "No, No" over and over, as if those words would erase the truth printed on the documents.

The news, news that unraveled the seams of my life, paralyzed my brain. My body responded as if facing grave danger or threats of losing something very dear to me. I was in the center of a fight-or-flight scenario. My heart raced and a film of sweat coated my skin, while my mind tried to move and search for the solution.

Do I stay and seek out the answers, or do I run from the truth? My pragmatic mind, always capable of calculated decisions, was gone. Character doesn't matter when one's picture of her life has been smashed. I wanted to shake my dying mother and shove the adoption papers into the chest of the man who had called himself my father.

I stopped screaming and repeated the line, "The man who had called himself my father…" Why? I had never questioned his love for me, but now I realized he had chosen to care for and love me.

My body folded on itself, my legs loosened under me, and I dropped to the floor. A deluge of salty water poured from my eyes and I lay my head on the carpet. In the midst of the papers, whose printing stripped away the history of my origin, I fell asleep.

WHEN I OPENED MY EYES, my head pounded and my body ached, as if the objects in my father's office, the ones I had abused the night before, had taken revenge on me.

As I glanced around the room, I realized the damage from the night before had to be reconciled. I cleaned, restored things to their proper place. I shoved papers back into folders, then arranged them into drawers.

I put everything back except the small wooden jewelry box containing the picture of the man who had haunted my life and the paper that read, 'father unknown.' They were mine, evidence my history had been altered.

CHAPTER 23

Later that morning when I pushed open her door, fresh flowers filled the vase. They had come to be a symbol of my mother's waiting and meant she still needed to be surrounded by beauty. The sender knew this about her and, incomprehensible to me, always knew where to send them.

My father seemed curious about the origin of the ever-blooming flowers, not allowed to die. A new delivery always arrived before the old had lost all life, but he came to expect them and believed my mother found their periodic deliveries as bewildering as he did.

Her eyes were shut, and the noise of the oxygen machine and the timed cranking of the morphine pump offered the best indication she was still alive. Very little was left of Rachel. Cancer had wilted her flesh into loose alabaster skin, and chemotherapy had peeled it hairless, morphing her into a pale amphibian. The muted morning light streamed down on her, spotlighting the bluish veins, thin arteries, and the outline of her skeleton. It was like looking at an X-ray of my mother.

My father slept in the corner chair. His round chin rested on his chest and his arm twisted between his belly and the edge of the chair. I shook his shoulder and leaned close to him.

"Dad, it's almost nine in the morning. Go home and get a shower, some coffee. I'll stay with Mom." I couldn't call him anything but 'Dad.' He had chosen the role and played it well, and I would not rob him of his part.

"No." His voice was groggy and hoarse.

"Yes, Dad."

"All right, but first let me make sure she's comfortable."

He hunched over and eased her to the side, straightening her pillow and pulling the covers around her shoulders while she slept. Then he bent his head and kissed her chin. When he turned toward me, a wet film coated his eyes. "Be sweet to her Abbey," he said and then swallowed deep like he had something in his throat.

"I will."

At last, he left, and I sat, twisting my hands around each other, thinking about what to say to my mother, the edgeless woman who had so many dimensions. I wasn't angry anymore, only intoxicated with the strange knowledge of the past, just enough to need more. I couldn't retreat any further. I had already hidden in the dark corners of the world, shielding my vision with the sharp lens of the camera. I had to look at her, to watch her eyes as she spoke.

When she woke, she smiled beneath the clear mask, like she did when I was a little girl. "Abigail," she murmured.

I scanned her face. She looked older than she did yesterday, with deep furrows digging into her forehead and bluish-black shadows resting under her hollow green eyes. A light blue Texas Rangers baseball cap, a gift from José, covered her hairless head. I looked away and then examined her face again, at first glimpsing a forlorn girl left alone.

Every time I turned back to stare into her face, another phase of Rachel appeared. For a moment, I pinched my eyes closed and pictured Rachel, my mother, the one waiting for me at the bus stop, the one laughing in excitement at my magic shows, the one kissing my skinned knee with her perfect red lips.

"Mom." I scooted a chair beside her bed, parallel with her, so she only had to turn her head to see me. My movements were quick and nervous.

"Abigail, are you all right?" She inched her hand to the edge of the bed. Her eyelids took long slow blinks as if, when shut, she had to coax them open again.

I thought about all of our hieroglyphic conversations, messages hidden in discussions focused on monkey social behavior.

"Why would the gorilla protect her young from its own father?" My voice trembled like a bad opera singer.

"Abigail," she said.

"I'm curious, because with the great apes—"

"Listen, I have waited too long to tell you this. This is not a story about a great ape. It's about a young girl, at the time, more than ten years your junior, who moved from a small town in Texas to New York in hopes of becoming a star." A tenuous smile crossed her face and she took in a forced breath.

"Did she become a star?"

She swiveled her head and looked at me. "In some ways, yes—"

"I saw his picture."

A knowing smile crossed her lips. "She met a photographer who was wild, passionate, and as you know, handsome." Her eyes gripped mine. "With his help, she became a model, and their love affair grew deeper, more intense. He seemed free from the constraints of society and he stripped the girl of her small town insecurities."

She swallowed and tilted her head back to look at the ceiling for a moment. "He had an accent that could make a girl run through mazes to find him. And I have to admit, when she first met him, she understood maybe a third of his words, but the Irish brogue had such a melody, mixed with the glide of his gait, she was like a mouse following after a pied piper."

A breathy giggle flew from her mouth and then a gay silence settled around us, decorating the small hospital room.

I wanted it to last so I could hang on to the air of happiness that surrounded us. Knowing the moment of joy would soon lift, letting the suffocating swamp of death envelop us, I left her side and edged toward the window, trying in wrenching desperation to hold back the tears.

She took a shallow breath. "He came from Ireland when he was seventeen and self-studied photography. By age twenty-two, he'd become rather successful, one of the most sought-after photographers for the top modeling agencies. He was my first love."

She stopped, her throat releasing an odd gurgling noise. "And I am reminded of him each day when I look at you."

I pressed my finger to the foggy window and traced a drop of rain down the glass, then drew figure eights in the sheer condensation that had settled overnight. I stared into the damp morning, wondering if the heavy clouds would lift enough to allow more light through. Without the sun, I didn't feel the difference between the night and day air; they had blended. One complete rotation of the earth on its axis and a family portrait has been retaken, members replaced, others given different parts.

"The man in the picture?" A statement and a question fused. I touched the tip of my nose to the cold window.

"Your father."

She knew the picture I referenced. She did not hesitate to say, 'your father,' not 'my lover.'

"Mom." My lips quivered. I puckered, squeezing them tight.

"You chose Frank for your dad. Abigail, come here, sit next to me," she said, her words reached my ear like a bird carrying a song too sweet to hear.

I shook my head and stayed by the window.

"Cahill and I had been together for almost four years and my modeling career had taken a surprising upswing. Things were perfect. I was with a charming, wonderful, attractive man who made me laugh. Then he changed, saying strange things, acting paranoid, nervous, like there were other people around."

She took a long breath. "One night he shoved me into an alley, made me stand silent for hours, because someone from the shadow government was following us. Something was wrong. His manic mood swings resulted in his losing photography contracts, but I couldn't stay away. I believed it would pass. Naïve, I know. The day I learned I was pregnant, I went to his apartment to tell him about you."

She hesitated, sucked in air and struggled through labored breath. "I knocked and then used my key to enter. I called for him, but he didn't answer."

My mother cleared her throat. "An inch at a time, I opened the door to his darkroom, thinking he might be working. One wall was covered with old pictures of the late President Kennedy and Lyndon Johnson, and the other wall was covered with photos he had taken of me... and on the edge of his workbench lay a gun. He had drawn happy faces on the photos of Kennedy, but on Johnson were scribbled black streaks. When he came home and found me staring at the walls of photos, he came after me and held a knife to my throat."

She sniffed. "He thought I was spying on him."

Like the snap of a tiny dry twig, she gulped. "Later, when he released me, he dropped to his knees, crying, begging for forgiveness. I never told him about you but I think he suspected. Soon thereafter he was arrested for conspiring against the president. Then he was admitted to a psychiatric ward, where they diagnosed him with paranoid schizophrenia."

The dark clouds suffocated the sun, making the morning feel long, tired. I breathed in the recycled hospital air that hundreds of sick people had expelled. "And Dad... Frank?"

"I ran back to Texas." She hesitated, brought the oxygen mask to her mouth, pulling in clean air, then gasped.

I spun around to look at her, to see if her chest still raised and lowered in a rhythmic pattern. "I moved in with my aunt in Dallas, and she helped care for you while I worked at a bookstore and picked up odd modeling jobs.

Most Sundays we went to the park and I would sit on a blanket and read while you played."

Her voice became light, like a young girl and her tone took on a poetic cadence. "You had on a light pink smocked dress and I wore a flowered sundress. I'll never forget that day because you knew."

I twisted around, leaning my back against the window. She had propped herself up and was watching the wall as if an old movie flashed on the blank light green screen.

"Me?"

"I would read a few sentences and then glance at you, then back to the book. I became good at reading and watching you. I looked up and you were petting a puppy held still by the arms of a broad man."

"Dad?"

"Yes. I was nervous, so I scooped you up in my arms and turned to walk away, but you cried and reached for the puppy. The man smiled, I nodded, and he brought the puppy closer. He asked my name, and then yours. I still remember his comment, 'Abigail, what a beautiful name,' and a moment turned into an afternoon and an afternoon into a lifetime," she said wiping the edges of her eyes.

"And a stranger into a father," I said in a plaintive tone as I lowered the metal rail and sat beside her on the bed.

She opened her eyes wide, like a child begging not to be punished anymore. "Abigail, how could I not love a man who loved you so much? So many different threads hold people together. Frank is a good man."

There it was, in her eyes, her confession. She had not loved the man who'd raised me. She knew he would be a good father and so she'd made a decision. A choice manifested from need that grew into a strong affection, and then molded, after years of familiarity, into a fond love.

I didn't know what to say. Should I tell her it was all right because she'd made a good decision, or should I feel betrayed that she'd kept hidden a secret of origin for so long?

I didn't want to ask the next question but I had to. "And the letters, you and Dad splitting up. Were you still seeing him?"

"Abigail... you must understand I've never stopped loving Cahill, or wishing a sickness had not taken him away. I did write him, mostly in an effort to keep him from hurting himself and because I knew he had not asked for this. Also..."

She lowered her eyes. "A part of me has never left him. But I never told him about you, because I was afraid he'd try to find us."

"Mom?"

She looked up at me. I meant to probe further, have the truth at last, ask her if she had been with him, ask her if she had loved him with her body while playing the devoted wife, but I stopped myself.

Why did it matter? She would love Cahill to the end, which meant more than anything two people could create between the sheets.

It's funny how marriages are threatened, torn apart by affairs, most often fueled by lust, but the intimacy of the mind and the soul is what binds us to another. No matter what she did using her body, my dad, Frank, must have known, lived with the terrible knowledge that another had whole parts of her he would never have.

"What is it, Abigail?" she whispered.

"Why didn't you just tell me?"

"Dad and I planned to when you got older." She covered her eyes with her bony hand. "But when the time came, he was apprehensive about revealing it. What you and Dad have is so strong. He's still afraid now."

I walked my fingers along the sheets until they reached hers, letting the tips warm to her fingers. "My father, Cahill is he—?"

"I don't know. For years he was at New York State Psychiatric Institute. But the last time I saw him was just after he'd tried to kill himself, so he had been read-mitted to Bellevue. I've tried to call a few times since, but I promised—"

"Where?"

"Bellevue or New York State Psychiatric Institute."

"I want to…" The next words stuck in my chest, drowning under a waterfall of tears. I clenched my jaw; if one tear fell, the faucet would open. All the tears, shed and unshed, exhausted me.

She shifted her body, rotating her shoulder toward me and resting her hand on mine. Her movements were mechanical, since cancer pressed down on her, making her bones brittle.

"Don't, Abigail. Don't overturn stones." Her tone held the gravity of a minister advising a sinner.

Some stones contain fossils, doors to the past, so one can make predictions about the future. I wanted to see my fossils, understand the look in the two young lover's eyes.

"Mom."

"You'll get hurt, that's what I don't want. Knowing is hard, but sometimes seeing the truth can poison us."

"I've been bitten before." I smiled.

It struck me that, when she died, I would lose a mother and a father; my family tree. I'd never heard the word 'father' without picturing anyone except the round-cheeked man I grew up with. I had to try to find my father, not out of some naïve quest to bond with him, since I already had a dad, but I needed to meet the man who was worthy of Rachel's soul. His presence in her life had nagged my blood, forcing me to turn from my mother, throwing myself to my dad.

She slid her hand around my arm, urging me in silence to be close, her watery eyes questioning me. "What about Dad?"

I allowed myself to shift into her, our faces close. A metallic scent came from her mouth. "Remember, I chose him?" I whispered. "I don't want to hurt Dad, but I have to go to New York."

She used my neck to pull herself next to me, resting her cheek on mine. "If you see him, tell him, Abigail, tell him I'm sorry and… good-bye." Her voice shook, and the wetness from her eyes moistened my cheek, blending with my own tears.

She tilted her head back and cupped both my cheeks in her clammy hands. My skin flinched from the coolness, and tears poured from my eyes, my shoulders shuddering against her bones. "Abigail, you'll be fine. You've always done it without me. Ran from my help. You've been a strong woman."

"But you were there. You ran after me," I said, between sobs.

She fell back to the pillow and shut her eyes. "And someday I'll catch up to you," she said, the corners of her mouth turning upward into a weak smile. Her hand dropped away and flopped to the bed.

I looked at her, wondering, when. "Mom?"

"Go to New York. I'll rest, you go."

"Will you be——?"

"I'll be here when you get back."

I adjusted the oxygen mask over her mouth. Her breath caught up with her chest and steadied. I stood by her bed, and the rage and resentment that had been my crutch for so many years drained from my body. I was sure, if I looked down, a puddle of green bile would circle my feet, spreading across the sterile hospital floor. I had been filled with anger for so long, and it was painful as it seeped from my pores and lifted from my aura.

Who was I, without hate for my mother? Without drinking until I was oblivious, using men just for a warm arm, running to exotic dangerous locations, taking risks, all in the name of hatred? Knowing my life represented the antithesis of the one she had chosen fueled my decisions. So, if I let go of the anger, who was I?

I shuffled my feet backwards, my eyes still lingering on her. I slipped into the hallway. Through the fine lines crisscrossing the glass on the hospital room door, my gaze skipped to the arrangement of fresh flowers.

Was I wrong? A glint of confusion flitted across my mother's eyes when I'd asked about the flowers, but she was famous for her posed, calculated expressions. Little could be read from her face that she did not intend to write.

Could Cahill have been watching her from afar, longing for her, even as she wilted from this world?

CHAPTER 24

The city was cloaked in white. An infinite number of warm flicking lights, like candles on the creamy white cake of a woman reaching her hundredth year, had transformed it. As if accompanied by the intolerable excitement when her family and friends gathered to marvel at each new breath taken from her aged form, Christmas was strung across one of the oldest cities in the nation.

It was late afternoon and vehicles jammed themselves through the streets. My taxi inched across town to Washington Square Park, central to New York University, where I attended school almost seven years ago, near the hotel where I would stay, and a brisk walk from Bellevue Mental Hospital. I calmed my breathing, aware my energy would not make the wheels of the yellow box turn any faster. I leaned back and my eyelids drifted almost shut, like slats of blinds tilted to keep most of the sunlight out.

The cab driver rattled off all the miserable aspects of the holiday season, his English skewed by a Middle Eastern accent. He mashed his words together so much, I was not sure where one ended and the other began.

He whipped his head around to glare at me. His voice took on a rush of anger when he plummeted into the disparaging facts surrounding our selfish American society, never as evident as it was during the Christmas season.

I understood with some certainty why this time of year claimed the most willing deaths. Why people would rather have a bullet pass through their head, or let the edges of a rope burrow into their soft skin, than slog through another holiday season where greed and demand blessed those with money, while a heightened realization of poverty and loneliness sentenced those without.

When we reached Washington Square Park, I handed him the fare, plus a generous tip. After all, it was the holiday season, and I didn't feel comfortable thrown into a pile with all the other money-hungry Americans who lacked regard for the hard work of others. Perhaps his speech was a routine, clever because it worked.

He glanced at the green paper in his hand, then jumped from the cab and lifted my bag from the seat. When he placed it in my arms like precious cargo, he smiled, revealing grayish teeth. "Tank you, Meddy Kissmas to you."

"Yes, Merry Christmas," I said as he jumped back in the taxi.

I stood still on the slushy sidewalk, the cold dampness seeping through the soles of my shoes, people bumping my stationary form as I took in the past.

Washington Square had been my canvas through graduate school. I never entered it without the strap of a camera circling my neck, like an ancient necklace. When someone interesting approached, I shot a photo of them, holding my encyclopedia of the world close and resting my finger on the shutter. I was territorial about my camera, acting like a jealous lover, never taking my eyes from it.

THE LENS OF MY FRIEND'S CAMERA first showed me the hidden wildlife of northern Wisconsin, and then revealed the primitiveness of State Street in downtown Madison, home to the University of Wisconsin. When we turned in rolls of film and later spread the pictures across our dorm room, she pointed at image after image, commenting on how my eye captured human and animal form in the most telling shots.

We smoked pot and made up fantastic stories about the photos. At the street side café, a girl bent forward just enough for her cleavage to invite as she served a cappuccino to an older man who wore wire rimmed glasses and a light tweed coat. Oh, the affair they had that evening, between our puffs of smoke, would make for a great French film.

The fawn stretched his neck to break the surface of a still pond with his tongue, his black eyes pouring toward his mother, making sure she hadn't left his side. The doe, neck arched and ears cocked open, awaited danger. Oh, and how they, mother and child, darted into the dense woods, eluding hunters by a mere whisper.

That evening, after devouring a bag of Cheetos and a whole pizza, along with sucking down a six-pack of beer and smoking too much marijuana, I told Alyssa, my college roommate, the only way I could see the world, with its painful beauty, was from behind a camera lens. Alyssa laughed and attributed my poetic spills to marijuana.

But the following Monday, during the last semester of my senior year, I made several phone calls, first to withdraw my application to both The University of Texas and Duke Law schools, and then to request an application to the graduate program in photography at New York University.

Next, I phoned my parents to tell them that winter was now melting off in Wisconsin and that I would not become a lawyer. A long silence lingered on the other end of the wire in Texas. Their confused and disappointed questions spilled over the line. My answer, simple, I had to see the world through pictures.

"Pick up a *National Geographic* or *Life* magazine," Mother said, "for God's sake."

Dad stayed quiet. Then, his voice laconic, he said, "Please tell me why."

I explained in sophomoric language and haphazard sentences my desire to slow time through my camera lens. Midway through came a click. My mother was off the line, but Dad's ear was still open. He'd offered no approval, just told me to call in a week and tell him the same thing.

So, for one week I debated how to say it better, how to communicate to Dad that my dream was real and not some whimsical quest of a young girl. My palms warm and sweaty, I dialed my parents' number seven days later, and through fatuous stutters, repeated my words, my father the only audience. My mother couldn't bear to hear me spout off like some kind of artist throwing caution to the wind. My father hung up the phone after a few sterile words.

That week I housed an empty feeling, every other moment questioning myself. Then a package arrived, a cardboard box, return address: my parents. I sliced the tape and lifted the flaps to find a camera, a zoom lens, a tripod, and lying under all the equipment, a cream-colored piece of paper torn from my father's work stationery.

> We want to see what you see!
> Love, Mom and Dad

It was Dad's handwriting, I don't know if Mom even knew about his seal of approval. He was the one to make the drive from Texas to New York to help me move when I started graduate school. Mom was occupied elsewhere, busy with charities helping others. I only understood that she didn't have enough time for her daughter. She never came to visit me in New York.

A few months later, Dad flew to New York, claiming he had business. Instead he spent the whole day with me, urging me to snap a picture of that bum or that lady with her colorful dress. He said my mom wanted to come, but she was too busy. I had stopped caring why she wasn't there and the gully between us grew deeper and wider.

MY MOTHER'S RECENT AVOWAL, her confession, persuaded me to see New York in a different light, as I whirled in small circles on the sidewalk, people eddying around me, taking in what New Yorkers refer to as 'the center of the world.' Perhaps to her it had been the core of the earth, better known as hell. Now I understood the greater meaning of my decision in her eyes.

Young voices with their lively harmony rose behind me. A group of carolers surrounded an old man dressed in a

Salvation Army suit. His hunched shoulders stiffened to a rounded erectness, like a wounded soldier trying to salute his country's flag. His twisted hand moved back and forth, ringing a small bell. One could set a watch to his bell, the timing was so precise.

The carolers pulled passersby into their circle, inviting them to share in a song of joy, encouraging New Yorkers and tourists to part with some green for the needy. I joined them for a song that had its roots in the twisted irony of Irish poverty and humor.

> *Christmas is coming, The goose is getting fat.*
> *Please put a penny in the old man's hat.*
> *If you haven't got a penny, a ha'penny will do*
> *If you haven't got a ha'penny, God Bless You*

It made me laugh and I was reminded of the paradox that clothed one of the most powerful cities in the world. I pulled my feet from the sidewalk and hailed a cab to the hotel. After checking in, I threw my bag on the floor and my body on the bed. For a few moments, I shut my eyes and was gone.

When I awoke, the sun was buried. I groped in the dark for the phone, pushed zero, and asked for the time: six-thirty.

I started an internal argument. Was it too late to knock on the doors of a mental ward? Was I afraid? I didn't know this man and he didn't know me, or that I ever existed.

With my coat pulled in close, I walked up First Avenue toward the hospital that provided the insane with a temporary home. I did not run or even maintain a brisk pace, as one might expect of a thirty-one-year-old woman searching for her biological father, her mother's lost love. I strolled towards my destination with the ease of a returning tourist, peering in shop windows, observing but not affected by the commotion of the big city during the holidays.

One cannot stroll the New York sidewalks without having all their senses bombarded. I tilted my head upward and snorted in the air, the aroma of every major ethnic group in the world united, then, with equal precision, poured into a perfume bottle and sprayed throughout the city. No other city in the world smelled like New York.

I gave permission to my senses, opening the door to the wave of memories locked in my mind. I passed an Irish pub. Like the Irish, pubs reproduced in great numbers throughout the city.

Often I had left that very bar seven years ago on different evenings with various men, adopting an attitude toward sex that encouraged me to use men for physical gain, leaving behind piles of my soul in strange beds and bars. Telling myself that was what I wanted when I awoke the following morning, whiskey bullets piercing my brain.

I didn't want them to love me, only to desire me, gifting me the control. So, I never needed them. Even the good ones, I just didn't.

As I converted into a self-avenging crusader for all women, I told myself that estrogen equated weakness. I disguised any overt signs of femininity behind sarcasm and aggressiveness that had its genesis in bitterness, a hollowing resentment toward my mother, because she had relinquished her dreams for the safety of normalcy to play a traditional role as a wife and doting mother.

Worse, my hostility had been magnified when I believed she failed in her role as my protector. Little by little, the bitterness had sucked out the tenderness of youth and the empathetic compassion unique to women.

Although I did not exert myself, my breath turned shallow. I wanted to retrace my steps down every road, through each bar, into all the stranger's beds, and scoop up the pieces of my soul and let them grow back together. Start over, decide who I was as a woman, not the girl who spit at the very thought of being anything resembling her beautiful and graceful mother.

Before, I had convinced myself she was all that for her own gain. And now, as my mother lay in a hospital bed clawing for every minute of life, only the shell of the woman she had been, I lamented for the little girl who had loved her and grown into the woman who would never have the opportunity to be her apprentice.

"Hey, lady, spare a quarter? I'm not a drunk." He approached me, a far-off look in his eyes and his words slurring. He came closer and I coughed from the stale smell of cheap liqueur and urine. "Really, I'm not."

I stopped. Should I keep walking, never making eye contact, or should I take a moment, a single moment to connect with somebody who looked as wretched as I felt?

"I have a few dollars." I took a five-dollar bill from my pocket.

He came closer, putting his hands with torn gloves on my shoulder. My body stiffened, but I didn't move.

"You're a nice lady, aren't you?"

My reaction, one day ago, would have been, 'Go fuck yourself and keep your damn hands off me.' Then my friends would have laughed, saying, 'Take it easy, Abbey.'

But now, I stilled my heart, taking shallow breaths. I was unsure of myself.

Black stubble covered his jaw and a greasy film coated his peeling lips and the tip of his nose, as if he had just eaten something fried. My eyes darted toward a traffic light, and I wished I had my camera so I could photograph him.

"You afraid to look at me lady?" He craned his neck up.

"No." I said, yanking my eyes back and examining his forehead.

"You are." He tilted his head closer, opening his eyes wide as if he could study mine. The odor from his mouth made me nauseous.

"No, I'm not." When I looked at him, I was sure his opaque eyes revealed a life resigned.

"I know, lady. I know why you're afraid." His hand slid off my arm and he backed into a dark alley sprinkled with scattered light that spotlighted the piles of garbage, the wreckage of homes.

"I'm not," I choked.

"I know." His whisper crackled as he disappeared among the spoils.

I took a couple of steps toward him and stopped, an outline of a figure vanished in blackness. What was I afraid of?

I turned around and ran hard, until I reached the entrance to the Irish pub. Sweat dripped between my breasts. I jerked my coat off, hung it on the back of the bar chair, and ordered a Guinness. I looked at the clock behind the bar, it was just past seven. I would go tomorrow, in the morning.

THE NEXT MORNING, I ARRIVED at Bellevue, entering a cheerful lobby decorated rather ornately for the holiday season. A large Christmas tree stood in the corner, draped in silver and gold, multicolored blinking lights were strung in half loops from the reception desk, and a large crystal bowl full of red and white candies sat on the edge of the desk.

Once the signs of the holiday season were boxed and stored, the area would still have been well decorated, with its velvet navy chairs and a burgundy-and-green rug, a canvas for several flowers. A grand chandelier hung in the middle of the room like a dismal gift wrapped with the most lavish paper. Upon receiving it, one would be so dazzled with its extravagance that the eyes would not be as appalled with the contents.

I took the elevator to the psychiatric ward. The receptionist was busy talking to an elderly couple. The old woman sobbed, her head swaying, between bouts of tears she pleaded for her daughter to be released for the Christmas season. Her husband rested his arms around her drooping shoulders. Life had forced her to beg to spend a holiday with a daughter who was considered disturbed.

"The holiday would probably be less stressful and agonizing if your daughter remained here," the nurse said.

"We only want to be with her during this time." the old

man said.

I wandered down the hall and stopped at the locked double doors. When I looked through the glass, bringing my face close, a muffled cacophony, along with erratic, solitary lives lived out behind the doors, further stopped me.

An assertive man spoke to a window, or perhaps to his reflection, as if participating in a heated political debate. He was poised, and throughout the few minutes I observed him, he often brought the fingers of his right hand to his chin and stared at the glass, nodding from time to time, as if considering the points made by the other debater.

I became so intrigued by his intent movements and his scowling eyes that I wished I could hear the words he exchanged with his apparition.

Two other men were involved in a serious chess game. After observing closer, I realized they weren't interacting with each other. They both played simultaneous parallel games, on the same board, without trade. They shared no words, exchanged no eye contact. Neither even considered the other's chess move; one could've been in the Bronx, the other in Scarsdale.

A woman who looked to be in her forties held her arms together, rocking the empty space between them as if cradling an infant, smiling down at the package she imagined in her arms. Her mouth shifted in a continuous motion, and I could almost make out the words of a popular lullaby.

A man skipped, in a way that looked like an awkward gimpy jog, from one wall to another, yelling. He crashed his appendages into the hard surface, caught his breath, then repeated the chanting jog.

I wondered for a moment about their lives before they entered a singular existence of a mis-wired brain. Had they been full of despair, agony, sheer poverty, and disappointment, leading them to madness? Or had they been people, like myself, successful, although sometimes on life's edges, according to those around me, in society, fighting with their own desperate minds to continue the life they began before their own brain launched its heist.

Mental illness, such a scary concept not to know or even to possess your own mind. I stared through the glass aquarium at those who had wound circles around their own paranoia and fear, plunged deep into the murky thick waters of insanity, their mouths, then their lungs, filled with a terror so great they could no longer see, much less reach, the water's edge. The small concentric circles never stopped until their lives were such that they lived in a bubble of madness.

While I watched the show before me, I wondered what it would take to drown? How much fear activates true paranoia? What degree of self-loathing and despair results in suicide? How many moments of surrealism is the mind permitted to have before one lives in a world constructed only within one's own mind? When is the heartache too much to bear? When does one become so isolated, and where does it start?

Perhaps it begins as a tiny pea of meanness, justified in one's own mind because of perceived unrighteousness of another, growing within the heart until only a festering anger remains to predetermine all decisions for the future. Maybe after the loss of a child or a lover, the heart atrophies from disuse, and despair replaces love.

I had never asked myself these questions. But standing on the outside, I realized that in some way I was connected to the madness before me, through genetics and environment. My mother's lover, my father, had served to fester an anger inside me that had determined so much of my life. The anxiety from behind the locked glass doors tugged at me, and I turned away.

The scolding stare of a large man in a white uniform met me. "Can I help you?" His voice bellowed down the hall.

My gaze scurried down the hall to see if he had gained the attention of the entire floor.

A slighter man, dressed in the same white uniform, approached from behind him. "Ma'am, we do not allow family members to loiter in the halls," he said over the larger man's shoulder.

"I wasn't loitering."

I had to tense my neck not to laugh at the contrast of humans before me, large and small bodies, deep and whiny voices, evident against the blank canvas of their white uniforms.

"All right, gawking. We don't encourage gawking."

I wanted to give him a speech on my decency as a human being, but I thought better of it, because, unless it pertained to animals, I was at a loss for examples. "I'm sorry, I was just looking for someone."

The large man shifted his eyes, pointed to the end of the hallway from where I had entered, and said with a tone of great authority, "That's why we have a reception desk. Besides, visiting hours are not for another forty-five minutes."

"Then, excuse me," I said, such contriteness in my voice, I thought I'd picked up a foreign accent in the past hour.

After retreating, I placed both my hands on the receptionist desk in an attempt to dispel the theory I may be armed, since both men had eyed me with intent suspicion. I said 'good morning' to the younger woman behind the desk, and even asked her, as customary in Texas, how she was doing?

She regarded me with a weary glance that reminded me I was not in Texas.

"Can I help you?" She threw her New York attitude on the counter. She had an accent (Queens or Brooklyn?), talking from the side of her mouth as if a cigarette dangled from the other side of her lips.

I stared past her, searching for an explanation that seemed sensible, since the real one sounded contrived.

"Hallo, take a pictcha, it lasts longa!" she yelled, standing up halfway, waving her hand in front of my face. She arched her eyebrows and repeated in a loud voice, "Lookin' fa someone? Maybe a close relative?" She rolled her eyes, as if the answer would indicate something about my state of mind.

"Yes, I'm sorry." I took a deep breath. "I'm looking for my... my uncle."

"Okay, now we're gettin' somewhere," she said, swigging down the remains of a cola she had behind the phone on the desk. She twisted her hips and the swivel chair slid in front of a computer. "Name?" she said, placing her fingers on the keys of the computer.

"Cahill Duncan."

She raised her hands. "Cahill?" her eyes opened wide, a faint smile flashed on her face. "I didn't know he had any relatives."

"Yes."

"Why have you waited so long to visit? All this time, he's gone with no visitors. The report in his chart says a woman has called to inquire and sent him packages all the way from Texas, but no visitors in over a decade."

"He's here?"

"No, I'm afraid he's gone," she said, accusation in her tone.

My heart jolted. "Gone?"

"Oh yeah, he'll be back closer to Christmas. He always comes back, either here or if he needs to stay longer, he goes to the State Psychiatric Institute. The holidays are too hard for these people."

Her gaze darted down the hall. "The staff doesn't mind Cahill. He's become somewhat of a celebrity with his Irish brogue and his habit of constantly snapping pictures of the staff and patients. Kinda charming when he has it together. But the other times, they say he's dangerous."

She reached for the ringing phone. "Bellevue... No, sorry, sir, he was transferred to critical care. He tried to... just passing on information."

How could she relay the information so lightly, of another life lost at the hands of a tormented mind?

She glanced up, twisting her eyebrows into a frown. "Sorry I couldn't help ya."

"Do you have an address for him?"

"Yeah. But that's privileged information and I'm not allowed to give it out. Leave a note and I'll give it to him when he comes back."

She seemed so sure he would return to the sterile walls of an institution to be protected from the outside world, which to me would incite madness.

"I can't wait until then," I said, seeking some reason to compel her to give me the information. "I have to give him something."

"Leave it here, and I'll see he gets it." Her words were blunt, even brusque, as she turned a page in some music magazine she'd kept glancing at.

"Please."

"What is it? Are you the woman?" She tilted her head back, taking in my face, scanning my body. "Nope, you're too young. The chart reports phone calls and packages back almost thirty years. Then they just stopped, maybe fourteen years ago, the packages anyway. I think she called again but he was gone and no information was given."

She stared at the computer screen as if studying someone's biography. "Say, is the woman your mother?"

"No, why would she be? No."

"Settle down. It makes sense since you're his niece, that maybe your mother is his sister. Jeez, maybe they could get you a sedative." She laughed at her own tacky joke.

I smiled, wishing I had caught on. "You're right, it was his sister and also my father's sister, my aunt. She asked me to give him something because she's very ill." Sincerity wrapped my words and I could tell I reached the woman.

"Sorry I'm so anxious, I just promised I would."

"All right. But not a word. I could get in real trouble."

As she wrote the address on the piece of paper, she said, "Says here he's lived there on and off for nearly ten years." She smirked. "You could say he has two homes, 462 First Avenue and Alphabet City." She tilted her chin and lifted her second and third finger together, as if she were smoking an exotic cigarette and a member of the pseudo elite.

"Thanks, really." I nodded my head.

"Merry Christmas," she said, as I entered the elevator.

CHAPTER 25

I thought about my mother's story and what lay beneath rocks she had hidden away. I had only seen a topographical map of Rachel's life. I wanted to rest, curl myself into a fetal ball, and lay my head on a park bench. Stare aimlessly at people's knees as they walked by and pondered, 'Oh, look at that pitiful woman, and she's so young, she must be a prostitute or a drunk homeless person.'

I told myself if I stopped, I would not start again. I would've seen enough, like when you're determined to climb a treacherous mountain, expecting the view from the top to be wondrous, but you stop halfway up and rest on a ledge. There you decide the view will do, you can't go any further, you did good enough.

I hailed a taxi because my legs were too weak to walk, the morning having left me in a state of emotional lassitude. Fatigue made me question whether or not I should go to the address the receptionist gave me, ten blocks away from the center of my graduate school career. In the course of those two years, I'd observed lots of people, staring into their eyes like mysterious subjects. What if I'd looked into his eyes and decided not to take his picture, because he was not interesting enough in my mind? I, whose photographs wielded the attention of professors and magazines, could have overlooked my own father, despite my keen eye.

During the short ride to the address on the paper, I flipped through my mind's photo album and realized I'd only seen very old photos of my father. Would I recognize him?

The cab dropped me off at the end of the street in the middle of a labyrinth of apartments, hidden escapes for future artists and the wealthy young who had made their way and were seeking to rekindle their artistic spirit. At the very east end of The Village, past the students, the artists and the yuppies, were dwellings of less than meager appearances.

The mailboxes were not marked. I had no way of knowing which buzzer belonged to him, so I pressed a random button. Through the window covered with a thin layer of soot, I spied a severely overweight woman shamble out of a door on the first floor. She pressed her wide nose flat against the glass and peered at me. I mouthed my father's name to her.

Within seconds, she opened the front door. She wore a stained smock nightdress, her flesh bulging between the front snaps. Her greasy hair was disheveled and a lime green scarf that might have been the Last Supper to a group of moths wrapped around her combination chin and neck. Her round face sunk in toward her mouth and cat-length white whiskers sprang from her chin. A malodorous smell seeped from her pores, and I stepped back.

When she opened her mouth, her lips disappeared into the toothless cavern. "What do you want? Ringing the doorbell in the middle of the day." She squinted, as if the cloud-shaded sun was too much for her hermit eyes.

"I'm looking for Cahill Duncan," I said, relaxing my stance.

She cackled, opening her mouth wider. Three lone teeth hid inside the cave. "What you want with that crazy kook?"

"I just—"

"He won't hear ya knocking anyway. He's got that damn Irish shit playing so loud." She opened the door wide and stepped to the side, pressing herself against the dirty wall. "Go on, he's upstairs, number 210."

I edged through the door, scooting myself past the woman, sliding close to the hallway wall opposite her. Still my shirt rubbed against the fat protruding from her stomach.

"Watch it!" She pushed my shoulder.

"Uhhh, sorry," I murmured, hastening past her.

As I ascended the stairs, the smell of curry, burnt cabbage, and a moldy dankness assaulted my nose.

I stood in front of number 210, while the faint sounds of bagpipes and drums marched under the large crack between the floor and the door. Staring at the door, my thoughts shifted to what my mother had said: I was turning over a heavy rock.

My hand went to knock and I pulled it back to my side. "Hello, I'm your daughter. Remember that model you loved? Well…" I said, under my breath.

I knocked, waited a second, and turned to leave. The door swung open and the man in the picture said, "Do come in," without ever raising his head to look at me. "Aye, Thomas, don't be fussin', the more the merrier. Aye, always enough whiskey to go around," he said laughing. He kept dancing and singing as if I was just another guest to a regular party.

A rubber band held his longish ginger and gray hair back from his face, silver and ginger lined his narrow jaw. He wore an old blue suit, several shoestrings tied together cinched the pants, and the jacket hung halfway to his knees, its sleeves kissing his knuckles. Pink digits peeked out from under the worn blue cuffs

I didn't move. All the emotions in my body reacted together: my heart, its erratic beat; my lungs expanded, speeding my breath; heat rose, gathering in my armpits; tears swelled behind my eyelids, and my knees trembled. I was there, aware of myself, but my mind was fixed on the jolly thin man before me. I prayed I could continue standing because while taking him in, my insides dissolved.

The tape ended, and he froze, one heel to the ground in the middle of a jig step. He swirled around and squinted at me. A vacancy inhabited his face. He jerked his head from side to side, scanning the room as if he'd just been spit from a time machine, desperate to discern his whereabouts.

For the first time since I saw him, I slowed my rapid breathing and took a couple of deep breaths. My fingers began their own dance, weaving in and out of each other while I watched him walk, catatonic, toward me.

His eyes were like an artist's palette, azure with gold specks through the irises, and red lines winding through the whites. As he approached, they grew wider and wider, transfixed on my face. A large blue vein on his forehead pulsed and his bulb nose, a reddish purple, resembled a plastic clown nose bought from a costume store.

He stopped a foot from me, close enough for me to

smell the swirl of liquor-tainted human sweat from his pores and fresh whiskey from his mouth. He stared over my right shoulder, jittery and hesitant, and then at last recognition dawned his face. "Jesus, Mary, Mother of God… is it you?"

I nodded.

"Oh, Jesus, Rachel. I thought I's banned to dancin' with ya only in my dreams."

My heart skipped at his mistake.

He finished the last of the jig, spun himself around, and stared into the faces of the airless characters who surrounded us. "Now, ya see, boys, I'm not a madman. She's here, she's here. Get out, all of you. I got some catchin' up to do with the beautiful lass. Go on now," he hollered, kicking the air around him. "You no good bums, the lady will think I'm mad, keepin' company with the likes of you."

He took my hand, guiding me past the door. He kicked some of the bums out the door. When he scanned the room, a few of his friends seemed reluctant to leave. He slammed the door behind him.

"Good riddance," he said, swiping his hands together. "Now let me have a look at you." He touched my chin, examining my profile, following the lines of my body. "You're in fine form," he whispered, proud of his discernment.

I forged my mind for composure, imploring my body to cease trembling, but I was struck with fear, yet not of physical harm. Something inside me wanted to shrink away from the madness before me, my own father.

As he examined me, he would probably not see Rachel at all, but rather her likeness. My pelvis felt uneasy and a queasiness washed over my body, a panicky sensation I had not experienced since early childhood when my parents had caught me misbehaving.

"The restroom?" I sounded breathy.

"Aye, forgive me." He removed his sticky fingers from my chin, his arm eased against his side, and he nodded to a chipped panel door at the end of the room. I would have mistaken it for a closet, had I not been instructed. "You go and I'll fix your favorite drink. It's indeed a celebration."

As I scooted through the door, I wondered what my favorite drink was. The bathroom was by mere inches big enough for me to turn around in. The shower wall was part tile and part plastic, with gray thick tape that drooped off the wall, but it was clean, free of mold and dirt. I caught a glance of my face in between the water spots that splattered the mirror. Red lipstick had smeared above my right lip and my hair was half up and half down. I tore the hairpins out and ran my fingers through my hair, then wiped the lipstick off with a piece of toilet paper, so he would see his daughter instead.

When I walked out, I realized the singular room with the small adjoining kitchen was the apartment. Along one wall, yellowed sheets draped in front of two narrow windows. Black-and-white photographs of professional quality, the caliber I had studied in graduate school, covered the other wall. To my right stood an old metal school desk, sitting on it an antique coke bottle, the vase for a plastic red rose, and on the wall above the desk, a museum of my mother.

The pictures told the story she only yesterday sketched of her life in New York. I slid myself sideways, inching closer to the display, so as not to distract the man in the kitchen as he prepared a drink in fastidious mode. I kept my eyes on him, shuffling sideways toward the wall.

His movements were meticulous. He took a kettle from the stove and poured boiling water into two clear mugs, swished it around, eyeing the movement of the clear liquid as it slid up and down the sides of the glass. Then he threw it into the sink, the water splashing against the sides.

The whole wall was a mosaic of my mother: magazine covers, torn pages from catalogs, black-and-white and color photos, some I had seen in the box that evening with Ethan. Stapled to the wall below every picture were worn pieces of paper with passages of verse, some Biblical and others poetic, each with a date. His creation must have cost him great effort, and perhaps great pain as well.

I could follow her evolution. The early pictures when she first came to New York, the shy Texas girl with her down-home coy smile, hands held in close, protective. Then, after time had passed and the essence of New York osmosed through her, her hands went to her hips and her chin tilted up in a cocky pose.

And when success at last lingered close and modesty had been extinguished by a free spirit, she threw her head back, and her hands moved away from her body. The camera had controlled her in the beginning, decided who she would be, but then she learned how to possess it, titillating the eyes behind it with such prurience that the imagination did not have to work hard to envision the model and her photographer.

What irony, considering my vivid and detailed assumptions as I glanced at him, and then again at her shrine. I had been proven rather pedestrian in my wayward fairytales. With such strength had I vowed to be the controller of my love, never the one on my knees. I would not be my mother, the one with warm tears on my face from a lost love.

So the few who gave it to me, opening their arms wide as unwounded lovers do, I treated with indifference, as if to prove something. As if my strength as a woman came from my ability to treat men in a cold and aloof manner, never giving, always taking, fueled by my naïve invention of my mother's life.

"Be patient, my fair one. I'm near the end," he called.

I turned toward the kitchen. He boiled more water, poured it into the mugs whose bottoms were covered with a combination of sugar and liquid gold, Irish whiskey.

The vision of my mother sitting on a blanket next to the fire, sipping watery gold from a similar mug moved into my mind's eye. A couple of times, when my dad was out of town on business, I had watched her through the railings on the steps, holding a mug with both hands, bringing it to her lips, while staring dream-like into the fire. She never ordered that drink in public or when my dad was home. I suppose it was Cahill's drink, his evening, when she could be alone with her thoughts of him.

With precision, he stirred his specialty drink, once upon a time my mother's favorite, and presented it to me, grinning. He stared at me, his round blue eyes were hollow, as if the madness had rooted in the orbs.

"To you. To me," he said, clinking his glass to mine.

"Yes, to you."

He gestured for me to sit on an old army green couch.

I chose a spot where the springs did not poke through the material. He sipped his sweet whiskey and peered at me over the rim of the mug. He scooted toward me, crossing the space between us, broaching to reach out, once again, to an old lover.

He snapped his head around, yelling at someone in the wild air to leave us alone, then bit his lip hard and squeezed his eyes shut as if wishing the pesky apparition away. In yet another abrupt motion, he looked at me, smiled, and laughed a faraway chuckle. He stopped, and words spewed from his mouth, his life history since I, Rachel, had left him, a rehearsed dissertation, as if he had prepared for this day all his life.

Fantastic stories about travels back to the old country, alluding to his stays in an institution. While he expounded, the cloudiness filming his blue eyes, his jerky and exaggerated movements, seemed to dissipate as he floated in and out of lucidity.

The more he talked, the harder it became to shut out the sadness that seemed to grow on itself. He was indeed a charming man, with a gifted eye, whose life detoured in such a way as if hijacked and forced to go to the middle of nowhere. He did not make the wrong turn; it had been made for him.

He reached toward me and placed his hand on mine, his gesture something between a father and a lover. Although the interaction between us felt strange, me listening and nodding as though I were my mother, I didn't stop him from believing I was Rachel.

I glanced down at his wrinkled hand. He wore a gold

ring, designed with two hands embracing a heart wearing a crown, the same ring I had associated with my mother's hand since I was a little girl.

When I looked up, his expression seemed puzzled; perhaps he would question my identity. His eyes stayed fixed on our hands as he told the story of his imprisonment, and how much he missed me.

Then I gasped when he said, "No worries for you. I stopped being angry years ago. I knew it was you who alerted the police. I understand." He looked at me. "Besides, I'd never have been able to pull the trigger, don't think I got it in me, and that's what I told them."

His eyes circled the room, peering at our onlookers who were, for the time, quiet. "They've asked me to do many evil things, but I've fought against them." He moved his hand from mine and made a fist, resting it on his heart. "There's, after all, a spirit in here stronger than their ceaseless badgering."

I turned my head away from him and squeezed my eyes shut, but not before a couple of tears escaped.

"They will always torment me as long as I remain on this earth. I've wanted to leave here many times, and a time or two I even tried to make my exit, but I know I cannot leave without my love."

I spun my head around, forgetting my tears. "What are you saying?"

"Oh, no, I won't have ya cryin'," he said, touching my chin. He reached in his suit pocket and offered me a handkerchief with embroidered green shamrocks lining its edges. I wiped my face and watched as he went across the room and put an old record on a player.

"Now we shall have no sadness. I've waited for this day for years and I won't have it that the most beautiful woman in the world is cryin'. Heaven's sake, this is about love, not sadness."

His gaze flitted to the back corner of the room and he placed a finger over his mouth, hushing the intruders. "Please, just this day," he said to them, a pitiful whine to his voice.

I wanted to plead also, ask them to leave him alone, so he could live out his days without torment, but that was not possible, not as long as he still lived. He had tried to tell Rachel exactly that, he had stayed alive because of her; otherwise he would have taken his own life, thus ending the lives of the monsters who lived in his brain. When he talked, it was clear that living was his hell, and dying would be a welcome relief from torment.

The player scratched against the old record and he adjusted it. He opened his hand to me. "I believe they'll give us a moment of peace." His eyes sparkled and he bowed. "Shall we dance?"

"I don't... I can't." I only knew how to move my hips back and forth, but, besides the two-step, I had never learned a dance that required footwork.

"Aye, Rachel, of course ya do, and what the body can't remember, the heart never forgets." He motioned for me to take his hand. "It will come to ya soon enough. The whiskey will get in your blood, then your legs will be dancin' and your heart singin'."

I placed my hand in his. I couldn't begin to know the

first step of the dance but the whiskey had made me warm, loose. I wanted to walk back in time.

He came to a sudden stop, holding my hand in the air, and peered at me. "You're stiff as Wedgwood, girl. Let yourself go," he said, pulling me closer until only inches remained between us. "Where are you, lass? It's time you unlock your soul."

Then he spun me to the end of his arm. I wanted to stop, ask him what he meant. He spun me back. "Ya only get one chance at this," he said. "Ya don't have to be perfect, ya just can't be afraid to fail."

My rigid self shook loose and I let the anxiety that surrounded me dissipate. I followed his steps, heel-toe and hands-on-hips, dance in a circle. As I did, the diamond gown floated around my body and the audience moved back into a distant circle, to watch with wonder at the happiness radiating from my smile.

"And heel, and toe, and around we go," he hummed, hooking his arm in mine, spinning me in the small apartment. "And there it is, my beauty. It is yours now," he shouted.

The music poured through my body as the words to the song etched in my brain. I let my mind believe the threadbare carpet was a field of grass sprinkled with tiny shamrocks. While my dress swirled around me, I imagined my bare feet twirling in the green grass below. Soon I knew the steps as if I had danced them my whole life.

"Aye, you were born to this, I say." He laughed again.

I laughed, a laughter straight from the heart. One I hadn't heard from myself since I was a young burden-free girl.

He tilted his head toward the ceiling. "I believe it's comin' back to ya, my fair one."

I twirled into him. He pressed his head close to mine.

"What?" I stared at the water-stained ceiling.

"The spirits are giving you back your soul, so don't be afraid to live with it, because to live without it is to perish." His arm wrapped around my back and he squeezed into me. The record stopped, he turned his head, giving my cheek a light peck. "You know how. You always knew."

He spun me away from his body out to the end of his fingertips. I reached behind me, fumbling for the arm of the couch. I had to sit, all the spinning had made my head dizzy and I had to remind myself where I was.

All around us, a magical madness came to life, but the backdrop remained a dingy sparse apartment, kept clean and organized to a meticulous degree. The sounds of horns and people yelling in the streets penetrated the thin walls, and the dreary hue which hung over the city never stopped tapping on the windows.

He dropped to the couch, his arms and legs flying into the air as he sat. "That was worth a lifetime of pain," he said sighing, trying to catch his breath.

"Nothing is worth a lifetime of pain." I stood up and walked toward the narrow windows, then peered through the slits of the dingy sheets draped over them. The falling snow made the air outside look dense, busy.

"Is it not, now? There are those who believe in protectin' their hearts, never feelin' any pain. That equals a lifetime of loneliness. I dare say, those are the losers. Aye, they may skirt around the pain, but they also miss the laughter and joy that accompanies it. I say, thanks to you, my life has held both joy and pain."

I pulled one side of the thin sheet aside and watched the snow glide to the ground. I felt like I was in one of those snow globes, turning slowly in a circle, without moving, while it plays music and white flakes flitter through the air, never melting. A still and deep silence enveloped the room, the kind that comes after a too sad or too joyous event.

"The little one?" His voice shaky.

"What?" I turned, squinting, when the question first hit my ears. I didn't know his meaning.

"The one you were carryin' when ya left. Boy or girl?" He kept his gaze to the floor as he spoke, but the inflection of his voice when he said 'girl' told me he already knew the answer.

"How did you—?"

"Lovers know."

"Girl." I lowered my eyes.

He stood beside me and peered through the dirty windowpane. "Heaven is callin', sprinklin' down the white carpet. Girl, you say?"

"Yes," I murmured.

He placed two fingers under my chin, lifting my head, his eyes pouring into mine. I met his stare.

"Question?" The index finger of his other hand settled on my cheek right below my eye. He studied only my eyes, as if searching for signs of Rachel. "Does she have the eye? Can she see what others miss?"

I opened my mouth, trying to answer, but nothing happened.

"She does, doesn't she?"

We met each other's eyes with fixed discomfiture, neither yielding to the muddled air. In slow but steady motion I pulled my head back from his stare.

"Shall I make ya another?" He picked up the glasses and walked to the kitchen. "I know. I know, don't be tellin' me stuff I know," he muttered as he prepared another drink. "Get on now, please, just this day, all right?"

"I can't stay," I blurted.

"Aye, so soon? I'd like to take ya out a bit. So many years have passed since I'd known ya."

"Yes, so many years," I whispered.

"Whadda ya say, just an afternoon before you're gone from my life for good?" He jerked his head, skittering his eyes around the room. "I promise, I'll keep them away."

"It's snowing."

"The white carpet for us. Let's go."

I grabbed my coat and we walked out the door. "Your coat?" I said, confusion threading my tone.

"Don't need one. But we do need this." He walked back in and grabbed an old Nikon camera off the kitchen counter.

I didn't ask again. He didn't have a coat, my father, the man who gave me the gift of sight through a lens, lives in New York without a coat.

I followed him through the front door to the outside coldness. He grabbed my hand, his grip loose, yet guiding, his bare fingers felt like an ice pack wrapped around my hand. "Remember the corner?"

I shook my head and let him pull me down the street. He

talked to his friends, and strangers stared, but I didn't care. I could now see New York through the eyes of the beautiful young Rachel, walking the streets with her fanciful lover.

He watched people, and then aimed his camera, as I had many times before. Then he brought it to my eye, showing me, as an instructor would, why humans are the best subjects, pointing out beauty in the prosaic activities of people living their lives. I'd always believed the sublime allure of New York belonged to its grandeur, yet through his eyes, the profound richness of the smaller lives being acted out within the larger life of the city itself was made manifest.

"Look," he said, pointing to a woman, early fifties, bending to brush snow from the tops of her high-heeled black leather boots before entering a store. "Snap as she arches her neck up, just before she stands. Get the boots and her face," he murmured behind my head. "Capture her retreatin' to her youthful sexiness with those new black boots."

Cahill turned a ten-minute walk into an hour of human observation. He missed nothing, except himself, where he was in relation to the people moving around him, to the city, to the world. He went through it, pointing and eyeing without inhibition, a child in a zoo for the first time, not caring about the disturbed glances or disgusted whispers of others.

"There," he said, pointing to a grandmotherly old woman dragging a young boy across the street.

I brought the camera to my eye and snapped.

"Zoom, zoom," he yelled. "Leave the bodies, 'tis the

eyes, the way he's lookin' at her hand, you have to get that. The eyes, remember?"

"Yes, yes." I refocused the camera on the boy's eyes.

Cahill was right. The boy stared at the old woman's hand, shifted to the waiting cars, and then back to the old fingers grasping his. I focused and took the shot, the boy's eyes locked in gratitude at the hand of security clutching his.

When I turned around, Cahill was arguing with two teenage boys. "Get the hell out me way. You just can't go bumpin' into people with no cares," he hollered.

"Hey, crazy old man, you fucking knocked into me, you're so busy staring at that woman," one kid said, pointing at me.

"She's with me," Cahill said, standing up straighter.

"Yeah, bullshit!" The other boy said, jamming his fist into Cahill's shoulder.

Cahill stumbled backwards, still standing.

I inserted myself in front of the boys. "Leave him alone."

"Fucking psycho. You better get away from him."

"No, he's not, he's my father."

"Shit," one of them said as they walked away.

"Are you okay?" I turned to stare at my father, the bum on the street, the schizophrenic without a coat, the genius photographer the world never knew.

He looked at me as if a light had come on, while his eyes investigated his daughter. His body shaking, he wrapped his arms around himself. "Let's get out of the cold. Come on."

We passed another corner and walked a few blocks. My cheeks felt stiff from the icy air. We plodded down a couple of creaky wooden steps into a dimly lit bar.

Torn barstools lined the wooden countertop, and old men were placed at their posts as if they all had assigned seats. Grunts and whispers filled the air, of a forgotten generation, the spirit of war, serving one's country, the old country some had fled, and how they'd go back someday, the extravagance and disrespect of the younger generations.

The bartender wiped the countertop with a soiled cloth.

"Marty," Cahill called to him, waving as if they were young boys seeing each other from down the hall the first day of school following a summer of separation.

When he saw my father, Marty shook his head. "Not today, Cahill."

"I got someone for ya to meet," Cahill said, grabbing my hand and dragging me forward.

The bartender's mouth dropped open. "It can't be."

The row of men craned their necks and one said, "Jesus, Cahill's kidnapped someone."

They all laughed.

"'Tis me daughter," Cahill said.

"Yeah, sure. What's her name?" the man at the end of the bar yelled.

A second slipped past before I realized he didn't know my name. He glanced at me, his mouth dropped open. A soft chuckle dominoed down the row of men.

I stepped forward, extending my hand to the bartender. "I'm Abigail." I smiled over my shoulder at my father.

He crossed himself and whispered something. Then he moved his fingers into the web spaces of my hand, clutching my digits, squeezing my hand the way only a father can.

One squeeze saying so much, I'm proud of you, you're mine, you'll be okay.

"Abigail, Abigail," he whispered, as if in disbelief. "Me mother's name sake, God bless you."

"Marty, give us two pints, will ya," he shouted to the bartender.

"Come on now, Cahill, I can't stay in business if I keep giving…"

I tilted my head at Marty and nodded. "It's okay, two pints."

He served us a couple of pints. We stared at the chocolate cure-all, Guinness, until it settled, then Cahill tapped his glass to mine, "Sláinté."

In the time it took us to drink the pints, Cahill talked non-stop about my mother, his words clinging to reality as if Rachel had been his lighthouse shining through the darkness of his cloudy mind. I understood the passion between the two young lovers as best as I ever would. With his stories, the life of the young Rachel, the girl who loved with abandonment, sprouted wings. I ordered two more pints, not wanting this moment to end, not for me, and not for him.

An old mirrored clock, most of the mirror worn to dull non-reflective, gun-metal gray, read 4:45.

"I have to go now. I need to catch my plane."

He nodded and slugged down the last of his second pint. Without attracting his attention, I reached in my jeans and laid two twenties on the bar. "Marty, thanks for taking care of us," I said.

He tipped his hand forward from his forehead, a bartender's salute.

Dusk had settled onto the city and we dashed back to his apartment. An unwarranted panic came over me. 'I'm glad I met you, I have to go.' I'd thought about what to say to him on the brisk walk back, but now I couldn't remember what I'd decided.

"Well, goodbye." I said, as we tarried in the doorway of his apartment.

He walked towards me with his arms opened wide, tears filled his eyes, and he bit his bottom lip. I wrapped my arms around him, trying not to register the pungent smell of unwashed clothes mixed with stale whiskey.

"Go now." He cradled my face in his hands, stretched his chin upwards, and kissed my forehead. His hands slid from my cheeks as he stepped away and watched me walk out the door backwards.

I shut the door, then ran down the steps. When I reached the bottom and opened the door, a gust of snow filled air rushed in, jolting my warm body. I stepped outside.

'Tell him goodbye,' my mother's weak voice sounded in my head.

I spun around and grabbed the handle before the door shut. When I reached the platform at the top of the stairs, I stopped. The outline of Cahill's face floated above me in the scattered shadows that wove through the stairwell. I froze one step below him.

Tears slid down his cheeks, hanging on the edges of his beard, making the hair glisten. We lingered on the stairs with only the suffused light leaking from the open door of his apartment filtering through the hallway.

"I forgot something," I said.

"Ya did, indeed," He held up the old Nikon camera we had used on the corner.

"I can't."

"Yes, please."

I reached up with both hands and took it, cradling it like a delicate porcelain doll.

"Thank you, Dad." I forced the words out. 'Dad' didn't seem to fit, but I used it anyway.

He hugged me again, clinging to me for a long minute. His hands moved to my shoulders and when he raised his eyes to mine, the cloudiness was gone, his eyes were clear. No one else joined us. He had managed to keep them away for a moment. He was as lucid as any man when he spoke. "Abigail, there's somethin' I want ya to tell your mother." His tears had dried, and his words were laced with conviction.

I nodded.

He lowered his gaze. "She's afraid to make this journey, I know. You must tell her, I'll not let her go alone. I'll be there with her." His hands tensed on my shoulders. "And I know she's ready to leave."

His grip felt as though someone had stabbed me with an icicle, sending a painful chill through my body. I could not keep my eyes dry.

"She told me to tell you goodbye, and..." I was about to say, 'she's sorry,' but he had already made it clear she had nothing to apologize for, and I would not dilute their love with such triteness.

He smiled. "She doesn't have to. I'm goin' also." A contented expression washed over his face, imparting a certain peace to his words. They were not spoken out of madness, rather a passion derived from an intolerable longing for a lost love that would be realized at long last.

I removed his hands from my shoulders, my arms shaking as I embraced him. After a drawn out moment, I pulled away. "I have to go. She said she'd wait."

"Hurry, child, she can't wait much longer."

I left him standing on the clearing and ran down the stairs.

"Remember, lass, how much you've been loved." His Irish brogue trickled down the stairs.

I hesitated in the open doorway, and then merged into the outside world, the door closing behind me.

The cold wind carried the snow to the ground, where it hovered, given a welcome home with the onset of the cooler temperature. I ducked my head against the wind, stood in the slush, the bottom of my pants saturated with dirty snow, and hailed a taxi. People raced by me in an effort to return to their warm homes before the weather made it any more difficult to move about the city.

I settled into the taxi and decided I should go straight to the airport, leaving my duffel bag with a change of clothes at the hotel. I couldn't risk missing the plane.

Cahill knew my mother was leaving. He'd felt her soul passing and I had to see her before she left. She had to know I understood her innate drive to protect. The reason I'd seen it so clearly in the eyes of the mountain gorilla mother cradling her infant was because I'd also seen it so many times in my mother's eyes.

CHAPTER 26

When the hospital elevator doors opened, my dad was standing outside my mother's door.

"Dad," I yelled.

"Abigail… you're… you're back."

It was strange to see my dad, the man who cared for me as much as any father could. As I drew nearer, he seemed almost unfamiliar. His face was drawn, already showing the lines of mourning. Tiny wrinkles sprouted from his down-turned lips, like cobwebs spreading across his face, and an anxiousness circled him as he stared at me. I couldn't tell if it was the loss of my mother or his fear of losing me. I suppose it was both.

I grasped both of his hands. "Dad," I said, releasing his hands and hugging his neck. My nose took in the scent from my childhood, when I used to rest my head in the groove between his shoulder and neck while we watched TV together. The smell of deep pine cologne and moth musk from his blazers, especially in winter.

I wanted to tell him he would always be my dad. The other man, my father, was also a parent, but in a way that makes him like a movie star. One of those people you think about, imagine their lives, and recreate them into more than they are, yet they remain someone you never really know. I had always known the man before me.

"How is she?" I pulled away from him.

"The doctor said she's taken a turn for the worse. They increased her dose after I demanded it." He blinked, a slow agonizing retreat of the eyes. "She was in so much pain. You need to go in and see her. She keeps asking for you. I don't think..." His voice cracked and he made an odd noise, like he was trying to block a sob.

"I'm sorry I had to..."

He nodded. "Mom said it was really important. I'm glad you're back." He touched my shoulder. "Ethan and José left a while ago to get some food."

I looked through the window, my eyes drawn to her motionless form on the bed. The flowers leaned over the edge of the glass vase, the vivid colors surrendering to a muted brown. I circled my hand around the doorknob, my eyes still fixed on the dying flowers.

"Oh, Abbey, by the way," he said in a hushed voice, arching his neck toward me, "your friend was here yesterday."

When I gave him a quizzical look, he said, "Ryan."

"Oh?"

" 'Oh' is right. He's been a devoted friend." My father turned to walk down the hall.

I smiled as I opened the door to my mother's room. Her lungs expanded as they struggled to get air. I crawled into her bed and squeezed myself between the metal bed railing and her bony form. As gentle as could be, I rested my head on her shoulder, curling into her, just the way the infant gorilla had squeezed into its mother for safety.

"Abigail," she sputtered.

I tilted my head up and gazed into her cloudy eyes, the vivid green overtaken by a murky swamp. "Thanks for waiting."

Rigid, in slow motion, she lifted her arm and her breath became more rapid, the effort laborious to her failing body. She wrapped her arm around my shoulder. The wiry muscle fibers contracted against my arm, begging me closer. I snuggled next to her, ignoring the rotten tinny smell of death. "Of course," she said, with a faint smile.

"Of course," I said.

"Did you...?"

Every word expelled seemed to sacrifice a breath of air. Her voice came out so weak, like holding a glass to a thick wall, trying to listen to a conversation in the next room, hearing only whispers of words.

I touched her mouth with my finger. "Shhh, don't talk, just breath. I'll talk."

She blinked.

I cleared my throat, not wanting to sound strained. "He said goodbye." I swallowed hard, sucking in a deep breath. "You're free to go."

"Did you tell him..." she gasped. "Did you tell him I'm sorry?"

"Mom... he said there was no need for that. You have nothing to be sorry for."

She shut her eyes for a few minutes, as if needing a short nap before she could say more. "There are always things to be sorry for. Anyone who gets to the end without regrets... never had to make choices." Her lids drifted shut again.

She slept. The low murmur of the machines and the

constant buzz of the air conditioner mingled with her fighting raspy breaths.

My father slipped in and out of the hospital room to check on her, kissing her forehead, squeezing her hand, resting for a moment in the chair beside her bed, and then leaving to pace the hall again.

I moved from her side only to do the necessary things of life, needing to be there every time she woke, have one more moment with her.

She woke after hours of sleep and she wanted to hear more about my trip, more about her prince. I told her about Cahill's life, how he lived in his own apartment, still took photos, and gave me his old Nikon.

The slightest hint of smile emerged from her thin parched lips. I didn't tell her he didn't own a coat, or about his pesky apparitions, or how he begged for pints at a dingy bar. I wanted her to have her prince, her fairytale, like the stories she had created for me, her little girl, while I snuggled next to her, rocked to sleep by the rise and fall of her pillowy chest, dreaming of my own prince.

"Abigail." She flexed her hand on my shoulder, her spindly fingers trying to squeeze me.

"Mom, I've always loved you. I was just…"

"Afraid," she said.

"Afraid," I repeated, but when I looked at her, her eyelids were closed. I shut my eyes and rested my head next to her. As my body lay nestled against hers, I thought she possessed great resolve, something I have not yet learned to access.

I fell asleep. She also slept. I woke. She did not.

CHAPTER 27

Dark suits, black dresses, and red eyes were stacked into the pews. The sea of faces seemed to fuse into one picture, washed together, like an open carton of eggs, with no difference between one egg from another. Faces held their thin veils of sympathy, masking underlying smiles of gratitude that they were still alive, they still had a mother, wife, or daughter.

I recognized most of them. Others were my mother's acquaintances from her various charities or friends of my father from the firm. So many hugs, so many condolences.

My father held his tears that day. He did not like appearing in public in a state of disarray. It was bad enough he had allowed himself to sink into dishevelment during the last weeks of my mother's life, but he refused to be the focus of pity on Rachel's day. He had even gone so far as to apologize to my brother and me for his bouts of confusion and outpouring of tears.

Clutching the familiar flowers between his hands, the identical small glass jar with the vivid wild flowers, Ryan walked to the front of the church and stopped to gaze at the framed picture of her on the table next to the coffin. He set the fresh flowers on the table beside her picture. He plodded back down the center aisle past me, his expression solemn.

I turned, watching Ryan as he sank in a pew in the middle of the church. Our eyes caught each other's; he brought two fingers to his mouth, kissed them, and then rotated them toward me.

'Thanks,' I mouthed.

The priest wore a white robe with an overlay trimmed in gold and red. His voice long and drawn out as he spoke of my mother's death and the great loss it was to her family and the community.

Wringing my hands in the folds of my skirt, I tried to remember some of the times she'd attempted to give me advice, but I had closed my ears. I spent my entire growing-up life rebelling against my mother, my perceived persona of her, letting most of her good words fall to dry ground. I would forage into the corners of my mind, find those ignored words of advice, and replant them in fertile soil.

My brother delivered a short, well-written speech. His voice shook as he spoke of my mother, his shelter from a sometimes cruel and isolating world.

The priest nodded for me to stand. "Abigail Gallagher, Rachel's beloved daughter, will now say a few words."

I raised my eyebrows at the formality of his words since he had known my family for more than two decades. When I stood, his face was flushed and he was trying not to choke as he spoke.

"Abigail," he said, nodding toward me again.

I brushed my long navy skirt straight and approached the podium. As I rested my hand on the edge of it, my eyes scanned the filled pews. I opened my mouth, but the emotion crept up, paralyzing my vocal cords.

I believed at that moment I would break down and cry, glimpsing first at her tranquil body, then into the sea of red eyes. I wanted to pound my fist on the podium and demand her return so I could grow up loving and admiring her. For several seconds, I closed my eyes and told myself she would hear my words.

My eyes focused on the sterile black ink I had taken great care to script across the white paper, my prepared speech. Like most events in my life, I had rehearsed the words for that day. However, nothing could articulate how I felt. Stirring noises echoed in the church, as people exchanged bewildered glances. Ethan mouthed my name, raising his eyebrows, his eyes asking 'are you all right?' Behind me, Father Andrew cleared his throat.

"My mother, Rachel." I spit the words from my mouth. I read the next line in my head, 'was an exceptional woman, she was a devoted wife, a wonderful mother.'

But when I searched the faces, I stopped on Ryan's liquid brown eyes, I knew what to say. I crumpled the paper in my fist.

> "Most of us look for our heroes on the front of magazines, gracing the movie screen, or flying through the air, sporting a cape. My parents taught me where the real heroes are...
> "Down the hall, tucking us into bed, kissing the scratches on our knees, and pulling our families together. My heroes were in the next room. I may not have realized that growing up, but I know it now.

"The real heroes live in neighborhoods, trying to create family as a tradition instead of something to pass time. I know this because you always want to emulate your heroes when you grow up.

"I hope when I grow up, I'm half the hero my mother was."

My father's shoulders shook as he nodded. Ethan slipped his arm around him. As I took note of Ryan's compassionate face, his eyes smiled at me over the crowd. He showed me the way, but the irony was, I had to lose a father, a mother, and someone who gave me unconditional love to understand the true meaning of 'heroes.'

I slid into the pew to sit between Ethan and my dad, the man who loved me enough to be content with Rachel's leftover heart.

Following the funeral, family and close friends retreated to my parents' house for food, alcohol, funny stories, and a spate of tears. It was a rather odd tradition and the house seemed strange without its hostess.

I wiggled through the people until I noticed a red dress with pink stripes, Dr. Seuss had made an appearance. "Thanks for coming, Sheila."

"Ab, how about it? I'm... well, you already know. I'll spare you the platitudes," she said with a rueful smile, extending her hands.

"Thanks." I grasped them. "I have to ask... what's with the outfit?" I smiled as I threw my eyes over the red and pink striped dress.

"What about it?... Not as shocking as you wearing a

skirt, so…"

"It's my mother's funeral. I had to."

"Well, your mother wouldn't recognize me if I'd worn some traditional black dress. She would've been yawning."

"You're right, your wardrobe has long been a subject of bemusement in this household."

"And…" She waved her hand, wanting more information.

I tilted my chin up and spoke with a high drawl. "Well, my mother says the clothing someone wears can tell you volumes about their emotional state." I let my eyes travel down the length of her loud dress again.

"Yeah, what's with your emotional state, blue jean girl?" she said, laughing.

"Dry," I laughed and gave her a light kiss on the cheek. "You do look wonderful."

I slipped past the dining room table, moving toward the kitchen. My Aunt Dolores was shoving pineapple upside down cake into her mouth. I crept behind her, hoping she wouldn't see me.

"Abigail," she yelled, yellow cake spraying from her mouth.

I stepped back.

"Oh, Abigail." She threw her hands into the air, as a short burst of loud melodramatic tears sprang from her.

I let her histrionic skit play out, hugged her with a rapid motion, and scampered away. I caught Ethan looking at me, concealing a laugh, leaning toward José, no doubt, to share the incident he had just witnessed. I rolled my eyes at him and walked into the kitchen.

I leaned against the counter, reflecting, as people do at funerals: my mother and her dreams, my mother and me, Cahill, his wild Irish eyes and the laughter that day in his apartment. The madness... and the sadness.

I shut my eyes, willing the vision of him gone. The image of Cahill committing suicide was unbearable to me. I tried not to think about how he did it, not to imagine the scenarios. I had called Bellevue yesterday, knowing the answer before anyone picked up.

He had taken his own life during the night of December thirteenth, same day my mother passed on, almost twenty hours after I had hugged him.

A large hand squeezed my elbow before grasping my hand. "Abbey, what you said about your mother was..." My dad struggled with his words.

"I just finally realized how much you both gave up for me."

He clutched my hand into his. "We gained, all of us."

I leaned into him, wishing I could absorb some of his pain, but knowing it would remain forever. She had been the cornerstone of his life.

"I'm not taking the Galápagos Islands assignment, not yet. Instead I'll be photographing the highest order primate, humans, for a Texas magazine. So I'll be staying in Austin for a while."

"The photo you shot in Africa of the mother gorilla is getting so much recognition. With that on your résumé, you'll have hundreds of offers from top magazines all over the world. Ethan and I can make it without you," he said, trying to sound light.

"Well, I can't make it without you." I smiled. "I'm just starting to grow up."

He leaned over to kiss my cheek. "I swear, your generation is taking a lifetime to grow up." He chuckled low. "But I guess if I could have things my way, I'd have kept you six forever." He shrugged as he strolled into the living room.

I walked outside. Gasping at the cool air brushing against me, I hugged myself as I looked at the dead stalks that would bloom roses in the spring.

At the touch of a hand on my back, I turned around to find Ryan standing close. "Thanks for coming," I said, speaking to him as if he were one of my mother's friends, not a man who had been my lover for over three years.

"Your speech was… it surprised me."

"Me, too." I offered him a small smile.

The corners of his mouth jerked back and forth, as he filed through his brain for words.

"How's the business?" I said to break the silence.

"Good, we're really growing."

"And the house?"

"The foundation has been poured," he glanced at me, "…and I think it's a solid one. It has settled well, but it hasn't been easy. The work, I mean."

"Okay, Ryan, enough about cement. When will the house be finished?"

"Probably a few months. And it will last forever, because the foundation is so strong."

"All right, stop with the metaphors, will you?" I chuckled, then paused. "I miss you, Ryan," I blurted out as a gust of wind whipped my hair around my face, a few stray strands sticking to my mouth, getting damp.

He nodded, then stepped forward to tuck my hair behind my ear. "I'll spell it out. I know my timing isn't good, but I just want..." He placed both his hands on either side of my head. "I'm a masochist for saying this, I know."

"What?" I tried to ignore the tingling from his touch.

"Maybe not forever, but I'm around."

"Around?" I raised my eyebrows.

His hands slid from my cheeks and rested on my shoulders. The smell of sugar circled his breath and remnants of icing glazed the edges of his lips.

"I'm not saying forever. Don't bank on waiting until they wheel my ass into an old folks' home."

We stared at each other. Lost in the silence that wove around us, I tilted my head to the side and studied Ryan. I imagined tasting him again, laying my lips to his, and ingesting the sweetness.

"Damn it, Ab," he whispered. "I never stopped wanting you."

I smiled. "Same here. My life learning curve is speeding up. Thanks to you."

I took his hand, holding it with one of mine, and traced the lines of his palm with the other. "What about the girl you were seeing? Jake told me."

He shook his head. "Jake was just watching out for me."

"Protecting you from the 'black widow?' " I smirked at him.

"How did you—?"

"I probably heard it before." I raised my eyes to his.

"Probably," he said in a hushed voice, pulling his lips

into his mouth, like he was fighting back a smile.

An impenetrable stillness rushed in, a quiet that held all the unsaid words. But they were ones I could say later, just not today. Unlike the diary that held my past, my future memoir would not be filled with 'could've, would've, should've.'

In a gradual rhythm, his hand fell from mine, he turned and walked toward his car. I watched him, his rangy legs extending a distance in front of his torso. It struck me then that even the ordinariness of Ryan provided so much solace in my life.

I wanted to run after him, circle my arms around him, and yell that I loved him, but not in the midst of losing my mother. Ryan deserved my whole heart, ready and capable of love. Wholly prepared to exercise care when handling his heart, a heart I had misused, taken for granted. I had, at last, learned that lesson. Something others learn in kindergarten.

When you mistreat a toy, letting it break into a million pieces, you don't get another one. Not until you've proven you're responsible, you know how to treat things with respect. Somehow, I had missed that lesson. Maybe I was sick that day.

I wondered if it was the life my mother led or the one she left behind that had a more profound impact on me. Had I heard the information sooner, learning a decade ago about my father, my mother's lover, would I have lived my twenties out with less destructiveness?

But perhaps if I hadn't unfolded the story of my mother's life in the midst of her death, my selfish mind would have allowed me to dwindle further into a nondescript ball of self-pity, fueled by an undefined anger toward her.

When I went back into the house, the party projected a hollowed out feeling. Not because of her death, but because she wasn't there to greet people, throwing her head back in laughter at the self-proclaimed humor of others. Her slim form would have waltzed through the crowd, encouraging people to eat more with her knowing smile and a glance toward empty hands. I even longed for the endless orders that accompanied these events.

I knew how to host a party, because I had learned from the best. I picked up a tray of hors d'oeuvres and swirled around the room. "Bob, do you need another drink?" "We have plenty of food," I said into a small crowd. "You look wonderful, Jacqueline." Sashaying across the room, touching all the lives. "How are you?" I said to one of my father's acquaintances, offering that perfect smile.

I am, after all, my mother's daughter.

CHAPTER 28

Today I brought some of my mother's old jewelry to an antique store. Some I have kept, but the other pieces I will offer for sale.

It has been almost three months since my mother's funeral, and Ethan and I have helped my father sell the house. He could not bear to sleep there without her. Now he's settled into a condominium near his firm. He has not, and will never, let her go. Even after her death, she is the center of all his conversations.

THE OLD MAN BEHIND THE COUNTER offers me fifty-two dollars for the jewelry, explaining that most of it is costume jewelry, not all that valuable. I don't argue, although I know it's worth more.

The antique store is cluttered, so I have to determine how to exit before I can proceed. I meander an indirect path toward the door, winding myself through old furniture, restored treasures, and junk.

Sunlight bouncing off a dull red object catches my eye. I look up and walk sideways toward the red beam.

Hanging above some toys, near the storefront window, is a boy's red bicycle, aged a few decades. The plastic handle grips are worn, frayed red, white and blue streamers hang from the ends, and a torn seat cushion exposes a metal seat, while rusty spokes hold the wheels together.

Nonetheless, it is the red bike. Perhaps it has seen its share of near crashes, wheelies off the edges of curbs, and lonely nights spent lying forgotten in the middle of a driveway.

But it can be restored if gifted to caring hands. Someone will have to take the time to repaint the rusted metal, straighten the wheels, and mend the torn seat. In time, the red bike will be someone's treasure.

The old man behind the counter says he'll sell it for forty-nine dollars plus tax, fifty-two dollars total. It used to belong to his son. Sentimental value, he explains. I agree that is worth a lot and lay down the money that just left his hands.

Although Ryan and I have often talked on the phone, I haven't seen him since the funeral. After loading the bike in my new black pick-up truck, I head toward his house.

I drove there a week ago, the evening he hosted a house-warming party, but when I arrived I couldn't enter. The thought of being surrounded by other people before I told him what I needed to say was more than I could handle. Instead, I sent him a card, thanking him for the invitation and explaining I missed his party due to illness.

I look in my rearview mirror and I am struck by the worn edge of my white t-shirt. I look down at my Levis, which have become my second skin, and I do the oddest thing. I drive to a clothing store and waste the better part of this Saturday afternoon crawling in and out of dresses.

The woman at the store convinces me to select one. Maybe she has grown tired of retrieving dress after dress and hearing me ask, 'people actually wear these?' as I look in the mirror. She says the periwinkle dress sprinkled with light green leaves is most suited for me and 'does wonders for my figure.'

I ask if I can wear it out of the store and she suggests I purchase a pair of stiletto heels, since hiking boots and dresses went out with dreadlocks.

In the parking lot, I march back and forth, trying to establish a rhythm for my body that seems natural while walking on heels. I fight the urge to cry, because at this moment I would give anything for my mother to be here.

I get in my truck and slide in the CD Ryan gave me when I arrived home from Africa, Guy Forsyth's *Steak*. I suck in a long breath and head toward his house. When Guy's low sultry voice thumbs into my shoulders with "Oohhh Monnna," I let the air slowly escape my lungs. By the time I turn onto the highway, Guy breaks into "Louisiana Blues," settling my body and strengthening my resolve to give the red bike to its rightful owner.

During the drive to Ryan's house, the sky takes on a gray hue and grows darker as I twist down the wide road. I pull into his driveway. His new home is in no way palatial; rather, it wears a simple look that coincides with its natural surroundings. I look up as lightning needles through the sky, followed by a large clap of thunder.

I drag the bicycle behind me, struggling to walk the length of the stone sidewalk in heels. I ring the doorbell and wait. My heartbeat has risen to my throat. I ring it again and wait.

I should have put on lipstick. What's the sense of wearing a dress if your lips look like a hockey player's in the winter?

The sky lets loose with a loud boom. I didn't expect the rain to come at such a pace. I huddle closer to the door after propping the bike on the side of the house next to me. One more time I press the doorbell. No answer. I leave the bike and try to run to my truck. The rain is slanting in and hitting my face with a force that stings my skin. My dress is plastered to my skin like a drowning person onto a life raft.

"Abbey."

The submerged echo of my name finds its way through the beating rain. I turn.

Ryan is standing in the doorway with a towel wrapped around his waist. He waves his arms for me to come. I wait, letting the rain soak every inch of me. Impatient, he gestures again. I take my shoes off and run toward the door.

"Christ, get in here," he says, pulling me through the open door and slamming it behind me.

I look down. The rain has shaded my dress, transforming it into a translucent sepia against my skin. I draw near to him and look up at his face.

He crests his head and steps back. He seems baffled, even shaken by my appearance. He knits his eyebrows together, confusion swathing his face. "Abbey?"

Heat rises in my blood and with it the flush that rushes to my face. "I wanted to bring you a housewarming gift."

He looks at my arms, and I realize he hasn't seen the red bike.

"And?" A perplexed smirk streaks across his face.

"It's outside leaning against the house."

Water drips from my body, making puddles around my bare feet on the tile floor. I shiver, feeling like a runaway, scared and tired of running.

"I'll get you a towel."

I scan his house. The furnishings are sparse, much of it the same furniture he has had since I met him. A pine plank table acts as a desk in the dining room. His kitchen table and chairs are Formica and metal, the kind used in my high school lunchroom.

He has a few pieces of art, pictures and photos. Some I recognize because I took them. They lean against the walls in the spots where I suppose he will get around to hanging them. Windows at the back of his house look out to the nature preserve that begins a mile or so away.

He returns with a towel and the tattered blue terry cloth bathrobe I gave him three years ago for Christmas, so he would throw away his other threadbare robe. Typical Ryan, he hates to discard things from his life. He has always been reluctant to replace the old with the new. He has changed into a pair of Levis with worn knees and two quarter-sized holes in the butt where his red boxers are peeking through, and a white t-shirt with frayed edges.

"Why don't you go in the bathroom." He hands me the robe and towel.

Ryan is being cautious. I can sense it in the stiffness of his voice and judged movements.

I change and when I exit, Ryan is holding an umbrella while pulling the red bike through the door. At once I feel unsure and hopeful about my gift. I wrap the robe around me and walk up behind him, wondering if he'll accept it.

He chooses silence. For a long moment he says nothing. He stares at the wet red bike. Then he bends down and wipes the water from its body as if it were a small child who had been caught in the rain.

"Ryan." I touch his elbow.

When he turns around, I move toward him. He pulls me close, nestling his face into my wet hair. He is familiar, like an old pillow you've had your whole life.

"Is this the bike?" I choke out, trying to push down the swell of emotion.

He nods. "Abbey?" he says as if it were a question. After a long pause, he seems to suck in a breath. "Does the boy get the girl, too?" He raises his head to inspect my face.

I focus on him, moving past the urge to roll my eyes and say, 'why the hell do you think I dragged this second-hand bike through rain?'

Instead, I say, "Yes, yes, I love you."

And, although I know it is not so, the sweet voice of my mother laughing and the melodious voice of an Irish man singing come to me from a shadowy distance.

"Oh, Ab," he gushes as he wraps his arms around me. "I love you, too."

As I lay my head in the sinewy groove where his arm and chest meet, pouring myself into him, I make a choice, giving my heart permission to love or to suffer, if either be the case. Knowing, no matter the ending, the joy of today will not be tainted and nothing is gained from fear, however cleverly it is disguised.

Book Club Questions

1) - As a child, how did you perceive your parents' marriage? Did you discover that some of your perceptions or assumptions were inaccurate? How did this impact your relationships?

2) - What is the significance of Abbey taking the photo of the mother-infant gorillas just before she returns to Austin?

3) - How much of Abbey's life outcomes are attributable to nature, nurture, or individual choice? For you, which of these three impacted your life outcome most profoundly?

4) - Would you say that your mother was protective when you were growing up? If you are a parent, do you parent similarly? Or are you less or more protective? Why?

5) - What scene made you most want to scream at Abbey? What scene made you most want to hug Abbey?

6) - Based on Abbey's realization in chapter 20, how much responsibility do you think parents bear to help their children avoid self-loathing?

ACKNOWLEDGEMENTS

It is my privilege to thank Cynthia Stone for her amazing editorial skills, plot advice, and creative ability to bring this project to fruition. A special thank you to Jennifer Imrie (IG: @imriecollegeplanner) for tackling last minute copy edits before publication. I am grateful for your attention to detail!

I want to thank Dr. Coe from the University of Wisconsin who taught Primates and Us, a class I took more than twenty-five years ago. This class piqued my interest in the primate world and how much we can learn from them. Daydreaming during this class was the seed for this novel.

My family, especially my parents, Denis and Julie, who think every story roiling around in my brain is worth telling and writing. Thank you!

I am surrounded by an amazing group of friends who encouraged me to bring this novel to the public after writing it more than twenty-years ago. Pam, Mary, Alyssa all recognized how much storytelling excites me! Thank you to all my family and friends who wrote letters for my birthday (2020), pushing me to publish a book written more than two decades ago and to continue writing fiction once again.

I am so grateful to my husband and my kids for just smiling when I enter a conversation midway after being lost in my 'writing brain.' Thank you to my children for letting me experience the potency of the mother-child bond.

My husband Bill always saw me as a storyteller/writer and pushed me to embrace that side of myself twenty-plus years ago. Thank you for the countless hours you have spent making sure my stories come to life on the page. (I don't write anything he doesn't read/edit… many times).

ABOUT THE AUTHOR

Tara Delaney was born in New York, but has lived all over the country, including, Wisconsin, Texas, and now California. She graduated from the University of Texas-Health Science Center in San Antonio with a degree in occupational therapy. Tara moved to Wisconsin to work as a pediatric therapist and attend graduate school at the University of Wisconsin-Madison. She fell madly in love with another Irish New Yorker and afterward moved to Austin, Texas.

The last move was to Northern California where she and her husband ran a therapy company for more than a decade and

had two children. She has published three non-fiction books (Autism and Sensory Processing related) and spent the past decade speaking throughout the country on a number of topics, including Autism, Behavior, Sensory Processing, and Dyslexia. She is fascinated by how early experiences impact adult behavior, including the cultural imprint from the various places one grows up.

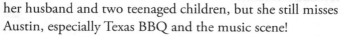

She lives in Northern California with her husband and two teenaged children, but she still misses Austin, especially Texas BBQ and the music scene!

Instagram: @author.taradelaney
Facebook.com/author.taradelaney
http://www.taradelaney.com
Author email: author.taradelaney@gmail.com